Red Horse

M.J. LOGUE

Copyright © 2015 M.J.Logue

2nd edition

All rights reserved.

ISBN: 151888931X

ISBN-13: 9781518889318

RED HORSE

DEDICATION

My thanks go to my boys, both the big one and the little one, for plot development, artillery titbits, and reading "The Furie of the Ordinance" when I really couldn't bring myself to. And for practising duelling in the garden all summer, not to mention seventeenth-century drill.

To my technical advisers (who know who they are) without whom this book would not, in a very real and practical sense, exist.

To my friends in the Wardour Garrison, who know what I am, and don't protest too much when I channel my inner Ironside over the embroidery.

Tam, Pixie and Geoff, Alan, and Antonia, for random canine company, clothing inspiration, friendship, silliness, and generally kicking me up the bum periodically. See? I do listen! And Tom, for reading the bugger....

And last but not least, this book is for my dad and the Wascally Woyalist, both of whom died before it was completed, and both of whom would have been so very proud to see it in print.

And there went out another horse that was red, and power was given to him that sat thereon to take peace from the earth, and that they should kill one another: and there was given unto him a great sword.

Revelations 6: 3-4

FOREWORD

Both King and Parliament needed capable and experienced officers at the beginning of the war. At this time there was no standing army and both sides were looking for men capable of commanding a troop of undisciplined, untrained, probably badly-equipped soldiers. Fortunately, there was still a pool of available talent in Europe where the Thirty Years' War was quietly bubbling away to itself, and there were mercenary officers available for the asking. Because there was no standing army until the creation of the New Model Army in 1645, the structure was considerably different to that which we recognise, particularly in the cavalry, where one troop of horse could be anything between thirty and a hundred men each commanded by a captain, with their own colours, some relatively autonomous, some brigaded together in regiments of around six troops commanded by a colonel.

For the disbelieving, there were several children baptised with the benighted handle of Holofernes during the period, as attested by parish registers. Lucifer, the Light Bringer, is another name for Venus, the Morning Star, and neither Calvin nor Luther considered it a name associated with Satan. (And they'd know better than I would!) The reason why Luce's parents chose to name him so controversially is a matter for another book!

Babbitt is fictional, but his commanders aren't. The Earl of Essex (*not* Oliver Cromwell - who was at Edgehill, albeit late) commanded the Army of Parliament until 1644, and was loved and respected by some and a source of infuriation to others, who couldn't stand his pedestrian style of command. For anyone looking for an overview of the English Civil War, I would recommend C.V. Wedgwood's "The King's War" as an excellent place to start.

M. J. LOGUE

1 TWO ENGLISHMEN, A GIRL, AND A BLUE CAT

Amsterdam, 1625

It was a raw night and there was a stiff wind coming up off the sea, bringing a driving rain and a tavern full of sea-captains and merchants with their pockets full. Margriete liked nights like this. The Blue Cat was full to bursting; there was a cheerful, rowdy, jaunty air to the place, the air full of the good smells of cooking and spilled ale and wet wool, with a hint of tobacco and spicy geneva. In the corner by the fire, the blond Englishman sat with his arm round his girl, running through his repertoire of bawdy drinking songs. Margriete liked the blond. Most people did. He was a good-looking lad; tall and broad-shouldered and sturdy built, with a sleepy, satisfied smile on his face most of the time that looked like he'd just come from someone's bed. Expensive black doublet and breeches, good linen, good boots. As vain as a courtesan, young Smith, for all the soldiering ways he put on and off as often as he turned his linen. But good-humoured and cheerfully conceited – a handsome enough lad, if you liked rather elegant pirates. Margriete had known enough real pirates – freelance traders, say, rather – passing through the doors of the Blue Cat to know the difference.

And then there was the other Englishman, the wolfish redhead – now he did look like a real pirate. Watchful and wary and slightly ragged round the edges in spite of his evident attempts to stay decent; wherever he'd come from. He'd taken a beating recently enough for the bruises on his face to be still blue. Red, they called him, predictably enough for the striking autumn deep red colour of his hair. Never looked like he had quite enough to eat. Didn't like to be around people that much. Not like Master Smith, who'd never been seen without at least three or four admirers in tow. This one was the latest regular one – Annit? Anneke? – but Margriete had had to speak to almost all the girls in the Cat quite severely at some point or another. Handsome, well-bred, charming, and rich, Smith should have been intolerable. And wasn't, which should have made him even more intolerable. But no – he was an engaging boy, with a good heart, a bottomless purse, and impeccable good manners, but he was still a boy, playing at soldiers. She had no doubt at all that at some point Master Smith would cease his play and disappear to resume his privileged life in England without a backward glance. Unlike most of the clientele of the Blue Cat in the winter months, for who battle was a profession, not a pastime. The Cat in November was the preferred haunt of half the mercenary recruiting sergeants in the Low Countries, all lounging around the fireside with their eyes on the latest collection of raw recruits, hoping to snatch up the most promising new blood for the spring's campaigning with tall tales of adventure and gold and loose women for the asking. All quick of temper and temporarily deep of pocket, full of stories of the dangers they'd almost faced.

The serving-girl Lynten swished past with a tray of empty tankards, giving Margriete a sidelong glance full of mischief. "I see your man's in this evening, *mevrouw*."

"My – oh, very funny, girl. I'm amazed you have eyes for anyone else but your own – after all, the contents of *his* purse are as golden as his hair, no?"

The blonde girl flushed. She'd been the last to receive warning that whatever he might promise under her skirts, Master Smith's romantic intentions were anything but honourable.

It was getting too crowded in the Blue Cat for Red. He preferred quiet places; places where people didn't stare at his height and his hair, and where he wasn't so busy trying to disappear into the background that he ended up tripping over his own feet. Come to think of it, he wasn't impressed with Amsterdam in its entirety, and he'd been here almost a month. Everywhere you looked there was yet another bloody food market – a cheese market, a fish market, a vegetable market – not the best when you were half-starved most of the time. He missed Lancashire, and he'd never thought he would: missed the moors, the wide open space for miles, nothing between you and the white sky and the black turf but the occasional lapwing circling. Missed the friendly, flat accents of home, too, rather than the gibble-gabble of a hundred and one strange voices. And he'd sort of got it into his head that when you signed up for a soldier of fortune, the fortune bit was supposed to come into it somewhere, and it hadn't so far – just the odd grudging stuiver handed over by a sergeant with a face like something dredged up off the bottom of the harbour. Far too quick with the flat of his hand, that one, as well. The odd friendly cuff here and there might work wonders on disciplining brawling puppies but it did nowt for Red. He wondered what would happen the first time he belted the old bastard right back because he would, one of those days. He'd spent the last seventeen years having the sin beaten out of him on a more or less daily basis and he'd made himself a little promise when he left England that no bugger was ever, ever going to lay a hand on him again without he wished it.

The stew was good here, though – and cheap. Hot and tasty and thick with beans and vegetables. He folded his hands round his empty bowl, hoping to catch the last bit of heat. There was one of the serving girls here – fat and sleek as butter, with a look on her face like she was doing him a favour by letting him clutter up the place. She'd have him out if she could as soon as she clapped eyes on an empty bowl. He saw her out of the corner of his eye; a tray balanced on her hip, flouncing at the Amazon – in spite of himself his heart sped up, as it always did, at the sight of the Amazon. There weren't that many women tall enough to look him in the eye, even in the milk-fed Low Countries, but the strapping lass who owned the Blue Cat was one of them. Fine lass she was, deep-breasted and heavy in the quarters like a little Brabant draught mare, with sleeves rolled up over solidly-muscled forearms. Well, it seemed the sin of lechery hadn't been completely beaten out of him. It was an oddly comforting thought.

Still, he was wary of outstaying his welcome. The Gasthuis was very well for travellers but he didn't think they'd look too kindly on a penniless soldier-apprentice in more or less permanent residence. The bench suddenly bucked underneath him as someone joined him in his smoky corner and he looked up sharply, recalled to more immediate business.

"Eat," she said, dumping a second bowl of stew on the table in front of him with a total disregard for civility.

He thanked God for dark corners and dim lighting that she hadn't seen his sudden fiery blush – laid both hands flat on the table that she wouldn't see their shaking either. Close up, the Amazon smelt of clean linen, fresh air and rosemary, and the combination of the near presence of her and the thought of her underlinen made him forget to breathe. And choke. Once she'd thumped him between the shoulderblades a few times he wasn't quite so overawed. "To what do I owe the honour?" he said warily. Couldn't help it; kindness was not a thing that came unearned, in his world.

"Don't let it go cold. And I have eyes in my head, Kersen."

Kersen. Cherries. He didn't dislike being known as Red – at least it was being called *something*, other than his own truly dreadful given name – but he suspected he'd have sat here with this same foolish moonstruck smile on his face if she'd called him Carrots. At least she'd noticed him. The Amazon stood up and he looked up after her. "Go talk to the blonde boy," she said kindly. "But wait till you've finished your supper." And she strode purposefully off. Straight-backed, strides as long as a man, shoulders fine and square in her clean violet-blue bodice. God send more women like the Amazon, he thought. The world needed more like her.

Well, he'd been commanded by a veritable officer amongst females, what else could he do? Other than present himself to the blonde boy, who he cordially disliked at best. They'd been matched with swords at practice before, being of a similar height and reach. Master Smith was a lithe, sinuous swordsman of many years' classical training, Red was more – what was the word? – pragmatic. The sergeant hadn't been impressed the first time he'd kicked the feet out from under the blonde boy, put him on his arse and took the sword off him. Apparently it wasn't what they were supposed to be doing. The next time they'd fought the blonde had got the hang of it and tried to knee him in the balls. That hadn't been so much of a duel as a brawl, and even the memory of it made him grin. For someone with more money than sense, Smith had the beginnings of a decent fighter - if he lived long enough to get over having more money than sense.

"God's teeth, it's Red. Out after bedtime tonight, aren't you, old son?"

He straightened his shoulders. He wasn't good at

being patronised. It made him itchy. "And good evening to you too, Master Smith."

"Sit down and have a drink, lad, you're making me nervous." He turned to the creamy blonde female at his side. Pretty. Bland as milk. "He always makes me nervous, this one. Dangerous man. I'll be offended if you don't have a drink, Red. *All* my friends drink with me."

"I am *not* your friend, Master Smith. And stop calling me Red."

"But I don't know what else to call you – *Red*. And sit down, or –" Smith suddenly shot one foot out and hooked Red's feet out from underneath him so that he sat down almost on top of the giggling blonde. "Or I'll do that. Let's be polite. This is Anneke, my girl. Don't forget that bit: she may be a whore, but she's *my* whore. Very friendly, is Anneke. Got to watch her."

Smith poured a cup of wine. It occurred to Red that the blonde lad was very drunk. "Let's drink to Anneke, Red. Very pretty girl. You got a girl?"

Warily, he shook his head – accepted the cup of wine poured, more successfully, by Anneke. She could be as friendly as she liked, and he still wasn't interested. She pressed her knee against his under the table, the plump line of her thigh against him under the layers of wool and linen. She smelt of scent. The part of him that clung to his father's joyless schooling wanted to assume it was cheap scent, but he knew Master Smith better than that, even if only by reputation. Probably very expensive scent indeed. He still wasn't interested.

"And you know me - or you damn well should, you've kicked my arse twice before now. Nat. Short for Nathaniel."

"*Not* Smith," Red guessed, and the blonde shook his head. Wisps of fair hair fell in his eyes and he pushed them back, grinning.

"Nah, not Smith, not really. But I'm not daft, old son –" he tapped the side of his nose with a finger, "if my worshipful father knew I was drinking with whores and ruffians in a *musico*, he'd cut me off without a penny. So he don't know. Nathaniel Rackhay is a *good* boy. He writes regular to his dear mother and everything. Nat Smith –" he grinned again –"Definite bad company, Red. Sort of bad lad your loving family prob'ly warned you about. Can't keep calling you Red. What's your *proper* name?"

Red took a deep breath. "Holofernes Babbitt."

Rackhay – he was going to find it hard to think of the blonde lad as anything but Smith – choked. Poured himself another cup of wine, thumping himself in the chest and blaming an errant crumb. "Holofernes? *Truly*? I can't call you that, Red... Be dead before I'd finished shouting that across the field, old son. Mind if I call you Hollie?"

Two new names in one evening. Two people who liked him well enough to notice him. "I'll grow used to it. *Nat*."

"Well. Let's drink to that, lad."

2 IN WHICH SERGEANT CULLIS IS NOT IMPRESSED

Powick Bridge, Worcestershire, September 1642

The long, slender shadow fell across the sunlit grass in front of him and Sergeant Cullis looked up, unimpressed, from the bridle bit he was cleaning. "Can I help you, sunshine?"

Pretty lad. Clean, plain, very good linen: clean, plain, good suit: clean, plain, brand new sword. Floppy, clean, shoulder-length fair hair, and eyes like a scared girl – he wouldn't last five minutes.

"I'm looking for Captain Babbitt," the lad said nervously. "I've a message from my lord Essex."

"Have you, indeed." Cullis grinned nastily and spat past the lad's well-polished, and equally new boot. "Well, now. Chances are by now he'll be down the horse lines. You know his horse, don't you? Everybody knows Tib, lovely beast, mild as milk he is. Tell you what I'd do if I was you – I'd go down there and pet Tibs while you're waiting for the Captain." He sighed ostentatiously, ignoring the sniggers from the rest of the troopers idly sprawled in the sun scorching bacon over a sulky fire. "Can't be no fun for that horse, tied up there on his own. He'd love a bit of fuss. Bet the Captain would thank you."

The lad looked slightly startled. "Wait for him? But the message –"

Cullis stood up, wiping wet grass onto his breeches. "I'm the captain's sergeant at arms, boy, not his pissing secretary. Now you can either go down there and waste some other bugger's time while you wait for him, or you can piss off back to my lord Essex and tell him you can't find him. Either way, I've got things to do."

The boy bridled. "I would remind you," he said with icy politeness, "that I am here on the orders of the commander of the Army of Parliament."

"I don't care if you're here on the Lord Almighty's business, lad, you're on my patch and you're taking up my time. Now bugger off." He jerked his thumb. "Horse lines. That way."

He watched the lad head off down the grassy slope towards the river where the horses of the troop were being watered. It had been a long morning, with half the Army of Parliament riding to and fro in the late summer heat looking for some mythical Royalist troop of horse. Some daft buggers had come skidding into Worcester just after dawn with a cock-and-bull story about the King's treasure convoy out of Oxford headed this way and ever since then they'd been quartering the countryside just outside the city like a pack of bloody hounds who'd lost the scent. Not so much as a loose penny on the road, of course, and the Captain spitting nails at being sent on a wild goose chase – especially running him in harness with Nat Rackhay. You didn't fly two old hawks like them two – and like Cullis himself, come to think of it – without a kill at the end of it. He squinted at the glare of the sun on the river, watching the boy slipping and sliding on the grass, which was what you got for wearing those damn' stupid officer's bucket-top boots instead of decent hob-nailed start-ups like a man of sense. Well, either Babbitt or his murderous horse would knock some sense into the silly lad.

Trooper Calthorpe stood up, rubbing his hands free of crumbs. "That weren't kind. He's nowt but a lad."

"Better grow up quick then, hadn't he?"

3 …AND IN WHICH LUCE PETTITT IS DISILLUSIONED

Lucifer Pettitt stood in the shade of the trees, admiring the dappled view. Such a beautiful autumn day, with the ripe blackberries like black jewels in the bushes and the spiders' webs still hung with dew despite the heat of the early afternoon. At the farthest end of the meadow, trees dipped their branches into the river, overlooked by a bridge of mellow golden stone. The horses were being taken down to the river to drink in relays; stripped of their harness, rubbed down, led into the water to stand hock deep in the ripples swishing their tails at the late September flies and snorting at the golden leaves falling into the river and swirling past. He sighed. It was a scene almost worthy of verse, the sun glinting off coats of chestnut and grey and black, of fine riding horses shoulder to shoulder with massive draught horses. He glimpsed his own dear sturdy grey Periwinkle, named for the country flower they called "Joy of the Ground", being led to the water in the company of an extremely aristocratic chestnut mare.

"Are you going to stand like a spare prick at a wedding all afternoon, boy, or are you going to get your sorry arse out of my way?"

Lucifer spun round, dazed and blinking, to find himself almost nose to nose with a massive fleabitten grey horse. He squinted into the sun framing the blowing horse's rider. A big, rawboned, unkempt trooper, unshaven and bare-headed, with reddish brown hair in a loose tail halfway down his back. "Lame, my arse," the rider said, to no one in particular, "bloody malingering beast - get on!"

The big horse shook his head with a blubbering snort, splattering Lucifer with foam and torn-up grass. "Get a shift on!" the redhead snarled, giving the grey horse a slap down the shoulder with the end of his reins and wheeling it into a lumbering canter that spun Luce aside like an autumn leaf.

"What a *remarkably* uncivil man," Lucifer announced aloud. No one answered him, but further down the bank, a lone black horse lifted his elegant, dripping head from the water and pricked his ears towards the sound of a human voice. They called Friesian horses Black Pearls and he could see why because Babbitt's black - and that beautiful beast could only be Babbitt's black - was incomparable, a thing of fire and shadow, as lovely and lonely as a fallen angel. The black came stepping up from the river floating across the grass like a feather and Luce was just stretching out his hand to caress the outstretched muzzle when he was suddenly grabbed by the collar and jerked, choking, off his feet.

"Have you got a bloody death wish, boy?"

Since the pressure of his own collar-band was throttling him against his windpipe, Luce was unable to either explain himself or identify his assailant.

"If you're lucky, that horse would only break your arm, you stupid –" Whoever he was, his arm must have begun to ache from shaking like a rat, because he let go abruptly with one final shove. Luce dropped sprawling on his face into the grass. "Oh, Christ, it's you again. Are you following me?"

"*Following* you? Why should I wish to follow you, you ill-mannered fellow?"

"First you pop up in front of me in a daydream and I nearly ride you down, and five minutes later I turn up to see to my own horse and here you are again, about to have your head stoved in? Did the name not give it away, boy? Tyburn? After the bloody gallows - bit of a clue? He's a warhorse, you gormless little bugger – he'd crush your bloody empty head like an eggshell!"

Luce scrambled to his feet and said with the remains of his dignity, "The Earl of Essex sent me to find Captain Babbitt, and his sergeant told me –"

"I'm going to swing for Cullis. Well, you bloody found me. What?"

"*You?*" Officers were men of good birth and manners, elegant and sophisticated. This dishevelled lout was a groom, or similar – some decayed tapster or low serving-man with ideas above his position, gone soldiering with his master. Officers did not go careering about the countryside in their shirt sleeves – dirty, and somewhat worn, shirt sleeves, Luce observed critically, looking at the smear of half-chewed grass down the man's less than impeccable linen where the grey horse had rested its slobbery head. "*You* are Captain Babbitt?"

"Unless there's more than one." The captain had a peculiarly vicious grin, too. "If you're looking for Hollie Babbitt, boy, then you found me. Now piss off and tell the grown-ups where I am, eh?"

Luce straightened his shoulders and brushed the grass from his breeches. "Then your rudeness does you no credit as an officer. My lord Essex –"

"If you throw that man's name up to me just once more, laddie, I'll knock your teeth down your bloody throat." Babbitt turned his back and started to walk back up to the picketed horses. "Whatever it is, I'm not interested. I've done enough chasing my shadow at his whim for the one day."

"I can assure you that I have no more taste for my new commission than you have!" he snapped, stung into uncharacteristic rudeness.

Babbitt's head jerked as if he'd been shot. He turned round again. "Commission?"

"I have been – ordered – to report as your cornet. *Sir*," Luce added sarcastically.

"Oh no. I need an cornet like a hole in the head."

"My lord –"

"If my lord Essex told you to put your face in t'fire, would you do it?" he said, in a reasonable tone. And then, abruptly, "Understand this, boy –"

"My name, sir, is Pettitt. *Lucifer* Pettitt."

"A boy called Lucey? How sweet." Luce stiffened, and Babbitt almost smiled. "Lord save us, does the boy have a backbone?"

"The *boy* is getting sick and tired of your incivility, sir! I have a mind –"

"One of Essex's lap-dogs? That'd make a change."

"If you weren't my commanding officer – allegedly – I'd knock you down for that!"

"Really?" The captain had turned his back, started to walk away. Contemptuously, as though Luce was of no account. That lanky build was deceptive. With a grace that would have been admirable in a man less determined to be unpleasant, he turned on his heel in one lithe movement and slapped Luce, hard, back-handed across the cheek. "Try it, boy. You just try it."

Luce wouldn't give Babbitt the satisfaction of seeing tears in his eyes – though he couldn't do much about the handprint that burned like a brand on his fair skin. Nor would he put his hand to his cheek, to rub away the sting like a child. He lifted his head proudly. "Touch you? I wouldn't dirty my hands. I might call out a man of honour, but not you."

Shaking his head, Babbitt simply turned his back again. "Piss off, boy, " he called over his shoulder. "Let's have this talk again when you're breeched, shall we?"

Suddenly Tyburn, restlessly pacing the shadows of the trees, lifted his head – ears sharply pricked – and

Lucifer saw the black horse's neck stiffen into a heraldic arch. He trotted to the end of his picket rope, head tossing. Babbitt stopped in his tracks. "What –" The black suddenly reared, ears flat back, and screamed an eerie, brassy stallion's challenge to the sky.

There was a long, waiting silence; even the gentle sounds of wind and rippling water had died down. Then, not half a mile away, came another horse's scream in response.

4 INAUSPICIOUS BEGINNINGS

"Can you ride, Pettitt?"

It seemed such a reasonable question, as the captain calmly untied his horse and sprang astride the bare back. As if that vicious interlude had never taken place.

"I can, sir, but -" Perhaps it was some kind of military initiation. Luce was confused. Uncle Essex had never led him to expect this kind of conduct. He stepped quickly out of the way of the black horse's restless forefeet.

"Which is your beast?"

"The grey mare – there -"

Babbitt followed Lucifer's gaze to Periwinkle, grazing peacefully hock-deep in the river. "Shit, boy, that's not a horse, it's a four-legged mattress. Ah, Christ, it's going to have to do – can you ride without a saddle?"

Lucifer shrugged. "I imagine so. But I -"

"Keep your voice down. There's another stallion hereabouts. One he don't recognise. Not half a mile away, by the sound of it."

"Doubtless, but -"

Babbitt reached down and grabbed his shoulder, hard. "Stop asking damn' fool questions and think. What kind of lackwit would put two entire horses in the line next to each other?" He let go and ran his hand down the black's neck. Tyburn was already beginning to lather. The smell of horse sweat was strong in Luce's nostrils. *"That's not our horse line."*

Lucifer gaped at him. "But my lord Essex said -"

"Oh, bollocks to him! I trust my horse more than I trust him. While he's been sat scratching himself me and Tib have been campaigning together for – long enough. Do what you're told, get hold of that misbegotten animal, and *ride*."

He started to walk the black back across the sunlit meadow. Slow, without a care in the world, with a hand flat on the horse's flank. Where his sword would have hung if he'd worn it. Lucifer pulled the mare's head up with a pat on her dripping muzzle, and kicked her into a canter – slowed her to a trot at Babbitt's ferocious glare. "Act like you're stretching her legs," he snarled. "There's summat up here. You're the cornet. Earn your pay. Go quiet – back to the men – tell them to prepare for an attack. Order them to form up – and do it *softly*, boy, d'you want the King's entire bloody army to know we're onto 'em?"

Tyburn tossed his head and sidled restlessly, barging his quarters into Periwinkle; catching the black's anxiety, she started to fret, and Lucifer caught at the slack makeshift rein of her halter quickly. "Perhaps," Babbitt said grimly, "we might risk a faster pace before that four-legged bedstead puts you on your arse?"

"But why don't we -"

Even as he asked there was a flurry of shots at the bridge and rooks rose out of the trees in a great cawing cloud. Babbitt kicked Tyburn into life, swearing. "For Christ's sake!" the captain roared, wheeling the black behind Periwinkle till the mare stumbled into a canter. "Form up, damn you – to me! To me!"

Jostling Periwinkle until he was close enough to wallop her across the quarters with the trailing rope end; men were struggling into armour, back and breast plates dangling loose, unbuckled, fumbling with weapons – half the horses a good half mile away, untacked, milling in the water. "Where the bloody hell has Captain Rackhay got to?" Babbitt roared at the nearest trooper, who stopped trying to shrug himself into his plate and stared blankly.

"Gone, sir -"

"What! Already? What the bloody *hell* does he think he's playing at, the -"

Lucifer, two yards behind on the blowing mare, exchanged a look of despair with the trooper. "Keep her up, damn you!" Babbitt snarled over his shoulder. "You're an officer - allegedly. You stay with me. *Now*."

"She -"

"If she can't, I'll put a bullet through the bitch's head! Cullis! Cullis, pox on you – get your worthless arse onto a horse and get those men into some semblance of battle order! *Move!*"

Babbitt put a hand out imperiously, snatched his sword without a word of thanks, belted the black horse with the flat of it, and took off at a flat gallop, scattering the ashes of the campfire underfoot.

M. J. LOGUE

5 MAKING THE BEST OF A BAD JOB

Leaving Lucifer very alone, cold, sick, and shaking, trying to load a pistol he'd never fired in anger whilst trying to control his labouring old mare with his knees.

"Good lad," Cullis said, suddenly knee to knee with him. "Bring the men up. No -" as he turned the mare's head blindly towards the river - "to the bridge? You'll be wanting the colours -" he gave Lucifer a mirthless grin, "what with you being the cornet and all."

"Yes - yes, of course, I -" The mare lurched, stumbling on a tussock of grass, and by the time he'd gathered rope bridle and pistol and colours and all, Cullis was gone.

He'd never seen so many horses and men so close to, and under it all the river kept on flowing and the autumn sun kept on shining, the bright fallen leaves floating away on the water. All Lucifer could think of was that if he kept close to the captain he'd be safe, because nothing on earth was mad enough to touch that bright berserk figure, and so he kept pushing on, edging his way forwards whenever he saw a gap in the fighting. Tyburn was screaming again, those weird unsettling shrieks of baffled fury: lashing out with both fore and hind hooves, forcing his way further into the press of horses and men in an attempt to get at his rival.

The other stallion was a big grey – almost white – almost the reverse of black Tyburn, tall and elegant with a flowing mane and tail like a knight's horse in a fairy tale, under the control of a rider in black plate. A tall man, almost as tall as the captain, with long dark hair that shone in the sun, falling in waves over his pristine white collar. He looked cool, in control, and distinctly unimpressed by the proceedings. Luce saw him point in their direction, glance towards the scarlet-sashed officer at his side, smiling as though the sight entertained them greatly. "Christ, it's Rupert of the Rhine himself," Cullis said. "Surely not even *Hollie's* fucking mental enough to take on the King's own nephew - "

And then one of Rupert's own lifeguard slewed his horse sideways into Cullis and the sergeant was gone, swirled away by the fighting.

In a brief lull, the captain jerked his head sideways, half-blinded with loose russet hair, saw Lucifer at his elbow and grinned fiercely. "Well, well," he said. "I know I said stay with me, but you do know the cornet is supposed to stay with the troop – not twenty yards in front of 'em?"

"And you do know it's usually a good idea to finish getting dressed before engaging the enemy?" Lucifer said furiously, gesturing with the colours at Babbitt's bloodstained shirt sleeves.

The captain shrugged, glancing around briefly at the mob of half-fastened armour and half-tacked horses. "No other bugger did.... Cornet Pettitt. Promise me one thing." His face was suddenly serious. "Give me your word."

"So far as I can, sir -"

Tyburn whirled on his hind legs. "Get rid of that bloody useless mare!"

And then he, too, was gone.

"How *dare* he –" And then Periwinkle, pushed to the boundaries of her patience by the frightening sights and sounds all around her, suddenly started to buck. His abrupt collapse down her shoulder probably saved his life. For a brief second he was actually surprised that some swine had actually shot at him - close enough for his ears to be ringing with the report of the shot - and then he scrambled back up on her neck and met the eyes of the damnable scut that'd done it.

"You bloody *bugger*," Lucifer said aloud, disbelieving – kicked Peri in the ribs, and yanked his sword free. A man on a big brown horse, backing wildly out of the melee, barred his way. Periwinkle simply barged through him. Just in front of them Peri's companion of the river, that lovely chestnut, went down squealing, her kicking hooves striking sparks from the stones of the bridge – came over onto her side, all white-ringed eyes and teeth, struggling to get back on to four feet that wouldn't obey her.

Lucifer and Peri were trapped against the bridge parapet. He felt the rough stone grind against his lower leg, harder and harder as the press of men and panicking horses moved, and hit out blindly with the flat of his sword. Peri shied as a man went down under her nose, shouting wildly, and Lucifer slid down her neck again, grabbing at her mane, dropping the rough bridle and almost losing the colours. Of the two, the colours suddenly seemed more important.

He could smell powder and sweat and, rather comically, horse shit, and then someone backed into Peri. The mare flung up her head with a squeal of pain and Lucifer hacked at the other horse's rump as she staggered. A line of blood appeared on the gleaming backside and suddenly the sunlight was glinting blindingly off the blade of a sword, off a well-polished breastplate. Luce had expected his first earnest swordplay to be slightly more distinguished. The two blades came together with an impact that made his arm tingle – he yelped, reflexively jerking his hand back, trying to back the mare but she was having none of it and he was hard against the bridge parapet again, frantically trying to parry the attack like a man swatting wasps.

And then by sheer chance Luce's blade slid along the

length of the other man's sword, with sparks like a blacksmith's forge, and a tiny thin ringing whine like a gnat's, and tore up his arm. Luce saw the fabric of his adversary's doublet sleeve part and the white linen underneath turn a sudden violent red, and the man's face turn as white as the linen. The young cavalier dropped his blade, pitched forward onto the horse's neck, slid limply sideways and was gone, over the bridge into the sluggish water of the Teme. Luce gasped – he wanted to bend over Peri's shoulder and see if he'd truly hurt the young man, to apologise, to make it all right. There was no time for more than a glance, and nothing to see in the slow brown water.

"Where's the damn' colours? Fall back, you sorry bastards, fall *back*!" Cullis suddenly back with him, standing in his stirrups and roaring, gripping the drooping colours one-handed. "If you're going to puke, boy, do it over the bridge," he said out of the side of his mouth and Luce gripped the mare's mane with one hand and thought that if the bridge would stop swinging dizzily about it was certainly an option.

"I do reckon we lost the captain again," someone said in a slow Somerset drawl.

"I do reckon we lost the bloody fight, mate," someone else said, and there was a burst of relieved laughter. Luce was cold, although the sun was still shining – hadn't moved much further in the sky, though the fighting seemed to have gone on for hours. He pointed mutely to the far side of the bridge. The distinctive figures of black Tib and the captain were returning. Babbitt looked shockingly naked in his shirt sleeves amongst the milling cavalry in their back and breast plates. There were still occasional shots, far-spaced and distant. The captain halted his horse a couple of yards away and sat, surveying his ragged troop with disfavour. There was a splash of blood across his cheek and across his less-than-impeccable shirt, and Luce doubted very much it was his own.

"Well." He crossed his wrists on the black's neck, and the horse threw his head up and down. "The first shots of the war, gentlemen." He looked coldly from face to face. "Pity they were on the wrong bloody side, isn't it?"

There was a glint of something. In the trees, on the far side of the river. Luce pressed the mare forward with his knees, an eye on that tiny gleam of sunlight on metal. A long straight line of light, like the sun on the barrel of a musket. He kicked Peri. She lurched forward, shoulder to shoulder with Tyburn, knocking the black off-balance for just long enough for Luce to throw himself across the mare's withers and shove his commanding officer to the ground. As the two of them hit the cobbles, there was an echoing crack that sounded like the only noise in the world, and Luce felt something sharp and cold slice his cheek. Babbitt was shaking under him. It was the first sign of humanity Luce had seen.

The captain shoved him to one side and sat up, bloody and white to the lips, and it crossed Luce's mind that he wasn't shaking with fear but rage. "Boy," he said grimly, "get out of my sight, and take your four-legged bedstead with you. *Now!*"

"But you - didn't you –"

Cullis leaned down and hauled him to his feet. "Best do as he says, lad. I'll explain later."

6 NOT A THING TO DO LIGHTLY

Luce thought he should have let the swine be shot. No, he had to be honest – the captain was ungrateful, sarcastic, vicious, unprincipled, bad-tempered, but he was *alive*. He led Peri down to the river's edge and let her dip her muzzle into the water.

Somewhere in that water there was a young man who'd also been alive, this time yesterday. He was food for worms – fish – now because Lucifer Pettitt had been in the wrong place at the wrong time. He'd looked so surprised as Luce's blade had torn up his arm. Luce dipped his hand in the ripples, feeling the linen of his sleeve turn chill and clammy as it soaked up the river water.

Remembered what – who – else was in the river water, and was very, very sick.

He lay for a long time with his face in the wet grass, breathing in the smells of water and late summer dusk as the sun began to dip behind the trees. His throat burned but he didn't feel any less sick. Peri lifted her head and whinnied companionably.

He rolled over – four white-stockinged, delicate, thoroughbred legs in the water, and he breathed an acid sigh of relief. Not black. Not Tyburn.

"Happen I owe you an apology." Not Tyburn, but the flat Lancashire burr of his master. Luce focussed his eyes on a beetle crawling up a grass stem, and determinedly did not look round.

"It has been known," the disembodied voice went on, "for me to cock things up. Not having eyes in the back of my head. Not summat I make a habit of, mind. And I wouldn't like you to get into the habit of knocking me off my bloody horse in front of the men. Under the circumstances, though... So." Babbitt sounded awkward. That had to be a first. "Aye, well. Thank you, lad. Er, Cornet."

"Captain. Go away." He buried his face in his cold, wet sleeve. "Sir." Took a deep breath because no way on this earth was he going to be sick again in front of that man. "Please?"

"Brought your horse. Well, she's got to be someone's, might as well be yours. She's not much use to that feller you kicked off the bridge –"

At which point he *was* sick, with nothing left in his belly to be sick with, in silent tears of misery and humiliation. Babbitt sat down beside him on the riverbank, stiffly, as if his bones ached. "You know summat? It's not a game. I've had twenty years of being shot at and I'm not like to tell you it gets better with practice because it bloody well doesn't. Christ, lad, what did you *think* was going to happen?"

Luce shook his head mutely. The captain wasn't looking at him anyway, staring out into the middle of the river, at the sun setting in rose and gold on the water. "It's not a thing to do lightly," he said absently. "If you've not the heart for it, boy, then go home, and no shame to you."

"Are you suggesting I'm a coward, captain?"

Babbitt turned towards him. He was still streaked with blood and the setting sun turned his loose hair to dark fire. "I'm telling you what I wish some bugger had told me, twenty years ago. I'll tell you summat else I wish someone had told me, as well." He stood up and flexed his wrist with a sound like a pistol shot. "Brandy helps, the first few times."

And with that he was gone, leaving Luce with a warm flask of raw brandy, a very expensive-looking chestnut thoroughbred mare, and far too much to think about.

7 A STEADY HAND ON THE BRIDLE, BABBITT

Autumn seemed to have set in in earnest overnight, and sharp gusts of wind set the wet leaves swirling over the Worcester cobbles in squalls. Hollie Babbitt hunched his shoulders against the drizzle and turned the black horse's head away from shelter, toward impending doom.

He wasn't in the best of tempers this morning – but then again, when was he ever, these days? – having spent most of the night under a dripping hedge in a field, unable to see a hand in front of his face for river mist. And with his new cornet for company. He was assuming the whining brat was male, based entirely on the assumption that it'd make an infernally ugly woman. Hollie wasn't sure what he'd done to deserve call-me-Lucey Pettitt, but he must have seriously upset someone somewhere. So he hadn't slept, hadn't eaten since breakfast yesterday (and Moggy Davies had cooked that, and his supplies were legendarily unreliable) and now he was stiff, chilled, and trying to persuade a bad-tempered horse into compliance. There were them as thought that Hollie and Tyburn shared some kind of unnatural affinity – and how wrong they were, he thought, rubbing his bitten forearm absently.

There was a hollow, echoing ring of hoofbeats and Nat Rackhay materialised out of the rain, shaking droplets out of his tangled fair hair. "Good morning, Red."

Hollie raised an undeniably-red eyebrow. "It's a morning, true enough, but I'll let you know what's good about it in about an hour."

"Oh, it won't be that bad!" He kicked his horse alongside Tib – an overbred and under-witted grey thoroughbred, Hollie thought sourly, bloody typical Rackhay. "What's the worst he can do?"

"Leave us kicking our heels in this arsehole of a place for the foreseeable future?"

Rackhay shrugged. "There's inns – and the Bishop's Mitre -"

"Trust you to know where the bloody brothel is."

"I didn't say I'd *frequented it*, captain – I merely suggested it for information."

Hollie snorted. "Of course. Never seen you in a brothel, have I?"

"Course you have, old son. I used to come round to your place all the time -" An armed sentry stepped out of the mist in front of them – Rackhay's thoroughbred went into an inbred panic, skittering all over the cobbles, and Tyburn stood disapprovingly still like the perverse black bastard he was.

"Who's there?"

"Rackhay and Babbitt, reporting as my lord Essex commanded," Hollie said – adding in an undertone, "as if you didn't know."

Leaving Tib tied in the courtyard seemed like the least destructive option. Rackhay's thoroughbred was led meekly round to the stable yard by one of Essex's staff while the two captains kicked their heels downstairs in a bare, newly-decorated room, awaiting his lordship's pleasure. It was newly-plastered enough to still smell of lime, but at least it was sheltered. It had been newly-swept, too, till two sets of wet riding boots had tracked dead leaves and mud across the clean boards. Two. Note that neither my lord of Essex nor any of his staff had seen fit to venture outdoors this morning.

Rackhay scrubbed his hands through his hair, making

it stand out round his head like a fox's ruff. "Not that he's making us wait a-purpose, of course."

"I don't care. It's not bloody raining in here." Hollie eyed the plainly plastered walls with disfavour. "Christ, Nat, I'd kill for summat to eat. I never had chance for breakfast this morning, what with being hauled in for questioning before the sun was up."

"You're getting soft, Red. You never used to eat breakfast."

"Getting old, owd lad, that's what it is. Turned thirty at Rheinfelden." He scratched, irritably, at his itchy stubble. "And don't be giving me any of your old buck about your sleeping under a bush wi'the rest of us, because you stink like a civet's armpit. Whatever bed you rolled out of, it had four bare legs in it. Am I wrong?"

Rackhay grinned at him unashamedly. "One of the things I admire about you, captain, is your ability to hit the nail square on the head."

Hollie shook his head. "You're an unprincipled bastard, Nat."

"Oh, for sure, but then it wasn't me who spent the night in a ditch with Sergeant Cullis's arse in my face."

"My lord Essex will see you now." The door had opened to admit a silent-footed aide: shiny-faced as a schoolboy, and dressed in impeccable linen. *He* hadn't spent the night in any ditches. Looking at the bare appointments of this new-plastered and empty hall, it was possible that he'd perhaps not enjoyed the full range of creature comforts – but at least the swine had had a roof over his head. Hollie was almost sure the wait wasn't intended as a deliberate insult – but only almost. "This way, please."

The staircase was wide and airy, with three long windows overlooking the courtyard, and an underwater grey-green light filtering in from the raw autumn morning. The catlike aide moved up the wooden treads with lithe grace. Damn him. Hollie eased his shoulders stiffly, uncomfortably aware of the difference between two middle-aged, somewhat well-worn officers straight out of the field and their elegant surroundings. Rackhay might have spent the night between four walls but he still looked like an unmade bed in a buff coat and he creaked when he walked – at least, Hollie hoped it was the buff coat that creaked.

Out of the corner of his eye, he glanced at his old companion in arms. It didn't seem five minutes since the Low Countries, and Rackhay had taken up his old position: at Hollie's right hand, two paces behind. They'd even managed to fall into step. It had been – not fated, exactly, that had a ring of predestination to it and he didn't hold with that, but there had been a sort of sense to it that two of the most distinctive lads in the troop had kicked around together: both tall and lean and bright-haired, you wouldn't miss either of them in a crowd. Rackhay's mouth had that sort of straight grim set it used to get before he got a right royal bollocking – that sort of devil-may-care pretending he wasn't bothered look. He caught Hollie's eye, and winked. Lengthened his stride and came up alongside. "Keep a steady hend on the bridle, Bebbitt," he muttered, in a near-perfect imitation of their old Dutch commander, and Hollie choked.

The commander-in-chief of the Army of Parliament was standing facing away from them, looking out into the rain-swept street, and he didn't turn round, not even to radiate disapproval at their levity. Very much like getting a right royal bollocking twenty years ago, then, except mostly in English. "Well, gentlemen," Essex said, addressing the window.

It wasn't the first time he'd set eyes on the Earl of Essex, but Hollie was slightly distracted by how much shorter the man was once off his horse. He found himself mentally calculating what advantage of reach he'd have with a sword over a man – five? six? – inches shorter than he was. He suspected the silence had been intended for Rackhay and himself to reflect on their disfavour, rather than an opportunity to Hollie work out the best way of disarming his commander. Force of habit. Essex was not a particularly imposing figure. There was a bit too much of the art of the tailor in that doublet for Hollie's tastes – he had no eye for fashion, the Lord knew, but he knew padding when he saw it and most of that manly physique had come off of the back of a sheep. He didn't quite dare look at Rackhay, who wasn't more than an inch or two shorter than Hollie but considerably more solidly constructed across the shoulders. The pair of them must look like they were looming over him like some cheap backstreet bravos.

Essex sat down, still without speaking, and then the silence began to grow uncomfortable. It hadn't gone unnoticed that he hadn't asked either of them to be seated. The Earl steepled his fingers and looked up at the two officers. White, well-kept hands. Hollie quickly put his own hands behind his back. Not for the first time, he wished he had the self-mastery not to start stripping the skin from round his nails when he was uncomfortable. The rain pattered gently on the window glass and trickled musically down the gutters. Essex wasn't daft; faced with two hulking roughs in a small space, he intended they should know their place.

Rackhay, still the master of dumb insolence twenty years on, picked idly at the gap where one of his canine teeth had been, with his little fingernail. Just to make sure Essex was aware they weren't in the business of being intimidated.

"The war has begun in earnest, then."

After so long a silence, Essex's voice startled the pair

of them. There wasn't supposed to be an answer to that, so they didn't give one. They'd been hauled over the coals before. They knew the drill. The Earl of Essex took a deep breath, and then lifted his head and let it out again. "You cocked it up, gentlemen. I don't know how two experienced field officers managed it, but you took a perfectly simple order and between the pair of you, you made a pig's ear of it. Any ideas?"

Rackhay was about to explain – which was more than Hollie could have done – when Essex held up a languid, humiliating hand.

"Please. I don't think I actually need to hear your excuses. The fact of the matter is I have two officers, one with a reputation for a lack of initiative, and the other with a reputation for intemperacy. Well, gentlemen, yesterday you appear to have changed roles, and it does neither of you credit. Captain Rackhay, how many men did you lose yesterday? Please?"

"Fifteen. Or so. Sir," Rackhay mumbled.

"Quite so. And Captain Babbitt? Your losses?"

"Um. None, sir. That I can account for." Head up, clear, distinct voice. Ears burning.

"Just so. Possibly, Captain Babbitt, because by the time your men arrived at the bridge Prince Rupert and most of the treasure convoy were in the next county?"

"That's not exactly true, sir –"

"No, no, I must be fair, I have heard reports of your, your, what's the word I should use? Enthusiastic, perhaps. Yes, your enthusiastic arrival. Obviously, I lack your experience as a commanding officer, Captain, but next time you seek to engage the enemy I should recommend that you finish saddling your horse – oh, and possibly wait for the rest of your troop to catch you up. I understand you were not the only man from your ranks who hadn't troubled to finish dressing, so I shall let that pass."

RED HORSE

Rackhay sniggered. Hollie turned his head and gave his old comrade a long, considering look. Essex hadn't finished. "Perhaps you could share the source of your amusement with us all, Captain Rackhay? I fail to see what there is to be proud of in your conduct – although it is something of an achievement to manage to miss a baggage train and a troop of armed men encamped in the next field to your own. A most remarkable achievement. You must enlighten me as to how you managed it?"

"Gets a bit misty down there by the river," Hollie said with a straight face.

Essex gave him a wintry smile. "Hold your tongue, Babbitt, you are neither of you schoolboys and you are each as culpable as one another in this. This is not a matter for levity. You –" he jabbed a finger at Rackhay, who shied off like a startled horse – "your lack of decisive action, your ill-informed weakness – do you have any idea how much harm you have done to the cause? You have lost us time, lost us valuable men, lost us the Lord knows how much plate was in that convoy, and most of all you, captain, lost us our good name! The first engagement of this war, and your men behaved like a pack of ill-disciplined cowards! What excuse was it you gave - an attack by Rupert's own Lifeguards, indeed! That was no retreat, you were routed! They were nowhere near you, man - what the hell were you *thinking*?"

Hollie was trying to work that one through in his own head. How the hell *could* you miss a baggage train and a hundred or so cavaliers milling round it like flies round shit? And all he could think of was that Essex was right, more's the pity - they hadn't been thinking. Not thinking at all – or rather, like every other bugger, thinking that the shouting and the finger-wagging on both sides was as good as it was going to get, because this was England, and wars do not take place on English soil. Much too complacent, Babbitt. Bet the bloody Spanish said that, too. And the Swedes. And the Germans. And every other bugger who'd had their blood spilled half across Europe in the last thirty years of assorted wars.

No, he reckoned that was it - that nobody thought it'd ever go this far, despite all the threats and the harsh words being tossed around by the great and the good since the King had raised his standard against Parliament three months back. They'd spent God knows how long riding round the countryside recently trying to look stern and soldierly without so much as a whiff of a perfumed cavalier. And that was half the problem, the buggers didn't have horns and tails, no matter what the likes of the Earl of Essex might like to make out – most of 'em would pass as his own troops, or Rackhay's: dreamy boys on highly-strung horses pretending to be Sir Lancelot, like that bloody wet cornet he'd been lumbered with; scared farmers on stolid draught animals; enough professional fighting men like himself to put the living fear of God into both kinds. They'd known there were enemy troops about, of course they knew that, they'd even met at the bridge earlier that morning without a cross word – well, apart from the customary idle exchange of pleasantries about the dubious parentage and antiquity of some of the Parliamentarian horse. "There's summat I can't put my finger on," he said cautiously.

Essex raised his eyebrows. "Would that be your harness, captain, or your armour?"

Hollie bit down hard enough on the inside of his cheek to draw blood, just to curb the reply that was on the tip of his tongue. He was still thinking, though. Something to do with Tyburn – he snapped his fingers. "That German twat. *That's* what kicked it off. *Him*. That bastard would start a fight in a nunnery if he thought there'd be glory in it. Bloody pot-hunter."

Rackhay was nodding. "That sounds about right."

"Bloody right that would be it. From what I've heard, he was probably teasy because he couldn't get his hair right – and I'll tell you what, if me and him ever meet on the field again I'll show him a trick or two that didn't come out of the officers' manual. There's many a sharp blade come out of a worn scabbard, the arrogant –"

"Am I to assume, Captain Babbitt, that the King's nephew has maligned your abilities as an officer?" Essex said maliciously. "That, I presume, would be the same Prince Rupert who had the forethought to line the lane with his dragoons in advance of your precipitate arrival and then held your men off for long enough to facilitate the safe removal of the treasure convoy? Surely not."

Rackhay, very gently, moved his foot so that his boot was pressing on Hollie's instep. Hollie took a deep breath and unclenched his fists. "That German twat's no more a bloody field officer than you are – begging your pardon, sir, but that being why we're slogging round the countryside up to the arseholes in mud and you're sat in here pushing the papers around. His mother probably kitted him out in shiny armour and a big shiny horse to get him out of the way because he's about as much use as a sick headache. We might not have pulled off the treasure convoy, sir, but at least we didn't start a bloody war. Wasn't *us* that fired the first shots, my lord."

Rackhay's foot pressed down slightly harder. Essex's thick black eyebrows were ascending his forehead. "Indeed, captain. I presume this little tirade is a diversion from the real crux of the matter, which is your professional negligence."

Hollie straightened his shoulders. He'd fought enough losing battles to know one when he saw one. Instead, he salvaged a tiny bit of pride by staring quite deliberately at a point six inches above the Earl of Essex's head. Wasn't often that Hollie was proud of being a hands'-breadth taller than most men – apart from Prince Rupert, of course, like that was any consolation – but if what he had was the ability to look down on Essex's bald patch, he'd take what little comfort there was.

Essex pursed his lips. "Gentlemen, you may consider this your final and only warning. There is no room in this fight for your –" he gave that thin smile again "- dare I say, *cavalier* approach. That may be how things were done In the Low Countries, but in this country we behave in war like men of principle. You are dismissed."

Rackhay slouched for the door, spurs jingling on the polished boards. Hollie, shoulders still rigidly braced, swung on his heel and would have followed but Essex called him back.

"You, Captain Babbitt, I am not done with you. Your reputation for arrogance and incivility precedes you, as does a reputation for –" Essex was hating every word of saying this, his lip curling as if someone had handed him a dead rat –"reckless brilliance in the field. Understand this, captain, I'll brook none of your insolence. I expect to see your deportment improve – *considerably* – to that befitting a senior officer, rather than that of a spoiled brat. And if I ever, *ever* catch either you or that damned ungovernable black beast of yours turned out in a state of personal undress such as yesterday's, I'll have you both shot. Are you clear on this?"

"Perfectly, sir." Rackhay was listening on the bloody landing, the sneaking swine. Impossible to be discreet in spurs, so the bastard just didn't bother.

"I am assured that you have the *capacity* to pass for civilised, Captain, by men whose judgment I trust. I hope that with appropriate correction -"

Hollie stiffened again. Correction. Interesting. He'd like to see Essex try it.

"I take it as my Christian duty to see to your

progress. I trust that your new cornet may act as a check upon your worst excesses of temperament, and that his confiding nature will not be abused by your company. His mother is a cousin of my lady wife's –"

Ah, well, that explained call-me-Lucey, didn't it? Essex's lady wife was somewhat legendary by her absence. Gone off with her fancy man whilst her lawful husband played at soldiers. Essex had been trying to pretend he was quite the big man ever since. Not, in Hollie's opinion, fooling anybody, but if the Earl wanted to pretend that all was sweetness and light in the Essex household by grooming his absent wife's friends and relations for prominence, that was his affair. Unfortunately, in the Earl's desire to promote the happy Essex family, he'd saddled Hollie with his own personal Rupert, some little inconvenience bought into a military career to get him out from underfoot. Rupert at least had balls, if little in the way of brains. Call-me-Lucey probably pissed sitting down. Hollie's jaw was starting to ache with the effort of not saying as much out loud. "I see," he said. His voice sounded distinctly odd, through gritted teeth. "Perhaps I might now be excused, sir? I was not aware of the family connection between yourself and Master Pettitt. I will take pains to behave accordingly." - and, he thought grimly, I'm going to kick his arse from here to whatever landed estate it came off of when I get hold of him.

"One other thing, Babbitt." Essex was pulling the dead-rat face again. "Your men held the bridge, Captain. Most of our losses were in the lane beyond – whilst Captain Rackhay and his troops were bolting in rank disorder most of the way back to the city in mortal fear of Rupert's lifeguard –"

Hollie coughed, trying to hide an unkind laugh. What was it they said about listeners in never hearing any good of themselves?

"Your men retreated in good order under your command, captain. Give them my commendation."

8 SUSPICIOUSLY ELEGANT LODGINGS

Rackhay was somewhat red in the face and elaborately casual as Hollie pulled the door closed behind him and headed down the stairs. "You done, then, Red?"

"Oh, I imagine you heard most of it."

"They probably heard your side of it in Scotland, old son."

"You reckon? I thought I was quite restrained."

"I thought you were like to *be* restrained at one point."

"What, by him? Don't worry, I'd let you hold my coat." He stopped on the threshold, noting that the discreet aide had not escorted them off the premises; they were seeing themselves out, like uninvited guests. Nat eyed the glistening cobbles and the billowing drizzle with disfavour.

"You notice he gets quarters with furnishings and we get to shift as best we can – not, you understand, that I'd not prefer to sleep with my horse than with my lord Essex."

"Didn't like to say, old son, but I've heard some funny stories about you and that horse."

Hollie gave him a narrow look. "That's only because my horse is better looking than your mother."

Rackhay grinned his foxy grin. "Now, talking of better-looking, and don't take this badly, Red, but you do know you and your lads are bedding down in the cathedral, don't you?"

He ignored Hollie's splutter. The two respectable burghers of Worcester passing by on the other side of the cobbles, well swaddled against the mizzle, gave them a horrified glance and scampered on. "I'll make you a small wager, Captain – if I'm laying my bedroll out next to yours in the vestry tonight, I'll stand you a drink. Done?" He spat on his hands and smoothed his hair behind his ears. It didn't, in Hollie's opinion, enhance his old mate's charms over-much, but mercifully he'd never been called upon to make a judgment.

"Lock up your daughters," Hollie said dryly.

"I don't do daughters, old son. Too much like hard work. I'd go back to last night's lodgings, but –" he lifted a shoulder with a swagger –"her husband's come home. I sent him out on patrol last night. Didn't see a thing but his horse's ears, poor old Blyth, but at least *one* of us didn't have a wasted night."

Shaking his head, Hollie mounted the subdued black horse. "You know what, Nat, I reckon you make it up." The mizzle was deceptive. Out from under the shelter of the overhanging eaves, it was raining in good earnest, and his saddle was slick within seconds. Tib laid his ears back and took a desultory bite at his rider's knee, but the black horse's heart wasn't in it and a flat-handed slap down the shoulder soon set him straight, though it sounded like a pistol shot in the silent streets. There was hardly a soul out this morning, and the two horses, walking side by side between the leaning timbered houses, sounded like an echoing army. Whether that was the weather, or fear of the real occupying Army, it was difficult to guess.

Whichever, it was unnatural. It made the space between Hollie's shoulderblades itch.

It was a relief to hear another set of hoofbeats advancing at a perky trot. Hollie glanced over his shoulder and stiffened. It was less of a relief to clap eyes on the pretty chestnut mare.

Rackhay craned round in the saddle. "That's your new lad, isn't it?"

Hollie turned his horse so that Tib's solid quarters

blocked the road. "Oh, Christ, he's following me again." He glared from under his dripping hat at his ill-wished cornet, who seemed oblivious. He also, damn him, seemed remarkably dry. "What?"

Pettitt reined the mare in: he even did that neatly, sitting there all bright-eyed and shiny, and Hollie felt every one of his thirty-ish years. He saluted, and one captain accepted it with a grave incline of the head and the other suspected him of irony. "Captain Babbitt, sir, I have instructions to direct you to your quarters."

"Do you, indeed. I shouldn't bother, Cornet, I can manage to find the cathedral with the use of my two eyes. It's the big stone building with all the men in it, right?"

"Sir?"

The little bastard had even shaved. Which was more than Hollie had found time or space to do in the best part of a week. That was always assuming call-me-Lucey had even started that particular masculine practice. "Don't play tricksy with me, cornet, I'm not in the mood."

"Sir?"

"That is starting to piss me off now, boy, so give over. What is it you want?"

"To direct you to your quarters, sir. But, as you know where the Cathedral is, you will no doubt be able to find the Bishop's Palace without my assistance."

Hollie took his hat off and ran a hand through his hair. It still felt like he was wearing the damn' hat. Be nice to get the tangles out of his hair, never mind wash it, some time soon. Something else to hold against the brat. "Is this something to do with your infernal lady mother?"

Pettitt looked innocent and affronted. "I'll thank you not to speak of my lady mother in that way, sir, and as she is at home in Witham I doubt if it's anything to do with her. She hasn't left Essex since my sister was born ten years ago, so what she might have to do with finding us accommodation in Worcester, I do not know."

Rackhay wheeled his thoroughbred round in a showy pirouette. "Would one of you two kindly explain why we're standing in the pissing rain talking about your cornet's mother, when we could be indoors having some breakfast?"

The aforesaid cornet dropped his gaze demurely and there was nothing exceptionable in his demeanour, but Hollie couldn't shift himself of the itchy-shoulderblade feeling of walking into an ambush. "My lord of Essex instructed that Captain Babbitt should be appropriately accommodated, sir. He made particular request that the captain's baggage should be brought to his new residence by noon."

"Which happens to be the Bishop's Palace. Not short of a bob or two, is our Master Prideaux, and scarcely a friend to the cause of Parliament, from what I understand. Is it purely coincidental, do you think, that that particular Croesus has been kicked out on his arse to make room for *us*?" Hollie said.

"Indeed, sir, I believe that Master Prideaux has left his lodgings on a matter of some personal expediency, although I understand that he may have left the household attended in his, ah, haste. When I set off, the cook was just beginning to prepare venison pasties."

"Was he, now." Rackhay sounded thoughtful.

"You can bugger off back to the cathedral, lad. You owe me a drink."

"Me buy *you* a drink, Red? You can whistle for it, old son – I'm sticking to you like a burr to a blanket. You've fallen on your feet this time. You *sure* you want rid of this lad?"

Surer than ever, Hollie thought grimly, wheeling Tib to follow back down the cobbles after Pettitt. Lucey had said nowt and done nowt you could take exception to.

Except innocently arrange to turn up with one of the most disreputable-looking officers in the Army of Parliament, and turn them loose, in the Bishop of Worcester's palace, amongst the Bishop's saintly neighbours, in one of the wealthiest districts of the city. Now, you had to ask yourself, was that intended as a sweetener for Hollie's temper, or was it meant for Hollie to make a bloody fool of himself and land him in hot water with Essex - again?

Well, this particular disreputable officer had no intention of falling on his arse for the personal gratification of the Earl of Essex's cousin, nephew, whatever the hell he was. And personal expediency, his lily-white arse. Prideaux was running scared, frightened that for all the King's promises maybe, just maybe, Charles Stuart wouldn't put himself out to haul the Bishop's chestnuts out of a particularly Parliamentarian fire. And if Hollie and his shabby troop had been used to put two fingers up to the Bishop, well, he'd been used to make insulting gestures before, it hadn't killed him then and it wouldn't kill him now.

Come to think of it, there probably wasn't much he wouldn't put up with, for the sake of a decent meal and a night's sleep in a proper bed.

9 TEMPORARY ACCOMODATION

Luce led the way into the warm, dimly-lit hall. Rackhay slouched after him, craning his neck at the arching beams and massive stone windows. "Nice," he said. "Very nice. You can see the river from here, Red."

"If it keeps on raining," Babbitt said ungraciously, "we'll be *in* the bloody river."

"Most amusing. I *mean*, unless the little bastards have got webbed feet, we're not going to be getting any surprise attacks from that way."

"Really?" The big redhead propped one elbow against the flawless plaster above the hearth and grinned. "That's a relief. I might get to lie a-bed tomorrow morning after all."

"Ah, that'd be nice – "

"I'll be sure and think of you when I look out of the window at the teeming rain tonight. Tucked up nice and chilly in the cathedral. With the rest of your bloody ruffianly lot." Babbitt hooked one boot under the nearest chair and sat down with a deliberate thump. "I could get used to this, brat. You got any more influential relatives you need to disclose?"

Luce was glad of the shadows, because they concealed the look of sheer loathing he directed at the back of the captain's head. "I would not consider my family to be a subject for common currency, sir. Do you have any further duties for me this morning, or –"

The redhead snapped his fingers. "Age, Rackhay, that's what it is. Told you I was getting on a bit. I forget things. Glad you reminded me. I do, Pettitt. Off you trot and find the rest of the troop, there's a good lad. I'd hate them to feel neglected."

Luce considered a protest. A look at Babbitt's face – innocent as a baby, and wholly unconvincing – and Rackhay's foxy grin told him that resistance was useless. "That's an order, brat," Babbitt added, in case the point hadn't been made.

"You are a bastard at times," he heard Rackhay say admiringly, and then the Bishop's hefty front door slammed shut and he heard no more.

Luce Pettitt did not swear. He was a kind, thoughtful, dutiful boy. People had always said that. Well, now he wasn't a boy any more, he was a man grown, and it was about time he started - and he was downright pissed off as he splashed through the puddles back towards the cathedral. "Bloody, buggering hell," he muttered, and the sentry on duty looked taken aback.

"Beg pardon?"

"I believe I may have been sent on a fool's errand," he clarified, with dignity. He had half a mind to turn round and go back to the Commandery and tell Uncle Essex in words of one syllable exactly what he thought of the calibre of his officers, particularly those large and uncouth ones whose idea of humour was to send innocent young men into a black, frigid marble hole filled with the best part of five hundred men – and expect him to pick out the right ones. He didn't even know how many men were *in* Babbitt's troop, and he couldn't pick them out of this Stygian gloom even if he had the faintest idea which faces he was looking for. "Do you happen to know where I might find Captain Babbitt's men?"

The trooper looked at him. "I haven't seen Captain Babbitt since this morning, mate."

"Yes, but his men – he *has* a troop here, I presume – where are they?"

"In there." He jerked his thumb into the blackness,

evidently presuming he was talking to an idiot, and Luce knew exactly how he felt.

"Oh, never mind."

There was a horse standing with its nose in the font, noisily drinking. That should have shocked Luce but by now he was feeling unshockable. Instead of an atmosphere of quiet reflection, the holy place was filled with the sounds of the inn and the stableyard. Well, if all the men were all as downright unpleasant as the two he'd just left, it was a wonder that the Lord didn't send down a thunderbolt to smite the whole boiling lot of them. It was no surprise they'd been defeated at the bridge.

A howling ghost in flapping white draperies suddenly went thumping past him and had it not been for the three other troopers who ran after the spectre and stripped off his stolen vestments, laughing like madmen, Luce would have thought he truly had entered Hell. As it was he was so shaken he had to lean on one of the great marble pillars in the nave until his legs were reliable under him.

"Here - it's Lucey – hi! Luce! This way!"

A friendly voice. He turned his head blindly – he was not going to cry, he was not lonely, he was not frightened, and he was not so angry under it all that he could spit – and saw his grim new sergeant. "Well then. What you done with the colours, boy?"

The temptation to suggest what he would *like* to have done with the troop colours was immense, but looking at the size of Sergeant Cullis, he didn't think they'd fit. By God, things had come to a pretty pass when the nearest thing you'd found to a friendly face looked like it had crawled down the side of the cathedral and stolen a soldier's coat. "The colours are at our new place of lodgings, sir," he said sweetly. "As is the Captain."

Cullis spat, deliberately, just past Luce's boot. "*Is* he. And where've *you* been all morning, lad?"

Luce leant forward until he was almost nose to nose with the sergeant's stony countenance. "*I* have been sorting out your bloody accommodation. Which I would have assumed was *your* job, no?"

"He got you there, sir." That was the big freckled lad from Somerset – the one who thought they'd lost the captain. There was a stained scrap of linen wrapped round his forearm. He was still grinning, though.

Cullis glowered at him, and then his gargoyle face slowly stretched into a grin. "You're a cheeky little bastard, Lucey. Where you got us, then?"

"The Bishop's Palace."

"You are having me on."

Luce shook his head and Cullis stared blankly for a second before he started to chuckle, then to snort, then to pound his fist on his leg in howls of laughter. "Aw, that's priceless! What the hell d'you do with the bishop? Tell him to move over in the bed?"

"Master Prideaux has voluntarily chosen to leave his residence on a temporary basis," Luce said, quite cool.

Cullis stopped laughing. "You're serious?"

"Of course. My lord Essex has requested that the troop take up temporary quarters in the house immediately. Captain Babbitt ordered me to bring the men hence."

"Shit. The. Bed."

"I suggest you try not to, sergeant," Luce said dryly. "The Bishop wouldn't like it."

10 A MATTER OF PRINCIPLE

There was a bright blaze in the hearth, and a chair pulled up on either side of it. The room was deliciously scented with burning apple-wood and fresh-baked pastry and spiced wine. Luce breathed a deep sigh of contentment. Civilisation, at last.

Unfortunately, the chairs were occupied, and the current incumbents showed no signs of moving. "Form the men up in the hall," Babbitt said, as soon as Luce walked through the door. Not hello, well done, you look wet – none of that. Luce gave the back of his head a silent hard stare.

"And you can take that look off your face as well, or I'll take your breeches down and paddle your arse like the brat you are," the captain added, apparently without looking up.

Resisting a strong temptation to hit him with something heavy, Luce stalked back out into the hall. Eighty faces schooled themselves from mirth into immobility. "Captain Babbitt wishes to address you," he said.

"Can't hear you at the back, mate!" an anonymous wag called.

"Shut *up*, then," roared Luce, "and listen!"

Babbitt leaned in the doorway, raising an eyebrow. He seemed to have the uncanny ability to materialise out of nothing, like smoke. "Impressive, boy. Be better when your voice breaks, mind."

"Don't hit him, Lucey," Cullis said cheerfully. "It only encourages him."

"Words of friendly advice, Cullis? I wouldn't bother. Pearls before bloody swine. Gentlemen." The redhead snapped upright and surveyed his troop. "I think we all know why we're here, lads. It's not for the sake of my pretty green eyes. Someone – I don't know *which* someone, but I've got a bloody good idea, *Lucey – someone* would like to see *someone else* landed in the shit. Now, as I reckon you all know, there's not a lot gets me riled -" he grinned evilly –"but backstabbers give me the arse-ache. So, gentlemen, you will behave according. I'll not be shamed by my men. I haven't had the training of you bastards long, but if there's a man of you who don't know his business yet, I suggest he speaks up now and gets back to sheep-shagging or whatever else misdemeanours caused him to end up under my command. So. There will be no riotous behaviour in this house. No cursing. No whoring." He didn't even glance over his shoulder. "Yes, that means you, Rackhay, you might be a bloody fellow officer but I know *exactly* what you're like. The whole damn lot of you will behave like you were in church of a Sunday, or you will answer to me. Personally."

"Best spend a blameless night looking over your weapons then, lads," Cullis growled.

There was a ripple of reluctant laughter and the odd underhand grumble. Babbitt's twitchy eyebrow flicked. "Well, I don't think there was a one of you got a shot off at the bridge. That's a *hell* of a lot of misfires. Dismissed."

The wag at the back passed a humorous remark regarding the captain's sexual preferences for dumb animals. Frankly, Lucifer had no trouble at all in believing him. He suspected nothing too low of that Judas-haired creature.

"It's all right, Lucey, I'm done with you, you can go out and play. I'm off to check Master Prideaux's bed for choirboys. I'm leaving you in the capable hands of Captain Rackhay, Lucey –" as he passed, Babbitt tipped

Luce's hat into his eyes – "watch your arse, eh? He's got form for pretty girls."

Luce removed his hat and set it down, neatly, on the table. Next to that platter of hot, juicy venison pasties, and the steaming jug of spiced wine, and two goblets. His mouth was watering – he hadn't eaten since breakfast, and the sun was presumably high in the sky, as far as anyone could tell behind a constant veil of grey rain – and he almost swiped a pasty off the plate. Caught Rackhay's sardonic glance and decided discretion was the better part of valour. This house smelt like home, that familiar scent of lavender and river damp and beeswax polish and baking. It felt like a violation to have those two brigands loose in it.

The men were breaking off into groups, particular friends finding a comfortable corner to settle in. Apart from anything else, it was such a lonely feeling, if you had no one particular friend to settle with. Even the gargoyle Cullis had his back to him, peering at a rust spot or something on the freckled lad's musket. It felt almost as though everyone was slightly embarrassed to talk to Luce. He glanced up at Rackhay, still sprawled out in his chair with his legs outstretched in front of the fire. Rackhay glanced back – raised one of the goblets of wine in a sardonic salute – and Luce blushed furiously.

He'd enlisted in the Army of Parliament less than a month ago believing, with his heart and soul, that the King was misguided and ill-advised: that Charles Stuart needed to learn that he could no longer ride roughshod over the wishes and needs of his subjects. He had expected to meet with other like-minded men, serious men, men whose dreams and ideals ran parallel with his own. He remembered sitting in his mother's cool, rosemary-scented garden in Witham, after he'd gone to see Uncle Essex at his house in London. Gabriel Pettitt was a quiet, gentle man, whose life revolved around the twin pleasures of his hearth and his home, and he'd passed on that love of peace to his son. Nothing had changed in that well-ordered black and white house since the reign of Elizabeth – the same uneven rose-red tiles on the roof, the same slightly faded bed hangings embroidered with gillyflowers and corncockles and daisies.

As far as Luce was concerned, the King's demands for higher and higher taxes from his subjects, to fund wars nobody wanted except his own stubborn Royal pride, were an attack on that peace and order, just as much as the King's Papist leanings were an attack on the established beliefs of good Englishmen and women.

Well, Uncle Essex had warned him to expect rough manners from professional fighting men both sides had bought in from Europe, but he hadn't expected deliberate intimidation from officers. It was almost as if both Babbitt and Rackhay cultivated an air of conscious menace. Neither of those two ruffians seemed to have a principle to spare between them, and Luce couldn't imagine why either of them would choose to hire their swords in a cause of honour. Still - Rackhay's voice had the clipped accents of an educated man, and whatever he was, he was no tavern bully. And Babbitt slipped between cultured and flat North Country, depending on to whom he was speaking - and, Luce was beginning to suspect, how much at ease he was in their company. Only a fool assumed that either was exactly as they met the eye.

And Cullis. Cullis seemed to have a proprietorial eye for the big redhead which implied a relationship of some standing; Luce had the distinct impression that the only reason Babbitt had been brought to apologise at the bridge, was on Cullis's say-so. Which implied that the captain listened to that old gargoyle. On the other hand, neither Cullis nor anyone else seemed to be able to curb his berserk temper.

"What about you, Lucey?"

Luce blinked. The sergeant had appeared at his side – squat and malevolent and grey: iron grey hair, mouth like a crack in a dry stone wall.

"What *about* me?" He hadn't heard a word.

"You going to take up Captain Rackhay's kind offer, then?"

The fair-haired captain looked even more wolfish with his eyes glinting amber in the firelight. Not a man to be trusted, not at all.

"Thank you, sir, but no. Most kind."

"Off you go, then, lad. Dismissed."

"But should I not wait for orders from –"

Rackhay chuckled. "Listen, old son. I broke Red's nose for him under siege at Nuremberg. Bloody awful place, we'd been sat outside the damn place for a month and we were sick of each other's company. He's snored like that ever since. I'd be delighted to enjoy your company, of course -" he leaned forward and winked ostentatiously, to the delight of several troopers – "but I reckon you've got an hour or so free before he wakes up. Go on, slip the leash. Nip up to the Bishop's Mitre. Tell Dulcie Nat Rackhay sent you. You might get one on the house."

"*Half* of that's true, " Cullis grumbled, "I wouldn't be spreading it about you were any friend of his. She'd likely charge you double."

Luce smoothed his hair back nervously, catching it in one hand and re-tying the ribbon he secured it with: there was a further burst of ribaldry from his new audience, who clearly looked on him as their own personal pantomime. "I am not going to the – I am not making myself presentable for company!"

"Brothel," Rackhay said kindly. "It's fine, laddie, we were all your age once."

Luce was outraged into silence – briefly. "I have no intention of frequenting such an establishment! I was going to - familiarise myself with the locality –"

"Go running to tell tales to Uncle Essex, more bloody like," – that distinctive Somerset burr at the back there, Luce was going to watch that lad like a hawk. The gossip had started already, then. He wondered who it was that had started that particular hare. He drew himself up to his full height and glared down his nose at the freckled lad, who grinned back at him, perfectly without malice, as if he'd passed some kind of test. "Weston, sir." The freckled lad stood up straight. "Isaac Weston. That there's my brother Luke. We'm up from Bruton, in Somerset."

"I could have worked that out for myself," Luce said dryly. Apart from the broad accents, the brothers were almost identical: they both looked like pigs. With their sandy, bristle-cropped bullet heads and stubby blonde eyelashes, they resembled nothing so much as a pair of prize baconers.

"The captain never troubled to tell us your name, sir," Luke Weston prompted, and Rackhay sniggered from the fireside.

"That's because he was hoping the young man wouldn't stay with us for long enough for it to be needed, lads."

11 STILL UNEARNED KINDNESS

Hollie stretched his shoulders with some relief, finally rid of the rigid weight of a well-worn buff coat. You got used to the weight of the stiff oxhide, but it didn't make the damned thing any more comfortable to wear. He had a permanent raw weal across the back of his neck, like a harness-gall. He left it where it fell, tempting though it was to give the thing a vindictive kick. Its military appearance seemed slightly indecent against the glossy polished boards of Master Prideaux's elegant bedroom.

Backsword where it always rested, standing on end in its scabbard leaning against the wall within easy reach. Got him out of more than a few scrapes, that habit of leaning his sword up against the wall next to the bed. He checked under the pillow for the left-handed dagger he always slept with. A habit that had driven his wife to distraction, it must be said, and that ten years of marriage hadn't broken him of. Possibly not the most domestic of arrangements.

Boots. Scuffed. Dirty. The Bishop's housekeeper would no doubt have kittens if she was made aware of the presence of one filthy cavalry captain in her best chamber. Or perhaps she wouldn't. It was not impossible that in the name of Christian charity the Bishop would be more than happy for one filthy - weary, famished - captain to lay his head for an hour or so, whichever side he favoured. There was still sometimes unearned kindness in the world. Even in these times. He twitched awake again. Falling asleep sitting up, never a good thing; he hadn't done it for years. He thought it was a rather more recent ability, something you picked up the ability to do when you got handed a command, with not enough hours in the day and not enough eyes in your head to stop eighty men from getting up to as much villainy as they could conceive as soon as your back was turned.

Well, whichever, he wasn't going to do it, so about time he bucked his ideas up and stopped sitting here on the edge of a bed the size of Wiltshire staring into blank space like a mooncalf. His fingers felt stiff and clumsy, fumbling with points and collar strings till he was about ready to scream. God almighty, he didn't remember fastening this many buttons on his doublet when he got dressed, did they breed in the dark like mushrooms under his buff coat or something? No point losing his temper and taking a blade to the collar strings, the state he was in at the moment he'd probably stab himself in the throat.

He gave a deep sigh of absolute contentment as the bit of torn silk that held his hair back finally worked loose, and the whole tangled lot of it slithered down against his bare back. Bliss. He reckoned he'd give up his chances of earthly glory, temporal riches and life everlasting, for the chance to spend the rest of this day between clean sheets. With his hair loose. Always amazed him how he never felt completely undressed till his hair was down. The sheets were clean and scented with the rosemary bushes they'd been spread on to dry. Funny how the scent of rosemary and the thought of cleanliness were still so entwined in his head now, even after this long.

He concentrated, hard, on the thread of voices downstairs. Moggy Davies, with his lilting up and down valley-voice. Cullis, rumbling along like an old grey mastiff. The Weston twins, as Somerset as cider.

Nat Rackhay, laughing in the room directly beneath

him, that maniac cackle that always set Hollie's nerves jangling slightly. At the same time it comforted him, like putting your hand on the hilt of your sword, or on the sweating shoulder of your horse; he could sleep easy, knowing that Nat was watching his back, for the next few hours at least.

That laugh of his still set Hollie's teeth on edge, though. He fell asleep with one hand on the dagger under his pillow, and a wry smile on his face.

He must have slept for a while, because when he opened his eyes the fire was lit and the light was starting to fade and there was someone else in the bed.

Hollie didn't move. If he moved, whoever was behind him would know he was awake. He carried on breathing slowly and deeply, willing his body into the semblance of rest while his hand closed more firmly around the dagger hilt and his brain worked out the best angle of attack.

He waited for the weight behind him to shift on the mattress and then rolled over, twisting into a fighting crouch with the pillow in one hand as a makeshift shield and his dagger in the other, trying to toss his hair out of his eyes. "What the *hell* –"

She just sat there with the point of the dagger dimpling her plump creamy throat and giggled nervously. Naked as a needle, blonde, fat, with about as much intelligence in her eyes as a cow in a field.

"Rackhay," he said grimly, and she giggled again. She was scared, he could see the muscles in her plump little neck working as she swallowed, but not bright enough to do anything but giggle. Definitely Rackhay. Just his type. She blinked her big eyes at him – and they were undeniably pretty, velvety brown eyes, give Nathaniel his due, when he chose to ignore an order he ignored it with style. Then she said, "Are you *cross* with me?"

He lifted the dagger away from her throat. Funny how much Nat knew about him, and forgot. Like that Hollie's loving father had gone out of his way to make sure that if his firstborn intended to sin, it had better be bloody worth it. Nice lass, no doubt. Not worth it. "No, lass, I'm not cross with you," he said. With an emphasis on the last word that he hadn't intended. "Put some clothes on."

She lay back on the pillow invitingly. "Do I not please you, then?"

"Please me? I'm sure you're delightful. Just not to my tastes." All the same, he was glad of the pillow in his lap. He might be particular, but he wasn't a marble saint, and it had been a *hell* of a long time. There was a limit to what flesh and blood could stand. "Lass, get dressed. I won't ask you again."

She stood up with a sniff. With a fine, fat arse on her, too. If she'd had a brain in her head she might have been worth a tumble. As it was – he was tempted, Christ, it had been too long since Griete –

And there it was again, the thing he didn't think about, and any consideration he'd had of taking the girl out of necessity, like scratching an itch, died a painful death. "Out. Now."

She glanced over her shoulder, grubby shift clutched to her breasts. Hollie slid out of the bed and jerked the door open. Grabbed the whore by the shoulders and pushed her bodily out onto the landing with her arms full of her clothes. Heard a sharp intake of breath and didn't want to turn round.

"Unhand that girl, you - !"

Well, of course. Who else would it be but call-me-Lucey, Lancelot Pettitt?

12 DESTRUCTION SHALL BE READY AT HIS SIDE

No one looked at Luce, or spoke to him, or invited him to join their game of dice. He wasn't wholly convinced by dicing in the Bishop's palace, but he suspected that were he to voice his concerns, he'd be laughed at. So he didn't bother. "I'm going out," he announced, and since no one troubled to respond – went.

First to the cathedral, and it still shocked him to the core that the Army were stabling horses in the cathedral, but he needed to go and find his patient childhood mount and bury his face in her rough mane just like he'd done when he was a little boy. But Periwinkle wasn't there. He could both see and hear the vicious black stallion Tyburn, picketed in splendid isolation in Prince Arthur's Chantry chapel where he could do least harm, restlessly kicking the carved marble to sparks. Cullis's old grey cob, gnawing the back of a pew. The two Weston mounts, built like plough horses, standing with their heads companionably together as if they were out in a field on the Levels rather than standing in the echoing nave of a frigid cathedral.

The lovely chestnut mare that he'd acquired at the bridge was standing perfectly still, her elegant head lifted anxiously. Luce felt a sudden deep sympathy with that poor anonymous mare. Torn untimely from her young master, thrown in with a pack of rebels, and now deserted. She pricked her ears in his direction. She didn't even have a name any more, poor dumb beast. A new master whose first act on making her acquaintance had been to slash her cruelly across the rump with a sharp blade. She buried her head in the bosom of his doublet as though he were a long-lost friend and he scratched behind her ears absently, feeling the fine coat on her as smooth as silk. There was good breeding in the mare, he'd say that – grudgingly – for Babbitt, the man had an eye for a good horse. Over in the chantry chapel Tyburn was flinging his head up and down with increasingly irritable bass rumbles, evidently in agreement as to the red mare's finer points.

"What bloody fool brought that mare in here?"

An officer he didn't recognise, an older man in a plain russet doublet and a very makeshift looking sash apparently torn from the bottom of a silk gown – scowling most ferociously. "You, boy, is this your horse?"

"Me? She – she – well, yes, in a manner of speaking, I believe she –"

"You believe. Ha. May Christ defend us from witless youth. Well, kindly take your mare, and picket her somewhere else. Bad enough I am blighted with that ungodly animal –" his lips compressed into a thin line as he tried to think of suitably godly words to describe the force of destruction that was Babbitt's black – "but for you bring a mare coming into season within his licentious compass –"

"I beg your pardon, sir, but –"

There was a crash of breaking glass from the nave. "Get. That. Mare. Out. Or I will not be responsible for my actions –"

Annother trooper sauntered past, whistling. He was carrying an axe over his shoulder. "I want that Popish screen down, Catterall. I'll not have idolatry in my sight."

"Right you are, sir." The trooper was barely older than Luce, a stolid lad with a rosy round face as shiny as a pippin. It sounded odd to hear fanaticism delivered in a homely rural accent. "Firewood, sir?"

"As you wish, trooper. As long as it's down."

Luce untied the mare with fumbling fingers. Under his hand her neck was hot and wet already, and her nostrils were blown wide and red-rimmed. Hardly the harlot she was being made out to be, poor beast. He doubted that the aggressive attentions of the black stallion were making her any more comfortable than anyone else within earshot. It would, he thought, be better for the both of them to be elsewhere. Luce wasn't sure he could stand idly by and watch the childish, wanton destruction of the church's beautiful carved fittings. The Lord knew he was no Papist, but he saw only joy and celebration in the loving works of men's hands praising God. There was another splintering crash and a rush of bitter air through the broken window. "I should not be so confident that the Lord smiles on your actions, sir," he said coldly. "Why else should he reward you with such intemperate weather?"

The grim officer bridled. "How dare you, puppy! Out of my sight, before –"

Luce inclined his head courteously. "With the greatest of pleasure, sir." He'd never actually seen a man foam at the mouth before, but bubbles of spit were gathering at the corners of the grim officer's mouth. It was quite fascinating, in a disgusting kind of way.

"And you may tell your commanding officer that I want that black demon gone from my presence with dispatch! I should have known you for a part of his godless troop!"

"Doubtless we all find grace in our own ways, sir. I bid you good day."

He backed out quickly with the uncomfortable feeling of having made yet another enemy. The mare was edgy – well, she wasn't the only one. He was glad Uncle Essex had billeted them in the Bishop's residence, even if it did mean sharing a house with those two wolves. At least the wolves were simply feral: they didn't break and smash and tear for the joy of destruction. A week ago if you'd asked him what he ought to do Luce would have guessed he'd keep his head, walk away, make his formal complaint through the correct channels, have it dealt with as an official grievance. And a week ago it wouldn't have occurred to him to do anything else. Yesterday, he'd killed a man, and today, he wasn't sure what he was capable of.

"Where's my mare?" he demanded irritably, stopping in the massive arched doorway and fixing the unfortunate sentry with a steely look. The man was staring up at the Malvern Hills, slowly disappearing behind a lowering white curtain of icy mist.

"I will lift up mine eyes unto the hills, from which cometh my hope," the sentry quoted, and Luce had had his fill of the devout for one day. He suspected the morning's boisterous surplice thieves were more to his tastes.

"What is likely to be coming out of those hills is a plentiful supply of inclement weather, trooper, and I wish you joy of it. For the last time of asking, where is my mare to be found?"

It was associating with Babbitt, that was what did it. Less than a week in the ruffian's company and Luce was already tainted with the big redhead's appallingly low tolerance levels. He jabbed the sentry in the chest with his finger. "Grey mare. Well-mannered. Which is more than I can say for most I've come across this day. She was picketed with Babbitt's troop last night. So what have you done with her?"

The sentry wiped the back of his hand across his moist nose. It was that sort of weather, and you couldn't blame him for it. Wholly. His mouth worked silently. "Gone out." His eyes rested, consideringly, on Luce's officer's sash. Luce could almost hear the ponderous roll of a penny dropping. "Sir."

"Clever lad," Luce said dryly. "I'm Captain Babbitt's new cornet, and that's my horse you've mislaid. And I want her back."

"Tethered out with the rest of the nag – er, riding horses, sir, with the baggage train. Out on College Green. Thought you must know, sir, seeing as it were on the Captain's orders she got took out, he said –"

Get rid of that bloody mare, was what the captain had said, and Luce's hackles rose at the recollection. Altogether too used to getting his own way, was that one – even for an officer. Oh yes, Luce remembered that conversation. Arrogant, high-handed, hasty swine, was the captain. He also remembered that Babbitt had threatened to have his dear old mare shot if she couldn't keep up with the rest of the troop. The sentry evidently mistook Luce's increasingly grim expression for a promise of vengeance, and started to babble his apologies. "I will deal with this myself," Luce said, narrowing his eyes in what he hoped was a menacing manner. He mounted the chestnut mare in the cathedral porch, swinging her till her hindquarters backed the sentry into the gap between the cold stone and the open door. Then, bending low over her neck, he rode her out into the rain.

13 A ROSE AMONGST THORNS

Praise the Lord for fresh linen and dry stockings, Luce thought wryly, rubbing his hair dry with a clean towel. This might almost pass for civilisation. With the door closed he could only hear the occasional burst of laughter from the men downstairs, and the soft hiss of the wind in the trees outside.

It was a closet, no more, a tiny room barely big enough for a bed and his saddlebags. A tiny chamber just off the Bishop's bedchamber, which meant there was a solid door between him and Babbitt. Captain Rackhay was right. Babbitt snored appallingly. Luce stifled a shudder. There was very little he could think of to commend that man.

Small as it was, though, the bed was soft and covered with a fine wool coverlet, and the air was fresh and cool with lavender. He lay back on the pillows and closed his eyes. In the darkness behind his eyelids, he could almost be back at home, listening to his mother bustling downstairs, giving the cook his orders, supervising the dinner – he could almost smell his favourite festival dish, chicken in spiced orange sauce; fresh bread baking, meat roasting, the exotic tang of cinnamon and cloves –

And then there was a giggle from the room next door, an unmistakably feminine giggle, and Luce sat up in shock.

The man was a whited sepulchre. He'd had the gall to lecture them about his expectations of their behaviour – no drinking, no cursing, no women – and all the while he had a woman in his bed. Openly. He had no shame.

Well, Luce didn't plan to lie here and listen to the filthy lecher take his pleasure. He slid off the bed and threw open the closet door.

Found himself faced with a plump, pink-cheeked, fair-haired lass without a stitch of clothing.

"Madam!" he squeaked, to his eternal shame.

She was clutching a shift to cover her modesty, and it didn't seem to be covering very much. To Luce's horror, he was not filled with a chivalric desire to right her wrongs. All he could think of was that – well, so this was what a real woman looked like without her stays. And whether she was as soft and – cushiony, that was the word he was looking for, cushiony – as she looked, and –

"Have her if you want, lad. She's paid for," Babbitt said sardonically, and turned his back on both of them.

The girl wailed. Luce threw his doublet round her shoulders: any excuse to find out whether she felt as soft as she looked and she did, it was like trying to button your coat over the softest feather pillow – left her trying to do the buttons up with a good hands' gap between the edges but that was no bad thing for a girl. "Captain Babbitt, sir, you are no gentleman!"

Babbitt turned back and favoured him with a malevolent grin, leaning one bare shoulder up against the doorframe. "Oh aye? Making something of it, are we?"

Luce was briefly shocked. The man really did have no shame. "How dare you treat a lady with so little courtesy, sir!"

"That's not a lady, brat. Ask her. I'm sure she can be very unladylike indeed, for the right price." He bent to pick up a length of rag from the floor, scooped his hair back one-handed.

Luce gave a contemptuous laugh. "And no gentleman would wear such scars as those with any pride."

The captain's bare back was crossed and recrossed with old silver scars, the scars of a beaten dog or a beast of burden. Luce was expecting bluster and shame and fury. What he got was Babbitt squinting down at his scars over his shoulder with amusement. "If you're trying to pick a fight, boy, pick something more current than them. I've had 'em twenty years and they don't trouble my sleep at nights. Now if you're that bothered about the lass, stop gawping at her tits and let her get dressed."

14 BUT THAT WAS IN ANOTHER COUNTRY, AND BESIDES…

Hollie kicked the door closed behind him, wishing to God the flower of bloody chivalry would either take his new plaything back to bed or go and be virginally affronted elsewhere. He could do without it, this night. Although he was getting better: the first thought in his head had been to go storming downstairs exactly as he was and tear the throat out of Rackhay and he hadn't and he wasn't going to. This was not a battlefield, it was a sober, godly household. Apparently. Damn, but it was tempting. Well, he was going to sit here on the bed and calm down, take deep breaths, put some clothes on. And then he was going to go downstairs properly attired and tear the throat out of Rackhay. Possibly with a brief pause on the landing to grab call-me-Lucey Pettitt by the scruff of the neck and shake some common sense into his virtuous little head.

And whilst trying not to think about the girl. Well, Hollie, you're not obliged to look at the mantelpiece while you're poking the fire. Too finicky, that was his trouble, he wanted the penny *and* the bun. He tied his collar-strings with a vicious tug – nearly throttled himself in the process – not sure if his hands were shaking with fury or thwarted lust. Still trying not to think about the lass. He shouldn't have sent her away. Christ, she was willing enough. Well, he didn't want *her*. He wanted his own lass back. Mostly, though, these days he just wanted to hit something.

The girl was halfway down the stairs, fully dressed.

Not nearly so appealing with her clothes on, a little brown country mouse in a goodwife's bodice, however low cut. Lucey took her arm and steered her out of Hollie's way. From which he deduced that he must be looking particularly intimidating. Good. So much the better. As he brushed past her the boy's hand tightened on her homespun sleeve, the fabric puckering under his fingers. The lad thought he was going to hurt her. He'd never yet laid violent hands on a woman, at least one who hadn't hit him first. Lord above, was that truly how he seemed these days?

Rackhay was cackling again, and that helped. Tempted though Hollie was to kick the parlour door open, he was aware of a dozen pairs of eyes on his back, all waiting for things to kick off. He *thought* if it all went to rat-shit he could rely on Cullis at the least to mind his back. Probably. "Captain Rackhay." Astonished by how remarkably cool and steady his voice sounded. Steady hand on the bridle, Babbitt…

Rackhay was sprawled in one of the chairs facing the fireplace, his back to the door. All Hollie could see of him was one knee, one hand on the chair arm, the gleam of firelight on a spill of amber hair. The gleam of firelight on a spill of cheap scarlet satin skirt across the floor and a whore's hand on Rackhay's thigh. "Come to join the party, Kersen?"

Cool and steady. Balls to that. It took him maybe two strides across the room and he just back-handed the blonde captain across the face, not really even realising he'd done it till he was licking the blood off his knuckles and coming back to his senses sufficiently to realise it wasn't his own. "Don't you *ever* call me that, captain."

And Rackhay stemming the flow from his bloody nose with his cuff and still managing to look faintly amused. "Sorry, old son. Didn't think you were still touchy about it. Where's –"

"Button your breeches and get out."

The second whore, half-laced bodice falling off one shoulder – sat back on her haunches, wiping her mouth with the back of her hand. Hard-faced little slut. "And you can get dressed as well, mistress."

"Oh, for God's sake, Hollie, just listen to yourself! Since when did *you* turn Puritan –"

The funny thing was, there was a bit of him that *was* still Margriete's Kersen, that shy soldier-apprentice lad from twenty years back - and he *had* been brought up Puritan. Rackhay shouldn't have reminded him of those days. It made it harder to draw your sword and rest the tip in the beating hollow of your best friend's throat. "I gave an order, Captain Rackhay. And you wilfully chose to disobey it. I will not tolerate insubordination in my troop. Get out."

His friend's eyes were slaty-grey and steady. He never blinked at the sword point. "You don't out-rank me, Red. Don't give me orders."

"I do in this house."

Rackhay shook his head, slowly and sadly. The tip of Hollie's blade made a tiny red zigzag on his throat but he didn't seem to care. "Sometimes, old son, I truly do think you've not been right in the head since Nuremberg. It's sad. But…" He glanced down with another sigh.

Like a bloody idiot, Hollie followed his gaze. Like the newest raw recruit ended up on his back with the breath knocked out of him and Rackhay kneeling astride him, grinning savagely. "I mean it, Red. I'll not be told what to do by the likes of you. Don't order me around, because if it comes to a battle of wills you will *lose*."

Hollie had caught his shoulder a proper smack, right on the bone, on the sharp corner of the hearthstone and it damn well hurt. Well, two of them could play at basic-level silly buggers. Rackhay was heavier set than he was – running to fat, too, if the weight of him was anything to go by. Hollie ran a quick mental inventory of what was to hand – pottery jug of what smelt like spiced wine warming in the embers of the fire, too far away to reach – his sword gone, kicked away across the boards when he'd gone down and what the hell are you thinking of, Hollie, to consider turning a blade on the man who's been fighting shoulder to shoulder with you for most of your grown days? Rackhay's nose was still bleeding. A warm drop fell on Hollie's face and he jerked his head away, sickened. Twisted under Rackhay and bit him, hard, in the soft meat of the thigh.

Rackhay rolled off him with an yelp and Hollie staggered to his feet, panting, rubbing his tingling shoulder. "You're getting slow, lad," Hollie said grimly. "Too much good living."

The blonde captain was on his feet now, limping slightly as he circled Hollie, pale eyes fixed on him. "You nothing," he snarled. "You dare to give me orders, you mongrel cur – you *dare*! I'll teach you respect for your betters, sir –"

"My betters? I don't think so. Get your whore. *Both* of your whores. And get out. Now."

"There was a time when you weren't so choosy about your whores – *Kersen*. I believe you married one, didn't you?"

There were a number of answers to that.. Words couldn't hurt her. He knew that. Words couldn't hurt Rackhay, either, so Hollie was going to have to punch him in the belly instead, and preferably keep doing it till the bastard stopped moving. Which was much more effective, and definitely more satisfying.

He was right, though, Rackhay was getting fat – didn't hurt Hollie nearly as much as it would have done once to bury his fist in the big blonde's gut. Too well-padded these days. Soft. Well, not quite so elegant now, Captain Rackhay, dribbling blood and snot on the hearthstone and retching – not quite so pretty as we were, are we? – but not quite sorry enough yet, no, not nearly sorry enough. Have to keep hitting him till he was, then. Rackhay was on his hands and knees, then suddenly rolling Hollie off his feet by force of weight with a furious roar, back and forth in the warm ashes, grabbing a handful of loose red hair and trying to crack Hollie's head open on the iron fire-dogs.

One single shot, echoing like the wrath of God around the ornate plaster ceiling, and the pattering of loosened soot down the chimney. Rackhay struggled loose and sat up, wolfish eyes narrowing. "By God, your cornet has just loosed a shot at me!"

Hollie leaned his back up against the great carved overmantel, still seeing stars. "Well, he missed, didn't he?" he said, fighting a wild desire to laugh. He wasn't sure if he was quite ready for the sight of Lucey Pettitt brandishing a pistol, protecting his maidenly virtue. His ribs ached enough as it was.

"Stop this. On the instant." Luce sounded quite convincing, though, for a brat.

Maybe not the best time to point out that they'd stopped already. The officious little creature might burst a blood vessel and God knows there was sufficient mess in here to be cleared up already.

"You should be ashamed of yourselves – brawling like – like –"

"I know, it's not the sort of thing dear old Uncle Essex would like you to see, is it?"

"You disgust me. The pair of you."

Hollie opened one eye. The room, he was pleased to note, stayed steady. "Lucey, if you tell me just once more that I'm not a gentleman, I'm quite likely to hit you. *That* is a gentleman." He waved a hand in Rackhay's general direction. "Edifying sight, ain't it?"

Rackhay snarled. Luce simply looked down his long

nose at the pair of them in grim silence, and eventually said, "I might remind you, *gentlemen* – and I use the term advisedly – that I have a brace of pistols. One has been fired. The other has not. Be still, the both of you. If you wished to make this into a house of ill repute, Captain Babbitt, you have made a *remarkably* thorough job of it."

Which Hollie thought was somewhat unfair, but since he wasn't the one with the loaded pistol he wasn't going to argue the toss. He got to his feet stiffly – there was a lump the size of a chicken's egg on the back of his head: he caught Rackhay eyeing him cynically and stopped fingering the bruise. Fine. Bloody Lucey Pettitt was eyeing him as though he'd just crawled out of a plague-house, and Rackhay was looking as smug as it was possible for a man with a fat lip to look. Gentlemen, was it? He'd give the whoring blonde bastard gentlemen.

The dark-haired tart was huddled by the chair, whimpering, her skirts soaked with the spilled wine. Another witless baggage. Any lass worth more than the time of day would have either made good her escape or brained him with that jug. With shyly downcast eyes, Hollie made her a bow. Stiff, but he hadn't fallen over yet. "Madam, my boldness wants excuse," he said. "I am dazzled by your beauty, as by the stars in the sky. Forgive my – *intemperacy*, madam."

And Rackhay needn't look so surprised, they'd learned the stilted phrases of court flattery – bi-lingual, if you please, in both Dutch and English – in the same Amsterdam *musico*. Not being a smellsmock, Hollie hadn't had as much cause to use them over the last few years. The trollop gawked up at him, her head on one side like a mongrel dog being offered a bone.

Mongrel. He wasn't going to forget that one in a hurry, either, Captain Rackhay. She stood up, still slightly wary, and he backed up a step. She was looking at him as if his wits had gone begging, but bless her, she thought she had him in her grasp now. Dazzled by her beauty. Ha. He'd seen more flesh on a picked rib. "Would you do me the honour of accompanying me into dinner, my lady?"

Rackhay choked. "Lady? Babbitt, I'll not brook this insolence !"

"Yes you will, Captain Rackhay. You *invited* these guests. Cornet Pettitt, would you be so kind as to relinquish the hand of your fair companion to the captain?"

Lucey evidently didn't know what he was playing at. He wasn't sure himself, except that he was murderously angry with Rackhay and it was probably better to humiliate the bastard than kill him. Although if Rackhay pushed him to it he'd probably consider that too.

He took the cocked pistol out of Lucey's nerveless hand. "Off you go, lad. We sit down to dine shortly."

15 COMING TO BLOWS

The sun was rising in great streaks of blood-red over the black crests of the Malvern hills, and a single heron took off from the bank of the river, wings beating tipped gold against the sunrise. The trees bending their branches low over the water were wreathed in mist. Luce had been sitting on the frigid stone sill of the window overlooking the Bishop's dawn-grey lawns for long enough to print every detail in his memory.

As dinners went, it hadn't been one of the more successful he'd attended. Babbitt sitting with a cocked pistol trained on Captain Rackhay across the table, very ostentatiously not drinking the wine. Rackhay sinking the stuff like milk and glowering at Babbitt. One increasingly sullen-drunk dark-haired whore pawing professionally at Babbitt and being almost wholly ignored, expect when he very politely and properly asked her to pass the condiments. One terrified and very young blonde girl – Luce didn't like to think of her as a tart, she seemed much too young and too timid – at Rackhay's side, picking anxiously at her dinner. Luce trying not to look too hard at anyone in case they took it amiss, and forgetting himself sufficiently at times to rest his gaze on the fair girl's ample chest – out of curiosity, mostly, at the feat of engineering which contained it. Cullis at one end of the table applying himself diligently to his plate as if he'd never seen food before. Well, between them Luce and Cullis had done justice to the good meal set before them, although having Captain Babbitt stone-cold sober on one side of you urging you with maniac politesse to take another helping of spinach tart, and Rackhay sliding under the table in a murderous rage on the other, was enough to curb even the strongest of appetites.

It had been enough to give you the nightmare, though; especially in combination with the most part of a spinach tart, gingerbread, mutton carbonado, apple snow and chicken fricassee. Luce was not naturally an abstemious soul but one glance at the dangerous glint in Babbitt's eye warned him off the wine. A clear head was probably going to be the safest bet. After a night spent dreaming of war and bloody murder, uncomfortably mixed with images of sweet-faced blonde girls in various states of inviting undress, Luce was glad to see the dawn come in – even if it was whilst sitting on a stone sill cold enough to give a marble saint the piles.

Rackhay and his coterie had gone, in the end, and Luce wasn't sure who'd been holding whom up at that point except that Rackhay was belligerently vertical and the dark wench had been equally belligerent in her desire to get him horizontal. She'd been shrieking half way across College Green. The little blonde had clasped his hand gratefully, looking up into his face with those big velvety brown eyes, and he'd been tempted, so very tempted, to smuggle her back up the stairs. "Thank you, sir," she'd breathed, and her very breath had been sweet and fragrant. "I'll not forget your kindness."

He wasn't sure if he imagined the sardonic snort from the shadows behind him, but it stiffened his sinews. He did not intend to lay himself open to ridicule from that quarter. He inclined his head gravely to the girl – lifted her hand to his lips in farewell – then turned about.

He hadn't imagined it.

"You must be out of your tiny mind, lad. You could have had that one for nowt, if you'd played your hand right."

Babbitt was leaning against the doorframe. Even in

the kind light of a dozen low-burnt candles on the table, he looked somewhat the worse for wear. "I have nothing but contempt for your manners, sir," Luce said stiffly. "I bid you a good night."

"No doubt you do, Lucey. Always found duty somewhat of a cold bedfellow, myself – and God knows I've had enough practice. But then you probably wouldn't know, would you? Good night, Lucey. Sweet dreams."

The redhead tipped his head back against the gleaming panelling with a thump, putting a hand to his bruises with a wince. Which was of course the point at which Luce should have sneered at him and gone up the stairs with his dignity intact, rather than being his mother's soft-hearted son to the fingertips. "That was a fair crack you caught on the hearthstone, sir. Does it pain you *very* much?"

"Only my dignity, lad. Only my dignity."

"Surely, but your head - does it, um, require attention?"

"According to Sergeant Cullis, brat, it's needed seeing to these twenty years and more. The sergeant is not best pleased with me this evening." Babbitt laughed to himself. "By, he knows his business, does our Nat. It's just as well you come in when you did." He sounded almost proud of it, too. "Not the first time me and the captain have been at each other's throats and doubtless it won't be the last. Fight like cats in a sack if you put us in the same place too long. Been trying to work out which of us outranks the other for the last twenty years, nearly. Vexes the sergeant summat appalling. He reckons one of these days we'll go too far."

"So I understand," Luce said dryly, thinking of Rackhay's earlier casual disclosure. He found it almost impossible to imagine the continuation of such a friendship had he been in Babbitt's place. "That said, captain, there is – there's blood all down your shirt. And, um –" he paused, touching a finger to his own eyebrow as a discreet hint –"bit of a mess, sir."

"Oh aye?" Babbitt rubbed the back of his hand across his cheekbone – looked at the blood on it with a near-comical look of surprise. "Bloody hell. The little bastard, I'll have him for that."

"What – what do you intend?"

Babbitt shrugged, and winced. "As little as possible, lad, tonight."

Which sounded to Luce like a declaration of truce, at least until daylight. He'd gone to bed with a sense of relief, tempered by the suspicion that leaving the captain downstairs, alone with whatever Rackhay and his trollop had left of the wine, was perhaps not a good idea. It was tempting to wake Cullis, who seemed to be the only person who had any influence over the redhead's erratic temper. The sergeant could have the dubious pleasure of putting him to bed.

But the rest of the night had passed peacefully, if restlessly, for Luce. Whatever went on downstairs, went on quietly, and when the sun was finally over the hills the house was as silent and still as a tomb. Luce slipped off the windowsill and went in search of breakfast. He was half starved.

The only sign of life downstairs was Cullis, hunched over the great polished expanse of dining table like some malevolent gnome. The previous night's debris had been cleared away; all that remained was a basket of bread, which the sergeant was abstractedly munching his way through, and a dish of broken meats.

"I take it, then, that you didn't have to put him to bed," Luce said.

Cullis glanced up. "What, His Highness? Haven't had to do that for a good few years, Lucey. Though I'll say one thing, he's teasy as a snake this morning, so watch your tongue."

"Surely not, sergeant? Captain Babbitt looking to pick a fight? I can scarce believe it."

Cullis refused to be drawn. "You got any head for figures, lad?"

"I'm not a clerk, if that's what you're asking." Luce helped himself to mutton (cold carbonado – not bad) and took a bite. "Why?"

Cullis raised his head and scowled. "Someone's got to, boy. Bloody troop don't run itself. So – you got a head for figures?"

"I believe that's the agitant's role."

"That be you, then, Cornet." Cullis shoved his pile of papers down the table at Luce. "Looks like you just got a new job. Don't trust our Hollie as far as I can throw him with the accounts. Bit of a creative accountant, is our Red."

"You mean, I assume, that he is barely numerate?" Luce said contemptuously.

Cullis grinned. "That I did not say. He's like most bleedin' officers - oh, sergeant, forgot to mention we're almost out of shot, make it so. Reckons the coffers are bottomless." The sergeant pulled one of the papers back with a grimy forefinger. "For the shoeing of six horses. Christ almighty, what were they being shod with, silver plate?"

"I suggest the captain learns to curb his profligacy, sergeant, if I am to direct the troop's accounts."

Cullis scratched his grey jowls. "You really have took a dislike to him, ent you?"

"I suspect it's mutual," Luce said ruefully.

"Not sure you've seen him at his best, mind."

"I suspect that might *also* be mutual."

Luce jerked his hand off the scattered bills at the familiar voice behind him.

"Bloody hell, Hollie, look at the state of you - it's just

like old times," Cullis sniggered. "I hope he looks worse than you do this morning."

Babbitt raised his intact eyebrow. "I imagine he does, sergeant, if you are referring to Captain Rackhay. And if his appearance is unremarkable, I would certainly guess he *feels* a damn sight worse than I do. I have business with Cornet Pettitt. Kindly leave us."

Luce bridled. The high-handed swine, who the hell did he think he was ordering around in that tone of voice? "I do not believe we have anything to discuss, captain. I was –"

"I reckon we have unfinished business, lad. I've seen you on a horse, and you ride like my maiden aunt. And I saw you fight, for want of a better word, at the bridge, and to be honest, out of the two of you I'm more scared of my maiden aunt. So. I'm at a loose end this morning, and I plan to see what you're capable of. And if as I suspect, it's not much, I'm going to let Cullis have you."

"As if I haven't got enough on my hands without nursemaiding the boy!" Cullis grumbled.

"I do not require nursemaiding, sergeant, I am a perfectly competent swordsman!"

"Are you, indeed." For someone who was black and blue from jaw to cheekbone, Babbitt seemed remarkably smug. He leaned, purposely, on the pile of papers in front of Luce. "Outside."

Luce shrugged mentally. The captain was stiff, bruised, and doubtless suffering from his debaucheries. If Luce, in the prime of life and well-rested, couldn't show himself creditably against such an opponent, his years of practice with the best fencing master in Essex had been wasted. Babbitt flexed his wrist with an audible crunch. "Scared?"

"Hardly. But Sergeant Cullis had asked me to look at the accounts. Which – with respect, *sir* -" he added sarcastically, "is apparently more than you've done in some time."

"I see. So Uncle Essex has gifted me with a clerk, has he? Well, brat, I've better things to do with my time than reckon up figures."

"I had noticed," Cullis muttered.

The captain drew his sword. A worn, scruffy, plain scabbard. A plain cavalry issue backsword, with a plain basket guard. How remarkably apt, for a worn, scruffy, plain man. "Put up, boy," he said softly.

Luce drew his own blade. It was scarcely free of the scabbard before Babbitt hacked at it, low and vicious, with his full weight behind the blow. Luce's wrist vibrated with the force of it. "Sir!"

"What? Did you think I was playing?" The captain stepped back, tossing his hair out of his eyes, feinted to the left and then while Luce went to parry that blow smacked him hard, back-handed, with the flat of the blade. Luce folded over with all the breath knocked out of him, free hand clutched to his side.

"Not a good start, brat. Bored now."

And then Luce was fighting in earnest, backing up across the wet grass with the sun in his eyes and Babbitt chopping relentlessly at him. Not using any skill a fencing-master had taught you, other than speed and which end of a sword was which. It was more accident than design that he skidded on a drift of sodden leaves, under Babbitt's guard, the point of his sword flicking upwards to catch the captain's cheek. It was hardly a cat-scratch. "You little bastard," Babbitt said disbelievingly. Touched his left hand to the scratch, looked at his bloody fingertips, and then at Luce scrambling onto his feet.

"I – I'm sorry, captain, I –"

Babbitt didn't say anything, and Luce was unsettlingly aware that whatever the big redhead was looking at now, it probably wasn't his cornet. The captain's eyes were steady and alight with a maniac glee. "No," Luce said firmly, taking a step backwards. It worked with dogs. He just hoped it worked with wholly berserk officers. "Captain Babbitt, sir -"

He brought his sword up just in time to avoid a backhand cut at his face. "Stop this, sir, I think you have made your point– "

Swaying back from the waist and he couldn't keep this up, even if he could continue to keep his feet in the slippery grass. The only thing he could do to avoid being hacked to collops was to counter-attack. As hard and as fast as possible, until he ran out of breath: possibly, if the look on Babbitt's face was anything to go by, permanently. All he could do was to block the captain's blows until his wrists ached – flinching like a girl, he knew, every time the two blades rang together. His every breath was burning in his chest and that Judas-haired ruffian wasn't even breaking a sweat. His arms were starting to shake. He caught Babbitt's blade on the guard of his own sword, felt the captain's weight shift, and then pushed back desperately while the bastard was off-balance.

Babbitt went down on his back with a yelp, arms flung wide, and Luce stood over him, gasping, hands on his knees. "Just *stop*," he panted.

The captain was grinning at him. Luce couldn't see what was so funny. Right until Babbitt reversed the blade and slammed the heavy, munitions-quality hilt of the sword up between Luce's legs.

Luce went down like a sack of grain, whimpering, unable to think through that appalling white-hot pain, but fully aware that Babbitt wasn't done with him. The redhead staggered to his feet, wincing. "You're quick, you little bastard. And you're not daft. But I'm damned if I'm going to have some whelp just out of skirts put me on my arse, boy."

Luce wasn't sure what would have happened if a skinny arm hadn't wrapped itself round the captain's throat, and a gravelly voice growl, "For Christ's sake, Hollie!"

Babbitt turned on the sergeant with a wordless snarl.

"Big as you are, you have a go at me and I *will* punch you in the head. And that's a promise," Cullis growled.

"Let. Me. *Go*."

"So you can murder the Earl of Essex's nephew under his nose? That's enough, Hollie. If you want to get the arse-ache with someone, take it out on some bugger who can stand up to you, not Lucey. He's done nothing to you. Now –"

The captain choked as Cullis yanked his head back slightly harder. "Stop it. Or *I* will put you on your arse. And you'll bloody well stay there."

16 RAHAB IS LOOSE AMONGST US

For once this week, it was not raining, and the Earl of Essex had the time to give second thoughts to delivering his right well-beloved nephew into the hands of Holofernes Babbitt.

Babbitt's reputation preceded him. Now he was, it had to be said, a competent – more than competent – officer in the field, when he chose to be. Essex's original intention had been that gentle, civilised Lucifer would be a calming influence on Babbitt, and Babbitt would be a healthy dose of reality for Lucifer. The boy was a dreamer, a sweet-natured lad with a core of stainless decency that had no place with the common clay. Less experience of life's harsh realities than most, bless the boy, which was possibly why Essex was so fond of him despite the tenuous family connection. Both Lucifer's parents were still alive, still living in their old-fashioned rambling house in backwater Witham: his sisters varied in age from ten-year-old Barbara to married and matronly Elizabeth at almost thirty, but all in good health. Gabriel Pettitt's fortunes as a member of the Guild of Glovers went from strength to strength, despite the King's best efforts to tax him into poverty.

No, there was no personal reason why Luce should feel so strongly about the battle of wills between King and Parliament, but he assuredly did. As did most of the county of Essex, to be fair; Gabriel Pettitt's hadn't been the only Witham signature attached to the petition presented to the House of Commons earlier this year in criticism of His Majesty. Always a quiet, dreamy boy, Essex thought, almost absent-minded in his bookishness. It was a joy to see his face grown passionate and enthused as he'd sat in Essex House in the Strand, and avowed his commitment to the Parliamentarian cause.

A dear lad, then, if innocent to the point of naiveté. Probably about time Luce was married, at almost twenty. Essex thought he might put his mind to that, cast an eye over some suitable girls of good family. Might settle the lad down, turn his mind from poems and politics.

Essex had thought at the time that Babbitt was other than what he'd turned out to be, when he'd put his dear nephew under the ruffian's command. Had known him, or known of him, when Babbitt was little more than a beardless lad out in the Low Countries. An odd boy, solitary except for his shadow Rackhay, with a conspicuous reputation for uncomfortable honesty. Odd, but not dislikeable, he'd thought at the time: and how long ago would it be, that Essex had first set eyes on him - seven years? Six?

"Corston. Corston, I have some unease about my nephew. Am I being reasonable?"

His orderly was probably not the best person to ask, as Tom Corston had likewise taken a wholly unreasonable dislike to the big redhead and his villainous sidekick on first acquaintance. The pair of them had made it fairly clear that they thought Corston was more ornament than military use. Which was somewhat short-sighted, as Tom could no more help being elegant and willowy than he could help having a mind for logistics with a grip like a man-trap. Corston looked up. "Um. Sir?"

"You know exactly to whom I refer, Thomas. Am I being fond and foolish, or am I right to be discomfited?"

"Not – unreasonable, I don't think. Perhaps if it would ease your mind, we could – you could – visit the Bishop's residence. To see how the boy is settling down, of course."

"Of course," Essex said dryly. "I'm sure we have no

more pressing matters."

"Speaking honestly, I should be glad of the opportunity to get out of the house."

It was a novelty to go out into the street on foot as a plain civilian, alone save for Tom Corston, without armour or fanfares. Smiling and passing the time of day with the residents of the city. He thought that Tom's idea of bakehouse mutton pies might be going too far, though.

Well, the Bishop's residence was still standing, though he carefully averted his eyes from the horses picketed on College Green. The cathedral looked like the aftermath of a house fire, piles of charred timber strewn on the grass, broken glass glistening in the sun like ice. It was very tempting to go into the cathedral and upbraid the officer of the day, but he caught a glimpse of the broad shoulders and russet coat of the fanatic from the West Midlands. He was known as Sariel in the ranks; some wit had dubbed him after the Angel of Death, and it had stuck. Essex couldn't think of him as anything else, once he'd heard that. He'd had the dubious pleasure of the man's company once for an hour and never again. Apart from the fact that Sariel seemed to view washing as the province of sinners and backsliders, the man thought it was his godly duty to root out evil wherever it lurked – and odd how his definition of evil seemed so often to involve whipping well-formed young troopers under his command.

Too late, though. Sariel's beady eye had lit upon him. "My lord! It's my duty to inform you –"

Essex halted. "Duty?"

"I have routed the Great Beast in his lair, my lord. Behold!"

It looked to Essex like a heap of torn paper and dirty linen, but Sariel was starting to foam at the corners of the mouth again, so best to humour him. "Foul baubles of men's vanity, sir. I endeavoured to bring your nephew to the light yesterday, but he turned from me in his pride –"

"What – *Lucifer*?" A less proud boy he found it hard to imagine.

"There are evil influences abroad, sir. Rahab is loose amongst us, the dragon, the Twisting One. We must ever be vigilant –"

"The man is a lunatic," Tom whispered, close to his ear, and he was inclined to agree. "Let us make our escape."

He was glad he'd removed Luce from the cathedral, though – apart from being away from the malign influence of Sariel, the boy had a solid roof over his head and the full complement of windows. He was met at the door, not by a liveried servant, but by a short, shabby trooper who hadn't troubled to shave that morning. "The Earl of Essex would like to pay a call to his nephew," Tom said smoothly. "Not a formal visit, trooper, so be at ease."

The man's eyes bugged slightly, and his mouth hung open. "Er – er – er –"

"Where is the lad?" Essex said kindly. "I'll find him myself. No need to stand on ceremony." He found it in his heart to be sorry for the man. Evidently not expecting the commander of the Army of Parliament on his doorstep shortly after breakfast, and without the wit to deal with unexpected situations. It did beg the question as to where all the officers had defaulted off to. "My nephew?" he prompted.

"I'll, er, I'll show you to the parlour, my lord, I think he may be –" the man's eyes darted towards the lawn and Essex raised his eyebrows.

"Outside?"

The sight that met his eyes was not wholly unexpected, although scarcely pleasant.

RED HORSE

Lucifer was rolled in a ball on the ground like a woodlouse, looking like a man in receipt of a mortal wound. The sergeant had Babbitt by the scruff of the neck and was giving him what, in Essex's opinion, was a long-overdue shaking. Judging by the marks on his face, it wasn't the first beating he'd taken. Essex hoped it was his nephew that had given the captain those bruises.

Luce uncurled gingerly and stood up. "Uncle. How lovely. What a delightful surprise."

"Lucifer." Essex nodded absently. "What the devil-?" His eyebrows were climbing rapidly up his forehead. "Is there an explanation for this, Captain Babbitt?"

"The captain was instructing me in the noble arts of self-defence," Luce said with a fixed grin.

Babbitt gave him a hard stare. "I can be trusted to speak for myself," he snapped, and Cullis let him go. Evidently the important part was that he could be trusted.

"Indeed." Essex met his stare in kind. "And your explanation?"

He cocked his head at Luce in sardonic acknowledgement. "As my cornet says. My lord."

"Really." It wasn't a question. It was a statement of flat disbelief. "Lucifer, I would speak with you. Privately."

"Sir?"

"Walk with me a little way, young man. Show me the sights of the river." The lad looked sick. Essex took his arm. "Are you sick, Lucifer? You seem – feverish. Not, I trust, an ague from any bad air, so close to the water –"

"Uncle, I'm fine." Unsteady on his feet, and very pale, but determined. "If you would like to go for a walk –" he frowned briefly with an almost imperceptible sidelong glance at the captain – "then let us go."

Out of earshot, Essex halted his nephew. "Look, Lucifer. A hawk." He pointed at a hovering shape over the far bank of the river. "Speak plainly. Are you well content?"

"Me?"

"I will be plain, lad. I have been having second thoughts about placing you in Babbitt's care, and what I have seen of his demeanour this morning gives me grave concerns."

Lucifer drew himself up to his full height. A good four inches taller than his uncle. When had the lad sprouted so? "My lord uncle, I am more than capable of dealing with Captain Babbitt's little - eccentricities."

"Are you, now. So the little scene I just witnessed was one of friendly sport, was it?"

"It was, sir."

"I shouldn't volunteer as a spy any time soon, Lucifer. You're not the best liar."

The boy flushed scarlet. "Possibly not, sir. But I'll not run away."

"Well. I'm proud of you, lad." He clapped his arm round Luce's shoulders – so slight, under the heavy doublet. Not a child, but nearly a man grown. It was easy to forget that, when you remembered receiving the letter bearing news of his birth. "Lucifer, if you are determined on this course of action, there is a service you could do me."

"Indeed?"

"Bring him to hand for me."

Lucifer shrugged off his uncle's arm. "You are not, I hope, asking me to act as your creature, my lord? I am no man's intelligencer."

Essex shook his head, smiling. "No, lad, I'm not. I'm asking you to make a reasoning creature of him. I'm assured it's possible. I just don't believe it."

The expression on the lad's face was comical. "Me? Do I *look* like Pygmalion?"

"No – but to be fair, Lucifer, I wouldn't say the

captain is much in the way of Galatea. He came with a reputation for independent thinking, shall we say, and on his present performance I should no more trust him with any real responsibility than I should trust one of my hounds in a chicken-coop. Such anarchy might have served him well in the Low Countries, but I will see him leashed before I trust him with any kind of autonomy."

Luce gaped at him. "But *me*?"

Before he had chance to reply, Tom Corston came over to them, stalking across the grass with his usual feline grace. "I have enjoyed a most edifying conversation with Sergeant Cullis, my lord," he said silkily. "*Most* edifying."

"Do we have an agreement, Lucifer?"

"Well, I – yes, uncle." He smiled suddenly, mischievously. "But only on the condition that *you* write to my lady mother with the funeral arrangements when he finds out."

"I think we need to return to the Commandery, sir. We have more urgent business." Corston glanced up at the sun with a frown. "I'm sure your nephew will be treated well."

"He knows where to find me, if he isn't," Essex said. "God be with you, lad. Let me know how matters progress with your education." He clapped Lucifer on the shoulder again, and Corston inclined his head in a grave bow of farewell.

They set off back across the grass to the house. Babbitt sketched a bow that was just this side of sarcastic, then ignored them completely. Cullis was deeply respectful and attentive. Of the two, that was the more suspicious.

"You were very keen to get us out of there, Tom," Essex said, as soon as they were safely crossing College Green. "What's amiss?"

Corston grinned. "That edifying conversation, my

lord? Sergeant Cullis said, and I quote, that if he caught me snouting round his troop's business again he'd rip my head off and shove it up my arse. I see no reason to doubt his commitment to his word. His loyalty to his men is laudable, don't you think?" The orderly smoothed his collar. "I imagine that any man that the sergeant had a care to, should be fortunate indeed."

17 COMFORTING WITH APPLES

Luce stayed standing by the river for a while after Uncle Essex had departed, watching the ripples of biting fish in the water. Pygmalion, indeed.

Well, he had no intention of being bullied into leaving this troop. His pride wouldn't let him. Even if he didn't believe with all the principle in him that someone had to take a stand against His Majesty and tell him that what he was doing was *wrong*. Even if his conscience wouldn't allow him to stand by as others took up arms in the cause that had suddenly wakened him to manhood - well, he was just *buggered* if he was going to let some scruffy bad-tempered ruffian chase him off. So Uncle Essex thought Babbitt had some redeeming features, did he? Could've fooled Luce. The big redhead didn't seem to be so much hiding his light under a bushel as burying it several feet deep.

"Don't chuck yourself in, Ophelia. I really can't be arsed to go to the trouble of fishing you out."

Luce turned round and glowered at him. "That was remarkably literate, sir, if every bit as worldly as I should expect from a man of your profane disposition. For someone so determined to be disliked, you seem to go out of your way to seek my company."

Babbitt blinked. "Me haunting *you*?"

"You could have gone back into the house, sir, if you were so set on avoiding me. But here you are."

"Here I am," the captain agreed, mildly. "Perhaps I just can't stay away from you, Lucey. There's a thought. Do you think if I made your life wholly insufferable you'd go away?"

Luce looked at him coldly. "Tell me, sir, have you

always been so angry at the world?" And with a final contemptuous flick of his head he left the captain on the river bank.

Hollie watched him go. "No," he said aloud. "No, I don't reckon I have." He'd always been solitary, but by inclination, rather than necessity. Not like Rackhay, who couldn't bear his own company for more than five minutes. But the constant and barely-governable rage, that was recent. That was only since *she* died. If he chose to look closely – and he didn't – that frightened him.

He'd not been entirely fair on the lad. It wasn't Pettitt's fault he was pretty and gently-born and elegant. Unlike Hollie. Not his fault he was so neat and nice that every time Hollie set eyes on him he wanted to rumple the lad's shiny smooth hair and roll him in the dirt till the whelp was as worn and scruffy as he was himself. Not, if Hollie was being honest with himself, Pettitt's fault that he had all the advantages that Hollie lacked. Well, wasn't it lovely to have a rich and powerful uncle whose arse you could crawl up?

No, that wasn't fair either. Honesty being one of Hollie's besetting sins, he was happy to admit to jealousy, but that wasn't Lucey's fault. Being a condescending, pompous little gobshite was Lucey's fault, but he wasn't to know that being right royally patronised put Hollie's back up. And he couldn't be entirely blamed for being stuck in the crossfire of one of Hollie's periodic spats with Rackhay; Hollie was even grudgingly willing to credit the brat with a degree of common sense in his prompt action there.

The up and the down of it was, Hollie had been looking for someone to take his temper out on for days, bored with chasing rumours around Worcestershire and jumping at shadows; Luce Pettitt had turned up in time to watch him and Rackhay make a holy show of themselves, and that was hard to forgive. It could have been anyone. It wasn't personal. *Mostly* wasn't personal.

Fine. Knock some of the polish off and see how sound the lad was underneath. And if that still didn't work they could always send him out as the forlorn hope. He scratched irritably at the nick on his cheekbone. He'd had worse cuts shaving. If he could break the brat of a tendency to apologise every time he drew blood, Lucey might make a half-decent little fighter after all. Stiff-rumped little bugger, but there was a flash of spirit, under there. Hollie shook his head with a rueful grin. Like he needed another one with spirit, to come to blows with on a regular basis. As if Rackhay wasn't enough of a handful.

He went back into the house by way of the kitchens. He'd always been keen on kitchens. Used to spend half his time in the kitchen of the Blue Cat, plaguing the life out of the cook. Acquired a taste for raw parsnip, in that long-ago life. There was a boy peeling apples into a basket, snug in a niche by the fire. Two maids slicing their way through a mound of vegetables. He sniffed appreciatively at the clean green scent of cabbage. One of the servants glanced up at him – fine dark eyes and cheeks as rosy as those apples – and nearly sliced her finger off in an attempt to look unconcerned by his presence. While she was flustered he palmed a handful of parsnip slices.

"Apples," he said indistinctly. "If you can spare one." He considered. "Two, even better."

The dark lass looked up – merry eyes, as well as dark. "Surely not in need of comfort, sir?"

Rackhay would flirt back. Hollie just stood with his mouth open, hoping it wasn't evident in the dim kitchen that he was blushing like a girl. "Ah. No. Probably not. Definitely not. Possibly. Where –"

"Best ask Master Thornbury first," the other maid said, nudging her. "He might not like it." She looked meaningfully at the depleted parsnips, and then back at Hollie. "Begging your pardon, sir. But. You know how it is, I'm sure."

He did, actually, know *exactly* how it worked in kitchens, but he wasn't sure the household staff ought to be so aware of that fact. "And where might I find Master Thornbury? I ought to present my compliments on last night's spinach tart–" which he remembered nothing about the tart other than that it had been on the table and that Lucey had been shovelling it in as if the last spinach tree had just died, but he did have *some* manners. Some people would be astonished to hear. "Most elegantly presented," he finished, nodding intelligently.

The dark-haired one was looking at her cabbage with an expression of stifled amusement. "Most of that dinner came back to the kitchens untasted, sir," she said. "We're not *that* daft."

"So I see." Not daft, merry-eyed, and handy with a skillet. If Rackhay had planted *her* in his bed he might have been in trouble. He wasn't sure he needed any more trouble. "Point me in the direction of the apples, and I'll get out from under your feet."

"Over there, sir. Will is making ready for tonight's supper, so please don't take too many."

The apple boy looked up from the peeling basket. A likeable young rogue, with a missing front tooth and more freckles than a custard. "Means I've got less to peel, though, don't it?"

18 PEACE IS RECEIVED, AND WRATH HAS NO PLACE

Luce was idly reading a copy of the Meditations of Dame Julian of Norwich, lifted from the Bishop's library. He wished he could be quite so confident that all shall be well, and all shall be well, and all manner of things shall be well. He wondered what Dame Julian would have had to say about Hollie Babbitt. And in a couple of hours he was going to have to face the mannerless swine across a yard of dinner table and engage in civilised conversation.

An apple plunked on the table in front of him. A fine, red, rosy, shiny apple. He jerked, startled, back into the less spiritual world.

Babbitt looked down at him. "Truce?"

"Pax?" Luce carefully moved the apple. "I don't think so, captain. I'm not that easily tempted."

"That's a pity. I seem to recall telling you not that long ago that I've been known to cock things up." He grinned ruefully and Luce made a startled downward readjustment of his age. Not so many years between them as Luce had imagined, after all. "It would be appreciated if you forgot the last couple of days ever happened, Lucey. Start afresh."

"Not calling me *Lucey* would be a token of your sincerity, sir."

"Not being so bloody sarcastic would be a gesture of yours, boy. Lucey. Oh, for Christ's sake!"

"Lucifer is adequate. *Captain.*"

"As someone once said to me, by the time I've finished shouting that across the field I'd be dead. I will go so far, *Luce,* and no further. I'm not asking you to like me. I'm asking you to forgive me for my filthy temper, these last few days."

"Something of an understatement."

"Are you determined to make me work for my forgiveness, brat?"

"No, Captain Babbitt, because I have no intention of having any dealings with you whatsoever beyond the obligatory. Taking orders from you is, regrettably, obligatory. Passing the time of day with you is not. I give you good day."

Babbitt lowered the Meditations of Dame Julian with one finger. "You can be a stroppy little bastard at times, can't you?"

Luce looked up at him quite coolly. "No doubt. I have learned from a master. Very recently."

"You realise, I take it, that this conversation could be seen as gross insubordination?"

"I do, captain. Frankly, were you to request my return to the ranks, or even better, to transfer me to another troop altogether, my joy would be unconfined. Now pray allow me to return to my reading. In peace."

The captain sighed. "Look, lad. I won't ask again. Like it or not, you're one of my officers, and if nowt else me and you need to be able to pass the time of day in front of the men without wanting to murder each other. Give us a chance."

Luce put his finger in the book and looked up. "Where our Lord appears, peace is received and wrath has no place."

"Am I to understand from that oblique little remark that I'm reprieved?"

"Temporarily paroled, I should choose to say, captain, on the advice of Dame Julian."

Babbitt grinned. "You want to stop reading them books, lad. It'll get you into trouble one of these days.

Right. Come on. Come and earn your pay."

19 A CLEAN SHEET

They stopped in the frigid darkness of the cathedral, looking up the aisle towards the great shattered windows where a thin cold rain was sifting through. The sulky fires here and there, fuelled by torn prayer-books and broken carvings, did little to alleviate the chill.

Luce gave an involuntary little gasp of shock and Babbitt looked at him, shaking his head sorrowfully. Such sacrilege if even the impious captain was taken aback -

"What a bloody mess," Babbitt said critically, and much more characteristically. "There's broken glass all up the nave. Any of my horses get lamed and I'm going to –" he glanced slyly at Luce, "have harsh words with your man Sariel there, since I understand this bloody mess was his doings. Probably beginning with telling you and everyone else within earshot that he was born good plain Penitence Chedglow."

Luce stifled a giggle. *Sariel* sounded menacing and zealous. Penitence sounded positively bucolic. "Very ominous," he murmured.

"Oh aye, behold thy handmaiden Chedglow. Round up the usual suspects, Lucey. I've not had the acquaintance of most of 'em myself more than a month or so."

"Speaking of Ched – um, Sariel – I forgot to tell you yesterday, with everything else that was going on. It seems that Tyburn's raising hell in the Chantry Chapel and Ched – um, Sariel – wants him out."

"*Owns* the cathedral, now, does he?"

Luce strode confidently down the aisle. He knew

where the men were now – difficult not to, with Tib shrieking furiously in the chapel like one of the minor demons. He didn't have a clue *who* they were. He was also determined not to make a fool of himself in front of the captain. He wasn't sure how far that truce went.

Babbitt slouched after him, whistling.

"Witless. My apologies. Witcombe."

A fat boy with dark eyebrows which met in the middle, surging to his feet stuttering apologies. "Witcombe is the regimental Anthony," Babbitt explained unkindly. "I believe every troop has one."

"M-m-my name's not Anthony, sir, it-it's Francis –"

"He *will* follow you around like a tantony pig, bleating. I find the best way to deal with him is to ignore him until he goes away. Takes a while."

"I was under the impression, captain, that the tantony pig was usually the favourite of the litter?" Luce said. Witcombe smiled gratefully.

"Well done, Lucey, you've got yourself a new pet," Babbitt said with a grin. "Here's Brockis. God alone knows what his real name is. Thieving bastard. It was a choice between joining me and being hanged for taking game. Not sure which I'd have preferred him to go for, myself, but he's got his uses."

Brockis, a gangly, rawboned countryman with a badger-streak of white in his rough black hair that had given him his name, grinned. "If I'd known what you was going to be like I'd have took the hanging."

"Calthorpe. Calthorpe is from Darwen, not ten miles distant from where I was brought up. He's been following me round Europe like some benighted shadow for the last ten years. Can't seem to get rid of him." Calthorpe was probably the homeliest individual Luce had set eyes on in a long day's march, a big shambling figure with teeth like a well-tended graveyard and rough grey hair that stuck out at all angles. He also had the kindest eyes Luce had ever seen. "Trooper Calthorpe is a Grindletonian, lad. Does that bother you?"

"If I knew what a Grindletonian was, sir..."

Luce caught a quick glance between Babbitt and the trooper as Calthorpe went to explain. "Go gently, trooper," the captain said warningly. "I imagine the cornet holds conventional views."

It would be hard to be offended by the gentle and unlovely countenance of Calthorpe, though, no matter what his views. Such a man could never be extreme, not with those eyes. "The Spirit is within all of us, Lucifer. Any man can preach, be he never so low, if he is so moved." He gave an unexpectedly piercing glance at Babbitt. "Can he not, Red?"

"How the hell should I know? I said tell him what it was, Aaron, not fucking convert him -" And the captain got up and stalked away, stiff with disapproval.

"Does the captain not share your beliefs, then, Master Calthorpe?"

"He does not, young man, although I can but hope he finds a path to the Lord's grace in his own time. As can we all, indeed, in our own ways. No, the captain is of good Puritan blood. His father is a lay preacher at Bolton. A good man, if somewhat - uncompromising."

Luce hoped his expression remained carefully neutral. "Am I to take it you're not a member of Master Babbitt's congregation, then?"

Calthorpe smiled. "Hardly, lad, though I know him by reputation. Not a tolerant man."

"Like father, like son, then."

The trooper shook his head chidingly. "Nay, lad, never think that. He's only kicking against what his father –" He glanced up, over Luce's shoulder, and stopped guiltily.

"I was under the impression that you were being introduced to the troop, Lucey, not holding a goodwives' gossip?"

Babbitt pointed to a knot of soldiers busily dicing. "That lot over there – the two with their backs to us and the gormless one stood looking at us scratching his head – yes you Eliot, yes you have seen me before, and yes I do know what you're up to – they're our lot, more's the pity. Eliot is not the sharpest knife in the box. He wants watching. Them two he's with – Ward and Archer – the whole boiling lot of 'em are villains. I tolerate Brockis and his thievery because he's useful. Them three are light-fingered, ill-natured, and malevolent. They're trouble, and the sooner I'm rid of 'em the happier I'll be."

"Your troop seems to lack men of principle, captain," Luce said with some disdain.

"Not sure they can stand the company, lad. I reckon they gave me this lot just to see if I'd scream and run back to the Low Countries. I seem to have acquired every malingerer, malcontent and dead-leg the rest of the Army couldn't do nowt with – and them three is the worst. I wouldn't care to rub shoulders with them lot myself if it didn't give me the opportunity to periodically belt one of 'em." He grinned maliciously and touched his hat to the furtive-looking Archer. "He thinks I'm summat like AntiChrist, does our Samuel. I seem to keep turning up whenever he's up to some badness – which nine times out of ten he *is* up to when you clap eyes on him, so it's not bad odds. He thinks it's because I've got eyes in the back of my head, the stupid sod. If that lot aren't playing with loaded dice I'm – oh, shite, that's *all* we need."

Sariel was stumping down the aisle with a face like thunder. At much the same time there was a roar of indignation from Archer's victims.

"They'm crooked!"

Babbitt raised an eyebrow. "See?" And then,

"Archer, you bent bastard, pack that in!" at full volume.

"Dice are the devil's playthings!" Sariel roared. "Sinners!"

"If there's one thing I hate worse than cheats, it's bloody preachers," Babbitt said irritably. Grabbed Archer by the collar and shook him like a terrier shaking a rat. "But there's not much to choose in it. Give them dice here."

Out of the corner of his eye, Luce saw Ward's hand jerk, tightening on his sword hilt. His own blade was three inches out of its scabbard before he had chance to think about it. "Do not even *think* about drawing on an officer, Master Ward," he said.

Ward mumbled something about scratching his nose. Luce didn't believe a word.

"In the mood for a whipping, Captain Chedglow?" Babbitt said cheerfully. "Be my guest, though I'll grant he's not as pretty as your usual victims." The big redhead cuffed Archer's greasy hat from his head and then grabbed the trooper by his equally greasy hair. "Now then, Samuel, say sorry to the nice man. Are you sorry, Samuel?" He rocked the trooper's head up and down, hard, by his ponytail. "Thought so. Ward, I believe you're the paymaster for this little scheme: hand it over, if you please. Christ, that means you're using Eliot as the muscle of the operation – you must be desperate."

Ward was quivering, his narrow face intent. He was up to something. The hairs prickled on Luce's neck, tingling with alertness. He felt the filthy little scut move before he saw it and his muscles reacted before his brain did, fist connecting with the man's bristly jaw with a force that sent the trooper staggering backwards into his grubby associates and knocked both dice and cup clattering to the flagstones.

Eliot and the troopers they'd been dicing with leapt

for the dice at the same time, four sets of fingers sending the bone cubes rolling amongst the pews. "Mine, gentlemen, if you please," Babbitt said calmly, resting his foot on the dice.

"And what about my silver, eh?"

"The wages of sin," Chedglow declaimed, "is death!"

"Aye and the wages of Okie's troop is sod-all, so give us my silver back, you cheating bastard!"

The trooper from Colonel Okie's dragoons reared up and took a wild swing at Eliot. Eliot grabbed him round the waist and bore him to the flagstones with a meaty thump. Babbitt released Archer – gave him a shove that sent him sprawling across the aisle with a grunt, all the breath knocked out of him by a well-polished wooden pew back – and danced back out of range as the two men rolled cursing across the stone memorials set into the cathedral floor.

Chedglow pulled his Bible out and leafed feverishly through it, eyes alight with godly zeal. "*Then I will draw near to you for judgment; and I will be a swift witness against the sorcerers and against the adulterers and against those who swear falsely, and against those who oppress the wage earner in his wages, the widow and the orphan, and those who turn aside the alien and do not fear me, says the lord of hosts* - Malachi three, verse five."

Luce trod, hard, on a groping hand, not particularly caring to whom it belonged. "Captain Chedglow, you're not helping…sir."

"Lad means shut up, *Penitence*," Babbitt added, also unhelpfully, grinning.

"Watch where you're shoving, arsehole!"

The scuffle had spread as far as the next troop and one big cavalryman was rising to his feet growling, having just had the legs almost kicked out from under him by rolling bodies.

"Dear me," Babbitt said. "Looks like Eliot's going to get a pasting, doesn't it?" And then without altering his mild expression, ramming his elbow into the pit of Ward's stomach as the trooper staggered to his feet. "That's not nice, Ward. Don't do it."

Chedglow was a-quiver with righteous indignation, finger marking his place in the heavy bible. "Brawling in God's house is an abomination!"

"Captain Babbitt, sir –" Luce was trying to discreetly indicate the figure who had just entered the cathedral. "*Sir.*" Babbitt was too engrossed in making sure Ward stayed where he'd been dropped on the flagstones, to look up, and the noise of shouting and swearing as more and more men were drawn into the scuffle made it almost impossible for Luce make himself heard without shouting. "Sir, it's –"

If it was possible, a pistol shot in the echoing cathedral seemed even louder than one in the Bishop's parlour. "The next bastard to lift a finger gets a ball between the eyes, are we clear on that?" Nat Rackhay drawled into the ringing silence. There was no answer, though Eliot and the dragoon from Colonel Okie's troop rolled sullenly apart trying to look as if they'd never set eyes on each other. Rackhay gave a thumping kick to the ribs of the prone dragoon. "I *said*, is that clear?"

Grumbling murmurs of assent. "Bit of trouble, Red?" Rackhay said, ostentatiously rubbing a spot of rust off the barrel of his pistol. Babbitt gave him a narrow-eyed glare and didn't say a word.

"Think nothing of it, old son. Anything to oblige a friend," Rackhay went on casually.

"Oh, shog off, you smug bastard –"

"Rackhay. Babbitt. Captain *Chedglow*?"

Luce happened to be looking straight at Nat Rackhay when the Earl of Essex came storming up the aisle. "Penitence," Babbitt said, looking innocent.

Rackhay was good, but he wasn't good enough not to stifle the immediate grin at the realisation of Sariel's given name. "*Penitence?*" he echoed delightedly. "For sure?"

"This is no matter for levity, sir!" Essex roared at him. "And Lucifer, I had expected better from you, young man! What is the meaning of this unseemly behaviour?"

"Gambling, sir," Chedglow spluttered, lifting his bible.

"And the prevention thereof," Rackhay added, shaking his head sorrowfully. "Disgusting behaviour, my lord. I was horrified. This ruffian –" he prodded the hapless Eliot with his toe –"I happened to arrive just as Captain Babbitt was endeavouring to discipline this shameless rogue. Who *knows* what might have happened had I not arrived in time?"

20 STARTING AT SHADOWS

"Penitence," Rackhay said again. He was still delighted with that titbit of information, almost a month later.

Luce grinned shyly. "I'm not surprised he prefers being called Sariel."

A narrow avoidance of a second bollocking in two days from Essex seemed to have put Rackhay's relationship with Babbitt back on a remarkably amiable footing for the best part of three weeks now. The warm glow had even almost included Lucifer, on the peripheries. "Although I'm not sure Captain, um, Chedglow will ever forgive you for that," Luce warned. "I don't think he liked being in trouble."

"Couldn't believe we got away with it," Babbitt said, again. Thoughtfully, Luce noted. Not like a man revisiting a favourite joke, but like a man assessing a future weapon for his armoury.

"Did you see his face though? When Essex started laying into him?" Rackhay chuckled. Again. "Christ, it was worth it just for that look alone. Priceless."

"I'm not sure we could do it twice." Although by the sound of it Babbitt was thinking about trying it, or something very similar.

"I'm not sure you *should* do it twice, sir. Although I will give you that it was quite funny. At the time. I just don't think he'll let it pass."

As usual, the captain didn't even give Luce's opinion the courtesy of polite consideration. "Thus speaks the voice of experience," he said, "consider yourself told, Rackhay. The eye of Essex is upon us." Cocked an eyebrow, stood up and went slouching across the hall with his sidekick at his heels, yanking the loose ends of his hair from under his buff coat and slinging his sword over his shoulder.

Luce took a deep breath and held his tongue – it was remarkable what an education less than a month's time in the captain's company had been. "Disapproving again, brat?" Rackhay said brightly over his shoulder.

"No, sir." Not entirely daft, and knowing when Rackhay was trying to bait him for the sheer joy of the argument. "Just wondering if this means we're marching out, sir, that's all."

They'd been woken just after dawn that morning by Nat Rackhay hammering gleefully on the door of the Bishop's residence. He'd looked quite elaborately innocent of the charge of deliberately making sufficient noise to wake every single one of the illustrious dead under the flagstones of the cathedral, never mind the immediate neighbourhood. He'd also formed up the whole of his troop, and led them across the Bishop's smooth green lawns. Eighty-odd mounted men going across the lawn at a smart clip to water their horses at the river left a considerably churned-up lawn.

Babbitt had hauled the blonde captain into the parlour, from whence the pair emerged half an hour later at the promise of breakfast and a spot of mild Chedglow-baiting. It was remarkable, Luce thought, no matter what time of day or night the redhead always managed to look just as wide-awake and just as dishevelled. Rackhay was grinning like a thing demented. "Marching out, young man? Whatever gave you that idea? Purely social call, old son."

"Four score mounted men in the garden, maybe," Babbitt said, abruptly not grinning and suddenly rather frighteningly businesslike. "Give me ten minutes to get this lot out of bed."

Luce had had the pleasure of his company for almost a month now and he was getting to know how far he could push it. "Are we, or are we not, marching out this morning, sir, or is Captain Rackhay trying to tease us?"

"Well, it's either march out, or have Charles Stuart up your arse by tonight, apparently. Unless you'd like that?"

"Oh, leave the lad alone, Red," Rackhay said, which brought Luce up rather sharply. Rackhay taking his side? Unheard of.

Babbitt hissed between his teeth and stalked off towards College Green. Rackhay shrugged and followed him. Luce thought about it, and then decided it was his duty to stay with his fellow officers, and followed both of them.

"Take no notice," Rackhay said cheerfully over his shoulder. "He's just arsy because I knew we were moving out before he did. That's what you get for soft living, Lucifer." He closed one eye in a knowing wink. "Virtue is its own reward, you see. I may be half dead of cold, I may have had bloody Chedglow hectoring me all night about my sins, but at least I know the Army's movements."

The chestnut mare lifted her head as he walked towards her and greeted him with an amiable whicker. He still felt slightly dishonourable leaving the faithful Peri in the baggage train, but he was under no illusions that the first time she faltered in a charge would be the last. There was no room for dead wood in this troop. He'd managed to keep her away from Tyburn though, which had been something of an undertaking in itself – even something as simple as where to picket his horse had turned into an excuse for Babbitt to criticise him.

It was, at least, dry today; they'd had three weeks of soaking drizzle since occupying Worcester, with the river lapping at the lawns of the Bishop's house and the whole place starting to stink of wet wool and damp leather. This morning had dawned bright, bitter cold, and as deep bloody-red as Babbitt's hair. Luce tightened the mare's girth and glanced up at the sky again. Rags of cloud were beginning to blow up from the east, black against the lightening horizon.

"Right, lads. Form up. On me." Cullis came trotting out of the cathedral door on his square cob, probably the only man in the troop who could come under that doorway without ducking. Luce had had a forlorn hope that one of these days either Babbitt or his equally erratic horse would have done something showy and brained themselves on that arch – didn't look like it was going to happen, now, though, and the Captain gave him a nasty little half-smile as they passed safely out into the city. "No such luck, brat," he said softly.

Which was another trick of his that Luce hated, the ability to read minds – or the outward show of it. "So where *are* we going, sir?"

"How the hell should *I* know? I'm only expected to get my damn' fool head shot off, you don't think anyone would tell me owt, do you? Round and round in circles, probably, just like we have done for the last month without any sight of an enemy you can get to grips with."

Rackhay said irritably, "Jesus Christ, Hollie! What the hell's the matter with you? Stop having a go at the bloody lad, will you!"

"What's the matter with me, Captain Rackhay, is that I am bloody sick of starting at shadows and false alarms!" And with a vicious slash of the reins down the black stallion's shoulder, Babbitt set his horse galloping down the cobbles, hooves skidding on the wet stones.

Rackhay watched him go and shrugged. "Arse."

"Never a truer word spoken," Cullis agreed. "He'll break his bloody fool neck one of those days. And you wind him up summat rotten, *and* you do it on purpose."

"Oh, God almighty, he's worse than a woman for

starting at shadows! Sergeant Cullis, *you* know and *I* know that we've more chance of stumbling across Hy Brasil than we have of coming across any bloody Cavaliers." Rackhay turned in his saddle and gave Luce a furious, feral grin. "Because if anyone would have advance warning of enemy activity, *Lucey* would - right, brat?"

"I don't believe I am so far in my uncle's confidence, sir, no." Though it seemed to suit people to believe it. Rackhay had a point, though. There wasn't sight or sound of a Royalist for miles, and as they set off on the road out of Worcester there was something of an air of festival - particularly in the continuing absence of the troop's commander. Luce caught sight of Babbitt's black horse fifty yards ahead of the troop, mixed up in the rear of Sir James Ramsay's disorganised cavalry regiment. No one was talking to him, and he wasn't talking to anyone else. In the thick of Ramsay's unregimented, cheerful squad, he cut a grim, and oddly lonely, figure. Luce could have found it in his heart to be almost sorry for the captain, if he hadn't brought it on himself.

"Looks like we'll be fighting on my patch, then, sir."

He glanced down at the little Welshman, Moggy Davies. In the mood to talk, and bright as a somewhat unshaven button. Thank God for the likes of Moggy, then. A little consistency of temper would go a long way, this morning.

"Your patch?"

"Oh yes, the Marches are just over that way, back the way we come. Me, I'm an Ewyas boy, proper little Marcher lord me."

"Indeed?" Luce inclined his head with grave courtesy.

"That's so, that's so. Now I do hear that you're an

Essex boy yourself, is that it?"

"I am from Essex, yes."

"And they were saying as you're first cousin to my lord of Essex, is that true?"

He laughed. "Now where would you have heard that? Not I! My mother is cousin to Lady Essex. The *second* Lady Essex. The present one."

"Oh, aye, yes, not the first, for sure."

It occurred to Luce that he hadn't even needed to mention that particular skeleton in the Essex family cupboard, because Moggy – in common with just about any of the other troopers who were aware of his background – didn't have a clue. All they knew or cared about was that their new cornet was a bit of a cut above – related to the Commander of the Army, don't you know, not just any old raff and scaff dragged up off the streets. "So, how came you to this particular mongrel regiment, Davies?"

Moggy shrugged, grinning. "As good as any other, sir, and the company's bearable. We're a bit of a bugger's muddle, tell you the truth. Odds and ends from all over the place. I reckon as we're made up of all the troublemakers as nobody else had room for. Poor old Captain did cop for it when he took us on – dunno as he knew what he was letting himself in for."

The mare was tossing her head now, sidling sideways and kicking up clots of half-dried mud from the track, making conversation difficult as she skittered and bucked. It was times like this he rather suspected he was going to miss placid Peri. "That mare needs to stretch her legs, lad," Moggy said sternly. "Like many a maiden – give her her head, but make sure she knows whose hand's on the bridle."

And the chestnut mare could run, to give her her due. He hadn't had a chance to try her paces since Powick, and when he put spurs to her sides she took off like a lightning strike, with a burst of speed that left him laughing aloud with the wind in his hair. He could have galloped for miles – *she* could have galloped for miles – with the breath pluming from her wide nostrils in great dragon-spurts and her dainty hoofs lashing the wet ground beneath her. He wondered if she jumped as well as she sprinted, and he was half inclined to set her at one of the thick hedges that barred this countryside, to find a suitable challenge for his new joy.

He didn't have to look far for a challenge, for the mare wasn't the only beast being given her head. There were heavy hoofbeats gaining on them. The big black horse pulled up alongside, rolling a mad white-ringed eye at them, and then cut ahead so that the mare was forced to slow her pace. "Care to explain what all *that* was about?" Babbitt said grimly.

Well, right now Luce didn't care. This beautiful red mare, this creature of fire and light, was his – "Did you see her? Did you see her run?"

"I imagine they saw you between here and the Isle of Wight, boy. Careering about the flaming countryside, I thought the bitch was running away with you. What the *hell* did you think you were playing at?"

Luce straightened in his saddle, stung. "Seeing what she could do. I believe you're quite keen on the evidence of your own eyes, captain. In my personal experience."

The corner of Babbitt's mouth twitched, almost imperceptibly. "Indeed. So you think that spindly little streak of nowt has got the edge on my Tib, do you?"

"I never said that –"

"Halt that mare, damn you."

Luce glanced quickly at the captain, horrified. Then, in some disbelief, saw the grim smile on his face. "I'll have a fair race or none," Babbitt said. "That mare's not half the horse Tib is. And them lot -" he jerked his head at the troop straggling lazily up behind them - "them lot reckon she's the better."

The black tossed his head restlessly and shied at his own shadow - "Be still, you witless beast –" walking shoulder to shoulder now back towards the marching troops, almost out of sight down the rolling lane, and the two horses were almost evenly matched stride for stride. "Barb blood in her, I reckon," Babbitt said, quite amiably. "Bit too light for my taste, but there's them as likes flashy horses, I've no doubt. Start from that oak tree. First man there and back stands the other a drink."

The mare was ready to run again, quivering in every limb as he halted her by the tree. Black Tib was acting up again, not wanting to stand, prancing like a parade horse –"And go!"

21 SOMETHING WICKED THIS WAY COMES

The red mare won, of course. How could she do other, with half the troop cheering her on? It was a near thing, though, with Tyburn finding a turn of speed at the last after fighting his master near enough every step of the way. The mare stopped, dancing, and Tib went past at a flat run.

Hollie was breathless and grinning like a truant schoolboy as he came trotting back. "Damn you, Pettitt, I would have sworn that bloody mare wouldn't have the edge on him! You give that bloody thing a name yet, brat?"

"Rosa, sir - Rosa Mundi, the Rose of the World. For her colour, you see. And if you spent less time fighting Tyburn, and more time training him," Luce said smugly – was rewarded with another panting laugh.

"Christ, brat, you're a self-righteous little bastard at times. *You* try it, and see how far you get. Tib don't own anyone his master – me included."

"No, well, you're not the best qualified to advise on discipline, are you, Red?" Rackhay brought his flashy thoroughbred back up to them at a brisk and businesslike trot, his face cold. "When you're perfectly ready to stop arsing about and take command of your own men again, I'll be glad to return to my own troop. Done with your little fit of the sulks, I hope?"

"Piss off, Captain Rackhay, there's a good lad."

"Don't be so damnably childish, Hollie. I expect better from you."

Hollie glowered at him, that uncertain good humour

evaporated again as neatly as water. "You know *damn* well what's the matter with me, Nat. We're not on our way to winter quarters, we're nowhere fucking near going to winter quarters, and that dilatory bastard knows summat he's not telling – oh, my apologies, Cornet Pettitt, your esteemed Uncle Essex – and it's me and you that's going to cop for it when he buggers it up. I've got a nose for trouble. It's kept my skin whole for nearly twenty years."

Rackhay swept an arm out to indicate the rolling autumn fields. Empty. The silence. The expanse of green and gold hills, still except for the moving cloud-shadows. "And you're *never* wrong, captain. Are you?"

The black stallion pranced heavily, swinging his hindquarters across the road and barging into Rackhay's thoroughbred till it skittered and bucked. Making Rackhay look a fool, jolted half out of the saddle and scrabbling for his stirrups as they arrived at the well-guarded portcullis of Warwick Castle.

Rackhay muttered something that he didn't catch, and then - "Stop being so fucking childish, Red. *That* is the castle, see, there, the one with all the walls still standing? And *this* is us, out here, you know, outside?" he said slowly and sarcastically. "Don't look much like Germany to me, old son. You note the total absence of, you know, siege paraphernalia? Lack of large bodies of armed men? You don't think it might be you that's being a bit of a old maid this time and jumping at shadows?"

"No, I bloody well don't. I think my lord of Essex has landed us in the shit, *again*, and not troubled to mention it. You're telling me Charles Stuart, having kicked our arses good and proper at Powick Bridge, has decided to bugger off to Oxford and he's stopped there for best part of a month twiddling his thumbs waiting for us to come knocking on his door? Not lay in wait for us somewhere around here, oh no. Right. And I'm the

Queen of Sheba."

"Captain Babbitt, sir, with respect –" Luce said stiffly.

"With respect, he's your uncle, and I'll endeavour not to call him a dilatory bastard to his face? I'll try, Lucey-lass, but I can't promise you anything." Hollie kicked the reluctant black horse onto the drawbridge - sideways. "Oh, for Christ's sake. I *hate* these bastard things."

So did most of the other horses. There was a lot of balking and squealing as the rest of the troop rode onto the echoing wood. "We'd have been better off swimming the bloody moat," Cullis muttered.

"You first, old son."

"Captain," Luce said again, still rigidly indignant, "I fail to see the problem with our present situation –"

"Do you, Lucey? Well, allow me to enlighten you." The brat was staring at him, open-mouthed. "Your Uncle Essex loves his sieges, doesn't he? Loves the idea of being all snuggled up on the inside while some other poor bugger sits outside lobbing missiles at him. Well, I've got this funny prejudice against being sat in there like a rat in a trap being slowly starved out. Oh, or dying of some foul plague or another. Call it bitter experience if you like, Lucey, but I'm just odd like that."

Essex couldn't be blamed for the fact that the prospect of a siege set the hairs straight up on the back of Hollie's neck; he'd been there before, at Nuremberg, and that was sufficient unto the day. He'd been having nightmares about it for years. It hadn't been the aftermath of the soldiers that had haunted him – compared to the wreckage the flux had left, the soldiers had been milk and water. He remembered riding through the shattered gates – even remembered the horse he'd been riding, a big grey gelding with a wicked streak a mile wide that they'd christened Hijo de Puta because it bloody well was one – Hijo had balked at something and gone straight up on his back legs, leaving Hollie bloody-nosed and cursing, and causing hilarity amongst his comrades under the command of Albrecht von Wallenstein.

"Nae bluidy use, yon horse," Wat Leslie had called in his broadest Aberdonian. "Best eat the bugger and save y'self the lead!"

Christie Illov laughed behind them and swung down off his neat bay mare – always neat, was Christie, even at the end, they said – to catch the dirty white blur that had run under Hijo's feet and spooked him. "No shame to fright," he said cheerfully. His English had never got much better. Hollie wondered if he'd deliberately cultivated that exotic, heavily-accented charm. He'd tossed the squirming bundle up into the air. "Want a keepsake, Babbitt?"

The keepsake yelped as Hollie had caught it, more by reflex than intention – Hijo had swerved wildly to one side, and Hollie and Keepsake had gone down in an undignified tumble of limbs. "Bluidy typical Englishman," Wat had called down to him, nudging his horse deliberately close to Hollie in the mud. "Women and bairns starvin' in the mud, and he's choosin' to grovel for a bluidy worthless dog."

"More worth than *your* useless carcass," Hollie had grumbled. "At least he can catch his own food. Rather than scrounging-" he cast a pointed look up at Leslie's well-filled cuirass, even the considerably less well-filled one of eleven weeks of siege rations – "off of every other bugger."

Hollie hadn't thought that minor witticism was worthy of the shocked silence that followed it. He'd sat up, with the trembling dog still pressed to his chest. Set the dog on its feet and prepared to catch the grey horse, standing stock still an arm's length away white-eyed and trembling. "*Hollie*," Christie had breathed, less as a warning than as a punctuation, and he'd spun round just in time to intercept a dead woman wielding somebody else's sword.

She wasn't dead, of course, although she'd died very shortly – and not by his hand, though he wished to God he had, having heard her raving in delirious agony. He couldn't get the smell of her off his skin afterwards. She'd thrown her wasted arms round his waist as she fell, and all he could do was to sit in the mud with her as she died, praying, clumsily, in slow English because he didn't know who she was - a Swedish camp-follower, a Lutheran, a Catholic, a German goodwife. He didn't know if she could hear him, if she understood him, or if she even cared, but she lay in the mud in her filthy shift with the rain falling on her face and her hand twined in his hair and she was alive and he couldn't leave her.

She died hard and the only way he could free his hair from her rigid grasp was to cut off the last inches of his braid, and all he could think of afterwards was his Griete, and the worn and dirty letter telling him of her death that had been following him round Germany these two months past, that had finally caught up with him. Had she died like that, alone, half-crazed with fever, and smeared with her own filth. She hadn't, of course. Couldn't have. The letter said none of it, just that Margriete Gerritszen was dead. Not Margriete Babbitt, because they thought he was a chancer and they'd not acknowledge that she'd married an eighteen-year-old mercenary soldier for the love of him - they wouldn't call her by her married name, because that was like admitting he existed. Margriete Gerritszen, it said on her grave marker, like she'd never been wife to Hollie Babbitt at all. Christ, it wasn't like any of her relations were in any hurry to spare his feelings, they'd have took delight in it. If she'd died hard they'd have told him and enjoyed the telling of it - that he hadn't been there, he hadn't sat by her and held her hand while she died. They said he hadn't prayed for her but he had, oh, Christ, he had, that night and every other night, even the nights he was too drunk to remember his own name he remembered hers.

It probably didn't matter, that he didn't know the manner of her death. But he didn't know that for sure. He'd never known, and he would never know - and that was what haunted him. One of the many things that haunted him about Nuremberg.

He took his pay and he left Wallenstein's service as fast as he could trot after that. Swapped sides, gone to fight with the Swedes, what was left of them after Gustavus Adolphus's death. Wallenstein hadn't been sorry to see him go, either. The more pragmatic of his officers saw him as an unpredictable liability; the more superstitious were afraid to cross him. And that, he thought, was the point it had all started to go to rat-shit. He thought he'd forgotten Nuremberg and the Thirty Years' War and he hadn't. There was no plague in Warwick – no starvation, no flux, no bodies unburied – and yet just standing here in the castle keep he could smell that woman, rotting while she yet lived.

The sentry on duty outside Warwick Castle failed to recognise him, or pretended to, what with there being a remarkable number of russet-haired cavalry officers with big Friesland stallions about the place to mistake for one other. The sentry had affected boredom and Hollie had been tempted to let Tib have his way and bite the man. He'd bitten just about every other bugger over the past few weeks. "State your business," the soldier had said in bored tones, not meeting Hollie's eyes, and still managing to look self-important.

"Between me and my lord Essex," Hollie said curtly. Possession of a shiny firearm didn't impress him much. Tib made a rude noise through his nostrils and rested his weight on one plate-sized hind foot. He wasn't planning going anywhere, either.

The sentry continued to stare through Hollie. "My lord Essex is too busy to see every dirty ploughboy who knocks at his door, so I suggest you go away, knock the mud off your boots, and come back with a better attitude."

Hollie took a deep breath. He doubted that punching the sentry in the head would improve matters, but it was tempting. He took his hat off and tucked some strands of loose, and very distinctively russet-red, hair behind his ears. The sentry at least acknowledged his existence this time. Hollie was bored now. He grabbed him by the collar and gave him one good shake, like a terrier shaking a rat, before dropping him back on his feet. "Now listen, arse-bite. You can tell your commander that Captain Babbitt and Captain Rackhay are outside awaiting orders. And that Captain Babbitt is getting fed up."

The gates came open slowly.

22 IN AND OUT OF GRACE

"Well, *you* turned up just in time, then, didn't you? Plenty of action here already, lads, without you lot turning up with the arse-ache as well. Been coming and going all day from bloody Banbury. Turns out the sneaky little bastards have left Shrewsbury two days since."

"Never!" Babbitt said, glancing sideways at Rackhay with a distinctly smug look on his face. "Surely they wouldn't try nipping off while our backs was turned. His Royal Majesty would never do a thing like that."

The trooper – Luce recognised him, vaguely, couldn't put a name to a face but remembered a surplice and a very poor impression of a ghost in a murky cathedral – grinned. "Headed for London, is what I hear."

"What on earth do they want to do a stupid thing like that for? Bloody horrible place."

"No idea. They never saw fit to tell me."

"What," Luce said patiently, "does that have to do with Banbury?"

"In the way, isn't it, mate? Bit of a bugger for the poor sods in the garrison at Banbury, if you ask me. Glad you two have finally turned up, because His Nibs is going mental up there –" he jerked his thumb up across the wide, peaceful sunlit courtyard. "All officers to present theirselves for briefing soon as they get in, no messing about. That be you two."

"Well, if by His Nibs you mean our lord and master the Earl of Essex, my lord can take a long drop off a short wall," Babbitt said, "I'm stirring nowhere till my horse is rested and watered. And you can tell him *that* an' all."

"You are an insubordinate ruffian, Captain Babbitt. And, once again, tardy, I see."

Tom Corston had appeared in his customary silent feline manner, presumably to see what was causing the hilarity. He didn't seem to wish to join in. It had to be noted that being on campaign had not impaired his immaculate personal grooming. He nodded abruptly and gave a curt greeting to Luce, who cringed as those few who hadn't known about the Essex family connection put two and two together and made four. Or worse, looking at Luce and the dapper orderly, and making five.

"Christ, that's t'kettle calling the pot brunt-arse, isn't it? Be late to his own funeral, that one – *and* he's come already kitted out." There was a badly-stifled ripple of laughter around the courtyard. Essex's habit of carrying his own coffin and winding-sheet on campaign – just in case - was a sore point. "Ah well, lads, looks like I'm about to get my – remind me, Nat, what is it now, second? Third? – bollocking this month off Essex. Assuming he's finished making his peace with his Maker by now."

Rackhay was nudging his horse closer to Tyburn, scowling, and Luce had the oddest suspicion that he was doing everything in his power to get the big redhead to shut up. Corston's face was showing the first sign of human emotion Luce had seen on it. He looked disgusted. "I think that's a sufficiency of your insolence, captain." He glanced round the sniggering troops until he'd quelled them into silence. "You may rest assured that I will make report of your insubordination. At a more *appropriate* time."

Babbitt shrugged. "Please yourself." His head was up and there was a wild glint in his eye and in another man Luce would have thought it was a sign of panic but not in Hollie Babbitt, the man didn't have a nerve in his body. He was simply trying to show off before an appreciative audience, that was all – live up to his stupid reputation as the Army's most insolent agitator, telling the truth and shaming the Devil.

"I'll take Tyburn, sir. *Whilst you receive your orders from the commander in chief of the Army.*" Decency compelled Luce to at least try to remind Babbitt of his position and responsibilities. Wasted breath, Luce guessed. He was a little tired of the captain's deliberate ill manners - childish, inconsistent manners, at that, diffident and vicious by turns.

"Well, there you go, I thought you were an officer as well, Lucey, so you'd come to the briefing - but clearly today you'd rather be a groom. It's a wise man who knows his limitations." There was a ripple of laughter from some of the troop starting to straggle in through the gates behind them and Luce flushed.

Corston glared at the lot of them. "Lucifer, get down off that horse, and –"

"I am not an officer of sufficient seniority to merit inclusion in your briefing," he said modestly. "I am watching and learning from my superiors how best to command."

Babbitt's eyebrow twitched. The captain was amused. Corston was mollified, or at the least, sufficiently flattered to seem it. "Clever bugger," Rackhay muttered from behind him. "Look to your arse, if you're going to flirt with Essex's bum-boy."

"You have half an hour, gentlemen, to see to your horses," Corston said, pretending he hadn't heard that.

The sentry winked at Corston's retreating back as he led the officers across the courtyard – those he could drum up, from an army straggled across half of Worcestershire and taking its time on an easy march in the late autumn afternoon. Babbitt and Rackhay were side by side, matched stride for stride in their own private conversation. It didn't seem to be a conversation that Babbitt was comfortable with.

"It's a dangerous game them two play, if you ask

me," the sentry said thoughtfully. "There's only so far you can push Essex. Look what happened to the first Lady Essex –"

"I know," Luce put in, before he got to hear any more scurrilous gossip about his own relations. "The *second* Lady Essex is my mother's cousin."

"Got you, you must be Luce Pettitt. Knew I'd seen you somewhere before, lad. It was you as rounded up your lot out of the cathedral in Worcester, wasn't it? I'm Edmund – Allaby. One of Ballard's lot. Infantry. He's a sod, isn't he, your Hollie? He's going to end up in trouble one of these days."

"He's not *my* anything," Luce protested, starting to lead his mare and Babbitt's black into the shade. Allaby grinned up at him, showing a rather engaging gap in his front teeth.

"I quite like him, actually. From what I hear, there was a bit of a bidding war on over them two. Which is why he gets away with murder. They know their business, those lads."

"What, Captain Rackhay and Captain Babbitt? You are, I hope, making fun of me?"

Allaby absently rubbed the mare's nose. "Absolutely serious, lad. Pair of them fought during the Thirty Years' War – and not choosy which side, from what I hear. I heard that's where our Hollie gets some of his more free-thinking ideas from. They're a broad-minded lot in the Low Countries."

"The man is practically an atheist," Luce said primly. Tyburn tossed his head restlessly with a jingle of harness, ears pricked towards the castle. Luce patted his neck with a degree of circumspection. The horse hadn't bitten him – yet – but both the black and his rider were showing an unsettling degree of edginess today.

Allaby shrugged. "Depends who you'd rather have on side, don't it? You never heard the saying, better the

Devil you know? Well. I'll leave you to it."

Luce had finished loosening the girths of the two horses and had just slid down the wall to rest gratefully on an upturned bucket with the sun warm on his face, when Babbitt reappeared. From the spots of feverish colour high up on his cheekbones, Luce surmised that the briefing hadn't gone well.

"Last in, first out, boy, but at least we're not like to be stuck in here for weeks on end. For which small mercy I must be grateful, no doubt."

"I'm sorry, sir, I don't understand –"

Babbitt dipped his hands into the horses' bucket and splashed cold water over his face. "I'm talking to myself, Lucey. An immediate march on Kineton to bring relief to Banbury," he announced in a mocking cut-glass accent. "Never mind. Option one, we march on this poxy place. Get intercepted, and cut to pieces, by the army of His Majesty. End up dead. Option two, we stay here, shut t'doors, and having starved out the garrison at Banbury they come back to finish us up. And we end up dead. You know what, I like the first one better. It's quicker."

He tossed his wet hair back. "I tell you what, Lucey, I've been trying to stall him every way I know till at least we get some back-up but he won't have it, will he? Mount up, lad."

23 THE VALE OF THE RED HORSE

Riding back out into the gold and green autumn lanes, Babbitt recovered what passed for equanimity with him almost as soon as he'd left the shadow of the castle. The captain's spirits were clearly rising with every stride he put between him and being trapped in the castle at Warwick. They didn't have a clue what might be waiting in Kineton, and Babbitt evidently didn't care as long as it saw some action. Rackhay and the redhead seemed to be in tearing high spirits, which was more than could be said for most of their troops. Cullis was even more morose than usual, and making it his business to cast a gloom over anyone else who dared to crack a smile. It grew dark early – and so cold, for late October, with a frost out of the clear sky making the wet leaves in the lanes turn to ridges of frozen mud as darkness fell.

"Maybe there's no such place?" one of the Weston brothers suggested, kicking his old farm horse up close to Rosa and hunching his shoulders against the biting wind that seemed to have sprung up from nowhere as the sun went down.

"Well, there's somebody around," Luce said, "listen."

Hoofbeats – a brisk trot – ragged, as of a band of mounted men straggling leisurely along a hedge line no more than a half mile away towards them, the sound carrying plain in the still, frosty night air. Laughter. Harness jingling.

His heart started to thump so hard in his chest that he was surprised it wasn't audible to the rest of the troop.

Luce saw Babbitt's hand lifted, white as an old bone in the near-dark ten yards ahead. There were advantages, he thought wildly, to having a fair-skinned redhead as your commanding officer. The men halted, muttering amongst themselves.

Babbitt wheeled the black and came back down the lane at a fast trot. "The fox is started from the covert," he said calmly. "No quarter, if you please. We owe them bastards from last time."

He waited for the troop to begin to move off – "Walk, for Christ's sake, don't trot, we don't need a bloody advance party!" Rackhay came out of the dusk on the far side, the pair of them herding the men like sheepdogs between the hedges. Like wolves, more like. "Keep a steady hend on the bridle, Bebbitt," a voice floated out of the shadows, and the big redhead jerked with silent laughter.

"Make ready to charge, gentlemen. Steady as she goes. Do *not* follow me. I'm riding a black horse on a dark night. Follow –" he glanced over his shoulder, at Luce and his bright chestnut mare, glowing like a lantern in the dark. "Follow Lucey."

And then quite abruptly he stood up in his stirrups with a wild yell like a hunting hawk, put spurs to the black, and was gone through a gap in the looming black hedge. Rosa took off in hot pursuit entirely of her own accord and before Luce knew quite what was happening he was in the vanguard of a pack of forty troopers going hell for leather in the darkness, crashing through the hedge into a stand of trees. It was briefly, wildly exhilarating. There was a clash of steel somewhere to his left and a scream and he thought now might be a good time to have his sword in his hand. He could just about see the mare's ears. His pistols were useless. Someone's weren't, and he saw a brief shower of sparks before the ball whistled past him – hit someone? He heard swearing, but that might just have been the stumbling horse swerve. Another clash of steel, and someone else came cannoning out of the dark. "Whoops!" said Rackhay, laughing maniacally. "Excuse *me*!"

Luce whirled the mare and ducked in time to parry a vicious downward slash from a sword, close enough to feel the wind of its passing on his face. Forced Rosa in to barge the Royalist horse

off-balance, and who had he picked *that* trick up off? He found himself swearing under his breath as he hacked wildly with his own blade. Felt it hit something – wrench in his hand as if it had struck something immovable: bite, and then stick. Couldn't work it loose in time. Felt the breath sobbing in his throat and the hilt go suddenly warm-slick in his hands and then something big and heavy came thundering out of the dark and slammed broadside-on into the Royalist horse. The horse went down with a shrill squeal and a snap like a green branch breaking. Someone carried on screaming.

There was a shot and the screaming stopped.

And then the lane was abruptly silent, save for an offended cawing of the rooks in the trees, disturbed from their late roost.

"That makes us about even, boy," Captain Babbitt said, leaning from his saddle, very close to Luce's ear. He wasn't even out of breath.

"I'm still none the bloody wiser as to where Kineton is," Rackhay said, in an aggrieved voice.

"We'm the scouting party, mate," a West Country voice called from the back. Could be Isaac, could be Lucas, distinctly Weston. "Trying to find the village. I do reckon they prob'ly lost it."

"Anyone missing?" Babbitt said, and there was a quiver in his voice that was either rage or barely-controlled laughter. No one answered. "Fair enough. Anyone want to declare themselves dead?"

"Me, sir. I'm bloody freezing."

"Thank you, Weston, that is not helpful. Given that I reckon we're mostly intact, does anyone object if we ride on? As I have no desire to freeze my arse to the saddle either."

"But what about –" Luce didn't like to be the one to ask, but there was a man down there, possibly injured, probably dead.

Babbitt glanced over his shoulder, his face a white blur. "I imagine he's quite dead, brat – and if he's not now he will be by tomorrow morning. It was bravely done, but I suggest you keep a tighter hold of the sword next time, eh? Leave him where he fell. I'm not in the business of looting. No doubt come daylight one of his pissy mates will come looking for him."

The tramp of feet and the crashing of heavy bodies through the branches, and a gruff shout of "Who goes there?"

"The Archangel frigging Gabriel," the mouthy one of the Westons muttered, just on the verge of hearing. "Who was you expecting?"

"Ballard's troop," Luce said quickly. "That's Allaby. I recognise the voice."

"He's right, you know." Rackhay sounded amused. "Quick lad."

"Oh, well, don't kill him quite yet, then, gentlemen. He's one of ours." Babbitt did not sound amused. "Am I like to run into the whole Army of Parliament blundering around in these benighted back lanes, Master Allaby?"

"Captain Babbitt. Sir."

"A salute is somewhat wasted, lad, I can barely see my hand in front of my face. We've – I hope – just been set on by a troop of Malignant horse. And kicked their arse, I might add. Don't trip over the dead one, gentlemen. First blood to Cornet Pettitt. Would you care to enlighten us as to what the hell's going on out here?"

"There are parties out all over the damn' place tonight, captain. We come out behind you lot – and some of us marched straight to the village like we was told instead of taking a short-cut through the hedge chasing after bloody Malignants, so we're nicely set up for the night thank you. At least one quartermaster's party gone out already that's not come back – and a few sentries out in the sticks that I know of."

Luce saw Babbitt's teeth flash in that nasty grin of his. "Dear me, Lucifer, I do hope you haven't just killed one of Master Allaby's sentries. That would be too terrible to contemplate."

"Doubt it," Allaby said cheerfully. "Been sounding like a bloody thunderstorm out here. We've been exchanging fire with *somebody* on and off all night while you lot was tear-arsing around in the bushes."

"Not guilty, old son, for once. Flushed the little bastards out of hiding, have we?"

"For sure. It's bitter cold out here, sir. We heard the shots and came to investigate –"

"Pity you wasn't ten minutes earlier, you gormless whelk," Cullis grumbled from the flank.

"So if you would care to accompany us back to the village," Allaby went on, pretending he hadn't heard that, "we should be able to accommodate your men. Er – somewhere."

It was a long, halting walk in the bitter dark, with the occasional branch cracking underfoot sounding like enemy fire, and the occasional burst of fire in the distance sounding like a bad dream. The horses were tired now, stumbling in the sodden clay, and they could only travel at the pace of the slowest. Weston's farm horse just kept plodding on, lifting each massive feathery foot out of the sucking mud with a deliberate squelch. Rosa's head was drooping. Rackhay was still whistling, in the vanguard.

It was nothing at all, in the end. A great white owl suddenly swooped out of the trees across the track in front of them; Rackhay's overbred horse shied, and dropped him down its shoulder. That was it. No more. He wasn't hurt - remounted, cursing – Babbitt caught him up and they exchanged a few words and that was it.

But Rackhay wasn't happy. The whistling had stopped and when they reached the village and he dismounted Babbitt was eyeing him thoughtfully. "Is something amiss, Captain Rackhay?" Luce said.

"Hm? Not a thing. Should there be?"

Not that Luce was fooled for a second. He didn't think Rackhay was hurt. The captain wasn't limping: there was no blood, no signs of damage – but there was something about the look of him that was frightening. Rackhay looked grim, and that wasn't an expression Luce had seen on those devil-may-care features before.

Kineton village was a straggle of limewashed cottages, snug in their hollow of hedges and deep in the hollow of the hills between Banbury and Worcester. The cottage where Allaby left them was small and dark, but it was warm at least, and someone had lit a fire. Luce's eyes took in the signs of a hasty departure – the child's shoe under the high-backed settle by the fireside, the unswept crumbs on the table. Wondered for whom the fire had been lit, exactly. Rackhay took his hat off and slumped down on the settle. The firelight gleamed like amber on his tangled hair. "Well then. Here we are. For which the Lord be thanked."

He tipped his head back against the rough plaster wall and Luce saw him shiver. "Are you cold, sir? Shall I put more wood on the fire?"

Babbitt glanced sideways at him. "Aye, do that, lad." Sounding almost amiable, and suddenly very North Country. As if in this place, with just him and Rackhay, he was a different, unguarded man. "It was a bloody *owl*, Nat. There's nowt to be afraid of in an owl – unless you're a mouse, that is."

"Afraid? Captain Rackhay?" It was almost an involuntary question from Luce, because if Nat Rackhay was afraid – Rackhay, who'd spit in the devil's eye and laugh – then there was something coming to be very afraid of.

"Shut up, Lucey."

"Oh, let the boy speak, Hollie. Yes, I'm frightened. Scared witless. Funny, isn't it? Me. Frightened. Of a bloody bird. A stupid bird. It's just an old wives' tale. It's not a bad omen. Course not. D'you remember, Red, they used to say we had more lives than a stack of cats? Well, that's my lot. I can feel it in my bones."

"It's a poor rat that only has one hole," Babbitt said absently. "Christ, Nat, I wouldn't trust bloody Essex to find his own arse to wipe it, never mind bring his Royal Majesty to bay. What are the chances –"

Rackhay shook his head. "You know damn' well what I mean. You've been seeing it coming for days and I never -" He covered his mouth with his fist, choking off the rest of his sentence, and stared into the fire. "Well, I'm sorry for it, Hollie. I should have listened to you. Always knew there was a touch of the witch in you with that hair." He giggled briefly. "Sorry. Sorry. Not funny, that. No, don't worry, I'm not going to disgrace myself by running away when it comes to it at the last. What is they say – those who live by the sword and all that? I just keep thinking – fucking hell, Hollie, is this it? I got so much to do. Hardly started to live yet, old son. D'you remember? Me and you? What we were going to do when we eventually resigned our commissions –" his laugh was almost a sob. "Don't think we had more planned than finding the nearest warm tavern and staying drunk for a week, did we?"

Babbitt swore, at some length. It wasn't in any language Luce was familiar with, but it certainly sounded descriptive. "Nat, *stop* it."

They'd forgotten he was there, Luce thought. Rackhay was intent on the fire, and Babbitt was intent on Rackhay. The big blond captain glanced up and gave Luce an absent smile. "Nothing the matter with me, Red. Nothing at all. It was a sign, that's all, for them with eyes to read it."

"It was a frigging *bird*, Nathaniel. It was nothing more than that."

"It was. A bird of ill omen. And it's coming for *me*."

Babbitt swore again, in perfectly plain English this time. "You are *not* superstitious, Nat."

"Oh, am I not? A bit rich, coming from the man who's spent last week skulking round Worcestershire croaking ill omens like Cassandra. "

"Christ, if I thought that bird was going to bother you this much I'd have shot it myself! Just bloody get hold of yourself, will you. It's no different from every other bloody time me and you have been somewhere at the front getting shot at. We've got no more and no less chance of coming out of it with a whole skin than we ever have had. Which is to say, somewhere between precious little and sod-all. You've got me through worse than this in my time, Nathaniel." Babbitt ran both hands through his already-tangled hair, then leaned across and shook his friend's shoulders. "I can't do this without you, Nat. I've not the temper for it. I'm not – Christ, man, you know what I'm like – we fight *together,* captain, you do the flirting and I do bitey-bitey. Give it a week before some bastard put a bullet in my ear, if I didn't have you to settle it for me."

Rackhay raised an eyebrow at him, and then nodded at Luce. "Little ears, Red. Mind your tongue. Don't frighten the boy."

"Don't be daft, Nat. He's not important."

Rackhay stooped and picked up the little shoe under the table, turning it in his hands. His face was thoughtful, under that deceptively piratical crust of blond stubble. "That was unkind, Hollie. The boy matters. Seems to me you take rather too much pleasure in baiting him, these days. You never liked it when it was you – *Kersen*." He fumbled for his purse, tossed it to Luce. "Take no notice. Old soldiers get like this, full of piss and wind. It means nothing. Go and find us all something to eat, there's a good lad. "

"The condemned man ate a hearty breakfast?" Babbitt sounded bleakly amused. "Or just working on the assumption that the best way to sweeten my temper is to feed me?"

"Always worked for Margriete in the old days, old son. Off you scamper, Lucey boy."

24 OLD SOLDIERS, SWEETHEART, ARE SUREST

Nat seemed to drop off to sleep with the ease of a clear conscience, and Hollie sat up until the sky began to lighten watching him. Probably not the best idea, with half the neighbourhood apparently crawling with the King's men, but sleep seemed to be evading him tonight.

After Luce had come back with the best that Kineton had to offer – a dozen wizened apples that he'd have hesitated to offer Tyburn, some admittedly very good new cheese and fresh-baked bread, and a platter of roast meat so hot that the boy was surreptitiously sucking burnt fingers as he dumped it in front of them – Nat had bucked up no end and if Hollie hadn't known him as long as he had he might have been convinced. Hunger and lack of sleep worked havoc with the nerves of the bravest men, God knows. It could have just been that. But it wasn't.

It was ridiculous, and somehow pathetic. It was a bloody bird. It hadn't been the best timing, admittedly, getting dropped on your arse just before you knew a fight was coming. And it was. Even if Kineton hadn't been riddled with god-damned Malignants, Hollie had a prickly, cold, sick feeling that he knew all too well from the old days. Storm coming. But that had been no more and no less than a barn owl, out on its legitimate business. Not a messenger from the underworld. Nat was a bloody Christian, for God's sake, not some heathen who knew no better. Even Hollie, whose beliefs didn't bear too much close scrutiny, wasn't feared of omens and spirits. (Mostly.) You might as well stake your life on the toss of a coin. Hollie had his faults, and gambling wasn't one of them. Life or death on the field was bugger-all to do with God's will. You lived or died depending on how determined you were to do either.

Rackhay was too calm, that was what bothered Hollie the most. There'd been none of his usual wild good humour, just a placid quietness, almost a peace, like a tired child making ready for bed. As if he'd decided what was going to happen tomorrow already. "And I'll not have it!" Hollie said aloud. They'd seen too much together, watched each other's backs for too long. Fought like cats in a sack at times but then Christ, what friends didn't, after this long knowing each other. It didn't mean anything, except that each knew where to poke the other where it hurt most and neither of them had the temperament to back down. His hand went unconsciously to the bump on the bridge of his nose, a little keepsake of the only real serious set-to where either of them had sustained any lasting damage. God alone knows what had appealed to them about each other in the first place, apart from a perverse sense of humour and a wholly undignified delight in brawling. Well, he'd ask Nat about it. Tomorrow. Yes, when the battle was all over, when they were sat in front of a fire somewhere, with the whispering dark outside, and he was taking the piss out of Nat's sudden turn towards the old-wifely, he'd ask him about that campaign.

The boy was awake, sitting up in his blankets and watching him, those big girlish eyes steady and serious and, damn him, sympathetic. Arrogant little bastard. "What?" Hollie said irritably.

"Are you worried about the captain?"

He was about to say something curt and then he remembered being told off last night about his manner with Luce Pettitt and Nat had a point, he was sharper than he had a right to be with the lad. And he hadn't been used to be cruel. There'd been a time – a long time - when it had been him on the receiving end of cruelty, and he hadn't cared for it. He sighed, ran a hand through his hair –"Aye. I am."

"Is he truly afraid?"

The correct officerly response was denial, Hollie believed. It wasn't one the brat was like to get. "Lad, if you meet a man who says he's not afraid of a battle that he knows is coming, he's either a madman or a liar, and for myself I shouldn't choose to serve under either. Captain Rackhay is a good officer." It was suddenly very important that after Powick the boy should know that. Neither of them had exactly covered themselves with glory at Powick Bridge. "I can't say I'm ungovernable with delight at the prospect of fighting, myself."

The boy smiled. Somewhat wryly. "I can't imagine either of you being frightened of very much."

There was probably a correct officerly response to that, too, and the lad wasn't going to hear that from him either.

"Aye, well, you'd be wrong, then. Queasy lot, officers. And there's a few I wouldn't care to stand downwind of on the eve of a battle, either."

Pettitt giggled, looking slightly less like a scared rabbit. Hollie wondered – very briefly – if he'd ever looked like that as a new recruit, and then dismissed it. He hadn't. He'd run away to the army as soon as he was tall enough to pass as of an age. He'd been less afraid in the ranks than he had been at home. And as Nat had pointed out, Hollie had been taking a grim delight in frightening the lad of late. Probably something he should feel guilty about, but if the brat couldn't cope with the reminder of his own mortality, he really ought not to be fighting. Ought to be still at home, sewing on his sampler.

Rackhay stirred, still stretched contentedly in front of

the dying fire rolled in his blanket. Hollie glanced down at him and then back at Pettitt.

"You care for Captain Rackhay," Luce said, wonderingly. Hollie thought about denying that too but what was the point? Sooner or later the brat was going to notice that despite first impressions, Hollie wasn't entirely barren of finer feelings. Pretty much entirely barren of an ability to articulate the bloody things, but he had 'em.

"I do, brat. He was near enough the first friendly face I set eyes on when I arrived in the Low Countries - neither of us hardly out of petticoats. We learnt our trade together. He liked me." He shrugged. "God knows why. I didn't go out of my way to be liked in them days."

"You still don't, Red," Rackhay said drowsily.

"Shut your face, slug-a-bed." Hollie prodded his friend's recumbent form with the toe of a muddy boot. "If your idle arse isn't up and on a horse in half an hour —"

25 VAIN THE AMBITION OF KINGS

There were leftovers from last night for breakfast, which was more than Luce had often had of late, and he stuffed a couple of the apples inside his doublet surreptitiously for later. Rackhay seemed happier. He caught Luce looking at him and winked. "Last night was just a passing fancy, boy," he said with a smile. "Old soldiers take these whims."

Babbitt looked ill, though. Dead white and heavy-eyed, and edgy as a cat on a hot griddle. Luce made himself a mental promise not to cross the big redhead any more than he could avoid. "What the *hell* is going on out there?"

Church bells, ringing insistently, A flurry of galloping hoofbeats, coming and going up the main street. Anxious raised voices. And then the initial stutter of drums – finding a rhythm and beating to sound the troops to muster. Feet. Marching feet. A large number of them. Babbitt rubbed his hands over his face. "Shit."

"My thoughts exactly, old son. Sounds like the hounds have found the scent." Rackhay buckled himself into his plate. Tied his sash. Stood up with his scabbard in one hand and his lobster-tailed helmet tucked under his arm, grinning like a fox. "Come on, then, Red. Let's go and earn our pay."

Cullis had the troop formed up ready, outside in a thick, swirling early morning mist that left tiny silver beads on hair and a chilly prickle on the skin. There was a cobweb on a bush just outside the front door, stretching from bush to rooftop, pearled with dew. One of the Weston boys had Tyburn on a short leading rein and the big black horse was snorting like a heraldic dragon, flinging his head up and down and splattering foam over his glossy neck. Cullis glowered at Luce and shoved the colours unceremoniously into his cold hand. "Enjoy your night with the senior officers, did you, Lucey?" he said. His eyes rested on the red-haired captain, leaning his head against the black's flank. "Looks like it was a good one. And the lot of you carousing on the Sabbath, too. Ought to be ashamed of yourselves."

"What's happened?" Luce hissed.

Cullis gave him another venomous look.

"I thought you'd know, with you being in with the officers. You remember last night – chasing round in the dark playing silly buggers with the King's men? Well, there they were all along, not five miles from here. Essex bumped smack into 'em on his way to church this morning. Fine time for you lot to go off on one - though I hear Master Rackhay's in need of a stiffener this morning, after last night."

Luce saw Babbitt's shoulders jerk. The captain turned round and gave them both a long, level look. "Watch your tongue, sergeant. I should hate any *unrest* to be spread amongst the men as a result of idle gossip," he said coolly. "Especially Captain Rackhay's troop."

The sky was almost totally cloudless– a clear white, shot with pink and gold. "It's going to be damned cold today," Cullis grumbled, his breath misting in front of his face. "Buggers could've waited till we'd had breakfast. Assuming that some of us could face food this morning – Hollie?"

His only response was another cold stare and then Babbitt moved off to join Rackhay. No closer than usual – within arm's length, far enough to be out of Tyburn's kicking range: nothing of remark, except Babbitt's odd watchfulness. Rackhay was still smiling to himself, very straight backed, very relaxed. The mood amongst the men began, almost imperceptibly, to lighten, as cold muscles warmed up at a brisk trot and the hock-deep mist on the grass started to thin.

Rackhay and Babbitt were gone. And then before Luce had chance to wonder where they'd gone, they were back. "Gentlemen. It seems we form up with Jamie Ramsey, on the left."

And the troops were starting to fall silent as the lane opened onto a great plain, a bowl of pearly mist deep shadowed by the long slope of the hill. They said that Edgehill had been covered by sea, centuries ago, and the steep hill rose above them like a towering wave. No one spoke, slowing their mounts to walk across the dew-white grass into the shadow of a thick hedge. Luce felt sick, his hands numb on the bridle as Rosa tossed her head with a jingle.

Babbitt halted the black horse, nodded at Sir James Ramsey absently, and turned to his men. "A few moments of prayer and reflection."

The big Scotsman nodded approvingly, the first ruddy light of early morning striking red and gold from his well-worn plate. Under of the hedge, someone coughed wetly and then retched.

"There's your first sight of the King's army, gentlemen." Babbitt inclined his head towards the ridge of high ground. "So I suggest that those of you who have souls to commend, spend your time wisely in contemplation. The rest of us – pray very hard that God loves a trier."

Luce shaded his eyes with his hand. There were a lot of them. They had a lot of guns. There were a lot of horses. One of the colours in the Parliament line unfurled in the breeze with a rippling snap and he jumped. "The, ah, hosts of Midian?" he hazarded, trying for humour.

"Afraid not, old son. Just Charles Stuart.

Somewhere up there."

"And that German twat, over the way," Babbitt growled, standing up in his stirrups as though Prince Rupert might obligingly appear within shot

"New officer?" Ramsey sounded amused and Luce flushed. Was it really that obvious?

"Not his first engagement," Babbitt said stiffly, "he has performed his duties to date most creditably." Luce just stared at him. "All things considered," the captain added, aware of his cornet's thunderstruck gaze. "Don't get ideas."

"They either get killed or they get used to it," Rackhay said, and there was a general consensus of amusement.

"Well, boy? What do you think?"

"It's big," Luce said stupidly. "There's a lot of people." He thought if he didn't keep talking he might join whoever it was in the ditch puking up his breakfast – caught Babbitt's coldly amused gaze and set his lips. "What happens now?"

Rackhay grinned. "We see who blinks first."

The morning wore on and Luce's initial terror began to subside into restlessness and boredom. No one seemed to be showing signs of blinking. Rackhay was wandering up and down the hedge line with his grey thoroughbred on a loose rein, trying to find someone to play cards with him. Babbitt was cleaning his carbine, for the fourth or fifth time that morning. If it was an attempt to look casual, it was failing utterly. The King's Army hadn't moved so much as a whisker. "Anybody bring anything to eat?"

Luce produced his apples with some shame. Babbitt ate his, core and all, without taking his eyes off Rupert's cavalry and without a word of thanks. Luce couldn't quite believe he was offering wizened apples to a man of Sir James Ramsey's standing but the old soldier ate his with every sign of pleasure.

Rackhay smiled and shook his head. "You have mine, Lucey-lad."

Then there was the sound of a cantering horse across the grass and all four looked round, though possibly only Ramsey didn't recognise Essex's officious young aide-de-camp in the terrifyingly neat figure on the equally neat horse. "Lord above, not a speck on him – where *does* he sleep at nights?" Rackhay said in a lazy and perfectly audible undertone – turning to grin at Babbitt with an expression that made it perfectly clear where *he* thought the young aide was sleeping.

"A message from my lord Essex for Captain Babbitt. You are to move your troop to the reserve forces behind the *centre*, under Balfour. At once."

"I am *what*?" Babbitt echoed. "What – what the hell is he *thinking*?"

Tom Corston drew himself up to his full height with great dignity. "I am not required to account for my lord's decision to the likes of you, captain. That's your order. Now move out to the centre, Captain Babbitt. Now."

"You must be out of your tiny mind. There's two men on this side of the field who know that German twat's little tricks - I'm one, and he's the other. And you're going to send us off over *there*?"

Corston shook his head. There was a faint, unpleasant smile on his face. "No, Captain Babbitt, I think you misunderstand. I'm going to send *you* over there. Captain Rackhay stays right where he is."

"When you two have finished calling each other names," Rackhay cut in, leading his horse up between them. He jerked his head towards the hill. "They blinked first."

The King's army was on the move. Pikes erratically waving down the hill like the antennae of some vast many-legged buff beast, and the midday sun glistening off back and breast plate. Artillery pieces rolling with a sound like distant thunder. Horses whinnying. Men cheering, calling. Flashes of colour – the scarlet sashes of the Royalist officers, the russet and blue and black and red coats of the troops, as their commanders' tastes and resources dictated. Rackhay whistled. "Praise the Lord, something's happening. My backside was getting numb."

"I see," Babbitt said coldly, disregarding him - and he wasn't talking about the King's army. So did Luce. He quickly dropped his eyes before Babbitt saw the sympathy in them. "Find Cullis, Lucey, and get the men mounted and formed up. *Again*."

Rackhay shrugged. "Oh, it doesn't matter. You'll be right in the thick of it anyway. All nice and cosy, hiding behind Ballard's lot. We're not going to see a bloody squeak out here in the bushes." He leaned, suddenly, from his saddle – poked Babbitt in the shoulder with one finger. "You behave yourself. No doing anything stupid without me there to keep an eye on you. You understand me – *Kersen*?"

Babbitt went dead white, jerking upright in the saddle like a man shot. "*Stop* calling me that!"

And he pulled the black's head up and spurred the horse into a wild gallop out of the left flank, scattering musketeers in all directions.

26 AMBITION, MADAM, IS A GREAT MAN'S MADNESS

Sir William Balfour surveyed the field with mild despair. Having moved perhaps a hundred yards, the King's army had halted again, with no sign of decisive action from either side. He turned to Luce with a sigh. "How did we get this far, laddie? However did we come to this pass?"

Once again, Luce had no answer. Now that it had come to it – pale, chilly sunlight glinting off arms and plate - now that he could make out individual faces and nervous smiles at comrades and wide, frightened eyes – he had no desire to hurt anyone. Not for a principle. He doubted the King did, either, not once he'd seen so many men prepared to lay down their lives in spite of their fear and their unhappiness: so many men of honour and certainty all lined up in row on row to tell him he was *wrong*. Surely then he would reconsider his ways and listen to what was right. He was a good man, an honourable man, otherwise he wouldn't be King – he would do what was right, once his subjects had made him aware of the limitations of their conscience. Thus far could they allow and no further. No man could expect less.

"I don't know, sir," he said uncomfortably. It gave him an odd, sick feeling to hear men the age of his father admit uncertainty in this fight.

Cullis slouched up beside him. "Go on then, where's he disappeared off to this time?"

Luce glanced around the restive cavalry troops for that distinctive horse – or at least the sun off a thick tail of cinnamon-red hair amongst the knots of men and resting horses. "No idea, sergeant."

"He's a bugger when he gets like this. He can't keep still. He's up to something… well, thank Christ they've split him and Nat Rackhay up or there'd be hell to pay, and no pitch hot."

Balfour gave the sergeant a dark look, frowning at the casual blasphemy, and nudged his horse into a trot, circling in a wide arc behind the troop, observing the Royalist lines. And there the captain was, weaving in and out of Ballard's infantry in the front lines with casual grace and total disregard for the artillery pieces lining up, managing to look both bored and sinister at the same time. The black horse shied at the waving colours, more out of perversity than fear, and Babbitt gave the beast a hard open-handed slap down the shoulder that echoed like a pistol shot around the valley in a still moment.

"Teasy as a snake," Cullis went on. "Do as you're told, keep your head down and don't answer back. I know that look, he'll go off and do something half-cocked just to get things moving."

The black was coming back up the slope towards them now, foam dripping from his bit. "You're going to wear that horse out before we get a sniff of a fight," Cullis called disapprovingly. "He's sweating like a pig."

"I wasn't aware you were related," Babbitt snapped back, pulling the horse to a blowing halt.

"Well, whatever half-arsed scheme you're plotting, put it out of your head right now –"

"Me?" Babbitt looked down his nose with an air of injured innocence. "Mind's a blank, sergeant."

"Aye, well, that's when you're most dangerous."

"Just making sure the sneaky bastards haven't sloped off while we weren't looking, sergeant. Keeping my eye on 'em. There he is, the little darling. *Nice* suit, Rupert." The captain sniggered. "God love him, he'd hate it if we didn't notice him, wouldn't he?" He waited till the elegant figure in the scarlet suit looked up the long slope. The sun glinted from the elaborate silver lace adorning Prince Rupert's shoulders and sleeves, and off the spyglass he was training on the Parliamentarian cavalry troops lining up on the left wing.

"Bleeding hell, shining like a shithouse door on a frosty morning," Cullis said admiringly, nudging his cob up alongside and following Babbitt's gaze..

"Different wig today as well, I reckon. You noticed his hair's never the same colour two days running?" Babbitt took his hat off and stood up in his stirrups, ostentatiously tugging at his own long ponytail. "Feast your eyes on that, old son - all my own, too." Sat back in the saddle, flicking his hair back over his shoulder. "Tosser."

"You really can't stand him, can you?" Luce said.

"Can't abide him, the pretentious little shit."

"Don't get him started," Cullis grumbled. "Be here all bleeding day once he gets going."

"Tell you what, brat. If we're both still here this time tomorrow -" the captain grinned - "I'll tell you all about the lovely meinherr Rupert. Book-learning, Lucey. That's all that is -" Babbitt waved cheerfully up the hill at the Royalist commander, and very deliberately blew him a kiss. The tall man in scarlet evidently saw him, because he turned away abruptly.

Balfour cantered back to join them. "Ah, Captain Babbitt. I see you've spotted the Robber Prince. Discreet choice of attire there, don't you think?"

Babbitt leaned over and clapped Luce on the back, and Luce flinched away, unused to such familiarity. "Brat, if our lovely fashion-plate over there don't rise to it soon, we'll likely be sat here till suppertime watching two sets of - pretty bloody ineffectual, it must be said - gunners popping away at each other. On the other hand, if the Palatinate ponce bites, we should be finished up in time for supper. Sounds like a result to me."

"I fail to see how you can treat this lightly!"

"Been doing it twenty years, Lucey. You get bored with it after a bit." He met Luce's eyes and raised an eyebrow in that irritating way he had. "Don't worry, brat. It'll all make sense when your balls drop." He pulled the black horse's head up. "Right. What's the plan?"

"You don't change, Babbitt," Balfour said wryly. "Still as hot at hand as ever. The plan, laddie, is that, seeing as we're the reserve, we stay put and look willing and hope we're not required, and you do what you're told. Which would make a first, but by the Lord's grace, it might finally happen. You're not racketing around with Wallenstein now. Speaking of which, where's that wild mate of yours?"

"Up there lurking in the bushes with Jamie Ramsay, plotting badness. My lord Essex thought it best to split us up for the duration."

"Can't say as I blame him, captain. One of you gives me enough trouble, I'd need two pairs of hands and four pairs of eyes to keep the both of you under control." He raised his own spyglass. "Ach, here we go." Handed it to Babbitt. "Feast your eyes on the magnificence of His Majesty's attire."

"What *has* he come as?" Babbitt said, remarkably mildly, and Luce remembered that Balfour was a legendary priest-biter - the Scotsman had once given a priest a thorough beating for trying to convert his wife, so Luce doubted that he'd take any of Babbitt's casual blasphemy. (And they'd clearly known, or known of, each other in the Low Countries. Did the whole command of the Army of Parliament have a past acquaintance - like a vast dinner party, where everyone either knew, or was related to, everyone else?)

RED HORSE

The redhead handed the spyglass to Luce without a word and then directed his gaze towards the King, making his way across the hillside in sombre black velvet with his household, speaking to each regiment in turn. Black velvet cap. Ermine-lined black velvet coat. Sunlight gleamed on the single pendant pearl trembling in his ear, and on the elaborate Order pinned to his coat.

"I *knew* I should have put my good suit on," Babbitt said, brushing the sleeve of his shabby black doublet critically. "I don't know that I can hold my head up for shame in such fine company."

"All right, Babbitt, that's enough," Balfour said, in a tone that brooked no argument. "Your point is made. Be still, and show some respect."

Behind him, Cullis snorted - turned it into a cough, thumping himself on the breastplate. "Frog in me throat, sir."

The big redhead seemed wholly unchastened. "Just saying, sir, that we must look right scruffy in comparison with -"

"Captain Babbitt, that is *enough.*"

"Hey up. Summat's stirring." Black Tyburn, mostly, round and round in restless circles. "Over there, brat. Look." Babbitt shaded his eyes with one hand and pointed.

"I can definitely see troops moving, but -"

"That, boy, is His Majesty's loyal Regiment of Arse-Lickers. Otherwise known as his royal household." He spat, having run out of adequate words to describe his opinion of the King. "Enjoying your first battle, Lucey, or are you as bored as I am?"

And without waiting for an answer he pulled the black's head up again and set off up the slope.

Luce didn't know how to respond to that. On the one hand, he didn't want to sound hopelessly naïve and staid, but on the other hand – well, that was the *King.* You didn't say things like that about the King. You could stand across a battlefield like a gentleman and demand that he listened to you, but at the end of it he was still the King and they were his loyal subjects. All of them. Still. Surely?

Cullis was shaking his head. "Take no notice, boy. He's always like this before a fight. Nerves, see."

"But he – he said – "

"If it suits you better, brat, that up there is His Majesty encouraging his loyal troops. Happier?"

And God forbid Uncle Essex should be so moved, Luce thought ruefully, because he hadn't seen hide nor hair of their own commander since Warwick. Still, listening to the faint cheering halfway up the escarpment, it sounded like the Royalists were having a lovely time. Still not sufficiently encouraged to mount an attack, mind, which left Essex's forces no further on. Like two strange dogs sniffing each other's backsides, neither of them prepared to be the first to attack without knowing the full capabilities of the other. Well, that was it, wasn't it? *Nobody* knew what the other side was capable of. They didn't even know what they were capable of themselves.

And then there was a bang the size of the world, and a sudden roar from the army of Parliament as the first shot in the war came from their guns, and Babbitt came back down the slope looking superior. "Someone got bored wi' the self-righteous little bastard strutting about, then. I know who I reckon it'd be. D'you remember Black Shuck, Cullis?"

Cullis snorted, did indeed remember that gun captain from the Low Countries, but Luce was too busy running his hand down the mare's sweating neck, over and over, to do more than give him a venomous look. Rosa's ears were swivelling back and forth, her hooves trampling anxiously in the wet grass – but she stood. God bless that unknown cavalier and his cavalry training. Most of Babbitt's horse were restless and sweating, but they held. One big bay in Stapleton's cavalry had panicked – was running loose back through the infantry lines with an empty saddle – but that was all. Luce found himself counting, like a man in a thunderstorm. One – two –three – four –

And then a barrage of cannon fire from the Parliamentarian artillery, echoing like the Last Judgment. Rosa went up on her hind legs, briefly panic-stricken, and every bird in Worcestershire seemed to rise from the hedge with a sound like a volley of fire. "Somebody else got bored wi' waiting, then," Babbitt said dryly. "Look at him go, dear of him. Like a little black beetle."

The King and his entourage had gone scuttling back out of range back up the hill. "If I were as short as he is, poor bugger, I'm not sure I'd want to ride horses that big. I'd feel like a flea on a drumhead."

"Captain Babbitt, *will* you be quiet!"

"Just making conversation," Babbitt said cheerfully. "Passing the time waiting for that lot of dilatory sods to - " And then another earth-shattering bang as the Royalists returned fire. "Thought they'd never get round to it," he finished, when the echoes had finished ringing round the plain.

Luce's first instinct was to throw himself to the ground and cover his ears, but Babbitt seemed perfectly cheerful – if anything, less restless under the sound of cannon fire than whilst he was waiting for battle to commence. It was oddly reassuring. "You will notice," the captain said loudly, "that they seem to be having trouble finding their range, poor things."

There was a ripple of weak laughter, and an infinitesimal slackening of the tension amongst the troop. "Making a hell of a mess of that field," he added critically.

It was true – most of the Royalist shot was ploughing uselessly into the earth, spraying great gouts of wet soil into the air at the bottom of the hill. Someone in one of the front ranks waved their hat cheerfully. "Hoy! Over here!"

Not that Essex's guns were any more better directed, as the jeering Royalist pikemen were keen to point out. Babbitt wheeled the restless black back round, halted at Balfour's right hand. "Just one thing, sir. If I come close enough, I'm having that overdressed nonce. He *will* come at us like the wrath of God. Er. Begging your pardon, sir. But that's his trick. He'll come careering down that hill like he had the hounds of hell on his tail and he *will not stop.*"

"And your point, Babbitt?"

"My point, sir, is that there's bugger-all use in trying to fight his lot like your men have been trained to do. No point at all shooting at the bastards, because they're not going to stop to fight. Not what they do. He'll come at you with a drawn sword, and it's size and weight that counts with him - that and a galloping horse. So. He learned his dirty little tricks from the same place I did, the bloody Swedish Army. Difference is *I* fought it, and *he* read about it afterwards. So when he comes screaming down that hill - move. Wheel to the left - and you let him bloody well go, because he can't *stop*. And once he's gone, halfway to the back of beyond, you can just trot after him at your pleasure and take him up the arse - "

Balfour's expression was one of horrified fascination. "How very remarkable, Captain Babbitt. Yes. Well, mercifully, I don't believe Prince Rupert is going to be our problem, is he? We'll have our hands full enough with my lords Wilmot and Digby - sufficient unto the day is the evil thereof, I think."

"You're not listening, are you?"

"A prophet in his own country, Hollie," Cullis muttered darkly. "Let it go, lad. It'll all come right."

Swearing not quite under his breath, Babbitt wheeled the big black horse and barged his way through the men.

Luce smiled weakly at Balfour. "My apologies, sir - he's not always -"

Balfour waved a hand. "Yes, he is. Always has been. He's probably right, too, but it's not our problem at the moment." The Scotsman squinted at Luce. "You're the new officer, yes? Hm. Welcome to the Army of Parliament, laddie, and I wish you joy of the company."

27 AN END OF IT

Rackhay took his helmet off and shook his hair out, running his hand through the sweaty mass "Bored now," he announced to no one in particular.

He missed Red at his side - not often they hadn't fought together, and he still thought it was a bastard's trick putting Babbitt behind the reserves while leaving him on the flank with Jamie Ramsay, whose troops were about as organised as a rat's nest. And Faithfull Fortescue, with the mud of the King's recent mismanaged Irish campaign still wet on his boots: a man who had a face like a well-slapped arse. Would've been good for a laugh if Red had been there. They would have teased Fortescue to the point of madness.

Well, there they were, playing cards under the hedge for most of the afternoon. He wished he hadn't turned down Lucey's apple - he was starved. Artillery duels bored the arse off him, especially pointless wastes of powder like this one - Cavaliers digging holes in the field and their lot digging holes in the slope. Vale of the Red Horse be damned, it'd be more like the Red Sieve if both sides didn't find their range shortly. No more and no less than a pissing contest - all about who blinked first.

He wished - again - that he could have the same sort of casual backchat with his men as Red had with his but he suspected to do that you had to be - well, not quite a gentleman. Cold, for October. There were still leaves on the trees, still an amount of cover from the hedge, but the year was definitely on the turn. He wondered if they'd go to winter quarters soon. Whether they'd go back to Warwick, where he'd have to put up with Hollie constantly bellyaching about being stuck in there if His Majesty decided to lay siege to the place, like as if he would, or whether they'd go elsewhere, and Nat could go home. Spend Christmas with Elizabeth and the children. They hadn't clapped eyes on him in almost a twelvemonth, what with one thing and another. Made for somewhat strained relations, when your own children didn't recognise you - worse still when you didn't recognise them, but they grew so quickly when you didn't see them from year end to year end. He'd brought a toy sword for Lysander, last time he'd gone home. The boy had looked at it, and him, in absolute disgust. Rightly so, to be fair; the lad was near enough to breeched and it had gone clean out of his mind. Could do with a proper sword, never mind a wooden one. And Cass was a pretty little thing - took after her father with her pretty ways, he flattered himself.

He wondered how Red was getting on with his new cornet. Glad he'd pulled him on it last night because Hollie hadn't always been so bloody nasty - if he wasn't so perpetually on edge these days he'd be a lot easier company. Well, Nat couldn't blame him for being edgy, he wasn't wholly comfortable with the way this war was headed himself. He'd been a bit on edge himself last night. It was just an odd feeling, being in your own country, speaking your own language, sleeping in your own bed, and firing on your own countrymen. Seeing faces you'd known since childhood, standing in the Cavalier ranks, facing you down the wrong end of a musket barrel. And not, in Nat's case, being entirely sure whose coin he'd choose to take, if he wasn't a professional soldier. Most of his home turf in Essex was for Parliament, but Nat wasn't so sure he would be, given freedom to choose. Was fairly sure that Elizabeth certainly wasn't for Parliament. Elizabeth was very much in favour of courts, and the rights of nobility. God knows she had enough knowledge of the latter.

Rupert was on the move. Conspicuous wasn't the

word, in that bright red suit. Overdressed, maybe, stalking about on his big white horse. Very occasionally, he thought he could see Hollie's point with His Majesty's nephew - other than the professional jealousy of one less successful, but otherwise equally tall, equally plain, equally bad-tempered, and equally sharp cavalry commander, for another. Christ, Nat knew he must have some annoying habits but Red's ability to get a bee in his bonnet about something and then keep harping on about it until the Day of Judgment, was phenomenal. "Mount up, gentleman, something's afoot," he said aloud. The Royalist dragoons were scurrying up and down the long slope like a disturbed ant's nest, and Nat's grey horse tossed its head at the crackling of musket fire and the snuff of black powder on the wind. Not the brightest of animals. For a cavalry horse it showed a remarkable lack sense in the matter of firearms. The beast had been bouncing around since the first exchange of fire and its dappled coat was dark with sweat before Nat had even mounted.

"Behave, witless beast," he said irritably, yanking its head up in an attempt to stop the lunatic creature from skittering off into a frenzy of bucking. For one thing, he had no desire for Fortescue to look down his aristocratic nose at his ill-disciplined mount, and for another, his arse was still tender from being dumped on it last night. Bloody bird. Bloody horse.

Here they came. "Steady, gentlemen, steady as she goes - let them do the work - " a glance to his left, Jamie Ramsay's face stern and forbidding unless you happened to be looking very hard in which case you'd see the almost imperceptible wink he gave Nat as his men started to urge their horses into a smooth trot. Difficult when you had every shape, size and denomination of horseflesh under the sun surrounding you. Rupert's cavalry, now - no expense spared in their horse, for the most part. There were some gorgeous brutes in there. One big dark bay with a white blaze and three white stockings that he had his eye on, and he wouldn't be crying in his beer if that beast's rider happened to go down. Nat was fairly sure that at least one of his own troop's mounts was the bastard offspring of a yard brush and a New Forest pony. And it scrabbled. He could hear the beast, ten yards behind and blowing like a bellows, and they hadn't even broken out of a trot yet.

Nat transferred the reins to his left hand, guiding the grey with his knees. Laid his primed pistol across his knee. Wait, wait, wait… another ten lengths - he glanced over his shoulder, feeling the grin on his face that he always got when he went into a fight. Bastards almost within shot now, and he could see the big bay's rider clear as day.

Gave the order to charge. The grey flattened its ears and shot forward. Nat sighted along his pistol - the bay's rider went down with a neat hole in the centre of his forehead and the bay went galloping riderless into the hedgeline. Someone was shouting behind him. He couldn't make out the words. He could see Rupert's scarlet and silver coat - *ludicrously* overdressed for the field - thundering down the hill.

And then there were horses in all directions, loose horses, mounts he knew and recognised, and Fortescue's troop were forcing their way through from the rear - and firing as they came. *"Turncoats!"* he heard one of his lads roar, just before a pistol ball took him in the throat.

Ramsay's horse was down, screaming, a foreleg snapped on the ridges of ploughed ground, and the big Scot was on his feet with his sword drawn, looking desperately for the next loose horse - Nat briefly, wildly, imagined him desperate enough to grab the misbegotten pony as it passed - but it was a big black and just for a second Nat thought it was Tyburn, and the sight of the empty, blood-slick saddle and the loose reins hit him like a punch in the belly. Then the black horse was thundering past him with Ramsay hauling himself into the saddle and it wasn't Tib, it was coarser built than Hollie's black, and somewhere on the other flank field Nat's best friend was still alive and still fighting as Wilmot's cavalry went smashing down into the right wing.

"Faithfull, my *arse*," he roared, spurring the grey into the fray. How dare he? How *dare* the man switch sides - what the hell was he playing at?

His men were fleeing - and he'd told them, told them and *told* them what to expect. They knew what was coming, Christ, he'd been through it often enough with Hollie after the fiasco at the bridge - knew the only way to handle Rupert's charges was to take the shock and let him go through. They weren't. Running like rabbits, buffeted this way and that by Fortescue's turncoats, firing uselessly as they fled.

Nat's grey staggered and he threw his empty pistol down, furiously. Drew his sword to meet the oncoming charge. The grey was blown. So much for its expensive thoroughbred pedigree. Balls to it. One last charge. Bring it on, you bastards.

28 I WILL RENDER VENGEANCE TO MINE ENEMIES

"Raise the colours, boy. Now."

Luce hadn't yet learned the trick of automatic obedience. "What –" And then realised that slowly but inexorably, the Royalist cavalry under Henry Wilmot and Lord Digby halfway up the slope were advancing downhill, inexorable as the incoming tide.

"Stick with me," Babbitt said grimly. "Hear me? Whatever happens, don't get lost. And stand your ground. *Stand your ground, Lucifer.*"

And then the tide hit, and Luce was fighting for his life, with the colours jammed into the soil beside the mare. The world narrowed to the space between a horse's ears, and the width of the swing of a sword. There was no room to discharge a pistol, after the first volley. It was close fighting, close enough to feel the press of a cavalier's knee against yours as he tried to drive his blade through your guts, or to feel the jolt of bone as you hacked at someone's wrist when they grabbed for the colours. He saw one of the men – he didn't know his name – go down with half his jaw shot away, choking and bubbling in his own blood. Saw Tyburn on his hind legs, screaming with rage and fury, smashing an unhorsed cavalier's skull like an egg with one lashing forefoot.

"Fall back, gentlemen. Let the bastards fight us uphill." Babbitt was spattered with blood and grinning like a fiend. "Come on, Wilmot, you fucker. Get it while it's hot, you bastard."

And then at last they saw Rupert's precious cavalry start to move downhill with the grace and precision of clockwork, straight down the hill towards Ramsay's troop. Luce, watching the captain, saw the oddest expression of mingled anxiety and envy on his face as he saw Rupert's troop sweep down.

It didn't last long. Wilmot's men hit the right flank, hard, and they were hard pressed again: bloody, aching hand to hand work. And then suddenly they were buffeted by the fleeing rags of men that Luce recognised from Ramsay's brigade, some turning to fire an ineffectual volley from the saddle, in panicking retreat. Rupert's troopers were in pursuit, overrunning the artillery, hacking at running musketeers, shrieking like apes as they gleefully followed, intent on bloody vengeance. Luce couldn't hear a thing above the screams of men and horses and the roaring guns, but he *felt* it. Babbitt's troop was abruptly swelled by cavalry from the shattered left wing, checked by Balfour's steadfast block of horse. He swung the mare about – planted the colours again – found himself almost shoulder to shoulder with another face he knew. One of Rackhay's troopers. "What are you doing over *here*?" he yelled.

The man wiped a hand across his grey, sweating face. "Lost the captain, sir."

"God have mercy on us." He had no chance to say anything more because now Fielding's cavalry were broken on the far right, flying for their lives, swept away in a rising tide of Wilmot's and Digby's advancing troops, and there was only the centre holding now. Two regiments of infantry left, and Balfour and Stapleton's cavalry reinforcing them from behind. It was nothing. He found himself praying, quite calmly, quite intently, under his breath. He wondered who would tell his mother. Babbitt suddenly halted the white-eyed black horse beside him. "Take up the colours, boy. I'm going through."

Balfour came up at a gallop, snatching at Babbitt's sleeve. "Captain, this is *madness* –"

"Likely." Babbitt jerked the black's head round with

such force that the stallion skidded on the wet grass. "Take your hand off me, Sir William. I'm having them bastards down there –"

He knows about Rackhay, Luce thought sickly. I don't know how, but he knows all right.

"I'm not asking you lot to come, don't fret." Babbitt grinned wildly. "I'll give them bastards forlorn hope. Right up the arse -"

Luce raised the colours, feeling suddenly cold and sick. What else could he do? "Gentlemen. Volunteers for a charge, please. The rest of you, hold your ground."

Babbitt laughed. His hair had come loose, was blowing on his shoulders, the colour of old blood in the setting sun. He looked almost entirely insane, and almost completely unstoppable. Cullis pulling up alongside him – Luce – Isaac and Lucas Weston -

"You will lead your men to certain death, then, captain?" Balfour said coldly.

"Me? I –" he glanced at Luce with a dazed look, as if he didn't quite believe what he'd just heard – "I didn't ask for - Christ, you're *all* as mad as I am. It would appear that *we* are going to charge the guns. Unless you're coming as well, Willie?"

Five of them. That was all. Just the five. Leaving Balfour gaping, Luce pulled the mare's head up, matched the black stride for stride, thundering across the meadow towards the Royalist artillery. All Luce could see was the cannon mouths yawning wider and wider, belching out foul sulphurous smoke – the screaming whistle as shot went overhead – and then more and more hoofbeats joining them as the remains of Balfour's cavalry joined the charge. A wild cheering from Ballard's regiment as they passed through the ragged gaps in the line. Edmund Allaby, thank God, unharmed, waving his hat and laughing madly. And then they were galloping uphill, the sticky ploughed mud pulling at their horses' legs.

"Shit." Babbitt was laughing out loud. "They've all buggered off, lads. Took one look at us lot and got off. *Now* what do we do?"

"We appear to have overshot the guns," Luce said, calmly, fighting a desire to laugh as he looked round at the abandoned Royalist battery. Not a scarlet sash to be seen. "Perhaps a – tactical withdrawal?"

"You mean bugger off ourselves, Lucey?"

"That would be it, captain."

"He'm getting sweary," Luke Weston said comfortably, "and that's never a good sign. Do 'ee want to do a bit of a job, while we're here?" He opened his hand, grinning. It was filled with string – nails – a snail shell – the assorted paraphernalia of a countryman.

"Oh, I do like you, Weston." Babbitt dismounted, managed to make it look leisurely. Picked the nails out of Weston's debris. Dropped several into the touchhole of the nearest gun. Unslung his carbine from his shoulder and hammered them in with the butt. "Any more where that come from?"

Balfour dismounted beside him, grinning. "Inspired, Babbitt. The Lord is indeed with us. Any more nails in those pockets of yours? That should give the Papists pause for thought."

"Next!" Babbitt yelled, with a maniac giggle.

29 SURELY GOODNESS AND MERCY

"Captain Babbitt – the King's household –"

Hollie glanced up in the direction of Luke Weston's pointing finger. Charles and James Stuart, two frightened young boys – James all of nine years old, barely breeched, Charles hardly older – and a handful of white-faced officers trying to escort then to safety. Children, the bloody lot of them. For Christ's sake, what bloody *fool* had thought it was a good idea to bring two children onto a battlefield and leave them in the care of half a dozen bloody trainee Ruperts, all shitting themselves at the prospect of an oncoming cavalry charge. "Calthorpe. With me."

Hollie trusted Calthorpe. Despite the unprepossesing exterior Aaron Calthorpe was soft as butter, and he wouldn't see two children hurt and frightened by their elders' idea of a character-building experience. Better yet, Calthorpe had known Hollie for long enough to know that *he* wouldn't countenance it. Not under my command, you bastards, no matter who their bloody father is.

"Give chase to the whelps –" he was in the saddle again and bent over the black's sweating neck and his old comrade was cantering up alongside, the ground shaking under the old mare. He nodded towards the scampering boys. "Close order, Aaron."

As if he could do anything else, with Tib staggering with weariness under him, but keep pace with the mare across the ploughed ridges of freezing earth. It was starting to turn bitter again as the sun dropped in the sky and the black's breath steamed.

Calthorpe had a sword cut across his forearm and his buff coat was splattered with blood, and God alone knew what Hollie looked like. The younger boy screamed shrilly, the older shouting defiance in a high, frightened voice when he saw the black horse and the patched mare come racketing out of the dusk towards them. Hollie winced inside his lobster-tailed helmet because that was no sound for a child to make.

Between the two of them, they were harrying the Royal household slowly but surely towards a little cluster of outbuildings, without a shot being fired. Praise God for witless junior officers with more good breeding than good sense, who clearly thought they were under attack by vicious desperadoes and were retreating in splendid textbook order, God bless 'em. Close enough for Hollie to see the smaller boy's set, tear-streaked face, stubborn and proud and bloody terrified. One of their household fired a single shot, high and wide, and the other lad cried out as if he'd been hit and that was enough for Hollie. He wheeled Tib away from the barn where the boys were scuttling for shelter, calling Calthorpe off like a dog.

"That's seen 'em off, then, sir," Calthorpe said comfortably.

He nodded stiffly. "Let's see who's left standing, then, shall we – oh, shite."

Balfour gone with his troop, Cullis's cob, gleaming bone-white in the dusk, in their train. The two Westons and their plough-horses gone – only bloody soft-headed Lucifer Pettitt still waiting for them, the mare fretting to be gone and Luce holding her with a remarkably resolute grip on the bridle and the colours under his arm. "I was beginning to think you'd got lost," the boy said sarcastically. "We're about to have company, so if you'd care to move?"

"Oh, bollocks to 'em, Lucey. Fine strapping lad like

you, you can hold off the King's Lifeguard for a few minutes, can't you?"

The ground was shaking. So was the brat, quite visibly. "You *will* retreat in an orderly fashion," Hollie said, and he thought he sounded reasonable. Between the bars of his lobster-pot helmet, the boy's eyes were unexpectedly steady. "Raise the colours, cornet."

His sword arm was aching, and he didn't know how much longer the black was going to be able to hold his place in the line. Some bloody line, straggling half way across Radway field, but at least he'd caught up with the back markers again. The mare was exhausted, too. The colours were wavering, the brat's arm shaking with weariness. Hollie could hear trumpets, faint and tinny in the frosty air.

"The German bastard's coming back," Cullis said grimly. "Been halfway to Worcester, I reckon."

"He can't be. He *can't*." Isaac Weston, shaking his head like a stunned bullock. Downhill again. Thank God. The horses were staggering with weariness. Back through Ballard's lines, with shot rattling all around them. As many men as there had been on the way out? He didn't know. The light was going. Surely they couldn't fight through the night.

Hollie wheeled the staggering black horse once more. "Rupert's back, is he?" He touched his hand to his helmet in ironic salute. "I'm having that fucker if it kills me. He *owes* me one."

Touched by a flaming sunset, he set the black horse back at a staggering gallop across the field. There was a single shot. The big horse stumbled - went down, rolling over and over in the long grass.

And then Essex sounded the call to break off engagements, and the sun went down.

30 BLOOD FLIES UPWARDS AND BEDEWS THE HEAVENS

It grew colder and colder as darkness fell, and the night was filled with the eerie whimpers of the dying and the hurt, and the occasional echoing report of musket fire.

Rackhay's men were stunned into silence, huddled in their troop staring into the bitter dark like animals waiting for slaughter, holding their ground because no one had told them not to. Luce couldn't bear it. He swung his carbine over his shoulder and paced out into the darkness.

Battlefields stank. Precious little in the way of honour or glory in the smell of blood and opened bowels and rotten, sulphurous gunpowder fumes. He didn't even know where to begin looking. Someone was sobbing at his feet, a hand groping wildly at his legs. The moon glinted on fair hair and he crouched, peering into the man's face, and then fled in sick terror. Not Rackhay. A boy. Not much older then himself, with a slash that had laid his face open to the bone and spilled his eye down onto his cheek. Luce crouched in the wet grass, throwing up the apple that was all he'd catcn all day. And then he went back, smirched and stinking and unlovely, and he sat with the boy until his comrades came for him, sat whimpering comforting nonsense that he doubted consoled the trooper in the slightest, but even that felt better than leaving the man in lonely, mewling agony.

There were too many bodies. Begin at the beginning, and keep on going, through the cold knee-high wet grass. Looking for a black horse or a grey, amongst the hundreds. He could see movement – stirring, weird, uncanny shifting – scurrying amongst the humped shapes, and he swallowed hard again.

"Looters, boy," Cullis said softly in his ear, and he

jerked upright and almost loosed a shot by accident. "Go canny. They won't thank you for interfering."

His boots slipping on the dew-wet grass, the moon bleaching all pale horses to grey and all light hair to fair. Turning over body after body, with Cullis stamping beside him like some squat demon familiar.

Luce was not going to cry. Every limb ached – he was shaking with cold and his shoulders were stiff with terror, but he was damned if he was going to cry. His mouth was trembling. He could feel it, in spite of his best effort, quivering like a girl's.

"Pettitt."

He spun to face Cullis, his boots slithered on the frozen grass, and he sat down hard. The sergeant's grim face broke into a reluctant smile. "You're all bleeding class, boy."

"What is it, sergeant?"

"Nat Rackhay's lads. I know some of this lot." Cullis glowered. "What's left of 'em, poor bastards. Cut to bloody ribbons."

He didn't say any more. Luce saw the thought flicker across his mind at the same time as it went through his own. Rupert.

"Vengeance is mine, saith the Lord," Cullis said, with a considering glance up at the hill where the King's troops had regrouped: too exhausted to fight, too proud to retreat. "Aye. Well."

They found Rackhay, in the end. He was almost unmarked. Only the blood soaking his orange sash, black in the moonlight, gave it away. A great sword slash across the join of neck and shoulder, parting muscle and bone just above his breastplate. He looked mildly surprised, but not pained. Luce almost expected him to sit up and curse all Royalist cavalry. He was the first dead man Luce had ever touched.

"I – I am sure he has gone on to a better place," he

said lamely, wiping his hands clean of chill blood and shrinking back on himself.

"Are you, boy?" Cullis turned on him and the sergeant was shaking, tears streaming down his face unheeded. "You know the first time I ever set eyes on him and Red, they was in a cheap tavern in Amsterdam, and neither of 'em was a day over sixteen. Not much younger than you, boy. I always said the pair of 'em would come to a bad end." He bent over Rackhay, stroking the dew-wet hair back from the cold face with awkward gentleness. "You daft bastard. What d'you have to go off and get yourself killed for, eh? Ah, Christ, boy, I'm getting sentimental. Might have been my own boys, them two. I was that proud of them – that proud –"

His mouth set in a straight line. "As you say, boy. Nat's in a better place, no doubt. He don't mind over much what happens to this –" his hand lingered over the captain's forehead – "You reckon he took any of these bastards out with him?"

Luce picked up Rackhay's empty pistol and turned it over in his hands. Cold. It would be. "Yes, sergeant. Yes, I imagine he did."

The sergeant stood up, wiping his hands on his breeches. "That's my boy. He showed 'em, didn't he? Gave 'em what for." He scrubbed his hands over his face. "Not the cleverest lad, our Nat. Left most of the thinking to Hollie. God help him. Kick one and they both limped. But brave. More bloody balls than sense." He stared round at the creeping shapes in the darkness. "Piss off, the lot of you. This one is mine, d'you hear me?"

"Stay here with him," Luce said, moved to gentleness. "I'll look for Captain Babbitt. I saw –"

"We *all* saw. I imagine the whole of fucking Radway field saw."

The moon riding high and clear and white in the sky

now and Luce could see every blade of grass as clear as crystal. The great tear in the earth where Tyburn had gone down. And the hoofprints leading away, up into the hedge line a hundred yards away, where the black horse was grazing with his foreleg through his reins, intact save for a long wet furrow on his shoulder. "Tib – Tibby – here, boy –"

He still had one apple left. The apple Rackhay hadn't wanted. He closed his eyes briefly, remembering Rackhay as kind, above else, at the last. The black lifted his head, ears pricked.

"Now what have I told you about that, Lucey?"

And Luce dropped the apple with a yelp, spinning round – slipping again on the soaking grass, would he never learn? – to see Babbitt, unharmed, alive, sitting under the hedge. It was, he reminded himself, unreasonable to be furious with a man for not being dead. It didn't stop him wanting to punch his commanding officer repeatedly in the head.

"Sir - are you - are you -"

"Dead? No. More's the fucking pity. Nathaniel is, though." Babbitt leaned his head on his knees, and then sat up, panting. "*Isn't* he, Lucifer?"

There was no other way. "Yes. Sir."

"Fuck. Are you any hand at writing letters?"

"*Me*, sir?"

"Yes, you, sir. Someone's going to have to write to Mistress Rackhay and –" he tipped his head back with a sobbing breath – "I'm not sure I can."

Luce wasn't sure he could, either. "Well, I can try, sir – I am told I write a fair hand –"

The captain straightened up and he was swaying slightly where he sat and Luce remembered with disgust the first conversation they'd ever had. Brandy helps, he'd said. It certainly smelt like it.

"I am sure his widow will be delighted with the

elegance of your handwriting," Babbitt snarled, "and if I could trust it to anyone but you I would, but – you have no *idea* how much I despise you. You're a smug little bastard, aren't you?"

Luce drew himself up to his full height. "Sir, you have been drinking," he said contemptuously.

"Not as much as I'd like to have been, boy." He pushed his loose hair out of his eyes with the back of his hand. "Not that you'd approve, would you, Mistress Mealy-mouth? And that's the *last* time I take an order from your hellbound uncle, though he breaks me for it. If I'd been stood with Nat on the flank they wouldn't have broken. I *knew* what that German twat was going to do. And he's not going to get another chance, if I have to stand there and pick the fuckers off one at a time -"

"Sir, this is not rational talk -"

"Oh, stick it up your arse, Lucey. If I wanted your opinion I'd ask for it, and it will be a cold day in hell before I seek guidance from any of *your* murderous kin. Want another surprise, puppy? You can stop turning your dainty little nose up at the smell of brandy, because most of it's on my hand –" He pulled his right hand abruptly out from between his knees. "That's going to be damn-all use to me tomorrow. Looks like you might end up doing quite a bit of writing for me, boy. Christ, Pettitt, why couldn't it have been you? You're no bloody use. Or better still, me. No bugger would miss me. He's got a wife, you know, has Nat. Wife and three babies. Children. Might be married and grown up for all I know - are you sure he's dead? *Certain*-sure? Not just hurt - you wouldn't leave him hurt, would you?"

Luce could *hear* him shaking. "I'll find Sergeant Cullis, he'll know –"

Babbitt put his head down on his folded arms again. "No you won't, boy, you'll stop right here and do what you're bloody well told." His voice was muffled.

"You're going to have to strap my hand up. Sweet Jesus, I'm cold. Are you squeamish, Master Pettitt – that's a stupid question, of course you are."

He glared at the top of Babbitt's head. "Frankly, captain, I have no issue at all with binding your hand. I only hope it hurts."

"Don't you worry, Lucey, it does." He sat up with a shaky breath. "Take a strip off my sash, it's clean enough. Tear a strip off me, won't be the first time. Christ it's cold, brat - are you *sure* Rackhay's dead? You wouldn't leave him out in the cold?"

The redhead was vibrating like a plucked lute-string, his teeth chattering. Luce was at a loss. "Captain, I - what can I do, sir? Does this fit take you often?" Without waiting for an answer he did the one thing he could do, he took his coat off – stinking, sweaty, heavy thing, he was glad to be rid of it – and put it over Babbitt's shoulders. He was miserably ashamed of being glad the captain was hurt. It gave him something to think about – anything other than Rackhay dead and cold. Tyburn screaming with fury smashing a man's skull with his steel-shod hoofs. The way it felt when your sword went into a man's belly.

"Keep talking to me, boy, or I may disgrace myself and faint like a girl. Then what will you do?"

"Straighten your hand with less discomfort, no doubt," Luce said drily. "And if you are going to faint - like a girl or otherwise - tell me, and I'll stop."

The captain had made a fair go of cleaning up the wound, wrong-handed and with raw spirits, but even in the moonlight the bruising was spreading black up his oddly-crooked wrist. There wasn't much Luce could do - he was beginning to get used to feeling useless, on this battlefield - but even he could tell a badly broken wrist when he saw one. "I think we need to find you shelter, sir. Sooner, rather than later."

"Oh, fuck off, brat. I don't want you -"

"Possibly not, captain." He looked up into the big redhead's face, smiled reassuringly, and took hold of Babbitt's fingers. "Unfortunately, I'm what you have to hand." And yanked his wrist straight. Hard.

Babbitt's head rested on his shoulder briefly and Luce thought the captain might have passed out. Then he took a deep, shuddering breath -"Christ, boy, I asked for that, didn't I?" he muttered thickly. Sat up again – greyish-white, and clammy as bread dough.

"It's not a thing you can do gently, sir."

"Hollie. Go and see Tib."

"What?"

Babbitt gave him a mute, furious glare, clamped his good hand over his mouth and jerked his head towards the hedge in an unmistakable gesture of dismissal. Luce scrambled to his feet. The black seemed pleased to see him. Nice to see someone was. He took his time feeding the horse with that wizened apple until the captain had finished being very sick.

Then he turned back with a casual air he didn't feel. "You were saying, sir?"

"Call me Hollie, boy. You might as well use my given name, God knows you've earned the right."

31 BECAUSE WE ARE POOR, SHALL WE BE VICIOUS?

Sarah Hadfield thought she would probably still be wakeful when the sun rose. She'd spent most of the afternoon flinching at every distant sound of battle, feeling as if the preacher was right and Armageddon was just around the corner. Sleep was a distant memory. Outside the frost lay thick and glittering on the rutted mud of the roadway and every time a horse passed she found herself jumping up and peering through the slits in the shutters as if she might indeed catch the Riders of the Apocalypse passing. It wouldn't have surprised her. She had precious little idea what was going on out there. She cared less, save that she'd had soldiers in the snug cottage she'd shared with her child and, not so long ago, her husband, and she felt invaded. And hers had been tidy officers, apparently: none of the casual contempt she'd been encouraged to expect from the gentry. Even so. Since Matthew's death twelve months ago she'd been expected to drop her eyes and flutter her eyelashes at anything in breeches that crossed her path in the hope of catching herself a nice new husband. She was thoroughly sick of it – both the whims and the capturing process. She didn't care whether it was the King or his Parliament who won the day out there, just as long as the lot of them left her well alone. The lot of them deserved to freeze out there. No, that wasn't true. She couldn't sleep for thinking of them – both sides, either side, she didn't care – poor toads lying out in the frost, alive or dead.

Small Matthew whimpered in his truckle bed and sat

up. "There, lambkin, it's a wild night, but Mam is here, I'll take care of thee, never fret."

It was a cold night, and getting colder. With her head bent over her son, she didn't hear sound of the latch, over the moaning of the wind in the chimney. A sudden draught blew her skirts tight against her body and she hugged Mattie close.

Peaceful and contented, right up to the point where she looked up and saw Luce on the threshold. She sprang to her feet and screamed. The sleepy little boy woke up and started screaming. Hollie leaned his good side up against the wall, feeling oddly detached from the proceedings. Luce braced him just in time as he started to slither down the rough plaster.

"Madam, be quiet!" Luce roared abruptly, and even stunned-stupid Hollie jumped.

The wench was half out of her seat, still yowling, and Luce was halfway across the room stuttering apologies, and nobody seemed to be paying the purple-faced infant the least attention. Its wails were reaching a truly terrifying pitch. "That child is like to burst if someone doesn't see to it," Hollie suggested brightly.

Luce shot him a venomous look, and the unfortunate infant's mother sat down again, pressing her howling offspring to her breast with one hand and grabbing her poker with her other hand. "Calm yourself, mistress! We mean no harm, we didn't know you were here – we were quartered here before the fight – we seek shelter, no more -"

He was a smooth bugger, was Pettitt, you had to give him that. Hollie would have probably entered into the spirit of things more enthusiastically if he didn't feel quite so much like a well-used pull-through. Since the lass was calming down without his intervention anyway, he was able to concentrate on not collapsing in a heap at her feet. "Get out of my house, or I'll bray the pair of you," she said coolly.

She set the wailing child on his feet and drew herself up to her full – unimpressive - height, lifting the poker to emphasise her point. She meant it too, Hollie had no doubt. Despite the fact that under better stars he could have picked her up in one hand and put her out the door without breaking a sweat, the wench was eyeing them like a mother wren facing a cat.

"As you can see," Luce went on, in that admirably calm and reasonable tone, "Captain Babbitt is hurt. In the name of Christian charity, madam, I would beg shelter for the captain on such a night, not for myself – I can shift for myself, if there's no room."

And he probably meant it, too, Hollie thought cynically – not that it was going to be an issue for the little bastard, noting how the lass had dismissed Hollie as beneath her notice and was fixing her attention on his cornet. Who happened to be tall, fair and handsome. How convenient. Perhaps he'd keep the brat after all. She hadn't softened, exactly – that poker hadn't gone anywhere – but the infant was snuffling against her skirts instead of wailing, and she was looking grim instead of murderous.

And you had to give Pettitt credit, he'd caught on quicker than Hollie ever would have. Sympathetic, understanding, gentlemanly – and all of a sudden, with a full purse. Christ, it was Rackhay's, that he'd given the brat to buy their supper last night, was it only last night, and Rackhay was dead - and Hollie shoved the back of his good hand against his mouth to stifle the kicked whimper that nearly escaped him.

The wren-girl looked up at him, stony-faced, at that helpless noise. "Well, you'd better come in, then. And shut the door behind you," she said.

The brat was steadfast. Give him that. He could have cut and run, several times that day already, saved his own skin and no one any the wiser. Maybe the lad really was that stupid. One thing he was, was solid, and without his support Hollie would have been flat on his face as he ducked under the low lintel.

Christ, his arm was aching now. More than anything else what he wanted was a drink. Whelp wouldn't approve of that, officers drinking on duty, but Hollie suspected the only way he'd get any rest tonight was numb. Which reminded him of Rackhay. The way you could always rely on Rackhay to turn up after a battle – late, as often as not, half an hour, an hour, after everybody else had been accounted for, looking pleased with himself and bearing gifts which didn't bear too close scrutiny. The only gift he'd left Hollie this time was his officer's sash, that Cullis had brought away. Lustrous tawny silk, with a deep gold fringe, not like Hollie's scruffy faded rag. Stiff with dried blood now, the silk crisp and brown as autumn leaves, fringe hanging in matted rags.

The lass was eyeing him. "I'll not have him die in my house," she said shortly.

"I'm sure Captain Babbitt feels very much the same way, madam," Luce said dryly. "I don't believe he's planning to die any time soon. With *rest and care* –" he emphasized the words heavily –"I imagine he will be perfectly well in no time at all."

"*Do* you. And I suppose you think he'll get it here, do you?" The wind moaned eerily in the chimney. She sat down again by the fire, and the boy scrambled into her lap. She pressed his head to her breast while he eyed them warily, thumb in his mouth.

"I do, actually. I don't believe for one minute you'd turn an injured man out on such a night."

"Then you'd better see to him, hadn't you?"

It was the nearest he'd been to a woman's bed by invitation for a long old while. Bloody inviting it looked as well, soft and warm and clean, tucked into an alcove on the far side of the cottage, and he sat on the edge of the bed abruptly and sat there panting and willing himself not to throw up. Not a way to endear himself to the wench, puking on her clean floor.

"Do you need my help, sir – er- Hollie?"

Yes, he damn well did, and he was equally damned if he was going to admit it to a brat who couldn't even call him by his given name without choking. Luce stood there, watching Hollie fighting a losing battle with his collar strings. If the brat had cracked a smile Hollie would have smacked him round the head – with the splinted wrist, it being the heavier. But he didn't. He just stood there with a carefully blank expression and never said a word.

With a final ferocious twist Hollie got the better of his collar, trembling like a dog shitting cherry-stones. Cold sweat trickled down his back.

"I think you should rest now, captain," the lad said, and even if Hollie had wanted to take it up with him there was no arguing with that tone of voice. The lad put his arm behind Hollie's shoulders – Hollie tried to summon up indignation at his effrontery but he'd gone past anything so definite as indignation, past feeling anything other than oddly cold and very sick. "Lie down," Luce said, and he sounded almost kind. For probably the first time in nearly twenty years, Hollie did as he was told without arguing.

"I'll wake you at daybreak," Luce said firmly, and pulled the blankets up. "Get some sleep."

32 ARMAGEDDON ON THE DOORSTEP

The girl was rocking the child to and fro on her knee, the pair of them watching Luce warily. She raised her head. "And I suppose the both of you'll be wanting feeding, as well?"

He took the purse out from where it was tucked inside his doublet. Rackhay's last gift. "I imagine all five of us will want feeding," he said mildly. "From memory, the cheese was very good. That's a fine boy you have there. What's his name?"

She looked at him. Then the corners of her mouth turned up. "Matthew," she said. "Mattie, after his da."

Luce nodded wisely. "A sturdy little chap." The admiring of children demanded a language of its own. Oddly, it seemed to transcend rank. His older sister, married these five years to a country squire in Norfolk, melted at meaningless words over her brood. Elizabeth's offspring, poor mites, took after their father, who was a good-hearted soul with a face like a midwinter turnip. Small Matthew had the advantage of possessing some discernible features as a means to flatter his mother. "He favours you, about the eyes."

"Does he, indeed." She sounded less than convinced. "Have you children of your own, then, to give you such experience?"

"I have not," Luce said, and looked up just in time to catch the flash of open appraisal in her gaze, and to see even in the dim amber light her flush of embarrassment as she realised he'd caught it. "My sister has a boy, of whom I have limited experience and considerable fondness. Now, mistress, would you do me the honour of sharing our regimental supper – and direct me to where I can find the makings of it?"

He suspected she might have preferred him to be rude and surly. It was easier to be cool with a rough soldier than a polite one. "I wouldn't put you to any further trouble," he said gently. "I think Captain Babbitt and I are sufficient evil unto the day."

"Any more trouble than Armageddon already on my doorstep, then, sir? That I doubt. Well, you can stop trying to charm me, for I've good broth and bread enough for both of you without the flattery."

"Than I thank you for it, my lady, and will see you recompensed." He gave her a small, grave bow, and she blinked at him, and laughed.

"Are you always like this, or do you keep it in reserve for special occasions?"

"Such as Armageddon? Always, or so I'm led to believe." He'd made her laugh. It softened her face, deepened the tender lines around her eyes so that she managed to look both younger and riper at the same time. With the little boy nodding against her breast, in her plain rosemary-blue homespun gown, he didn't think he'd ever look on those idolatrous images of Mary the Virgin in quite the same way again. "In truth, mistress. Will the presence of both the captain and myself be an intolerable burden on you?"

The corner of her mouth lifted again. "How should I know? He's precious little trouble at the moment, that's for sure."

Luce leaned forward, partly the better to speak to her above the moan of the bitter wind in the chimney, but mostly because she looked so soft and warm and comforting. The cold of the battlefield seemed to have got in his bones and being near her warmed him. "Do you know anything about healing, mistress? For we rejoin the Army tomorrow, and I wouldn't like him to be hurt. Any more than he is."

"Tomorrow?" Her fine, dark eyebrows twitched. "In that state? And you call yourself his friend?"

She didn't know much about Captain Babbitt, Luce thought glumly, if she thought he'd be put off by anything so mundane as a broken arm. "Not a friend-" No, not a friend. Just a man who had been given a duty of care that he'd see out or die trying. "I promised to wake him at dawn, and I will hold to it."

Her lips set in an uncompromising straight line. It didn't flatter her. "Then I hope you can live with your conscience." She hoisted the drowsy Mattie onto her hip and settled him back in his truckle bed. Smoothed his quilts, tucking the coverlets about the little boy's shoulders and then smoothed the blankets over Babbitt with the same abstracted tenderness. It spoke of long practice, and jealousy was a new, and uncomfortable, sensation.

"Madam, it is my *duty* to –"

"Fine."

"I don't break promises -"

"Good." She sat down again– straightened her skirts, still without looking at him, and picked up a little shirt from the basket of mending at her feet.

He sighed. He knew when he was beaten. It worked on him at home, too, with his baby sister. "I promised the captain, madam, and I'll not break my word. But if he is unfit to ride at dawn, then you may continue to enjoy the pleasure of his company."

"A delight, I'm sure," she said drily. "Sadly, my conscience will not allow me to turn him out to die on the doorstep. Neither will yours, I think."

Luce was grateful for the semi-darkness, because it hid his blushes.

33 LUCE WAKES UP

It was late, well into the night, though still before dawn, when the captain started to stir restlessly in her bed, and Sarah sat up on her pallet of sheepskins by the fire.

What was odd was that he and the other one looked so much alike – similar long, lean build, both with dead-straight hair tied back in a tail as thick as your wrist, same fair skin, same long straight nose, like one of the less forgiving angels off of the big carved rood screen in the church - and yet the blonde one managed to be handsome and the big redhead managed to be plain as a pikestaff. She smiled to herself. All right, so the fair-haired lad was handsome. She wasn't so set against men that she hadn't noticed that. Handsome, and kind, and gentlemanly, and *incredibly* young. Not a good idea on all fronts.

Lord, what fools men be, she thought ruefully, and women for letting them get away with it. These two were just two of – she couldn't even begin to guess how many had joined battle yesterday afternoon. And some woman had birthed every last one of them, counted out little fingers and little toes, kissed bumps and grazes, sat up nights over childhood ills; and for what? To end up cold clay on a battlefield, if they were unlucky. Or damaged beyond repair – conscientious beyond his years, like the fair-haired officer, or haunted, like the redhead. Neither of them yet in their middle age, and already the blonde lad wore a perpetual, faint crease between his brows. Sarah must be twice his age, and she didn't have that look of constant watchfulness. And the redhead, whimpering and twitching in his sleep, dreaming imaginary battles, and losing. She'd changed her mind. Whoever had begun this war had earned her hatred, if this was what their cause did.

"Is it time?" the fair-haired lad said sleepily, propping himself up with one elbow on the settle and rubbing his eyes with his fist. Tousled and blinking, he looked like a little boy woken untimely, for all that he was old enough to bear a sword. The corner of her mouth curled up and she shook her head and then realised that the light from the banked fire was likely too dim for him to see her do it from that distance.

"No," she whispered back. "He's just restless. I don't want him to wake Mattie." - although precious little woke Mattie once the boy was down for the night, save hunger or colic. The redhead had managed to throw most of his covers off, and was cursing in English and various heathen tongues. Fluent lad, give him his due. Sitting on the edge of the bed demanding to know where Margaret was, and getting quite cross about it. Well, the precious little that woke Mattie probably included noisy soldiers. Sarah got up, wrapping a blanket over her shift – well, if the pair of them were planning rape and murder they were probably leaving it a bit late in the night – and went to her son. Dead to the world, four chubby fingers in his mouth. Went to the redhead. "Hush," she said softly. "Go back to sleep. You're amongst friends."

He turned his head abruptly and looked straight at her and called her Margaret. Whoever Margaret was he evidently held her in great affection. She smoothed his sweat-tangled hair back off his face. He rested his cheek against her wrist with a great sigh of contentment, called her Margaret again, and in all charity she left her hand against his cheek as he lay down again and she said, "I'm here. All will be well." And he smiled – she felt him smile against her palm – suddenly relaxing into sleep.

The fair-haired one was awake now, his eyes – blue,

she thought, or green, but definitely pale in colour even in this light – alert and once again wary. "That was kindly done, mistress," he said quietly. "Though I would guess your name isn't Margaret."

"It isn't." She shivered and pulled her blanket tighter about her shoulders. "It's Mistress Hadfield. Sarah. Sir, if you would be of use, make up the fire. Your friend will be cold, and I need a cup of tea."

He inclined his head gracefully – manners of a courtier, she thought wryly, even in her little cottage at something after midnight – and padded silently across the floor to the fire to poke up the embers into life. She watched him, fascinated by the play of soft amber light on his face. Handsome, and yet not. Not beautiful, his features weren't even especially regular, and yet he had an odd intense charm all his own. He was intent on his task, bending over to blow on the glowing ashes, with his hair held away from his eyes.

She freed her hand from under the redhead's cheek, and went to join him. "Mint," she said, and the lad blinked up at her as if she'd broken his dream. "I should normally suggest chamomile, were I wakeful and alone, but I suspect you mean to resume your duties at sunrise. Which is not far off, I think."

"You are most kind." He stopped, and his lips curved into a shy smile. "Sarah."

"Kindness costs nothing, sir. It's about all that doesn't, these days."

"Lucifer. Lucifer Pettitt. Though I – I prefer to be called Luce, if you don't mind."

She ran a hand through her own sleep-tangled hair, catching halfway down her braid. "Very well. Luce. There is a jar of honey in the cupboard on the wall, if you would be so good. Set it down on the table, please. We breakfast on bread and honey."

"That's a better breakfast than I enjoyed yesterday,

mistr – Sarah."

She closed her hands around the rough pottery cup, inhaling the fragrant steam. Closed her gritty eyes. "Young man, you will forgive my plain speaking, but remember that I am but a foolish countrywoman." And wondered whether he'd recognise sarcasm when he heard it. "Both of you are ill-fed and ill cared-for. You're worn out and he's hurt, and you're both wretched. Can you explain it to me, what it is that drives men to throw their lives away on a cold winter's night in such a battle?"

He opened his mouth to answer her and she was making herself angrier by the minute just looking at him, with his sleepless-bruised eyes and his childishly knobby wrist. He should be at home still, tucked up in his bed. And he was one of the lucky ones. He had a roof over his head this night, and not a few inches of frozen Worcestershire clay.

"It's a matter of honour, Sarah," he said stiffly, lifting his chin. "The King cannot continue to act the tyrant unchecked –"

"Ah," she said, nodding, "I wondered whose colours you wore. As if it makes any difference to the likes of me. Honour - there's a man's word! Where's the honour in leaving your wife and your children behind to starve, sir? Tell me that! Good men marched away with those soldiers of yours, good men who will be much missed at home. What will become of *their* families when they don't march home again? Will honour put food in their children's bellies, or tend their harvests? I doubt it very much. And –"

He put his hand, very gently over her lips. "That's enough. I'll not hear it." And he wasn't a boy, for all his sweet-faced charm. Lucifer was most definitely a man grown, and she was suddenly very aware of wearing nothing but a thin shift under the blanket. And aware of him – of the breadth of his shoulders, and the warmth of his skin, and the curve of his mouth. "Every man must be willing to make sacrifice for the safety of the things he holds dear, Sarah. If such is the Lord's will."

"Easy enough to say, sir," she said wildly.

"Not as easy to do, though. I know." His eyes were mist-coloured in the firelight, and steady on hers. "I'd not *choose* to die in the morning with so much yet to do. But if my death goes towards giving England back her freedom, then – yes, I'd be willing."

"And what can *you* sacrifice, at your age?"

He never looked away. "I've never as much as kissed a girl. An oversight on my part, no doubt. I always imagined I should have time enough to tend to such matters…later."

She leaned forward and took his face between her two hands - definitely not a beardless boy, the fairness of his bristles was deceiving - and kissed him. That was all she'd meant to do - a mother's kiss, light and comforting. She hadn't meant that the lad should kiss her back, with such eagerness, nor that his innocent fire should wake something in her that had lay sleeping since Matthew died. His mouth was soft, and at the same time certain, and he tasted of apples and honey. She buried her hands deep in his soft hair, feeling the length of his lithe young body against her -

She didn't know where it would have ended, nor where she would have wanted it to end, if Luce hadn't put his hands on her shoulders and disengaged himself gently. For a moment she was too dazed to think why he'd stopped. Then she remembered they weren't alone.

The big redhead was propped up on one elbow, watching them with an expression of fascinated contempt. When he was sure they were aware of his attention, he smiled. It was not a friendly expression. "Are you done, brat?"

Luce brushed her cheek with his fingertips. It was both a caress and a gesture of defiance. "When thou hast done, thou hast not done, for I have more," he whispered. Sarah wasn't sure how to reply to that.

The redhead snorted. "Poetry for breakfast, for Christ's sake, and Donne's damnable papist doggerel at that. I should have shot you yesterday and been quit of you."

Luce opened his mouth furiously, then looked at Sarah and set his lips. Not that the captain was paying him the least attention, struggling up and being currently engaged in trying to fasten his armour one-handed. She let him struggle himself to a standstill, and then caught the loose buckle dangling from his breastplate, holding it still for him.

And then started back at the heat radiating from his body. "Sir, you should not - you have a fever, sir, you need your bed -"

"We haven't got time for this, brat," he said, perfectly civilly, as if she'd never spoken. And then he turned his head and gave her a disconcertingly sweet smile that had no recognition in it. He'd forgotten who she was. "God bless you and keep you, mistress."

And then he was gone, and after one bemused glance over his shoulder, Luce was gone after him.

34 PROVOKED TO ANGER WITH A FOOLISH NATION

Essex looked round at the tattered rags of his officers. Balfour, aged thirty years in a night, stubbled with silver. Stapleton, with his immaculate linen black with powder and his cheek laid open to the bone. Ballard, blinking owlishly with exhaustion. Ramsey, glaring accusingly around him, and the other officers carefully avoiding his eyes. Babbitt, with his broken arm in a makeshift sling fashioned from a bloodstained tawny silk sash. And the gap where Rackhay would have been, on Babbitt's right, that no one wanted to look directly at.

Luce wondered which of the two was going to drop first, Thomas Ballard or Hollie Babbitt. A betting man would have guessed Babbitt – no more than two or three hours' sleep in the best part of two days. But the redhead was grimly vertical, and leaning, surreptitiously, on Luce. His weight would occasionally rest against Luce's shoulder – brace himself – jerk upright again. The only outward sign of the captain's exhaustion was an even scratchier mood than usual. Luce wasn't sure how much longer he could hold the captain up as well as himself. His sword arm ached. His eyes felt dry and gritty, and his head throbbed in time with his heartbeat.

The pearly grey light of early morning started to spread across the plain. "I am – proud of you, gentlemen. One last push, and the day is ours." Essex's voice sounded raw and strained.

"It cannot be done, sir. Cannot." Stapleton was shaking. "I cannot order my men to mount another attack, in all humanity."

"And I *won't*." Ballard flung his head up. "I cannot expect it of them, my lord. They fought bravely, but they must rest, sir. Eat. Sleep."

"Are you defying me?"

Babbitt turned his head and looked at Luce with an expression of uncharacteristic docility. "I knew you wasn't dead, Nat," he said softly, with a happy sigh.

And Luce - tall, fair-haired Luce, who bore no other similarity to the dead man than an passing accident of height and colouring - shivered involuntarily, glancing over his shoulder for fear Rackhay should be standing behind him cold and bloodless-white. "Sir?"

Babbitt smiled faintly. "You had me scared last night."

"Sir, I am not Captain Rackhay. You mistake me. I'm - I'm Luce, Lucifer Pettitt, you recall? Captain Rackhay died - honourably and bravely, in the commission of his duties, yesterday -"

He half-expected the redhead to hit him. He certainly expected foul abuse. What he did not expect was that the captain would blink at him like a hurt and astonished child, his sound hand creeping to his mouth - "Died? You're - and you *left* him? To the crows, and the looters?"

"I thought it more needful to bring you away, captain, hurt as you were-"

"Oh Luce, that was not well done," he said, and turned on his heel. The scarlet rays of an autumn sunrise glinted from his wet cheek, and Luce had to shake his head to clear the unnerving impression that the captain was weeping tears of blood. The fact that he was weeping at all was unnerving enough. "There's a messenger coming down the hill," Balfour said sharply, breaking the awkward silence.

Thomas Ballard giggled. "And what a messenger. God almighty, where's *he* been hiding?"

"Under the bed, by the look of him," Stapleton said, grinning. "Wish I had his clean linen, this morning."

"Wish I'd had it last night," Balfour said irritably. "Could have done with that coat just before dawn. Bitter, it was."

The elegant messenger was picking his way, carefully, down the hillside from the King's stand atop the hill, bearing a white handkerchief aloft. His hair was loose and carefully curled on his immaculate black-clad shoulders, the scarlet feather in his crisp wide-brimmed hat pristine. His single pearl earring gleamed in the wan sunshine. His horse was fresh, groomed, fine breeding in every line of it. Stapleton sniffed. "Daddy, buy me one of *those*," he breathed. "By God, what could I not do with that mount."

"Be glad of one with four sound legs, myself," Ramsey grunted. It was possibly the first time he'd spoken to anyone since Rupert's charge had put his loosely organised cavalry to flight.

There was a long pause whilst the officers present – those that Tom Corston had been able to find, those that weren't dead, drunk, or incapable of sitting a horse – stood watching the King's emissary advance. "Son of a bitch," Ballard said, shaking his head with some admiration. "Will you look at him. Not a bloody mark on him."

Babbitt shoved his matted hair out of his eyes. "I'm having that fucker," he said calmly. "Fucking Revelations, gentlemen. Behold a rider on a black horse, and a pair of scales in his hand. I'll give you famine, you son of a fucking bitch."

His voice was pitched to carry, and the emissary winced as he drew his glossy white horse to a halt. "Gentlemen, I bear a flag of truce," he said, dismounting with a graceful flourish – Essex stepped forward, every inch the experienced courtier greeting his equal with dignity and grace. Ramsey spat, accurately, past the Royalist's shiny boot.

"My lords. I am privileged to be given the task of delivering a message from your rightful sovereign," the emissary said, ignoring the big Scot with difficulty. It was rather harder to ignore the sudden outcry in the Parliamentarian artillery and the wild hoofbeats coming down the hill. Cheering.

"Cheeky *bastards*," Babbitt said, and shoved rudely past, heading towards the horse lines at a flat run.

Cavalry officers were not designed to sprint, Luce thought, stifling a grin. Essex was blinking as though trying to clear the vision from his sight.

The messenger looked somewhat taken aback. "What –"

"Do try and keep your friends on a shorter leash," Stapleton said coolly. "Rupert's men – again. Interesting flag of truce you have, sir."

A dozen or so of Rupert's troops had come careering down the hill, surrounding one of Essex's abandoned field pieces, and were dragging it away with screams of wild delight. Ramsey barged past the emissary after Babbitt. Caught up with the big redhead where he was struggling to mount his horse, and practically heaved him into the saddle. Babbitt's distinctive accents were clearly audible across the field, describing Rupert's wild young bloods in terms of scatological anatomical correctness. "They mean no harm, I'm sure. High spirits," the King's messenger said uncomfortably. A shot rang out, followed by a stream of furious Scots invective.

Essex's eyebrows twitched. "As Sir Philip says. Interesting flag of truce."

"Those are *your* officers taking the offensive, my lord. Not ours." The emissary drew himself up with some dignity. "Rupert's troop are given to youthful high spirits, no more. 'Tis a game they play, of no more significance –"

"Say your piece, my lord," Stapleton snarled, "And be gone."

"As you wish." He inclined his head gracefully. "In recognition of your years of loyalty, His Majesty would possibly be prepared to overlook this ill-advised transgression, and, like the return of the Prodigal Son, forgive your rebellion."

"Would he, now." Stapleton sounded amused. "And what does His Majesty get out of it, other than a warm glow inside?"

"In return," the messenger went on, coldly ignoring him, "His Royal Majesty asks no more than that you lay down your arms and return to the commission of your lawful duties. In his generosity of spirit, His Majesty would guarantee that no reprimand will be meted out to either yourselves or your unlawfully raised troops."

"So, allow me to be clear, here." Balfour. "His Majesty is prepared to pardon the whole boiling lot of us, no questions asked, no more to be said, so long as we just lay down our weapons and go home?"

"That is, roughly, correct, my lord. Yes."

Essex was wavering. With astonishment and contempt, Luce could see his uncle's dark eyes dart from face to face, looking for guidance. The Earl of Essex was irresolute. His heart was not wholly given to the Cause. He wanted another to make his decision.

"My – my lords, may I speak?" Luce stammered. Essex frowned at him.

"Yes," Stapleton said quickly. "You may, Cornet. You have earned the right to speak as freely as any of us."

"For my-myself, sir, I would ask – given the weight of our concerns, the fears which led us to take such – such desperate measures as to take up arms against our rightful King – which of our apprehensions will His Majesty address first?"

Stapleton was nodding. "Aye. I'd be interested to hear that one."

The emissary shook his head. "Boy, you have the matter on its head. His Majesty has no case to answer. He is not a plaintiff, to be questioned which way please you. In his graciousness, your sovereign is offering his forgiveness for your unprecedented act of anarchy. Be grateful for his generosity, that he does not demand your heads on Traitor's Gate, as would be his right. Now will you hear his words, or no?"

For a very brief second Luce was so angry he was speechless. He spread his hands, wanting to take in the whole field: the shattered men of both sides, the hearths that would go cold and empty this winter at His Majesty's caprice. Men who'd sat down to breakfast yesterday laughing with comrades, lying cold with the frost thick-furred on grey lips and open eyes. He'd had faith in his sovereign's reason; that he'd see the weight of his subjects' concerns when he set eyes on the ranks of Parliament men opposing his whims. Instead, His Majesty spoke of godlike forgiveness, of welcoming his wayward subjects back into his royal bosom as though they were naughty children. Luce's hurt and disappointment and fury went too deep for words. With a sob, he slapped the King's messenger across his well-scrubbed face.

"Reckon the lad says no," Balfour said lazily. "I'm inclined to agree with him."

"Lucifer!" Essex was appalled. "How *dare* you –"

"You agree with this," Luce gasped, tears running unchecked down his face. "After all we lost?"

"No, boy, I did not say as much, but in all courtesy –"

"See him off, boys." Balfour was grinning now. "You can go back to His Majesty, laddie, and tell him the

Army of Parliament says thanks for the offer, but we're all right where we are."

Ballard put two fingers in his mouth and whistled in a most ungentlemanly fashion. The nearest officer of his infantry troop came heading up the slope at a run. "Sir?" he panted.

"Take this gentleman off the field, Little, and return him from whence he came. Preferably through the ranks, and be sure that some harm comes to him." Little grabbed the emissary by the collar. "As you wish, sir," he said, grinning.

"My lord Essex, will you be led by –" the Royalist choked as Little's hand tightened on his neckcloth , and he glanced at Luce with loathing – "a stripling and a pack of rebels – will you not reconsider this foolish choice –"

Essex blinked, slowly. "My whole trust resides in my officers. I respect their opinions as my own." He turned his back, very deliberately, on the emissary. "As you were, gentlemen."

There was a great cheer as Little cheerfully cuffed the elegant messenger's hat from his head.

35 DARKNESS AND THE SHADOW OF DEATH

It had been a fool's errand, Hollie thought bitterly. Daft idea in the first place to go careering after Rupert's pack of young ruffians, but the sight of them yelping and hooting like Barbary bloody apes dragging the field piece away like a trophy had set his hackles up. He hadn't been thinking straight and he hadn't expected anyone to come with him. Evidently Jamie Ramsey wasn't thinking straight either. With hindsight – wonderful thing, hindsight – he should have known the big Scot would have jumped at the chance of having a bit of revenge for yesterday. They'd no chance of catching the bastards, of course. Well-rested and on fresh horses, they were halfway to frigging Oxford before Hollie was even mounted.

Under different stars, the sight of Sir James Ramsey careering across half of Worcestershire in pursuit of an escaping field piece, purple in the face and sweating like a pig, using language no upright and godly man should have known, would have had Hollie helpless with laughter. Seemed quite reasonable, this morning. They'd returned, in a mutually sullen silence, to their respective places – past Thomas Ballard, with a battered scarlet plume proudly displayed in his hat. Hollie brought Tib to a halt beside the limp colours. Cullis brought his cob up alongside, grim as ever. "What did I miss, sergeant?"

Cullis sniffed, rubbed the back of his hand under his nose. "Bugger-all, lad. His Majesty's fancy boy got sent home with a bloody nose and we're back to seeing who blinks first."

"Ah." Both armies formed up again on either side of the vale, then, just like yesterday. Maybe it *was* still yesterday, and he had it all to fight over again. Nat would be down on the left flank – or had Essex ordered him somewhere else, today? Cullis was frowning at him. Hollie glanced at him warily. If the grim old bastard cuffed him again, he'd have him this time. Too free with the back of his hand, was Cullis.

No, Cullis hadn't laid a hand on him in the best part of fifteen years. He was Cullis's commander now, and he wasn't fifteen any more. He kept forgetting things, today. A fair-haired officer came trotting up, mounted on an elegant chestnut mare. "What are you doing over here?" he snapped. "I thought you were supposed to be –" Down on the hedgeline with Ramsey, but it was the wrong fair-haired officer. Not Rackhay. Looked nothing like Rackhay. Wishful thinking, Babbitt. This was Essex's whelp, not Nat. Nat was dead and this little bastard had left him to the looters and the crows - oh Christ, the crows - he went for his pistol and realised his wrist wouldn't answer. Fumbled left-handed for it, almost dropped it, and tried to sight on one of the rags of carrion black beginning to drift down to the frosty grass.

"*Hollie*," Cullis said warningly, "put that down."

"I'll not have those fucking birds -"

"It's all right," the brat said. "Ballard's lads are sorting it out." He leaned over and put his hand on Hollie's sound wrist, and just for a second Hollie still wasn't sure it wasn't Rackhay's fingers on his arm. So bloody cold - well, he would be, obviously, he'd been dead all night. "I promise," the boy said earnestly, and no, that wasn't Rackhay. That bugger never kept a promise in his life, though he always meant to. "It'll all be done decent, captain. You have my word that Captain Rackhay's body will be honourably interred."

"Oh." Hollie looked at the black horse's mane for a minute, then shook his head, hoping to clear it. "So what are *our* orders, brat?"

"Well," Luce shifted uncomfortably in the saddle,

"Ramsey's been complaining about you." He affected a thick Scots accent. "Says yon laddie's off his heid."

"Not sure he's wrong," Hollie muttered. "But not that off my head he wasn't keen to come with me in the hope of giving the Malignants a bloody nose."

"No, sir, but off your head enough that he wants you relieved of command."

Hollie took a deep breath, feeling suddenly like the ground had opened up under his feet. Surely to God they couldn't strip him of that too - "And he said what?"

"He said if you were mad enough to charge the Royalist artillery by yourself he thought you were probably sufficiently mental to keep Rackhay's men as well as your own for the time being."

"Christ." It was probably the first favourable thing the Earl of Essex had ever said about Hollie Babbitt. Pity Essex's good opinion mattered slightly less to Hollie than that of one of the horse turds scattered about the field.

They waited. The sun rose higher in the sky. Some of the frost melted, but not much. Nothing else happened. Was it Hollie's imagination, or were the ranks of Malignants thinning? He was damned if he was going to point it out, had no intention of looking any more stupid or any more cracked than the little bastard already thought he was, but he was almost sure of it. Rupert's cavalry had gone, melted away from the field like the frost. The Robber Prince was distinctive enough to be conspicuous by his absence.

"Quiet, ain't it?" Cullis said, and Hollie glanced at the old gargoyle. Not his imagination, then. Not unless the sergeant was indulging in a like fiction.

"They're pulling out."

"Good. My feet are sodding freezing."

"It's not warm, is it?" Luce agreed cheerfully, and Hollie raised an eyebrow at him.

"You two are supposed to be soldiers, not bloody goodwives. Give over whining."

Luce trotted off. Came back a few minutes later. "They're definitely pulling out."

"And what are we supposed to do, stop here till we freeze?"

The brat shrugged. "The intention is to return to Warwick, as I understand. So we wait till my lord Essex gives us the order to withdraw."

"Waiting on Essex to make his mind up? Surely not." And Hollie pulled the black horse's head up and headed off at a canter.

36 LUCE SETS IN ORDER THE THINGS THAT ARE WANTING

Slowly, orderly, the Army of Parliament withdrew from the field, battered but defiant. It was past noon when Babbitt's troop came to move.

Most of Ballard's men had been left on burial duty – those who were still left standing, and that was less than half. The sound of shovels on iron-hard ground rang across the cold air. Luce realised with a sense of deep resignation that he seemed to be the most senior officer left in Babbitt's troop. Which meant he was in charge of an organised withdrawal. Cullis gave him a sour grin. "I reckon we must be at the bottom, 'cos the shit keeps on coming downhill."

"What?"

The sergeant jerked his head towards the advancing form of Captain Little. "We got company."

Little was filthy, and looking somewhat embarrassed. He was being followed by Edmund Allaby – praise the Lord, still whole and smiling, even if he was leading Tyburn. The black was limping and draggled. His rider was equally filthy and astonishingly biddable. "We always cop for the dirty jobs," Little said cheerfully. "Some smartarse –" he shot a wry look at Allaby – "suggested that Captain Babbitt might be overdue for burial."

"Well, he don't look too clever, do he? So he got in the hole quite willing-like, thinking to save us a job later," Allaby said. "Wasn't expecting that, mind."

"Had a bugger of a job getting him out, as well. He's all yours, cornet, and I give you joy of him. Right-ho,

Allaby, back to shovelling. We got a bloody big pit to dig yet." He gave Luce a big grin. "See you in Warwick, lad. Keep us some ale by, eh?"

Leaving Luce with a smirking Allaby and an uncannily meek Captain Babbitt. Even the black horse was unnaturally compliant. "Truly? In the burial pit?"

Allaby shrugged. "Look at the state of him. What do you think?"

"I think," Cullis said coolly, "that you keep your nose out of our business and your gob shut. Is what I think."

"If you reckon I was intending to go round telling everyone your commanding officer's run mad –" Cullis took an involuntary step forward and Allaby dropped the black horse's rein quickly. "If that was what I thought. Which it ain't."

"Oh, come on, Lucey, let's get him out."

Babbitt turned his head and looked at them. Without that habitual scowl, the big redhead seemed oddly young and vulnerable. Luce edged the mare closer and took Tyburn's slack rein. "Up we come, there's a good lad."

"Stick him in the middle of the troop – in between Calthorpe and Moggy Davies, they're sound lads, they won't make a fuss," Cullis suggested. "He's been like this before. 'S just a fever…he'll come about. Prob'ly. Lay you a drink by time we get to Warwick he'll be teasy as a snake, back to normal."

Calthorpe raised his bushy brows and said not a word, other than to put his hand, gently, on Babbitt's splinted arm. The captain smiled absently at him, which didn't reassure Luce much. Hollie Babbitt in his right mind did not smile at anyone, absently or otherwise. Davies just trotted along prattling away, glad of an audience whether it responded or not.

"Leave him wi' friends," Calthorpe said, and Luce thought, yes, you would say that. No matter what – if the captain had run stark mad, foaming and raging,

Calthorpe would have been as willing to stand by him. "You go and pick up your duties, lad. You can rely upon we two. Known Red a long ol' time, I have. Poor lad."

And Luce rather thought he could. There was a core of absolute steadfastness to Babbitt's troop, from taciturn Cullis to quietly zealous Calthorpe to the garrulous Davies – even Babbitt himself was resolute, in his own ungovernable way. Once committed, they did not turn aside, not a one of them. Which was more than could be said for my lord of Essex, who had led them into this pretty pickle. Luce would not forget the nervous darting of Uncle Essex's dark eyes, flickering from face to face as he sought for someone's opinion to shore up his own. He couldn't imagine any of this troop seeking for approval to justify their actions. An odd mix, those committed to the Cause standing shoulder to shoulder with battle-hardened mercenaries, and yet a blend that would withstand trial by fire, he thought.

He could lead such men. Yes, he could give his heart and soul to such a command. And they seemed to be – not humouring him, that wasn't fair, but they seemed eager to help him in his first commission. He hefted the colours and clicked his tongue to the mare. May the Lord continue to smile upon his endeavours, he thought wryly, because in spite of a deadlocked battle and a distracted captain, he thought he'd had it easy so far. And nothing lay between them and Warwick Castle but a few miles of leafless open country, scarcely ambush territory. The worst they had to fear was the cold. No, God willing, Luce might yet pass this first command off quite creditably, with the aid of Sergeant Cullis. A shadow seemed to pass across his sight – the shadow of the Rider on the Red Horse, no doubt. The first command of many, after today. Whether he gave his word wholeheartedly or not, Essex had committed them all to a course of action that would see this day repeated time and again until King or Parliament achieved mastery.

"Lucey – er, sir!"

Isaac Weston's voice broke him from his reverie. Weston's broad Somerset accent was not made for panic, yet he sounded alarmed. Luce drew his pistol sharply. "What is it, Weston?"

Twenty yards away there was an immovable obstacle in the highway, around which Babbitt's troop ebbed and whirled like the current around a rock in a river. It was black Tyburn, standing stock-still with an empty saddle. Cullis came up from the rear – looked in the direction of Luce's horrified gaze. *"Bollocks."*

"One minute he was there, and the next minute – nearly rode right over him, I did, sir," Isaac Weston was saying, sounding deeply apologetic. "Just as well old mare's slow, ent it?"

Cullis exhaled through his nose. "For fuck's sake, Hollie."

The captain was lying in the road, limp as a dropped glove. *"Hollie."*

Luce dismounted and knelt down. Gingerly – half afraid of what he might feel, and half afraid that Babbitt's calmly closed eyes might suddenly fly open – touched his fingers to where he thought the beating pulse in the captain's neck might be. Nothing. He felt suddenly dizzy and sick. "Sergeant Cullis, would you – could you –"

"Move, boy. Let me see. Fuck. *I* don't know what I'm looking for, for Christ's sake – " Cullis kneeling the other side of the captain, both of them fumbling at the redhead's motionless body like a pair of grave-robbers.

"Let m-me through, please."

Witless. Francis Witcombe, the fat boy, pushing his way through the knot of men and horses with an unrecognisable expression of resolution on his pimply face. "I w-w-was 'prenticed to a surgeon," he said over his shoulder, gently but firmly moving Luce out of his way. "Before I joined the troop."

Handed Luce his bridle-gauntlet and put three of his chubby fingers on Babbitt's neck, feeling his way gently. The lad was frowning. Luce thought probably every man in the troop held his breath. Witless shook his head, and Luce felt a icy chill down his spine.

"His heart is beating steady enough," Witless said, sitting back on his heels, and Lucey didn't just think there was a collective sigh of relief – he heard it. Also heard Calthorpe's brief and heartfelt prayer. Witless also took a deep breath. "I – think –" he screwed his eyes shut between words, as if he were forcing the words out, "that he is stunned only. The fall from his horse." For all their fat pink clumsiness, Witless's fingers were gentle as he examined the captain. "In my –" his lips pursed again in the effort of forcing the word out whole – "*professional* opinion, his skull is not cracked."

"More's the bleedin' pity," Cullis growled, his natural bad humour restored. "It might let some bleedin' sense in."

Witless looked up and grinned. "I would not recommend bleeding, sergeant. Not in this case."

"Don't get smart with me. Come on, then, sawbones. Earn your pay. What d'you reckon?"

"You're the troop surgeon," Luce added, with a smile. "As of about five minutes ago."

"Me?" The fat boy blushed a deep and mottled scarlet. "I wouldn't want to be the captain when he regains his wits –"

"I like the 'when' part," Luce whispered to the sergeant, who was startled into a brief bark of laughter.

" – he will have something of a headache, but it will be no worse than that, God willing." Witless shrugged uncomfortably. "That said, sir, I w-w-will promise nothing. I have known cases where a man had little more hurt than a clip to the temple and died an hour later. It's im-possible to tell how deep the hurt goes till he wakes."

"What," a cold voice said, "is the meaning of this delay?" And then, "Oh, God's teeth, I might have known it would be this troop at the bottom of it."

Luce stood up and bowed with as much grace as he could muster, splattered to the thigh with freezing mud. "Master Corston. We are honoured by your presence, sir."

"Are you, Cornet Pettitt. Are you, indeed. Would you care to be honoured sufficiently far away from the highway that the rest of the army can pass, or do you plan to use the opportunity to present an interesting new engine of warfare – a barricade of stupidity?"

Cullis stepped forward, scowling, and Luce stopped him with a look. "Captain Babbitt has met with an accident, sir –"

"Cornet, Captain Babbitt *was* an accident. I imagine his father would agree – if he could identify the gentleman in question." Corston smiled thinly. "I don't care what –"

"Well, I believe your master does care, sir. My lord Essex spoke highly of the captain's bravery this morning –" sort of, in a roundabout way – "and his hurts have been honourably gained in carrying out my lord's orders. I do not believe that *my uncle* would see a man wounded in the commission of his duties and punish him for it. Do you, Master Corston?"

Essex's elegant aide looked flushed and furious. "No, cornet, but –"

"Well, then."

Babbitt stirred restlessly, twitched his head away from Witless' probing fingers, sat up, coughed, and then was sick at Corston's feet.

Someone sniggered. "You did that on purpose,"

Corston said, in horrified disgust, looking at his besmirched boots.

Witless shook his head. "No, sir, 'tis common with such injuries, I assure you –"

"I am sure," Luce interrupted smoothly, "that not even Captain Babbitt is capable of such malice." He wasn't, actually. But he was prepared to give him the benefit of the doubt. "However, *if* you are so certain that the matter is so urgent you must have the troop move on without Captain Babbitt, I will give the order for the men to fall in with the body of the army, under Sergeant Cullis's most experienced command, and I will follow on with the captain shortly, when Master Witcombe – who is almost a trained surgeon, Master Corston, an expert – is happy that he should do so. Does that satisfy you, sir?"

There was a long, baleful silence.

"*Nicely* done, brat," Babbitt said, just quietly enough for Luce to hear.

37 THE BEGINNING OF REVENGES UPON THE ENEMY

It hadn't been one of his more illustrious engagements, Hollie thought ruefully. Those parts of the last two days where he'd been upright and in full possession of his faculties seemed to be as rare as hobby-horse shit. It hadn't done much for his dignity to be lay in a ditch being poked, prodded and generally groped by Witless – who'd have thought the stammering tub of guts would turn out to be a competent bonesetter? – while the tag-end of Essex's army slouched past. Sniggering, probably. And he'd been lectured – *lectured*, damn it all – by fat Witless on his expected conduct for the next few days, and the importance of meekly reporting to be doctored if he noted any disorder in his temperament.

Corston had had a face like a well-slapped backside though and it was almost worth being handed over into the brat's dithering care for the sheer joy of pissing Essex's aide right off. Come to think of it, it *had* been worth it, for the once in a lifetime, never to be repeated pleasure of puking on Corston's mirror-like boots. Probably tomorrow he'd feel differently about it, when the bruises stiffened up. Christ, the brat had been worse than a girl. Sit down. Be still. Drink water. Small sips or you'll make yourself sick. Shame Corston hadn't stuck around. Hollie could have had him a second time.

And now here they were at dusk tottering along behind the rag-tag of the Army like a pair of old maiden aunts on market day, Hollie on the mare because between the two of them they hadn't been able to get him back on to his own taller black without his screaming like a rabbit. Lucey was not gentle. Or rather, he *was* gentle, in a slow, deliberate, clumsy kind of way. The Lord clearly did not intend Luce's future to lie in tending the sick.

He wondered, idly, what the pup would say if he finally admitted defeat and fell off the mare. Could all too easily imagine the smug, self-righteous expression on the boy's face. All the more reason why he was going to stay upright and lucid if it killed him. It was remarkable how crippling such a simple hurt could be. The mare's every stride sent jolts of pain up his arm, and she was a fairly easy-gaited animal. That said, Tib was so stiff and so exhausted, poor beast, that he was plodding along like an old cart horse.

He wrapped his good hand in the mare's coarse mane, closed his eyes, and tried to think of sunshine and flowers. Not that it helped, really, there only being two things in the world these days that cheered Hollie Babbitt up. The lack of a working sword arm currently debarred him from relieving his feelings by laying violent hands on someone, and he really couldn't face food at the moment. "Boy. Lucifer. Stop, damn you."

The black horse was twenty yards ahead and he hated himself for it but he just couldn't go any further. Without waiting for the boy to stop he slid down the mare's shoulder – sidesaddle, like an old dame on a mule – stopped, panting, leaning against her solid flank. Sat down in the grass to wait for a sudden wave of dizziness to pass. He wanted to cry. He hadn't felt so wretchedly ill for a long old while. He wanted to quietly crawl into a ditch and die.

"You look rough. Sir."

There was probably a suitable response to that and maybe it would come to him some time tomorrow. At times like this the sardonic eyebrow of least resistance came into its own.

"I'm not sure we should try and go any further. Do you want to rest for a while?"

Hollie shook his head. What he mostly wanted at this moment was for either a swift and merciful death, or for the boy to go away. Either would be good. What he really didn't need was a shiny little cornet peering hopefully down at him and dithering. "Go away," he croaked. "*Right* away."

To his profound disgust, Pettitt grinned. "You sound just like my baby sister when she's eaten too much marchpane – although she normally goes and hides under the table to be sick. Well, I can hardly leave you in the middle of the road all night, can I?"

Luce caught hold of the mare's bridle. Tib seemed pleased to be relieved of his duties, standing broadside across the highway with his nose in the deep grass at Hollie's side. "I'll leave you my pistols, sir. Both loaded. I imagine the neighbourhood is still fairly crawling with Malignants."

"I imagine it is, brat. I lack the will to care." Hollie suspected the brat was laughing at him. Tyburn dropped his slobbery black head onto the captain's shoulder with a grunt that sounded suspiciously affectionate and he was oddly comforted. Being mocked by your subordinates and dribbled on by a bad-tempered horse was not normally grounds for comfort. He was getting mawkish in his old age.

Luce dug his heels into the mare and headed her back up the lane. There was no way they'd catch up with Essex tonight now, even if he thought the captain was fit. He'd seen better looking corpses on the battlefield. It was probably hysteria, but that expression of Hollie's did remind him frighteningly of Bab after a surfeit of sweetmeats. He wasn't more than about fifty yards back up the lane before it became apparent that Hollie had something else in common with his little sister: an inability to be quietly unwell. It was unkind to laugh, so Luce tried not to.

Back to Kineton, then. And hope that the enemy had moved on. The sun was low in the sky by the time he rode back into the village, noting with relief the smoke from Mistress Hadfield's cottage chimney. The sky was a darkening steel blue, slashed across with orange: storm coming, no doubt, and a rising wind rattling the leafless tree branches like a hundred tiny swords in their scabbards. The street was deserted. He couldn't see any patrols – either scarlet or orange sashed – so he could only assume it was safe. To be sure, he stuffed his own orange sash under his saddle. He'd left his weapons with Hollie – which was, on reflection, a stupid thing to do – but on a weary and mud-splattered horse, he could be anybody. Almost. "Mistress Hadfield?"

The door was latched. She opened it a crack, one eye appearing suspiciously in the gap, and then pulled it open with a cry of joy. "Oh, Luce, thank the Lord for your preservation!" And amazingly, she drew him into her warm, safe cottage, threw her arms round him, and kissed him with a fierce abandon. "I was afraid I should never see you again," she said against his mouth. "I am so glad to see you whole. *So* glad. Come you in, and get warm. I was so *frightened* - Oh, Luce, come in, out of the cold! 'Tis another bitter night, no night to be out there in the dark –"

It was a welcome he could grow accustomed to, and he returned her greeting with enthusiasm. "You are truly pleased to see me, mistress? Truly? Even after -"

Her nose was almost touching his, and her eyes were alight with an honest joy. He gave a shaky sigh of relief as she nodded, and leaned his cheek against her neat white cap, folding her into his arms.

"And your friend?" she said against his shoulder.
"Is still alive, mistress. Hurt, and - wandering in his

wits, a little, but alive. Could you give us both lodgings again for the night? Not if it will put you in danger. But if you could find a bit of room and a crust of bread for the pair of us, I'd be grateful."

She gave him a rueful grin. "Luce, dear lad, you are too nice for your own good. " The soft wrinkles at the corners of her eyes deepened as her face softened. "Mattie's early to bed, mind, so I'd have the pair of you stay quiet as mice." She twined her arms round his neck again and put her cheek against his, quick and hard. "I prayed you'd come back safe, Luce." And to his shame and guilty delight, there were tears in her eyes. "I'll have a good supper ready for you, and a – a - You take care, Lucifer. There's still plenty strangers in the village, and it's a cold night. Here, now." She stripped him quickly of his own doublet and bundled a heavy, rough homespun garment into his arms. Evidently Matthew Hadfield had been somewhat shorter and broader than Luce. Even Sarah turned her face away to hide a smile. "It fits where it touches," she said dryly. "Still. It'll keep the chill off."

She smoothed the rough wool over his chest and he was almost sure she must be able to feel his heart suddenly bounding under her fingers at the nearness of her. He pulled his own hat down over his eyes; it was shabby enough now, having spent the night after the battle being used as a pillow. The coat smelt appallingly of sheep, and he suspected was lousy with ticks. "And try and walk a bit less like a gentleman," she said kindly. "Keep your hands in your pockets, and not so straight in the shoulders. Can't say you'd fool anyone close to, mind, so you'd best be off and bring your captain straight back here."

"Sarah –" He didn't know what to say. Thought he should say something. That she was lovely, that she was kind, that she talked more sense than most of the great and the good of the Army of Parliament? "Thank you," he said lamely, and closed the door behind him.

The mare was sufficiently rested to go again, though sluggishly. He turned her head back up the lane towards Banbury. The thought of riding past the battlefield in the dark – worse, under a rising moon – made his skin crawl. It was a long, slow ride on the shadowy dusk, and he thought he heard voices at every turn, behind every hedge, in every shadow.

And then he did hear voices.

"Now what, I ask, is this?" It was a well-bred, young, amused voice. It was the sort of voice that was attached to a well-bred, young, amused bully. "It's a plough horse, gentlemen. Do you think it bites?"

He kicked Rosa into a trot, calling, in his best playhouse yokel voice, "There 'ee be, Reuben!"

"Another plough horse, gentlemen. No – I stand corrected – this one is presumably the plough horse's mother."

Luce felt a wave of indignation on his horse's behalf. She might be dirty but she had better breeding than this poisonous toad. At least Tyburn was dirty and scruffy *and* incorrigibly vicious. "Is that you, Reuben?" he said, louder. "Sarah be looking for 'ee, boy. Where you to?"

And then, praise the Lord, Hollie answered. "Here, you fool, where else'd I be? Owd horse has gone lame, see." It wasn't a wholly convincing Worcestershire accent, but at least it was neither aristocratic officer nor Hollie's natural Northern burr. "'Ee be stuck in this old ditch here, I do reckon."

There were only the three of them, one scarlet-sashed, all well-mounted. Tyburn was still barricading the road, and Hollie was on his feet, arm out of its sling, in his shirt sleeves. Oh, thank God, he had *some* wits left. It was difficult to imagine anything less like an officer than Hollie Babbitt in his less than impeccable linen. "You look as if you've been in a fight – *Reuben*."

"I 'ave, sir. Aye, I 'ave at that."

"On whose side, pray?"

Luce prayed Hollie didn't try anything stupid. A brace of pistols and a backsword in the grass at his feet, a carbine rolled up in his coat behind Tyburn's saddle. It wasn't as if he was short of arms. He stifled a wild giggle. No, what the captain was short of, was – well – *arms*. Unless he was a competent left-handed swordsman. Oddly, Luce doubted it. "For the King, bwoy, who do 'ee think?"

The scarlet-sashed officer dismounted, tossing the reins to one of his companions. "Well, Fanshawe, don't just sit there, help our loyal comrade get his beast out of the ditch!"

Hollie shook his head almost imperceptibly at Luce, and then shuffled a few paces forwards. "Don't 'ee fret, zur, I'll have 'en out." He was turning into one of the Weston twins. Luce was sure of it. "Don't want 'ee getting thy good coat dirty with my owd horse, now. Come up, lad –" He leaned against Tyburn's shoulder, chirruping encouragingly. "Get out of these fine gentlemen's way, Blackie."

The black, belly deep in long grass, looked much like any other shaggy, unkempt working horse. The Royalist officer and the man called Fanshawe joined Hollie at the head end. Fanshawe was chortling. "Out you come, my rustic Bucephalus!"

And with a resigned snort, Tyburn backed out of the ditch. Stood four square in the middle of the lane with his elegant, definitely not shaggy, well-bred legs quite clearly outlined in the light of the rising moon. "That," the officer said sharply, "is not a plough horse, my lad."

"By, you're quick," Hollie said, with resignation. And shot him with one of Luce's pistols, tucked into the top of his boot.

Left-handed, his aim wasn't what it should be, but the ball still went home – the officer went down screaming, clutching his belly, and Hollie threw the empty pistol in Fanshawe's astonished face. "Lucey, *do* something – oh, for Christ's sake -" Smacked the black horse, hard, across the muzzle with the flat of his sword. Tib wasn't used to that kind of treatment. He went straight up on his hind legs with a furious squeal, knocking the stunned Fanshawe flat.

"Lucey!" Hollie roared from the ditch, recalling Luce to his duty. Just in time, as the remaining Royalist trooper came at him, yelling wildly. Luce took one look at the white-faced trooper - who looked scared out of his wits – and one look at the sword he was waving, and dug his heels into the mare. Rosa took off up the lane at a gallop with Luce bent low over her neck, expecting a bullet in the back at any moment.

He could hear hoofbeats, a jumble of hoofbeats, somewhere up ahead and when he heard a single shot behind him he cringed lower still, his face pressed into her mane, eyes screwed shut. Confused voices in front of him and then suddenly a chaos of hooves and shouting and whinnying and he appeared to have ridden full-pelt into the middle of half a dozen Royalist reinforcements who weren't expecting him, judging by the panic-stricken disappearance of several of their mounts. With a wild yell, he wheeled the mare, meaning to head her straight at the remaining troopers and hoping to God they'd scatter again. He was unarmed. He hoped they hadn't noticed.

Another single shot, and a voice from twenty yards away said, "Ill met by moonlight, gentlemen."

Luce sagged with relief. If nothing else, Hollie's reappearance had given him a moment's respite. The troopers were all staring past him, at Babbitt. The captain and his black horse looked like creatures of nightmare, halted in the lane with icy moonlight glinting on the carbine resting across the pommel of his saddle and running down the wet black edge of the backsword slung over his shoulder. Tyburn pawed the ground restlessly. "You might want to go back and pick a couple of your mates up. Master Fanshawe's dignity is bruised, but he's perfectly sound. If somewhat light in the weaponry department." Hollie grinned. "Consider it a donation to the Cause, lads. Now bugger off."

Luce brought the mare round to stand at Tyburn's shoulder, lifting his head in what he hoped was a proud and defiant stare. "Unless these gentlemen would like to make a like donation?" he suggested. His voice didn't shake at all.

"*There's* a good idea." Hollie lifted the carbine and rested it across his wrist. His right wrist. Well, his aim would be perfectly steady, Luce thought: Hollie was resting it on his splint.

Luce dismounted and walked across to the first trooper. "Your sword, sir, please."

The man was twice his age, with the ruddy cheeks and faded eyes of a country squire. Soft-bodied under his crabshell of plate, with grey eyebrows and a crust of grey stubble on his pouchy face. This was somebody's father, some countryman in his middle years, not the sort of spoiled aristocrat he'd imagined wearing the King's colours. "You insolent puppy," the old man blustered – handing his sword over. "How *dare* you – "

"I imagine we could make use of the pistol too," Luce said politely, holding his hand out. The trooper slapped it into his palm. "Thank you kindly."

The other two were meek as milk – and who wouldn't be, facing the archangel with the fiery sword, or at least his earthly representative? "Off you go, gentlemen," Hollie said. "We're done with you. That was painless, wasn't it?"

"I am not done with you, you –"

Luce stepped just that bit closer to the older man. Looked him in the eye. "Sir?"

"I'll not forget your face, boy! I will remember this indignity!"

"Luce, how many horses did we lose in the fight? Strip the bastards."

"You wouldn't dare!"

"Want to try me and see?" Even Luce had to admit that the captain didn't look entirely open to sweet reason. "Off you get, old son. Don't worry, Luce, first one to argue gets a ball between the eyes."

The squire's horse was sidling, ears flickering anxiously; a big, square-set grey cob, a countryman's mount, bred for rough ground and long hours in the saddle. Not a gentleman's horse, not like Tyburn or Rosa, but a working farmer's horse. Not a poor man's mount either, the beast was well fed and well taken care of, but a working mount nonetheless. Luce couldn't look at the old man's eyes again because he was suddenly ashamed that the Army of Parliament should be so dishonourable as to strip an old man of his horse and his weapons on a winter's night and turn him into the darkness. "Sir – this is not the cause for which I fight, Captain Babbitt. To strip the gentlemen of their arms is sufficient indignity, I -"

"Then I suggest you get back on the mare and piss off back to your village tart, Lucey."

Luce took a deep breath. He had a choice – turn and walk away, or swallow his pride and take the grey's bridle. He suspected if he turned his back he'd be shot before he mounted the mare - probably by his own commanding officer. Tears stung his eyes. "Please, captain –"

"Take the horse, boy. It pains me to see a lad so hurt by his conscience." The old squire kicked his feet out of the stirrups. "There is yet honour amongst thieves. I judged you harshly."

"Pains you? He gives *me* the arse-ache. Oh, get back on your horse, Lucifer, you spineless brat. Leave the old bastard his mount, if you're going to create about it. We've not got all bloody night." The captain flicked the carbine barrel up against his shoulder with the back of his hand, leaving the butt propped in the crook of his elbow. It looked very menacing and casual, and not like a man whose useful wrist was immobilised between two stout staves of good English oak. He turned Tyburn back up the lane.

"I won't forget *you*, you Judas-haired rebel," the squire shouted after him. The black horse stopped again. Striped by moonlight and the flickering shadows of tossing branches, horse and rider looked less human than ever.

"*'For I will make mine arrows drunk with blood, and my sword shall devour flesh; and that with the blood of the slain and of the captives, from the beginning of revenges upon the enemy.*' Mark me well, you Malignant bastard. Pettitt – here. *Now*."

Luce stuffed the weapons into the mare's saddlebags – glanced up the lane at the waiting figure, well, what's the worst he can do, kill me? "I give you good evening, sir. Sirs," he said politely, mounted the mare, and set off at a trot.

He passed Babbitt, refusing to even look in his direction, and sooner or later he'd come to the village and there was light and warmth there and he could pretend that it was all a bad dream. The mare shying at the dead officer in the lane, blood black on his scarlet sash – all a dream. He'd wake up soon. Part of him wanted to go home and bury his head in his mother's apron, but he was a grown man now, grown enough to have blood on his hands. He wanted to forget that he'd raised a sword in Parliament's name.

"Lucifer. Will you *stop.*"

"Not for you, sir, not if you shoot me like a dog on the highway. Not after this night." And his voice did wobble and he did not *care.*

"Oh, don't be so bloody dramatic, boy. And if you used your brain for something more than keeping your ears apart —" The black horse swerved in front of him, forcing him to halt. "How the hell can I shoot *anybody*, Lucey? Have you ever *tried* loading a gun one-handed? Christ! I had one carbine. Your two pistols. That's three shots, Lucifer."

"You mean that was an *act*?"

"I shot the officer twice, and that was only because I can't bear to see a man dying gut-shot. I couldn't hit the side of a barn with my left hand, brat, though I reckon I'd best start getting in practice."

"You let me face three men — *unarmed* — while you sat there with an empty pistol?"

The captain grinned. "I wasn't sure you'd do it if you knew. Give you credit, you've got more balls than I thought. I wouldn't have had the brass neck to have their guns as well."

"But you said —"

"Fanshawe? Long gone. That was the third shot. God alone knows what I hit with that one, but it didn't slow him down any."

"Take your horse out of my path, sir. You have abused my trust — abused an old man — committed acts of shameless piracy — oh, you *disgust* me, Captain Babbitt! That my uncle considers you a fit person to hold a command — assaulting old men and boys, sir, for shame!"

The redhead was laughing at him, shoulders shaking with silent mirth. "Don't do that again, Lucey, for Christ's sake. If I fall off this bloody horse you're going to have to pick me up. Old men and boys, indeed. What d'you think *we* look like?"

Luce looked at the captain. There was no arguing it, the redhead was no longer in his salad days, either green in judgment or cold in blood, as Master Shakespeare would have said. "I see your point, sir, you are indeed in your dotage."

"I'm thirty-three, you cheeky bastard. And *you're* on borrowed time. Come on. It's getting bloody cold out here."

38 SAFELY GATHERED IN

Sarah had felt unsettled all day.

It wasn't, odd though it sounded, anything to do with the fighting. That had been frightening, and it made her anxious and fretful and reluctant to leave her own safe walls, but it had little enough to do with her that it didn't disturb her. It had frightened her like ogres in fairy stories, or fireside tales of ghosts and witches; raised gooseflesh on her arms in the telling but it wasn't real.

And now it was real, because those two fantastic shapes of the King and his Parliament had taken on flesh, in the form of a lithe, not-quite-handsome boy with misty grey eyes. Luce was a soldier - he was an *officer*, for all he didn't hardly look old enough to shave. This time tomorrow he could be dead in a ditch. That thought frightened her - frightened her for all of them, every last mother's son on that battlefield. Even the red-haired captain.

It wasn't just the stillness after the battle that had made her so nervous today - that frozen stillness was no more and no less than you could expect from the beginning of winter in Kineton, when all was safely gathered in and the fields stood bare and empty to the frost. It was almost too still, after what had happened - but only almost. You could almost believe that the battle had been a bad dream. She'd heard the army - not sure whose army - marching out, the rumble of the carts and the guns rolling unevenly on the frozen ground, the tramp of boots, the occasional snatch of raised voices. Barely a shot fired this day. The few reports she'd heard had been so widely spaced that they'd made her jump.

Mattie had spent most of the morning staggering back and forth across the cottage trying to get the door open and see.

No, life would settle back into its winter rut, was settling there, like a stone into mud, as if Kineton had never been a part of this mysterious war; the harvest was long in, the sheep settled in their winter cotes, the fields ploughed over ready for the spring. Those thousands of men drawn up in the fields these last two days had made no more lasting impact on the long rearing flank of the hill than a fly buzzing around the flank of an ox. It was over. It was done, and Sarah, and she suspected, most of the village, little the wiser as to the part they'd played in it.

The tiny domestic pleasure of making bread had eased her restlessness that morning, allowing her to beat the bread into submission till her arms ached and the dough was soft as a lady's hands. She hadn't thought she could bring herself to take the dough to the baker, to slide into his big oven with the rest of the village's baking – even assuming that normal life had been so far resumed that there was a baking, today. She'd set her bread to rise in the hearth ashes, the old-fashioned way, to bake under a pot when it was risen. Her shutters were still tight-barred, slats of the sunlight falling across Mattie's dark head where he played on the floor by the settle, rolling a piece of firewood back and forth pretending it was one of his beloved soldier's horses.

That first night had been terrifying, when the soldiers had come and Sarah and all the others had been forced to quarter them - and she couldn't face that, she couldn't bring herself to smile at strangers occupying her home and make civil conversation with them, and so she'd fled up the village to Hester Whyte's house, taking Mattie with her. Imagining drawling fine gentlemen or lawless rebels, as gossip dictated, in occupation - and all the time it had been Luce. And she hadn't known, till last night, and he'd been so sweet and so apologetic and so nervous about it, poor boy. She was glad, fiercely glad, he was safe. She'd been *shamelessly* glad to see him.

"Out you come, young man," she said firmly to Mattie, wrapping him in layer on layer of wool till the little boy in his warm skirted gowns looked like an onion. "Let's me and you go and get some air before it gets too dark." And some food, she thought, something more festive than bean soup. It wasn't as if there wasn't food to be had: not in her little household, though she feared that not all of the village had fared so well under their unwelcome guests. Even her little square of vegetable plot had been ransacked, although not devastated; a mercy that kale was near-indestructible, and a trail of booted footprints across her plants had left the leaves bruised but not ruined. A row of gaping holes in the frozen earth showed where her straight young leeks had been.

Kale, then. And herbs. Bread, and beans, and onions, and cheese, and ale. She had apples, plenty of apples, and honey in the pot, and eggs a-plenty; she considered, briefly, whether it would be best to wring the neck of one of her hens and feast for a day or two. The Hadfield household was, by Kineton standards, a relatively comfortable one. Matthew had left her bodily wants provided for, and her needs were small; there were a few sheep left, enough to make her marriageable, she thought wryly. Even though soon, probably before the end of the year, she'd need to knuckle down and find herself a man - even if only to market the sheep next spring.

Sheep. Of course. Up the chimney, safe from prying eyes, was a leg of mutton ham, well-smoked over the last months. One of the worst things about being a widow of some independence was that every wastrel in the village seemed to think you were an easy mark and tried to batten on you like a leech. It would have become their Christian duty to call on her daily if it'd been known she had a goodly supply of meat in her chimney. Mattie was stumping across the kale now, with a somewhat disenchanted slug dangling from his fat fingers. "Mama, icky! See!"

"Lovely," she said, dumping the offending object back on the frozen ground and giving it a hearty stamp. "Home we go, jiggety-jig." Holding her apron up in one hand, full of battered kale and earthy roots, and Mattie's cold, wriggly fingers in the other, she set off back home.

The cottage was warm, and as she set the dough in the ashes to bake and the water on to boil for the mutton stew, her thoughts strayed back to the fair-haired officer. Not, necessarily, comfortable thoughts. She'd have almost preferred him to be ill-favoured. The prospect of idle gossip linking her name with that of well-born, well-mannered, decent, not-quite-handsome young officers was not as disturbing as it should have been, for a respectable and godly matron. Knowing her luck, the neighbours would accuse her of setting her cap at the redhead. He was, after all, likely more her age. Well, there was nothing so ridiculous as idle gossip. It was very sweet the way the fair-haired boy's eyes went wide and dark when he looked at her - the way he blushed and looked away when she glanced at him, obvious as a baby, bless him - very flattering that the boy desired her, at her age. And that, Mistress Hadfield, is as far as it goes, she told herself sternly. Flattery. Certainly no more thoughtless passionate greetings on doorsteps - no longing thoughts, no stolen glances, none of that. Lucifer Pettitt is a nice boy, and that is *all* he is.

"Ba," Mattie said firmly, poking a less than spotless finger into the mound of kale. "Mattie *like*."

She handed him a scrap of cheese rind, which he gnawed with every sign of relish. "You like everything, young man," she said, putting her hand on his soft hair.

And then there was little to do, for once, until the stew was ready, but sit with her mending and listen for hoofbeats in the lane. Like the greenest of shy virgins, at her age. The stew already smelt thick and rich, when she took the lid off to check on it, simmering gently in the kettle over the embers, stiff with rings of glistening onion and rags of mutton.

"*Horsie!*" Mattie said urgently, and she smiled at him absently, hearing nothing over the shush of the fire and the bubble of the good stew.

"Lots of horsie, sweeting. All gone, see?"

He shook his head mutinously. "No - horsie *now*." And stumped to the door on his chubby little legs, heaving it open. "*Back* horsie!"

"Black horsie," the big redhead agreed from her threshold, clinging one-handed to the black horse's mane in the gathering dusk. "Want to put him up, Lucey?"

"I do not," Luce said frostily behind him. "I'd like the child to retain the use of his limbs."

"*One* of us ought to, that's for sure."

Sarah wasn't sure she ought to laugh at the redhead, and she wasn't *entirely* sure he meant her to. She stood in the doorway and folded her arms, barricading Mattie in the cottage with her skirts. "It's a kind offer, I'm sure, sir, but it's bitter cold and my door is open and you're in the middle of the road for the whole world and his wife to gape at. So please - could you get down and come indoors?"

"If I could, lass, I would, believe me. Unfortunately without the aid of my lovely assistant -" he trailed off. Shook his hair out of his eyes abruptly. "Being, as you see, a pitiful cripple."

"And a bitter one, by the sound of it." Luce dismounted. "Here's my shoulder, and go gently."

She could see chinks of light over the lane appearing

as doors were cracked open, the better to overhear what scandal might be gleaned. "Please, sir, as much haste as you can -"

"I'll turn the horses loose in the sheep cote," Luce said. Something else she was beginning to find appealing about the fair-haired lad was that he never argued, never complained, he just got on with it, in as good-humoured a way as you could imagine. "In you go, sir."

Mattie wailed, behind her. "Want to go horsie!"

"Determined little bugger, isn't he?" the redhead said. "Fine, child. If your mother agrees Luce will take you for a ride on his horse. *Tomorrow*."

"*Back* horsie," Mattie said stubbornly.

Luce turned round, hearing that from ten yards away, and gave the redhead a stern look. "Don't you even *think* about it, Captain Babbitt."

"Don't pester the captain," Sarah said quickly. "Be grateful for what you have." And stood aside to let him pass.

Mattie had evidently taken to the redhead. He stood in front of the captain, fingers in his mouth, eyeing him critically. "Dirty?" he said, after completing his inspection.

"Can't disagree with you, child."

"Mattie," she said warningly. "Be quiet."

"The boy's fine. I'm used to dealing with small children. Half my troop are barely breeched. Anyway, I *am* filthy. Spent most of the morning helping some of the lads dig a hole. Bloody great big one, it was." He looked at her blankly, and then shook his head, frowning. "Saving your pardon, mistress. Forgot the company."

"I have hot water, sir, should you care to wash," she said warily, not quite sure what he might come out with next.

"Oh, Christ, call me Hollie - sorry. Done it again. Just Hollie. I'm in charge of nowt, not any more." He laughed, and Luce was right, he *was* bitter, bitter as wormwood. "Worthless and worn-out."

"I have no idea, sir, of your personal shortcomings. But there *is* hot water."

"Mistress, I'm not sure I can be ar- bothered. And I'm not sure I'd waste the water, were I you."

She looked at him, bruised black and stiff with clotted mud and old blood. "Well, sir, since you're clearly a man who values plain words - you're a mess. So if it's a choice between having you in my clean bed like that, or cleaned up - I don't care if I do it or if Luce does it, but cleaned up you will be."

And Sarah doubted that many people spoke to the captain like that. He looked at her, frowning, as if he wasn't quite sure what he was hearing, then raised an eyebrow. "I see," he said mildly.

Luce reappeared, pink-cheeked with the cold and carrying both his and Hollie's snapsacks. The redhead turned his head, wincing as she dabbed with a wet rag at his bruised temple. "You're back, brat. Thought you'd got lost."

"Lost? No. Gathering some wood for Sarah - ah, for Mistress Hadfield's fire whilst I was out."

"Virtue is its own reward," Hollie muttered sarcastically. Luce didn't say a word, he simply dropped his bundle of firewood in the hearth and smiled at her as if only the two of them existed.

"Thank you, Luce. That was a kind thought." She held her hand out, quite deliberately, and took the fair-haired officer's chilly fingers in her own. "'Tis a cold night, to be scratching about in the hedges. Will you sit down to your meat now, sir?"

The mutton stew was good. Sarah tried not to catch Luce's eye and neither of them dared to look at Hollie, chasing his stew round the bowl left-handed with grim determination, with Mattie watching round-eyed in amazement, clearly wondering why a grown man with such deplorable table manners wasn't getting the rap across the knuckles that a small boy would have received. Eventually Luce took pity on the captain and untied his sling so that he could brace the bowl with his splinted wrist. It wasn't a tidy operation, but at least he was fed. Luce thanked her prettily, and evidently gave the redhead a hearty nudge under the table, for he shied upright like a startled horse before muttering his thanks.

Sarah cleared the table, hiding a smile at the sight of Mattie and the big redhead side by side, both blinking owlishly at her, Mattie leaning against the captain's side drowsily. "*Someone*," she said meaningfully, "is needing their bed." More than one someone, at that. The little boy was past his bedtime anyway. Luce gave her a quick, shy glance, and she caught her breath. There was a promise in that look.

39 COVER HER FACE. MINE EYES DAZZLE

Whether it was the warmth, or being full-fed for the first time in God knows how long, or the humiliatingly tiny amount of the widow's ale he'd had – or whether it was just that Hollie wasn't as indestructible as he'd once thought he was – he was so tired he felt drunk. Not in a necessarily pleasant way, although the muzzy-headedness stood comfortably between him and any number of things he preferred not to think about. The little lad was warm against him, and that was unexpectedly comforting. Even his wrist was only a dull throb.

He closed his eyes. Only for a second, the widow had no call to poke him in the shoulder – the good one, mercifully – so forcefully, he wasn't asleep. Quite. He still hadn't got used to seeing the brat where Rackhay had been, looking at him across the table with the firelight on his yellow hair. Wouldn't *ever* get used to the brat in command, looking down his nose and giving orders like he owned the place.

Well, Hollie had given up, hadn't he? Had said as much to the widow – in charge of nowt. Didn't want it, wasn't going to have it. If the brat wanted to take over a troop half full of blank-faced strangers and half full of every reprobate and dissenter the Army didn't want, then it was all his. Someone had to be stupid enough to do it. Oh, but they paid well. Ha. That was the argument every bloody tavern bravo threw at him, when they wanted to pick a fight - as if what you got paid made up for being treated like the cheapest whore in Southwark.

Oh, Christ, they could have paid him all the gold of the Indies and it wouldn't make sod-all difference to him now, because Hollie had nothing: nothing and no one, and even the lowliest bloody worm had a hole to slither back into to lick its hurts, and he didn't even have that. Even this sharp-tongued piece hadn't looked at him twice, and he'd have thought she'd be glad to take what she could get. Not that he'd have looked back. He wasn't that hard up.

He *was* that hard up. It had been nearly ten years of miserable loneliness since Griete had died - ten years of being lost and adrift and, oh, hell, Babbitt, you're a man like other men, it's not only your heart that aches of a night -. He stifled a wild giggle. Aye, well, even *that* release was presently denied him, with his right hand strapped rigid.

It's a battle, Red, men get killed. He remembered Nat saying that to him, a very long time ago. It shouldn't have been Nat, with his lovely lady at home putting these tiny stitches into the lovely silk sash she'd made for her lovely husband. They'd made a right bloody mess of it, as well, between them, what with Nat bleeding his life out on it and Hollie tying it in knots. No, it should have been Hollie on the left flank, getting hacked to bits by Rupert's cavalry, and he hadn't even been able to get that right. If he hadn't pissed Essex off, he'd have stayed at Nat's side, and Nat wouldn't be dead. Simple as that.

And he was so bloody tired, and if the brat thought he couldn't see the pair of them holding hands under the table he was dafter than Hollie took him for. Done it himself, half a lifetime ago, and wouldn't that thought make the brat stare? Had it really been that long ago, that he'd sat opposite Nat and one of his friend's casual girls, in the warm spot beside the chimney breast in the 'Cat, with Griete's knee pressed against his under the table and her warm, capable hand held still, for once, in his? It was just tiredness that made his vision blur, that was all. Not tears. He hadn't cried then, and he wouldn't now.

Someone touched him and it felt like part of the dream, and he was taken quite aback to see the widow sat there. "Luce, would you put some water on to boil," she said over her shoulder. "I'll make tea. Do you know how chamomile looks?"

"Got it," the brat called cheerfully. Got his feet well under the table already, hadn't he?

"Don't trouble yourself." Went to push his hair out of his eyes – caught his breath, wincing. Changed hands. Tried again, because he would not be betrayed by his own contemptible weakness -

"Then I'll see to the bed, then," she said, and turned away quickly, as if she couldn't stand his company. Which made two of them.

"I'll help," Luce offered.

"I bet you will," Hollie muttered, just loudly enough to be audible.

Truthfully, he was glad to be left alone with the silence, all but the crackle of the flames and the child snoring softly against him – he peered anxiously down at the little lad's head, wondering what the hell he'd do if the damned infant woke up and started squalling, given his total inexperience with small human beings even without his current infirmity.

Then stifled giggling from the far end of the cottage, and he was trying not to listen. He'd been a giggler himself, once. Ticklish. It was something Griete had used to do if she thought he was looking too grim – she'd poke him in the ribs in passing and he'd used to collapse like an undermined wall. Nobody left alive who knew that, now. All gone. It was an odd feeling, to think he was all that was left.

His wrist was starting to ache now, a dull grinding

ache, not unbearable, just the sort of pain that kept you awake at nights. Move his fingers, and it sharpened to a stab. Keep his fingers still, and his arm tingled as if he'd lain in a nettle bed. What had the camp surgeon said, six weeks? He'd go stark staring mad with six weeks unable to use his right hand. He was useless. Couldn't even bloody well manage to get himself killed properly. They wouldn't hear if he whimpered in the night, or if they did, they wouldn't care. They wouldn't pay him any mind, the two of them, rolled in their blankets and each other.

It wasn't the coupling Hollie missed, since he'd lost her. It was the having someone in the dark to turn to – someone's warm shoulder to lie your head against, to whisper your secrets to. Someone who cared if you were hurt or unhappy and didn't look to turn it like a weapon against you. Someone to call you her big daft lad, her *lieveke*, her little sweet one. He'd talked to her, in his head, every night since she died. It was only of late she'd stopped talking back, and he wondered if that was because he was forgetting her or because she was going away from him. And what would become of him when she was wholly gone.

There was a rustling outside against the shutters and he couldn't decide if it was rain or dead leaves and he wanted it not to be rain because somehow of all the things he couldn't bear the one that hurt him the most was the idea of Nat lying in the dark with the rain falling on his face. Hollie slipped his splinted arm out of its sling and very deliberately leaned his full weight on it. If he was going to cry he was going to make damn' sure he had something to cry about.

40 PULL DOWN HEAVEN UPON ME

Sarah set the big pottery jug in the ashes to steep. Meadowsweet for a fever, chamomile to soothe, honey for sweetness.

Well, she'd told Luce she was expecting trouble from the redhead and he hadn't disappointed her. That first night he'd barely spoken two words to her before putting his head down on the table and falling asleep. Which she hadn't grudged him, rest being the best medicine that she knew of. Mattie had snuggled up to him and the pair of them had been dead to the world before the supper dishes were cold.

She'd thought, that first night after the battle, that the big redhead was jealous, and now she didn't think he was. Despite what Luce said, she didn't think he was mad, either. So hurt - in his head, if not his body - that he'd withdrawn into himself like a snail into its shell. Crazy with fever betimes, but not mad. He'd frightened the wits out of her more than once, unexpectedly sitting up to have what sounded like perfectly commonplace conversations with people who weren't there. Sarah thought, by the one side of the conversation she could hear, that she didn't mind sharing her cottage with the invisible Margaret, who sounded like a lady of good sense and tolerance.

Lucifer, though. Awake, Luce was thoughtful and gentle and courteous. Asleep, he cried like a babe in arms and fought his battles over and over again in dreams. He'd come awake with a stifled gasp, his hair matted to his forehead with sweat, blinking the dreams out of his eyes. And she'd put her arms round him, because how could she leave him uncomforted, and he'd put his head on her shoulder and drifted back into a restless sleep, twitching and muttering. Over and over again, throughout the night. By dawn she was gritty-eyed and irritable with weariness, and Luce had worn himself out and was sleeping the limp, motionless sleep of exhaustion. Then he'd put his arm across her in his sleep and she'd cuddled close to him because he was warm and solid and she was chilled and weary. And then he'd woken up. And he'd been innocent, and she wasn't sorry he wasn't now.

She felt almost guilty, watching him sleep: tousled and peaceful for once, those level dark brows relaxed in what must be the first restful dreams he'd had in a week and more. He was lovely, and sweet, and funny, and kind, and gentle, and he had a way of looking up at her under his lashes that set all her skin to tingling, but - that was all it was. He was a dear boy, and she was twice his age, and she was a widow who'd never left Warwickshire and he was a gentleman's son. And that would have been fine, if it had been her heart that had been set to tingling. And it wasn't.

She pulled the blankets up over his bare shoulders, her hand lingering over his warm skin. She could have stayed and watched him sleep for hours. It wouldn't get breakfast made, though, nor tend the redhead. She stood for a few seconds breathing in the clean scent of meadowsweet, clearing her head.

And then a hand closed around her ankle, and she jumped back to wakefulness as Luce stroked her instep with a look of astonished delight on his face.

"And good morning to you, too, young man," she said briskly. She was wearing her shift, and nothing else. Which said something about something, even though it was a perfectly clean and very respectable garment. "Would you care for breakfast?"

He propped himself on his elbows and smiled up at her. "A fair sight, for this early hour, if I may say so."

She couldn't help smiling back, though she suspected she probably ought not to encourage him. "You may say so as often as you like, Lucifer."

He gave a contented sigh, and his eyes rested on her face with evident satisfaction. "Mistress Hadfield, I love you," he said calmly. She almost dropped the poker into the big earthenware jug, which would have done neither the jug nor the tea any good at all.

"*Me?*" Which was all she could think of to say.

"You. My dear Vesta, my goddess of the hearth – the sweetest of meadowsweet –"

She knelt down beside the pallet of sheepskins where they'd spent the night, and kissed him briefly. "Pretty words, my lad, but they won't get breakfast made."

"I am yours to command, my lady. Direct me." He stood up – well, he wasn't perfectly respectable or perfectly decent, and her eyes widened slightly as she realised how not decent he was.

"Lucifer," she said sternly, with a twinkle in her eye that belied the severity of her tone. "Get dressed, young man."

"I don't believe you mean that, mistress."

"No," she said with a sigh, and pulled her shift over her head quite brazenly. "I don't."

41 A MAN'S HEART DEVISETH HIS WAY

He shrugged his shirt on, buttoned his breeches and left it at that. The floorboards were warm under his bare feet. Her little wrist was warm under his hand. "Is there nothing I can do to help?"

Her gaze came up sharply. She had lines in the soft flesh round her tender mouth, and he hadn't noticed them. Older than he'd thought at first glance, as if it mattered. (First glance had stopped somewhat short of her face, Luce, and well you know it.) Pale eyes, almost colourless in the milky early morning light, under fine dark brows. She looked at him thoughtfully for a few seconds and he thought his heart might stop beating. Then the corner of her mouth curled up. "I have been better, Lucifer, I'll say that. But thank you for asking."

"You have only to tell me, and I'll do it."

She put her hand up and rested it on his cheek. "You're a good lad. I know you would. Too soft for your own good at times, you are. But no, love, there's nothing you can do. It's just frightening at times, being on your own, out here."

Her hand slipped down to rest on his shoulder and he moved closer to her, not to press home any advantage but because there were tears glinting on her lashes and she looked as lost as an abandoned child. "I'll - I could take care of you," he suggested.

She glanced up at him sideways and sighed. With pleasure, not in resignation. *He* hadn't done anything wrong, then. The top of her head just tucked nicely under his chin. She smelt of sunshine and sweet herbs.

She laid her cheek against his shoulder. "I wish *somebody* would."

And he put his arms round her - slightly awkwardly, because she was probably the first woman he'd laid a hand on who wasn't related to him, and he wasn't altogether sure how she'd take to it in daylight - running his flat hand up and down her back as if he was soothing a fractious horse. He could feel the bones of her shoulders, like wings. He wondered what she'd do if he put his hand under her chin and tilted her face up to be kissed. Whether she'd let him. She sighed, and leaned her weight against him, what there was of it, poor fragile little maid.

Then she stepped back, neatly disengaging herself, and he thought how easily he could get used to this. "No," she said firmly, and he wondered if she'd read his mind. She frowned over his shoulder and he sagged with relief. The little boy had finally extricated himself from Babbitt, which was a blessing. He was tottering towards the fire with a scowl. "Come away from there, young man. Sit up at table."

Luce hoisted the little boy into his arms, smiling at the warm weight of him. The warm and slightly soggy weight of him. Not so fragrant, either. "I wouldn't," Sarah said. "Not till I've changed his clout. Not lovely in the morning, are we, caterpillar?"

She stepped quickly into her skirt and shrugged on her bodice, lacing herself in with an ease of long practice that Luce rather envied. He pulled her hair from under the back of the bodice, marvelling at the soft, fine weight of it in his hands. Last night he'd never been unchaperoned with a woman and today he was helping to dress the one that he'd helped to *undress* last night. Quickly, he dropped a swift kiss on her shoulder. Clumsy: he knew it, and didn't care.

But the captain never appeared at the table. Luce

spooned in his last mouthful of frumenty –blander than that he was used to at home, but it was hot and filling and he was just going to have to grow accustomed to it unspiced – and looked up at Sarah.

"What do you want me to do today?"

"Mattie and I will go out," she said, "into the village and see if there's any that need help."

"*I* might need your help, my lady – you behold a man sick of love -"

She raised an eyebrow at him fondly. "I don't think you're like to die of it, Luce, in a couple of hours. And looking innocent isn't fooling anybody." She ruffled his hair. "I want to make sure there are no others in your case and worse in Kineton. We're comfortable enough. Not everyone is so fortunate."

Luce looked down, shifting uncomfortably. She suspected he'd imagined the bunches of herbs drying from her ceiling were there for cooking, or flower arranging – depending on quite how elegant his household actually was. Bless the boy. "Is there not *anything* I can do to help, Sarah?" he muttered, sounding chastened.

"You can stay here, and look after your – " she didn't know quite how to refer to the captain – "He's quiet, and like to stay that way for a while. Try and get him to drink the tea, if he wakes up. It won't do you any harm if you're tempted, either. There's bread and cheese if you get hungry – what you two have left of the frumenty –" she smiled down at Mattie tenderly – "and if you get bored you can always chop some wood. Is there anything you need?"

He shook his head. "I'll be fine. Just don't be away too long." And then a slantwise smile, like the sun coming out. "I'm not sure my poor heart could stand a lengthy separation, mistress."

42 THE HEART KNOWETH HIS OWN BITTERNESS

Luce chopped wood till his arms ached – which, given his limited experience of the activity, was probably not as long as it should have been for a young man of his age and condition. Then he glowered at the pitiful pile of chippings, set his teeth, and chopped some more.

There must be something he could do for her. It was – unjust – unreasonable – cruel – that Fate should have served the lovely widow so, left her alone and unprotected. Life had been harsh to Sarah Hadfield and if the Lord had seen fit to send him to take care of her then that was how it would be, and if the world didn't like it they could – they could – he gave the last log in the pile a resounding wallop and it split with a satisfying crack. Then he pulled his sleeve down and wiped his sweaty forehead with it.

"Where are you?"

He jumped at the sound of Babbitt's voice behind him. "I'm here, captain. Right here, getting some wood for the fire."

"Don't you go off and leave me."

"I'll not be going anywhere, sir. I'm staying put, as commanded."

Luce turned round, bracing himself for the expected malicious comment. Instead the big redhead was looking at him enquiringly, eyes fixed on Luce's face. "Have I said summat to upset thee, lad?"

Luce paused in his stacking of the wood, somewhat lost for a reply. He'd been in the company of Hollie Babbitt for less than a month, and he still hadn't got the measure of the wretched man, and he wasn't sure he ever would. The redhead was lying propped up on his good elbow, looking at Luce with an expression that was both quizzical and slightly hurt. "Not - no more so than usual, sir," Luce said warily, and Hollie laughed in acknowledgement.

"Aye. I'll give you that one."

Luce turned his back and carried on stacking logs. Harder work than he'd suspected, actually. The things had a bad habit of rolling out of his neat pile - they weren't anything like an even shape, and getting them to lie flat was the devil, and the splinters kept snagging his hands, which stung. "Can I help you at all, sir?" he snapped, nettled by the feel of Hollie's eyes on his back. Contemptuous, or at least mocking.

"Oh Christ, I doubt it." The redhead lay flat again with a thump, one arm across his eyes.

And he sounded so bleak that once again Luce's soft heart was touched in spite of everything the wretched man had said and done to him - "At least let me make you a bit more comfortable, sir."

"Hollie," he muttered, muffled by half a yard of tangled red-brown hair. "I'm not your fucking commander, brat. I'm not *anything* any more -"

"Hollie, then. And yes, you are. You were appointed as such by the Commander-in-Chief of the Army and you will remain so -"

"Oh Lucifer will you *fuck off* - and take the Earl of fucking Essex with you - " He struggled upright again, and glared at Luce furiously. "Christ, but you are a sanctimonious little prick at times -"

"No doubt! And you - *sir* - were given a command to hold, which by God's grace you retain -"

Unexpectedly, the redhead laughed. "Oh aye, and I'll do a fine job of it. Do I *look* any use?"

"Well, you've looked better." Carefully, Luce freed the captain's blood-stiff hair from under the stained silk sash. "If you don't mind me saying so, sir - Hollie - you've probably been more fragrant. Sir."

"Are you saying I stink, you whelp?"

"Um. Yes. Like a shambles on a hot day, I'm afraid. I really do think you'd feel better if you were to let Mistress Hadfield tidy you up a bit, you know. *I* always feel better when I've had a wash and a shave -"

"*You* bloody would. Leave me alone." He turned his head abruptly on the pillow, the ends of his ragged hair scraping across Sarah Hadfield's clean linen with a sound like tearing silk. His eyes were closed, but Luce didn't think he was trying to sleep.

"No," Luce said. "I will not."

"I don't *want* you!"

"Probably not, sir. Hollie. But I'm what you've got." Luce leaned over and pulled the blankets up, giving his shoulder an awkward pat. "I might lack military experience, but I do have some facility with fractious invalids. I have two sisters, remember."

It had been intended as mildly humorous – clumsily done, he knew, but not meant to wound.

"And presumably I am to be admitted to your happy little family, am I?" Nothing could have prepared Luce for that look of utter loathing. "Stick it up your arse, boy. I don't want your pity, I don't need your charity, and I don't want your fucking company."

"Sir," Luce said stiffly. "I will burden you no further with my unwelcome presence."

He stalked out and was about to apply himself to the rest of the log-pile, narrowing his eyes at one obstinate branch. Was just limbering his shoulders ready to take out his irritation at that ungrateful, disreputable liability taking up Sarah's clean bed-

"Oh Christ I'm sorry."

"What?"

"I'm *sorry*. Just - leave it, all right?"

"Sir."

"*Hollie.*" There was a deep, shaky breath from the bed. "Not Red. Just Hollie. Please."

"I should not presume. *Sir.*"

"*Hollie!*" Covering his eyes with his hand again – "There's no other bugger living to whom I'm any more than *Captain Babbitt*."

"Luce, sweeting, I think – I think the captain is tiring, love. I think that's enough –"

He hadn't heard Sarah come in. She left the door ajar, the clean, pale sunlight glowing in a wedge across her clean-swept floors, and smiled up at him. Mattie, trailing after her in a spatter of mud, braced himself with his fat little hands spread on Luce's knees. "Horsie?" he said hopefully, and Sarah diverted Luce's kiss onto her cheek. "That's a good idea. Would you mind, Luce? While I straighten up –"

"The captain is *very* tiring," Luce breathed, very close to her ear, and her expression never changed, though her eyes danced with humour.

"I do believe it's time for your physic, sir. Mattie, love, can you fetch the honey –" the little boy beamed with delight and staggered off to fetch the precious jar – "and there's no need to pull that face, captain, it's good for you, and you *will* drink it. To the last drop. And *then* you can have honey."

"You're enjoying this," Luce said, and she gave him a sly sidelong smile.

"Oh, absolutely, young man. Now out you go, and take Mattie with you." Mattie squawked in protest, fingers tightening around the spoon. "Honey after chores, caterpillar! Out!"

43 THE RIDER ON THE RED HORSE

Luce, hand in sticky hand with the purposeful Matthew, and the pair of them stamping on the cat-ice in the ruts in the lane for the joy of it. He was very aware of eyes on his back, of the wary glances of the few passers in the lane. He wasn't sure he minded. They'd get used to him, when he came back after the war – it would all be over by Christmas, surely, and he could get on with the business of loving Sarah.

There was a cart, a heavily laden cart, slowly creaking up the lane, and he pulled Mattie out of the way of the two great beasts that hauled it. "What news?" he called civilly to the carter, an amiable-looking gentleman as massive and stolid as his oxen.

"News, sir? And who might be asking – and you with Sarah Hadfield's boy? She know you're out, Mattie?"

"Go horsie," Mattie said, freeing his fingers from Luce's to point into the field. The mare pricked her ears and Tyburn, grazing alongside her, lifted his head and rumbled an unexpectedly civil greeting.

"I see." The carter's eyes were surprisingly sharp on Luce's face. "Don't seem to have taken much hurt, sir. From the fight."

"They've had a few days' rest," Luce admitted. He hardly dared to ask which way the man's loyalties lay. Which was funny, because he had the oddest feeling the man didn't like to ask which way *his* loyalties lay, either. A world turned upside down, where a gentleman and a carter could stand in a lane exchanging coded pleasantries. "I hope to catch up with my – uh – duties, soon."

"Ah? Wouldn't be in too much of a haste, sir. Been

fierce over Pillerton way, where I come from. They say there was a cobbler paunched like a rabbit, and all over daring to ask what all the fuss was. Soldiers attacking a wagon, I hear."

"Indeed. For –" he gulped, "for whose cause, do you know?"

"Me?" Those sharp eyes rested on his face. "I do hardly know. Now, sir, who's to say which side has the right of it? Not for the likes of me to know. 'Tis all the Lord's will, no doubt."

"With the Lord having no better use for men's bodies than to see them broken in the name of vanity," Luce said sharply, without thinking.

"Looking pretty well on it yourself, sir, if I may say so." He clicked his tongue to the oxen. "Up you come, boys. You tell Mistress Hadfield Tom Wayton sends his remembrances, sir, and if she needs anything just to shout up next time I'm by this way. Give you good day, sir." And he gave Luce a polite nod, and the cart lumbered off.

He unlatched the gate, and the two horses started to walk towards him – Tyburn in the lead, head up and ears pricked, mane bannering out in the chilly wind. Snuffing Luce's hands and coat politely enough, but distantly, as if the big stallion was waiting for his own master, and renewing Luce's acquaintance out of civility. Mattie tore up handfuls of the frost-blasted grass and held them up to the black's muzzle, and the big horse snuffed politely and then turned his head, limping away. Luce called him back, running a hand down the long, swollen gash on the horse's shoulder. Healing nicely. He wouldn't have fancied the task of telling Babbitt his demon familiar was permanently lamed, though he suspected the wound would scar. Then, the big horse was scarred enough already – old, white scars round his mouth, as though he'd been ridden in a cruel bit: newer raised battle-scars on his chest and shoulders.

Tyburn flung his head up again, snorting. Luce smiled to himself, remembering his first impressions of the black horse – the incomparable black pearl, he'd thought at the time. Well, either the horse had mellowed under fire, or the stallion preferred human to equine company. Hadn't occurred to him that a horse as cantankerous as Tyburn might get lonely – or, indeed, that the big horse might enjoy the company of a handful of sheep and the undivided attentions of the red mare. Rosa was *distinctly* giving the black melting looks over her shoulder.

That said, Rosa was giving *Mattie* melting looks. "Madam, you are a shameless flirt," he said sternly to his mare, and she came and buried her head in the breast of his coat while he pulled her ears through his fingers. Her winter coat was coming thick and cinnamon and shaggy. She needed grooming, badly. She politely submitted to his disentangling her mane with his fingers, while Mattie patted her chest and shoulders, and she bent her head and licked his honey-sticky fingers with every sign of appreciation. Tyburn gave her a hard stare, and then barged her rudely aside to sniff the boy's hands.

"No more sweetie?" Mattie said forlornly. "Horsie not have sweetie?"

"I imagine you are lucky to have all your fingers intact, young man." And made a mental note to supply the big black with sweetie, next time he visited the horses.

"Me go ride," Mattie said firmly, and wound his hands in the black's trailing mane. Tyburn threw his head up, ears back, and Luce grabbed the little boy just before the stallion laid him flat. "Not on him, you don't," he said, "you'll fall off and break your neck, and your mother will kill me."

Rosa wasn't at all sure about having the wriggly

little bundle placed on her back, but she was as willing and courteous as ever and she stepped out smartly when Luce held her forelock and trotted her up and down the field, scattering sheep.

"There. You. Go," he stopped at the gate, panting, and the mare gave him an affectionate nudge with her nose, wanting more. "Hey, missy. You've got four legs, I've only got two. Give me a rest, hey?"

"Again," the young emperor demanded.

"Let me catch my breath, child! What d'you think I am?"

"Go *fast*," Mattie said ominously, and Luce gave the boy what he hoped was a stern look. "Over my dead body."

Which seemed to make sense to the boy, who let go of the mare's mane and deliberately slid off. Luce caught him just in time – it was a miracle all mothers didn't take to drink, if small children were all this hell-bent on self-destruction – and then tried to grasp the squirming little body.

"Back horsie now!" Mattie demanded gleefully, pointing with the hand that wasn't belabouring Luce about the head, and Luce and Tyburn exchanged a look of mutual resignation ending with the big horse standing, braced to receive his wriggling burden. Deeply unhappy about the proceedings, but warily willing to trust that Luce knew what he was doing.

A lesson his master might do well to emulate, Luce thought wryly.

44 A SILLY LAD, BETIMES

"You and I," Sarah said sternly, "are going to have a little talk, young man."

Hollie closed his eyes and turned his face to the wall. She'd go away. They all did, in the end -

"You've given up, haven't you?"

Oh yes, he'd given up. Didn't reckon he had anything else left for the Lord to take off him. He said nothing, but lay resolutely still, concentrating on the rhythmic throb of his wrist in time with his heartbeat. Wondering if it'd be worse to will it to stop, or -

"Well, if you're planning to lie there and starve yourself to death, sir, you can do it under someone else's roof. You might be fooling Lucifer with what a poor sick creature you are, but you're not fooling *me*. I nursed my man through his last fever in that bed and you, young man, have *not* got a fever. You've been in your right mind this day and more, and don't you try and have me on that you haven't. There's nothing ailing you but stubbornness and pride." He felt her shift on the edge of the mattress, and caught his breath as it jarred his tender wrist. "All right, you're a *bit* hurt," she added. "Bones heal, don't they? Well then."

He turned his head back and gave her a look of utter loathing.

"Let me guess, I don't understand? Saw my man burn up to nothing in that bed and I couldn't do a thing to relieve a minute of his suffering - but no, I don't understand? But *you* can't stand to lose a stupid battle, so you'd rather not play any more - right?"

He stubbornly said nothing. Wrong. But if that was what she wanted to think, the hell with her. "What a daft thing to want to die over," she said conversationally. "As if it's going to make any difference to the likes of me or you who's sat in London. It could be the Archangel Gabriel and I wouldn't care, so long as I've got food on the table and clothes on my back."

"Neither would I," he said wearily, and then remembered too late he wasn't speaking to her.

"That's better," she said. "Now I know you have got a tongue in your head, when you're in your right wits. Now. You'll drink your tea up, young man, and then we'll have that talk." And she put her head on one side like a little wren, and narrowed her eyes. "*And* you'll drink it sitting up like a Christian."

It was nasty stuff - angelica, she said, for sweetness, since he evidently possessed precious little of his own, and bitter all-heal - and she sat and watched him critically till he'd finished the last drop, and then she gave him a great spoon of honey just as if he'd been a fractious babe. "Well, you're acting like one," she said, when he expressed that thought aloud. "You mope worse than Mattie, and he's not yet three. Are you hungry?"

"No," he said - sulkily - and his belly growled to give the lie to it, and she raised her eyebrows.

"Surely. Not hungry enough to have a bite of bread and cheese to keep you going till your Luce comes back? This morning's baking," she said innocently, and he admitted defeat. "But you'll not sit at my table till you've changed your linen, sir. And put a comb through your hair."

She scolded like a magpie, he thought, not actually listening while she tended to his somewhat sketchy toilet. She and the brat would mar another couple, she hectoring him on his personal shortcomings and the brat giving him hell about his dereliction of duty -

"Ow!"

She stopped with her comb stuck in a particularly

recalcitrant tangle. Stopped, tugged, tugged again, and then took a knife and simply sawed the knot out. "You have no vanity, sir," she said sweetly, "so you won't mind resembling a scarecrow when I'm done."

"According to bloody Rackhay, I already do," he grumbled. "He always says -"

"Well - says what?" she said after a long silence, holding his ponytail in her hand to drag out the rest of the tangles, and Hollie turned his head as far as he could to look back at her.

"He says nothing, lass. Not any more. He died in the battle. It's not important."

She ruffled his hair loose on his shoulders with her fingers. In spite of everything - in spite of the fact that he'd seen more meat on a butcher's pencil, she had no tits and no hips to speak of, and she was bedding bloody wet Lucey Pettitt - a shivery tickle went down his back, and he clasped his hands together quickly so she wouldn't know they were shaking. It had been that long since he'd had a girl, then. "Then I'm sorry for it," she said briskly. "A good friend, I take it?"

"Sometimes," Hollie said honestly. "But he was all I had."

He glanced over his shoulder again, expecting to see pity or contempt on her face. Instead, she was looking at him with mild amusement, and he didn't know how to take to that. She put her hand on his shoulder, and squeezed it, not unkindly. "Oh, you are a silly lad, betimes."

45 AN ALARMING DEGREE OF HONESTY

Luce almost dropped his firewood when he returned at dusk with Mattie to find Hollie up, scrubbed shiny, shaved so recently he was still bleeding, and with his wet hair confined in a neat ponytail at the nape of his neck. "Good Lord," Luce said, and Hollie looked at him and didn't quite smile.

"Aye. Well."

"He decided to rejoin the land of the living," Sarah said, setting her hand on his shoulder, and Luce felt a brief stab of jealousy.

"Sir?"

"Don't start that again, Lucey."

"You look - better, " Luce said warily.

The redhead certainly looked different, though still somewhat battered. He just looked at Luce, and then looked away - down at his splinted hand, then back up - and his mouth twitched. "Better," he echoed. "Aye."

Mattie squinted up at him warily, and then backed against his mother's skirts. Sarah rested her hand on the little boy's dark curls. "So different I'm not sure he knows you," she said wryly. "Amazing how much of a difference a bit of a wash makes, isn't it? - well, I'm sure you feel better for it, though."

Hollie's splinted hand twitched again, but he said nothing, just looked sardonic. "Now, then," Sarah said. "Who's for supper?"

And she presided over the meal with as much command as if she'd been the Earl of Essex. Luce tried to lead by example, bowing his head politely over a distinctly halting grace led by Hollie, as the senior officer present. The redhead had to be prompted once or twice, but all things considered, that unregenerate ruffian remembered his duty to God and, reluctantly, his superiors - and in that order, too.

"May I help you to more mulled ale, Captain - Hollie?" Luce said, and the redhead looked up at him with that odd half-smile on his face.

"You *may,* Lucey. Whether you *should,* is questionable." He curled his good hand around the mug, nestling the warm earthenware against his chest with a sigh of gratitude that Luce suspected might have been involuntary. "It's good, Mistress Hadfield."

"*Supper* was good," Luce said sternly.

"Aye, I suppose it was." He fell silent again, staring absently at the firelit shadows on the wall.

"It's getting very cold of a night, isn't it?" Sarah said, after the awkward silence became almost unbearable, and Luce agreed with her, wondering if there was some kind of coded message about the warmth of shared blankets in that remark. She hadn't been *looking* at him, but -

"Can I get anyone anything more? There is a little of the apple tansy left."

Mattie squeaked and bounced, and Hollie looked at the little boy, then at Sarah, and without a change of expression said, "Shift over here, child. I can't do nowt right-handed. One dish, two spoons. Dig in."

"You will end by spoiling that boy, captain," she said sternly, and he looked up with a faint smile.

"Ah, well, the Lord never blessed us wi' one of our own. Ceased to be after the manner of women, with my girl." Mattie ignored the two stunned grown-ups at the table and shovelled apple tansy into his mouth with more enthusiasm than accuracy, and the big redhead nudged the bowl with his elbow to catch the drips before digging in himself with an equal lack of precision. "God alone knows what any get of mine would have come out like, mind you," he added thoughtfully, "so probably for the best."

Sarah's eyes rested on his badly-mended shirt with a sort of horrified housewifely fascination, and travelled upwards to the ragged, unbarbered ends of his russet hair. "You are a married man, captain?"

"Mm? *Mine* -" he swooped clumsily on the last spoonful of tansy, to Mattie's displeasure, then looked at the little boy's crumpling face and popped the spoon neatly into the child's gaping maw. "Not any more, mistress. She died, God rest her." And just in case anyone was feeling sorry for him, the pair of them applied themselves with frightening and rather unlovely efficiency to cleaning the bowl.

Luce averted his eyes. There was tansy over a wide area, and it wasn't pretty. He was curious, though. "Don't you ever get, you know –" he glanced at Sarah – "lonely?"

"Oh aye," Hollie said cheerfully. "'Specially while I've had my wrist strapped up like this."

Sarah got up hastily. "Bed time, Matthew," she said.

They sat in cautiously companionable silence for a while, listening to the fire burn to ash and Sarah settling the sleepy child. "You must have been very young, to marry," Luce said cautiously, and Hollie gave him a somewhat rueful grin.

"Seventeen. And before you ask - she was two score years, give or take. You know how it is."

"I, um, do?"

"When you're seventeen you'd poke a hole in a bloody mattress, Lucey. Before God she was beautiful, though, my Griete. She was about shoulder-high to me - fair hair, bit lighter than yours, all wavy when she took it down at night. Christ, she was a bugger for clean linen.

If she knew what I look like these days she'd turn in her bloody grave. Cleanest wench I ever come across."

"And you *married* her?" Because Luce, at twenty, had never given serious consideration to the blessed state of matrimony. Not really. Not before Sarah, he reminded himself quickly. The redhead gave him an austere look.

"Of course I bloody married her, what d'you take me for? Jesus, brat, have you got *no* bloody morals?"

He bridled, and then realised, belatedly, that he was being teased.

"She had lovely tits, as well," Hollie went on dreamily, gazing into the fire. "Cleavage you could drown a mouse in. I told her that once and she had me sleeping in the kitchen for a week. I thought it was quite a pretty compliment, myself. You can use it, if you want, Lucey. Stick it in one of your poems."

Luce was just taking a mouthful of ale at that unhelpful point. Hollie looked at him sternly as he choked and spluttered. "Shut up, or you'll wake the child. What in Christ's name d'you want to be a soldier for? Nobody made you – not like you was running away from owt, or had a choice of enlist or be hanged, like Brockis."

"Well – you finished with that bit of cheese? Pass it over, then – thanks. He just wants telling, doesn't he? The King, I mean. Enough's enough. No more funny taxes – none of this hole-and-corner sneaking about with Papistry– getting into bed with the Scots. He's just gone too far. I'm sure he's a nice man, but you've got to draw the line somewhere. He's not the King for his own personal benefits. He does have *some* responsibilities –" Luce finally finished his ale and then lifted the jug again. "Good Lord, Hollie, I think we killed this one."

"Didn't take much finishing off," Hollie said cheerfully. "I *thought* you was getting a bit uncharacteristically fierce, brat. Had me frightened for a minute there."

"Indeed. Well -" Luce squirmed, "look, if in the morning you'd rather I forgot this conversation-"

The big redhead stifled a yawn. "I'm not *that* pissed, Lucey. I've not said nowt I wouldn't say to a mate, sober. Shove that bit of cheese back this way, there's a good lad." He leaned his head back against the wall with a thump. "Ah, hell, brat. Honour's all very well, but it's a *bugger* for getting in the way."

"I do think a man has to have some code of honour by which to live."

"Do you?" He sounded genuinely curious.

"Well, what is it that *you* fight for?"

Hollie scratched the back of his neck thoughtfully. "Good question. Me and Nat were never fussy whose gold we took, back in the day, so long as it was forthcoming. Ask me a week ago, and I'd have said we was both in it for the money."

He was eyeing the last of Sarah's good bread thoughtfully, and Luce pushed it over. "And now?" he prompted.

"Now?" The redhead gave a slow, cold smile. "Vengeance, brat. Sheer bloody vengeance."

46 BACK TO THE DAY JOB

Luce would have stayed, if he could. Forever, if she'd have had him. He hadn't asked, and she hadn't said anything, and Hollie was sufficiently mended after another day or two to be getting restless.

Sarah had done her best to get the bloodstains out of the silk sash, with little success. The silk had faded in patches, and the stains had darkened to a stiff muddy brown. About as shabby as the rest of the captain's wardrobe, though Luce's was in no better state, despite all Sarah's best efforts.

Hollie's belongings were unexpectedly neat, and few, strewn across the bed as he tried to put his shirt in his baggage one-handed - a selection of well-thumbed pamphlets. Bridge's Puritan tract "Babylon's Downfall". The seditious works of Lilburne, published whilst that rascal lay in the Fleet jail. Luce's eyebrows rose. All recent, published within the last two or three years, and mostly on the inflammatory side of Dissenting. A comb, missing teeth, and a faded blue silk ribbon. Clearly, the captain had some vanity, even if only a very little.

"Gracious, sir - Hollie," Luce said mildly. Still finding it hard to call the big redhead by his given name, even after several days of truce. "Somewhat seditious reading material, surely."

"Ah, not really my thing, brat," Hollie said, flushing a faint but definite shade of rose. "Just looking after 'em for a friend. Anyway -" a characteristic rally and counter-attack, "it's not *me* that's writing pornography. Rustic pleasures, by God!" He leaned over and casually plucked one of Luce's poems from his snapsack.
"'*Awake, awake, thou fire!*
Let Vesta's white hand raise

Thy tongues of flame to praise' – Christ, brat, since when have you been knocking off an arsonist?" He threw the paper back on the bed, shaking his head. "I reckon it's best we get back to the day job, Lucey. You stop here writing that rubbish and you're likely to end up as degenerate as them bloody Cavaliers."

"You *what*?" Luce squeaked. "Back to the - Hollie, you can't go back like that!"

"Like what?" He flexed his splinted hand consideringly, stiff in an armoured bridle-gauntlet. "It's fine. Fuck-all use, but it'll do. *'Have I not kept this in reserve and sealed it in my vaults? It is mine to avenge; I will repay. In due time their foot will slip; their day of disaster is near and their doom rushes upon them.'* Says so in the Bible, owd lad."

"You are off your bloody head!"

"Aye. Probably. But you wasn't planning to see out the rest of the war skulking under Mistress Hadfield's bed, were you?" He shoved loose hair out of his eyes. "Not with your code of honour, surely?"

Luce blushed - felt himself do it, and looked hard at the wall over Hollie's shoulder. "Me? No."

Tyburn was pleased to see Hollie, burying his head in his master's shoulder, while the captain pulled the horse's ears awkwardly, and Mattie clung to Sarah's skirts and grizzled. Well, the boy could have his bed and his mother's undivided attention back - for now. And then it was time to go, and there was nothing else to say but his farewells.

"Lucifer. I give you God speed, dear lad, and a safe journey." And she put her dear, work-roughened hands on his cheeks and drew his head down for a chaste and cousinly kiss. Then she looked at Hollie, with sword and harness and snapsack slung over his shoulder and his plate half-buckled because he still hadn't got the trick of doing it one-handed -

"Come here, you," she said, with a laugh that touched Luce with a most unwarranted jealousy, and the redhead pulled his ponytail free of his buffcoat and stood patiently to be fastened in to his armour.

"I'll let you do it this time, as well."

He didn't touch her, and other than her fingers deftly tugging the fastenings of his plate tight, she didn't touch him. He didn't even look at her - frowning absently into the distance - and Sarah was concentrating on her handiwork. There was no reason why Luce should have a sudden sense of understanding between his lady and his commanding officer.

"I'll come back," he said suddenly. "I *will* come back, Sarah. I'll –" He had his hands on her shoulders: so much unsaid, so much he needed to say, on the tip of his tongue, when he was interrupted by a brief flurry of cursing and squealing as Babbitt and his horse re-established their relationship of armed neutrality. She smiled. "I think it's time to go, Luce."

He mounted his mare with a filthy look at the captain. Hollie didn't even look back, but registered his cornet's presence sufficiently to set his heels into the black's flanks with a whoop and take off up the Banbury road at a neck-breaking gallop, disregarding frozen puddles and deep ruts in his haste to be gone.

"We should be able to catch up with –" Hollie began, and Luce glared at him

"You have no soul."

"Just saying, if we keep cracking on –"

"Sir, I have just left behind the woman I love - how *can* you?"

Hollie pulled the black up alongside Rosa, and nodded gloomily. "You're right, brat, you're right." He shook his head mournfully. "Hell of a good cheese she had. I'm going to miss that cheese."

"Sir!"

"Hollie," he corrected cheerfully.

"Hollie. Sir. You have no -" Luce paused, struck by a sudden thought. "As a point of interest, sir, what *is* Hollie short for? I don't believe I've heard anyone call you anything other."

There was a long silence. Tyburn tossed his head with a jingle. And then - "Holofernes," the redhead said, through gritted teeth. "Puritan father, brat. Bloody inappropriate name for an officer, ain't it?"

"Provided your wife's name wasn't Judith, I fail to see the problem."

"True. Not being prone to getting pissed up and falling into bed with decent young ladies, I'm probably safe." He turned and looked straight at Luce, his eyes shaded by the bars of his lobster-pot helmet. "Brat. I'm sorry I was such a cock, all right? I never give you much of a chance, to start off with. I didn't ought to have give you such a hard time. I just thought your uncle had wished you on me as some sort of bloody penance. Thanks, lad." He gave a sharp laugh. "You're all right, Lucey. You'll do."

"Don't be so daft, Hollie," Luce said without thinking. "Uncle Essex just thought if he put me in with you, I could keep an eye on you for him, keep you in line a bit -"

Tyburn suddenly went straight up on his hind legs, squealing as if Hollie had dug his spurs into the black's flanks, then came to a skidding halt, barricading the road. "He. Fucking. *What*?"

"It's not important," Luce said quickly.

"You're a fucking *spy*?"

"And *you're* being stupid. It might have started off as duty, but -"

"How long have you been sneaking on me to your uncle, you little *shit*? Is that what you've been scribbling - that what you keep noting down in your little book, you fucker? Give that here -" He grabbed for Luce's snapsack, and the mare shied wildly.

"That is *verse*, captain, as you well know-"

The big black horse reared again, massive chest like a battering ram forcing Rosa off-balance, "You *are* on our side, aren't you, Lucey? You're not a fucking cavalier as well -?" Hollie lunged without warning, grabbing at Luce's snapsack - jerked it free in a brief tug-of-war, and then Tyburn snaked his head in and his teeth tore into the red mare's neck, Rosa reared, hooves scrabbling on the frozen lane, and that was the last thing Luce remembered.

His next clear recollection was opening his eyes from a horizontal position, the trees in his vision swirling dizzily. The chestnut mare skittering, and Babbitt kneeling over him looking embarrassed.

"You all right, brat?" he said awkwardly.

Luce struggled into a sitting position, and the redhead passed him that increasingly battered, flask of raw brandy. "Might as well finish it up, if it'll help."

It didn't help. The few mouthfuls of brandy burned in Luce's throat and made him feel even dizzier. The captain gave him a quick sidelong glance. "Aye. Well. Thee - ah, Christ, lad, I don't - I'm sorry. It was an accident. I didn't mean - You all right?

Luce squeezed his eyes closed. The world kept swirling. He thought he might be sick. "Fuck off," he said hoarsely. "*Captain Babbitt.*"

47 AN UNDESERVED LOYALTY

They spent the night, in mutually uncomfortable silence, under a hedge five miles outside Banbury. Banbury was in the King's hands, so the pair of them were stripped of any kind of distinctive harness. Hollie with his distinctive hair bundled roughly up under Luce's much-abused felt hat, and Luce scruffy and unshaven – their own mothers wouldn't recognise them. They even passed the time of day with a troop of Malignant scouts, pounding by with less than the expected malignancy.

"Going somewhere special, lads?" the captain had laughed, and Hollie had grinned back at him amicably enough and shaken his head.

"Anywhere with a roof over it will do me."

"Looking for anyone in particular?"

And it wasn't as amicable as it seemed, was it? "Captain Little," Luce said indistinctly. "Lost him at Edgehill. I wouldn't mind, he still owes me a drink. You seen him? About my height, grey hair to here, quite, er, sturdy built - "

"Don't know the name, mate. You got the toothache, lad?"

Luce nodded gingerly and Hollie looked anywhere but at the lad, expecting at any second that the brat was going to denounce him as a rebel officer.

"Good tooth-drawer at Deddington, about six miles hence. I'd keep going if I was you."

And Hollie had surreptitiously wiped his sweating palms under Tyburn's mane and blithely agreed, you couldn't be too careful in these uncertain times, keep riding.

He regretted that row. It had been an accident, there

but for the grace of God it hadn't been the other way about and *Hollie* on his back in the road, that bloody overbred mare hadn't the wits of a flea, and - aye, well, yes, Hollie had lost his temper and now the lad was sulking. All it had done was make it impossible to find lodging in any of the inns on the Banbury road. The last had been so uncomplimentary about the appearance of two ragged, disreputable soldiers in their tap-room, that Hollie had decided to give up and make their own arrangements. And the boy was looking distinctly the worse for wear. The bruises were all too visible, even in spite of his efforts to cover them by wearing his hair loose. (Which was a loyalty Hollie probably didn't deserve.) As night came on and a fine, freezing rain started to fall the brat was hanging white-knuckled onto the mare's mane whilst swearing in a slurred voice that nowt ailed him, and not convincing Hollie one bit.

"That's far enough," he said, dropping the reins on the black's neck and leaning from the saddle to catch the plodding mare by the bit. "Lucey, that's enough. We're making camp."

The black stood like a rock with his backside turned into the gusts of rain and his head drooping with boredom, whilst Hollie led the mare into the shelter of the bare hedge. "Off you get, brat," he said briskly, holding her bridle so that the brat could use his shoulder to hold onto without having to ask for help. Luce looked at him blankly, and then slid down the mare's flank – staggered and would have fallen.

"Best leave off the brandy next time, Lucey."

"*Not* drunk," the lad said mutinously. Hollie turned his head – almost nose to nose with the brat draped across him – and grinned in spite of himself.

"It was a joke. Not a very good one. Sit down before you fall down, child."

"Not a child, neither."

Well done, Hollie. The lad was miserable and hurt – and he didn't get that way by himself, either – and you were *still* baiting him. He kicked about the ditch, scuffing through the rotted leaves, towing the brat and the mare with him, till he found a patch in the lee of a fallen tree that was almost dry. Whistled to the black. Tied both horses to a rotten branch, though he wouldn't trust to the security of any knot he'd tied left-handed. Left the brat sitting on the tree trunk and headed off into the darkness to find some dry wood.

It wasn't the best campfire that had ever been lit, but considering the circumstances Hollie was proud of it. A perfectionist might say it was on the smoky side, and it could have been warmer, but it was alight. He tugged his cloak from behind his saddle and draped it across the lad's shoulders. "Cold, brat?"

Denying it, of course, and shivering like an aspen tree in a high wind. Well, Hollie had slept out in worse. He'd never seen the lad look so wretched, stripped of all his cool assurance. Wrapped in Hollie's thick cloak Luce looked like a ruffled hedge-bird in midwinter – and when had the lad got so thin, he was nowt but skin and bone under his buff coat.

"Get some sleep," he said gruffly. "I'll mind the fire for a bit." And the lad didn't argue, simply pulled Hollie's cloak tighter about his shoulders and lay down. Hollie tossed another rotten log onto the fire and settled his back against the tree. On the edge of the circle of firelight, the black horse raised his head at the sound, eyes gleaming. Not the first time the pair of them had stood watch together through the dark, and likely not the last.

RED HORSE

48 A RECURRENCE OF FEVER

It was almost dusk by the time they rode into the little village of Strand Green, on the banks of the Thames on the London road; stiff and cold and mired to the ears in freezing mud. They passed a picket on the outskirts of the village, looking about as cold and miserable as they felt, with a thick mist rising off the river wrapping itself about their horses' legs. "Who's that?" one of the sentries rapped.

"Looking for Captain Babbitt's troop, gentlemen. Parliament men, the both of us, as you may see for yourselves –" Luce turned his head and glared at Hollie, then edged the mare forward into a gap between the trees so that the sentry could make his own decision.

"Babbitt? Never heard of him." And there was a rustle and a breaking of branches in the undergrowth behind them as a second trooper cut them off from any possibility of retreat.

"Fair enough," Luce said grimly. "Try this one – the Earl of Essex's nephew and a fellow officer, new come after the Edgehill fight." Considerately tipped his hat back so that the man could scrutinise his face. "Were you at Edgehill, gentlemen?"

"Might have been," the second trooper muttered behind them.

"Then you recall Captain Babbitt's troop as the men who charged the Royalist guns, don't you?"

There was a long silence. Then the first sentry sniffed. "Well, he was a bloody madman, that one. Anyway, he's dead, ent he?"

"Not last time I looked," Hollie said.

"Take 'em in, Rob. Buggered if I know whether to believe that half-arsed story or not, but I don't want to turn round to Essex and say we left his nephew out to be eaten by Malignants."

"Thanks," the faceless Rob said, without enthusiasm. "Right, you two. I want to see the pair of you with both your hands on your bridle reins where I can see 'em –"

"So would I," Babbitt said with deep feeling, Luce snorted with unwilling laughter, and Rob stalked in front of them with a face that would crack a glass.

"Nobody likes a smartarse. *Sir*."

The big redhead flexed his splinted hand conspicuously. "Not being funny, lad. Much."

"Walk on, pair of you. Bear in mind Hall's got a brace of primed pistols in his belt if you're thinking about doing anything stupid."

It wasn't quite the glorious return to the troop Luce had envisioned, being led down the main street of the village by a suspicious trooper who didn't recognise either of them, muttering darkly about bloody donkey-wallopers. In spite of everything Luce could do to flatter, persuade and cajole, the sour-faced Rob refused to leave their side. "Somebody's going to have to let on to one of youse, eventually," he said, spitting phlegm accurately into a puddle. "Or back to your prinking masters you bloody well go."

Under other stars, the idea of Luce, who hadn't shaved in the best part of a week, and Hollie, looking like the fifth horseman of the Apocalypse, being mistaken for scented Cavaliers would have been comical. It was only by chance that Luce walked into Sariel Chedglow, crossing the street in front of the church looking as dour and judgmental as ever, and not a scratch on him. "Captain Chedglow, sir!" he called, and Chedglow's head jerked.

"*'And lest I should be exalted above measure through*

the abundance of the revelations, there was given to me a thorn in the flesh, the messenger of Satan to buffet me, lest I should be exalted above measure.'"

"I reckon he's pleased to see you," Rob muttered sardonically.

Hollie just laughed, humourlessly, and gave him back quote for quote. "'*Behold, I give unto you power to tread on serpents and scorpions, and over all the power of the enemy: and nothing shall by any means hurt you.*' As you see – *Penitence*. Pair of us, delivered from the mouth of the dog."

"Fair enough, if you're one of *them*, I'm out." The sentry turned round and tramped back the way he'd come. He wasn't sprinting, but he was going at a fair lick. Sariel Chedglow had that effect on people.

"Miserable unbelievers," Chedglow began, and Hollie evidently wasn't in the mood to listen because before the final drops of sibilant spittle had landed the big redhead was off his horse and had Sariel by the throat.

"Where's my fucking troop, you canting *bastard* –"

At which point two of Chedglow's devoted adherents pounced on the redhead with howls of evangelical fury and had Luce not insinuated himself into the fray with his most winsome smile and a free sword arm, things could have taken an unpleasant turn. "No harm done, captain, I'm sure," Luce said sweetly, backing Babbitt up against the churchyard wall out of harm's way. "Glad to see you unharmed, sir. Captain Babbitt and I are just going to bespeak ourselves some lodgings – never fear, sir, I'm sure we'll find something suitable – and a bite to eat before we rejoin the troop. The captain is as eager as ever to rejoin battle, sir, that's all – as hot at hand as ever he was -"

Chedglow inclined his head grimly.

"You say a word," Hollie muttered over Luce's

shoulder, "one *word* about the fucking eager bridegroom, and I swear I'll take your head off."

Chedglow didn't seem inclined to bandy further Biblical references with the redhead. With a pointed look at Luce, he chivvied his two ragged acolytes down the road out of range. "Like we're catching," the redhead said irritably.

"I think, captain, you grow too excitable," Luce said, with a frigid courtesy that would have set a brass monkey at arm's length. "I would not have you laid low with a recurrence of your fever, sir – the night airs –"

"Worried I might start a fight, you mean. I'm not dead yet, brat. You're not in charge yet."

Luce was actually thinking on inns, and the possibility of a hot meal and a bed for the night and surely to God having five minutes where he wasn't having to look over his shoulder and see what trouble his intemperate commanding officer was stirring up now. Their appearance hadn't improved in the week since they'd left Kineton, and that was before they'd started sleeping in ditches. Of the three signs he could see down the narrow village street, the shabbiest seemed to be the Green Dragon. So that would be the one he'd try first.

The quietest, the shabbiest, and oddly, the kindest. There were a few – a very few – officers in the tap-room, most of whom he didn't recognise, who looked up and smiled at him absently, seeing the sash and the buff coat and knowing him for one of their own but no more. A tall, fair-haired young man with a lovelock tied with a red ribbon, brushed past him in the doorway, murmuring apologies, and Luce stayed him with a hand on his elegant slashed sleeve. "Sir – my apologies, sir, do you by any chance know where Captain Babbitt's troop of horse are quartered?"

"Babbitt?" The fair-haired man shook his head, frowning. "Not a name I recognise. A cavalry troop, you say? No. I don't believe I know of such a troop." He bit his lip, gnawing at a well-kept moustache. "No, wait. I do recall the name. Captain Babbitt was killed at Edgehill, I collect. His sergeant, though –"

Luce heard a sharp intake of breath behind him, and glanced over his shoulder.

Babbitt was very much still alive, but in the firelight he looked like a man who'd taken a sword thrust to something vital.

One of the younger officers leapt from his chair by the fireside, bowing and almost tripping over his own feet in his haste to vacate his place for the redhead. The captain sat down, staring blankly into the fire, unblinking.

"An old wound?" the fair-haired man said solicitously.

"You're the second person tonight to tell him he was killed a month ago," Luce said. "I imagine it's somewhat unsettling."

49 LOST AND FOUND

Luce left the captain under the somewhat startled eye of the merry band, and ordered supper – limited, by his old standards, but a feast in comparison to what they'd enjoyed in recent weeks. Broiled mutton, a pigeon pie, an apple tart, a dish of winter cheese. The tavern-keeper's wife was a plump, motherly sort with a breast like a pigeon and a distinctly softening glint in her eye when she looked at Luce. The lady was perfectly open about it. "I've a son your age," she said, almost before he'd spoken, and then proceeded to whip a comb out of her pocket and tidy his hair before tying it back with a length of ribbon from the same capacious garment.

Which made him smile at the same time as it tugged at his heart, thinking of Sarah and her habit of tidying him up. He submitted to being straightened and combed, while the lady chattered on at him about her son, out with Captain Denzel Holles's men in the garrison at nearby Brentford, and then she lectured him about taking better care of himself, which he suspected would lead to an extra dish unasked-for on the table at supper and that was even before the lady set eyes on the unkempt Babbitt. Dear God, between them they could corner the market in maternal impulse - Luce dishevelled and Babbitt underfed - they'd end up provisioning half the Army.

"I'm looking for our sergeant, madam – about so high, somewhat, uh, stocky –" – how did you tactfully describe someone as the regimental gargoyle? – "grey hair, cut short –"

She was shaking her head blankly and had no one heard of Babbitt's troop – had they even got past Banbury, or had they deserted, been slaughtered, got lost? He shouldn't have left Cullis in charge – should have left Babbitt to his own devices in Kineton, or even better, to die in a ditch – but then he'd never have met Sarah and never had those three weeks of delirious happiness. He'd learned a lot in those three weeks. Some of it he could probably even share with his parents, if he ever got back home to Witham. "Two brothers – large young men from Somerset – twins, with freckles –"

"Westons," she said promptly, and he sagged with relief.

"Do you know where they're quartered, mistress?"

"No idea, love. I'd try the Chequers, up the road a ways. Doubt they sleep there, mind, but I imagine they drink there. Most of the boys do."

50 TAKEN AS A BETRAYAL

Hollie ducked his head under the lintel of the Chequers, narrowing his eyes at the sudden haze of tobacco and woodsmoke. Feeling sick and very cold and shaky because he didn't know what the hell he was going to do if Cullis and the men weren't here, and determined that the brat wouldn't know it.

And then the knot of shapes at the fire resolved themselves, and in the midst of the babble of sharp Essex voices he heard Calthorpe's flat Lancashire voice, as familiar and comforting as an old coat – Cullis growling like a bass mastiff – the Westons, as country as milkmaids. He pushed his way through the crowd – dicing again, damn it, what had he told the men about gambling, it always ended in tears – came to a halt in front of Cullis and stood there, waiting for the sergeant to look up from his conversation.

"Consider yourself relieved of command, sergeant."

Cullis looked up, narrow-eyed and snarling, and then his stony faced relaxed into what passed for a smile. If you hadn't known him for twenty years, near as, you wouldn't have known he was pleased to see you. "Captain Babbitt. Sir." The sergeant grimaced. "Heard you was dead, captain."

Hollie ran his good hand through his hair, light-headed with relief and weariness. Very much underdressed, he felt, very much off-duty with neither plate nor buff coat and his doublet slung over his shoulder "Not for want of effort on the part of our Malignant associates, sergeant, but no."

Cullis didn't smile. "Where've you left the lad?"

He shrugged, awkwardly. "Tagging after me, like he has been half across the country. What have I missed?"

"Not a lot. Your pissy German mate's been busy –"

"Had Banbury back after all, didn't he? We got warned off Banbury – run into a patrol just outside the town, might have gone nasty if Pettitt hadn't acquired some fictional mate in the King's army that we were apparently trying to catch up with." He laughed bitterly. "Good little liar, is Pettitt. Never think it to look at him, would you?"

"Wish *meinherr* Rupert had stopped with Banbury. He's had Aylesbury and Reading as well while you was laid up. Well, if he's got his heart set on picking London off like a nice fat sugar-plum out of a pie, he's in for a nasty surprise, God bless him. 'Cos we're going to be sat there waiting for him."

"Christ, that'd be a first, for Essex. What's he done, sent his coffin on ahead this time?"

Cullis sniggered. "Behave your bloody self, Red. Show a bit of respect. The commander of the Army likes to be well prepared, that's what."

"Oh aye, the end of the world is extremely fucking nigh. You sound just like Willie Balfour. How is the miserable Scots bastard? Does he thrive?"

"Last time I saw, he was in fine fettle. About a week ago calling down the wrath of God on some dilatory dragoons. He's -" The sergeant stiffened, grizzled eyebrows knitting together. Then he stood up, a hand lifted in abrupt salute. "Ho! Boy! Here!"

"What –" Hollie was half-turned to see what was happening when the brat barged past him, flying at grim grey Cullis, grinning all over his face and pounding the sergeant on the back with sheer delight. Worse, the sergeant was pounding him back, the pair of them thumping each other like a pair of hound puppies. Hollie opened his mouth to pass some unhelpful remark on this uncharacteristically joyous reunion and then realised half the troop were leaning back in their seats, grinning indulgently.

Wished just one of them had been that pleased to see him back, though. As he looked round the circle of faces the grins were fading – not unhappy to see him, but serious, the expressions of men recalled to their duty, awaiting orders. And Luce with his hand on Cullis's shoulder, beaming like a sunrise. Like *he* commanded the bloody troop, and it was Hollie that was the newcomer. The brat was mid-tale now, telling his story with gestures and looks, a sudden burst of laughter from his audience: and not one of them had so much as glanced up at Hollie.

"Oh, you little *bastard*," he said, softly and with feeling. Waited a second, hating himself for allowing that weakness, just to see if anyone did turn round – put a hand out to him, to draw him into that enchanted circle. They didn't. Well, balls to them. To the lot of them. He turned on his heel and went back out into the night.

51 TRIBULATION WORKETH PATIENCE

Luce looked up as the busy, smoky tavern stilled briefly, and the door slammed shut on a gust of cold air. "That's it," he said to Cullis. "That is finally it. I do not understand that man, I do not wish to understand that man, and he can finally have his way. I'm going to ask for transfer to another troop."

"Wouldn't blame you a bit," Cullis said, nodding sagely. "You had some supper, lad? Pair of you look like you ain't seen a decent meal in weeks."

"I have, actually." The sergeant lifted his hand anyway, and one of the serving-girls trotted over to see what she could get them.

"Stew's good," Cullis said. The girl dipped her head in polite acknowledgement, and then gave Luce a look that was rather unsettling in its appraisal. He looked back quite without thinking - worth the looking at, if you happened to like small and plump and fair - and the corners of her mouth turned up. "Can do room service, sir, for two shillings extra?"

"Well, well, well," Cullis said after she'd gone, swinging her hips tantalisingly in passing. "Look who's all grown up, then. *That* where you been for the last month, is it?"

"Oh, I wish," Luce muttered. "Ever had one of those days when you'd have willingly exchanged your present company for that of AntiChrist?"

"Frequently, with this lot."

"Well, I've had one of those *months*."

Cullis snorted. "He has that effect on a lot of people." And then the grim sergeant paused as Luce's stew was set in front of him, waiting till he was halfway down the bowl. It was good stew. It was also hot, filling, and deeply satisfying to be eating in the sort of company that didn't make your palms itch.

"Don't give up on him, Lucey," Cullis said, quite out of nowhere. Luce was so surprised he swallowed a mouthful of bread unchewed, choked, and had to be pounded on the back by one of the Westons till he could breathe again.

"You - *what*?"

"You heard. He stands in want of a bloody good hiding, I'll give you that."

"I'll hold your coat," Luke Weston muttered, not quite inaudibly.

"But he's nowhere near in the state I thought he'd be in, after Rackhay. He ain't dead, for one thing. Teasy as a snake, but that's nothing new, and I'd rather have him teasy and breathing, lad. I was scared to bloody death when we left, what I'd find, but you done a good thing, Lucey. You kept him in one piece."

"*I* did?" Luce echoed. "Does he have some history of this appetite for self-destruction?"

"Red? Oh Christ, yes. I known him twenty years, and -"

"Sergeant, spare me the sentiment. Had you known Captain Babbitt for twenty years, he would have been barely thirteen at the time of your first acquaintance. By his own admission. Which I think unlikely."

"Ah, that's true." Cullis was idly gnawing Luce's leftover crusts now, and Luce had a suspicion that the order of stew hadn't been entirely altruistic. "He was *seventeen*."

"Get on!" Luke Weston propped his elbows on the back of Luce's chair, all agog, and Cullis nodded. "He was. Lying little bastard told me he was nineteen, and you know - the size of him - I believed him. Had his eighteenth birthday outside bloody Breda, in, what - '24? '25? - him and bloody Rackhay, pissed up on filched Spanish sherry. Now I know he was eighteen, cos he *told* me. Trying to start a fight with some bloody Dago mercenary, twice his age and twice as wide. Fierce little bugger, even in them days, he wouldn't take no shit from anyone."

"Still don't," Luke said, sounding proud. "The King hisself don't cut no ice with Captain Babbitt."

"I have no desire to hear the captain's life story," Luce said coldly, and Luke peered up at him.

"I bloody do! What happened to the Dago?"

"Oh, he wouldn't take him on. No honour in it, see. You reckon you're a bit of a coming man, Lucey, I tell you you've got nothing on Red. He had his first command when he was your age."

"Impressive," Luce sneered, and "Bloody hell," Luke Weston said, counting on his fingers. That was the odd thing. The disreputable little crew gathering round Cullis seemed to be on Babbitt's side. He was even-handed, Eliot said, and Ward had snorted and said he was that right enough, he was a bad-tempered arsehole to everybody - but he'd laughed when he said it. Davies reckoned the captain was one of their own, not too high and mighty to rub shoulders with his lads. "And he's a great lad for a scrap," Isaac Weston had said comfortably, "can't keep him back from it, can 'ee?"

Luce didn't think any of it was recommendation for an officer, but looking at their eager, indulgent faces he had the suspicion that Babbitt was something of a favourite.

They didn't think he'd been unfair to Luce - to a man, they thought it was perfectly reasonable to be suspicious of a poetry-writing nob with relations in high places, who wrote to his mother twice a week and changed his shirt before supper. Luce had come late to the party, it would appear. What he saw as incivility, they saw as rough camaraderie. Eliot was *grateful* that Hollie hadn't, as he put it, grassed him up to Essex for the incident with the crooked dice in Worcester. The fact that Hollie had kicked his sorry carcass round the cathedral in front of half the Army didn't bother him in the least - he seemed to be happier with an outcome of being casually assaulted by the captain, than subjected to formal military discipline. Even godly Calthorpe had a soft spot for that ruffian, and Luce simply couldn't understand it.

Someone had stood Cullis another drink, and the sergeant was growing expansive, telling tall tales of the wild youth of Rackhay and Babbitt - stunts they'd pulled, grandees they'd insulted, brawls they'd been in. There was much hilarity, and much amazement. Luce found it hard to believe they were thinking of the same man. That surly brute, who read Puritan sermons and seditious political tracts for pleasure, and who knew the writing of Shakespeare and Donne. A foul-mouthed rogue, who'd treated Sarah and Mattie Hadfield with as much courtesy as if they'd been members of the King's household.

A man, and neither a plaster saint nor a minor demon. A man who could feel every bit as hurt and lonely and frightened as Luce, but did a better job of hiding it. "Oh, Lucifer, you can be a *bloody* fool at times," he said aloud to himself.

Cullis looked up, didn't pause in his relation of some anecdote featuring a mule, a laundress, and part of Colonel Butler's baggage train at Magdeburg. But he definitely winked.

52 BEING NOT CONFORMED TO THIS WORLD

The alarms came late on into the next day. Part of Lord Brooke's regiment of foot were stubbornly setting themselves in the way of the whole of the King's army at Brentford, to cut off His Majesty's advance on London - and more particularly the Parliamentarian train of artillery at Hammersmith.

Babbitt's troop had been mounted since midday, restlessly trotting the horses up and down the main street without so much as a whisper of an order, and the alarm came out of nowhere. "What the hell's going on?" Cullis demanded of a passing infantryman in Hampden's green-coated livery.

The man shrugged, hefting his pike over his shoulder, clearly wanting to rejoin his comrades as they marched across the fields towards Brentford bridge. "Lieutenant Colonel Quarles has took the better part of Holles' men already, mate. Brooke's lot left under Lilburne, and not so much as a peck of powder between 'em."

Luce stiffened. "*John* Lilburne?" That pamphleteering anarchist?

"Captain Lilburne, that's right. What I hear they had to raid every house in Brentford for what shot they've got. The garrison there is hard-pressed, boy, so if you're done asking questions, Holles' troop are in retreat and being hammered by Malignants -"

"Then you'll be in need of a troop of horse, won't you?" The black horse skittered to a crazy halt on the cobbled street, lathered and steaming. "Form the men up, Pettitt," the captain said. "We're going in. Go on, tell your fucking dilatory uncle that."

Luce looked at him. White-faced and panting like a hound on a leash, and with that wild unreasoning glint in his eye? "No," he said. "I'll not put my men in danger at your whim, sir."

"*Your* men, cornet?"

"Yes, *mine*, captain, when you're in this humour. If you want to make an end of yourself, sir, you go right ahead. But I'll not stand by and let you take good men with you."

He could *hear* Hollie trembling, hear the breath coming shaky between his teeth. "Are you defying me, you whelp?"

Luce astonished himself. He felt perfectly calm. "Indeed, sir, I am countermanding that order."

"Bring them up to the bridge with Hampden's troop," Hollie said, louder. "We're going to cover Holles' arse. Did you hear me?"

"You're out of your fucking mind." Cullis simply put out a hand and caught Tyburn by the rein, jerking the black's mouth hard. "The boy has the right of it. *I* will not countenance throwing good men after bad. The light's going. You heard what he said, Holles and Brooke are in retreat. *Look* at 'em, Hollie. It's over. You can see them from here. Cavalry's no bloody use on a ploughed field against pike and shot!"

"Christ, will you *both* defy me?" The redhead was almost sobbing. "Well, damn the lot of you, I'll go myself!" He drew his sword, left-handed and clumsy – yanked the horse's head out of Cullis's grasp and wheeled the black in a tight curve to face the muttering troop – "Have not a one of you fucking cowards the balls to come with me, pox on it?"

No one moved. With a curse, Hollie lashed the buckle end of the reins down the black's shoulder and the big horse galloped away, steel-shod hooves skidding and sparking on the cobbled street. "Shite," Cullis said wildly. "He means to finish it, doesn't he?"

"I'll not have it," Luce said. Quite matter-of-fact, without a thought in his head other than that he wasn't going to stand idly by and watch Hollie Babbitt jeopardize his immortal soul. Gave the sergeant a quick, ironic salute. "You know my mother's direction, if I fail to return. Been nice knowing you."

"You are *both* out of your –" And that was the last he heard as he sent the mare thundering after Tyburn. The black was bigger and the mare was faster. He knew that. At this breakneck speed Hollie was like to run himself and his uncontrollable mount into a forest of pike. Which gave Luce barely a hundred yards to head him off.

He swerved the mare to avoid colliding with the first of Holles' retreating infantry – was sworn at profusely by a few troopers, but most of them were too spent to do more than snarl. The black was hardly five lengths ahead now, Hollie bent over the horse's neck with his sword drawn clumsily left-handed.

One last burst of speed. For the first time since he'd had the mare, he jabbed his spurs viciously into her heaving flanks and she lengthened her stride and he'd known the horse could run but this went beyond speed, this was storm and lightning and thunder. Her nose was level with the black's massive quarters, close enough for Luce's face to be spattered with the mud of Tyburn's passing.

And then there was no help for it, as the black began to pull away again and they were almost in the thick of the retreat. He wheeled the mare and slammed her square into the galloping stallion's flank.

Both horses went down in a tangle of flailing legs. Luce felt the turned winter earth under his cheek, lying there with all the breath and half the sense knocked out of him. He was dragged up by the scruff of his neck by a big pikeman: shaken like a rat, cuffed and set back on his feet, while the mare staggered up a few yards away. Babbitt was up, dragging his lobster-tail helmet off one-handed. "You little *shit*, if you've lamed my horse I'll gut you like a rabbit –"

And Tyburn struggling to get up, and Luce simply put his shoulder to the steaming black flank till the horse was on his feet, shuddering with fright. It was a measure of the horse's distress that upon being smacked round the backside by a burly sergeant of pike he trotted unsteadily in the direction in which he was pointed, back towards the village, rather than kicking the pikeman's front teeth out.

The mare was sound. Luce grabbed Tyburn's trailing rein – dragged the black into a limping canter, across the ridges of turned earth. Away from the clash of another staggering charge by Hampden's gallant infantry, still trying to cover the desperate withdrawal of Holles and Brooke from the winter fields.

Near dark. The cold rising off the damp ground, and the rooks flying like ashes above the bare black trees against a fiery sunset.

Luce was too angry to speak. And then he wasn't. "Captain Babbitt, I am *buggered* if I'm going to stand by and let you kill yourself!"

Hollie looked at him, cold and level and absolutely calm. "You'd even take that off me if you could, wouldn't you?"

And he turned on his heel and limped away.

53 BLESSED ARE THEY WHO MOURN

Windsor
December 1642

Luce ran a hand through his hair: needing, badly, a wash and a trim, and he'd probably get round to it much the same time as he got round to shaving, which was likely to be the twelfth of never.

The big redhead hadn't spoken to him since Brentford. They occasionally passed each other and at first he'd spent the whole time he was within Hollie's range with his pistol to hand, just in case. He was fairly sure, now, that it wouldn't end in blood.

Staid, sensible Edmund Allaby, quartered with the rest of Ballard's infantry just outside the town, often found his way to Luce's quarters and they often went for a quiet few drinks together. Luce was grateful for the company, and the young man's unimaginative friendship. Allaby was a nice, quiet, well-brought-up young man who thought and behaved exactly as was proper. He was exactly what Luce's mother would have approved of.

Allaby was a nice lad. He was no more and no less than a nice lad. And try as he might, Luce kept comparing him with Hollie - not the desperate, wounded Hollie of Brentford, but the shyly companionable comrade of their last days at Kineton. At a loose end, at winter quarters, the captain was utterly lost, utterly bereft. You came across him in odd places, at odd times, just looking dazed, staring at nothing, sitting there in his unmended linen.

The troop didn't help, although God knows they thought they were being kind. Treated Hollie with careful civility, which was hard enough at the best of times for that rabble, and spoke to him with slow kindness like he was either deaf or daft. There were times Luce wanted to bang their silly heads together - peace and quiet being the last thing Hollie needed. He *needed* to be pestered. He needed to be in the thick of things again.

Witless had had the splint off the captain's wrist a week or two back, poked and prodded, and then shaken his head. Not mending as well as he'd have liked. "Why did you n-not have your fingers set, at the time?" he'd demanded, and Hollie had looked blank because the only person who'd gone anywhere near straightening his hand out at the time had been Luce. So Witless broke two of the redhead's fingers again, in the hope of putting them anything like straight, and then he'd splinted up the whole enterprise till it was armoured like plate and Hollie was completely left-handed for another month.

"But that's all right," Cullis had said with spurious cheer, "cos you ain't got nothing to do anyway, except write begging letters, and Lucey can do that - right, Luce?"

Luce muttered something non-committal. Hollie stalked out balefully, dramatic exit spoiled by the fact that he couldn't manage both thumb-latch and handle on the kitchen door with one good hand until Eliot helpfully held it open for him. And that was how they were - they thought they were being kind and they were just making Hollie feel worse. Anyone with half an eye could see that, not that you could say anything because he'd be even more unbearable if he thought he was an object of pity. Although Luce thought he could probably administrate the troop as capably as Hollie, while that troop was safely contained in winter quarters. And he liked their winter quarters, though the house was somewhat damp. He liked *Windsor*, though like every other town it had its rough district, mostly down behind the marketplace; the wide grey skies were not unlike his own home turf, the place was not unfriendly, bustling yet civil.

The men were well cared-for, the horses well fed, and the whole lot of them were bored witless and that couldn't be helped whilst most of southern England was waist-deep in frozen December mud; the Army did not move in the winter and that was the end of it. It was a good house, if you ignored the damp; not as elegant as Luce's own home, but a good, solidly-built timbered building that leaned out over the busy High Street and had a snug walled garden to the rear with an apple tree and a tiny, scrubby patch of herbs. There was even a bakehouse, two streets away. He often found himself in there of an early morning, when the pies were hot and fresh from the oven. It was warmer than the kitchen of their quarters – and the breakfast, despite the efforts of Moggy Davies, was a hundred times more savoury.

He'd even started to put down roots in Windsor over the last weeks – regular invitations to dine with the better sort of merchant, for which he normally found time and brushed off his good suit. Three months on campaign had changed him and he rather fancied it was for the better. He was also not entirely blind to the fact that he was leaner, fitter, and broader in the shoulder, and that it wasn't entirely unnoticed. One of the reasons he normally found time to dine with the local merchants, if he was honest.

No, Luce had the oddest feeling that he'd suddenly become one of Windsor's more eligible bachelors, which was slightly unnerving. He was young, not ill-looking, in – God help us all – a position of some responsibility, with the ear of the Earl of Essex. He'd made himself a reputation for being honourable, polite, and honest. There seemed to be an irresistible glamour about a soldier's coat: even Cullis made the occasional visit to the house of a well set-up widow at the bottom of Peascod Street, although as he usually came back looking just as grim but considerably tidier Luce suspected nothing more sinister than that she did his mending for him.

He missed Sarah, though. Thought of her often, and dreamt of her more often than that. These days, though, he also dreamed of the goldsmith's housemaid, who was a dark, saucy-eyed wench with a naughty smile, and a habit of brushing her hip against his shoulder when she was serving at dinner. A very friendly miss, indeed, and it would have been churlish of him to refuse her offer to show him the shortcut that ran along behind the marketplace - very dark, it was, and she'd got somewhat nervous on the way. She'd had to show him four times now, and she still got nervous at the same place, and he couldn't keep the route in his head. She was going to show him again tomorrow afternoon. That was different, though. That wasn't love. That was just - bedding.

He'd just come in from the street, shaking the rain out of his hair, and still smiling to himself. The house was silent, still, comfortably warm.

And Hollie Babbitt was sitting alone in the kitchen, with one of his pistols on the table in front of him. Staring at nothing, not even turning to look at Luce. Grey-white and suspiciously red about the eyes, not that Luce was stupid enough to mention that.

"Sir, are you - are you all right, captain?"

"Fuck off, Pettitt." And he was shaking like a leaf in a stiff breeze.

"Are you *unwell*, sir? It is a perfectly reasonable question, captain. If you require assistance I will go and get it. It's all right," Luce snapped, nettled into uncharacteristic sharpness, "I'm not going to impose my company on you any further than that."

"No. Well. You've done enough damage."

He could have walked away. Shrugged his shoulders and said the hell with it and gone upstairs, read, worked on the verse he'd had in his head all day. "What do you mean, *I've* done enough damage?"

"*'I've just been called in to Uncle Essex, Cornet Pettitt.'*" The redhead giggled wildly. "Looks like you got rid of me. You got what you wanted. I've got my marching orders, whelp. Uncle Essex don't reckon you're doing a very good job reining me in, it seems, so looks like he's going to get Sir James Ramsey to do it instead. Having walloped this fucking lot into some order, he's taking the troop off me."

"But he - you - what on earth *for*, sir? I thought - reports - but we - I had heard nothing but praise for this troop after Edgehill, captain?"

"What for?" Babbitt mimicked unpleasantly. "My lord Essex has been receiving complaints about my demeanour. Can't imagine where *they* might have come from, can you?"

"Complaints?"

"Oh, don't play innocent with me! You're out every afternoon God sends, disappearing for hours on end, coming back with that smug look on your face -"

"Captain," Luce said cautiously, "you are aware of Master Cookson, the goldsmith? With whom I dine, um, regularly?"

"Oh I am *aware* of him. So what?"

"I'm - ah, his housemaid and I have a - she is a remarkably attractive young woman, and I -"

The redhead bridled, looking as if Luce had slapped him. "You're *fucking* the goldsmith's maid?"

"I should not care to put it like that."

"You hypocritical little bastard!"

"It's nothing to do with me!"

"Oh, *really*. No one's been telling him tales. Or -

what? - *God* told him, did he?"

"Taking the Lord's name in vain, sir, will not help."

"The only thing that will help, Pettitt, is putting a pistol ball between your eyes. Or mine. I have had it up to *here* with you. You wanted my command. Fine. You've fucking got it. You got *everything*, didn't you? You *used* me, Pettitt. I think I've got every *right* to be pissed off with you. And now if you'll excuse me, I have some personal effects to collect before I take up my posting under Sir James." Luce saw the big redhead scrub fiercely at his eyes with the back of his hand. "I bid you a good afternoon, sir. And I wish you joy of your new command."

He almost took the door off its hinges, and almost collided with Cullis on the way out. The sergeant raised his eyebrows. "Now what's up?"

"Me," Luce said gloomily, "saying the wrong thing. Again."

"What - and you're going to go after him, in that mood? Lad, I'll say this for you, you've got mettle, though I reckon you might want for sense."

"No, I think I'll let him calm down." He sighed. "I suppose I'm due a visit to my uncle. I reckon I owe him that much."

"What, your uncle?"

"No. *Hollie*. I think Uncle Essex and I need to have a little talk."

54 AN UNEXPECTED ALLY, BOR

Tom Corston was conspicuous by his absence, and Luce was slightly ashamed that Uncle Essex was lodging not fifteen minutes' walk away, and he'd never set foot in his uncle's quarters, despite finding time to dine with assorted wealthy burghers. Also slightly embarrassing was the fact that Cullis's refined widow was walking up the road towards him, with a maid in unsmiling attendance - knew who he was and greeted him with a gracious tilt of her neatly-capped head. Quite a well-preserved old lady, if your tastes happened to run towards the antique. Somewhat humiliating to think that your regimental gargoyle was sniffing around her skirts, though. He shuddered at the idea. The sentry on duty at the door of Essex's lodgings grinned.

"Bit chilly, is it, lad?"

"Brisk," Luce said. "I should say, brisk."

"I'd say bleedin' freezing, meself. Go on in, I know your face. His Nibs is keeping bachelor's hall at the moment, so the house is all upside down." He stepped aside to let Luce pass him, taking a step into the dark hall, smelling of woodsmoke and wet wool. "Never thought I'd miss that prim bugger Corston, but he'd soon set this place to rights, wouldn't he?"

"Why, what happened to Corston?"

The sentry sniffed. "Sword through the arm on the way up here after Edgehill, and it took bad ways, poor lil lad. Reckon as if it takes me more than two weeks to get on wi' dying I'd like somebody to put a ball between my eyes. Cleaner."

"Quite." He agreed, most wholeheartedly, with the sentry – on the matter of clean deaths, but also, somewhat forlornly, on the matter of Tom Corston's absence. He hadn't taken to the fastidious aide in life, but evidently Corston's chilly efficiency had been necessary to the smooth running of Uncle Essex's staff.

"Turn in his grave, lad would, if he could see this slummocky mess," the sentry went on gloomily.

"Is my lord currently unaided, then?"

"Hoping for a vacant tenure, sir? Afraid not. Picked hisself up a new one – nice enough soul he is, catching on quick but –" he shrugged. "You know how it is. Learning on the job."

"What we up to, then, Trooper Heron – gossiping or gathering information?" Luce spun round to see the speaker – a big, fair, freckled young man, deceptively burly, and quiet as a cat on his feet. As far removed from the spare and elegant Corston as it was possible to be. "Who's this, then?"

Trooper Heron blushed and stuttered in evident embarrassment and Luce decided to finally spare him. "My Lord of Essex's nephew, sir. I have a troop – er, I'm a mere junior officer, but our captain is currently –"

"From what I do hear," the freckled lad said cheerfully, in a suddenly broad Norfolk accent, "you can tell your captain, but you can't tell 'en much. Andrew Venning from out at Diss, at your service. Guessing from the look of you and being my lord's nephew and all, you'd be the famous Lucey Pettitt?"

"I am," he said warily. "It's Luce. Not Lucey. If you would be so kind."

"Best let His Lordship know as you're here, then, bor. He be suffen savage if he do know me an' you been a-stood out here mardlin'."

The accent was so comical that Luce couldn't help but laugh, and Venning's broad, plain freckled face relaxed into a friendly grin. "That's better. Come on." Gave Luce a familiar clap on the shoulder, and steered him round towards the stairs.

Thank God, someone in the Army of Parliament who wasn't either evangelical, mad, or melancholic. Luce begun to think he'd strayed onto the stage during a performance of one of the bloodier revenge plays, of late. Venning knocked on the door of Essex's private chambers.

"Cornet Pettitt, my lord." In a polite, cultured, and suddenly accentless voice, eyes modestly downcast. "I'll seek out refreshments." Glanced up at Luce and winked, almost imperceptibly.

But he made Uncle Essex laugh, for which Luce would forgive him much – the wink had not gone unnoticed, nor had it been intended to. He suspected there had been altogether too little humour in his uncle's life of late. Essex looked older, much older, and there was silver in his moustache and the dark hair on his shoulders. Tired, too, pouch-eyed and worn. "Luce. I am delighted to see you, boy. You keep yourself too much apart." He stood up, spilling papers to the floor. "They can't fall any further," he said, with a smile. "Drew will deal with them."

Clasped Luce's hand warmly, and he might be older and wearier but by God the man still had a grip like a carpenter's vice and Luce resisted a temptation to check his fingers, deciding instead to give his uncle an awkward hug. "I am truly sorry to hear about Master Corston," he said. "I trust he died in the Lord's grace, sir."

"As do I, Luce. He deserved better. He was a loyal man and he served me well." Essex straightened up, patting his nephew's back. "Boy, you're as thin as a winter wolf. Your mother will skin me if I return you to her in such case. What's the use in commanding armies if you can't command a decent dinner?"

"I dine out, my lord. Not infrequently."

"So I hear," Essex said dryly, and Luce felt a familiar boiling blush rising up his cheeks. "Don't colour up, boy, I hear nothing but good. Will you dine with my officers tonight, or do you prefer the company of your own?"

"I tend not to associate with my fellow officers, sir," he muttered. Fortunately at that moment Venning rattled the door handle. "Here I be, sir, got my hands full!"

"He's a good boy, is Master Venning. A little rough in his manners, compared to Master Corston, but what he lacks in polish he makes up for in enthusiasm. And resource. I would hesitate to question the nature of some of his supplies."

"Come up out of the cellar, my lord," Venning said blandly, putting a dusty bottle of wine on the table. "Still got spiders on it." Which didn't answer the question of *whose* cellar, Luce noted.

"Bespeak us supper, Drew, there's a good lad. My nephew will stay to dine. I imagine we could all do with the festivity. A cold winter, and a long one."

"A green winter makes a full churchyard," Luce said absently.

"Then God send us more cold nights, for it saved many a life after Edgehill. Will you send for the rest of your officers to dine with us, Luce?"

Luce remembered the last - the only - time he'd seen Captain Babbitt and Sergeant Cullis dining formally, and it hadn't been a high point in anyone's history. "I – I think not, my lord."

"I'll see to it, sir," Venning said, somewhat obliquely, and went thumping off down the stairs sounding like most of a troop of cavalry.

"Well, then, Luce." Essex lifted the dusty bottle. "What brings you out to pay me a visit on such a miserable day? Familial duty?" He sipped his wine. "That's not out of *this* cellar. I'll have words with

Venning on his return. That's good stuff, that is!"

It was. Luce thought he probably needed to drink considerably more of it before he felt sufficiently able to say his piece. Fortunately the wine was easy enough on the tongue to make it a pleasure, rather than a chore. "I need to speak with you about Captain Babbitt, sir. On a matter of some delicacy."

"I thought you might."

"Uncle Essex, I have to - sir, have you given Captain Babbitt any suggestion that I was your intelligencer?"

"Me? No, why - should I have done? His behaviour has been discreditable in the extreme, Lucifer - he has left you almost *entirely* in charge of the troop, these last few weeks -"

Luce gave a wan smile. "That's my job, sir. I'm his junior officer. I'm *supposed* to deal with the paperwork."

"Young man, you are my nephew, not a clerk!"

"No, sir, I am an *officer*. Although, obviously, proud of our family connection. Uncle - answer me truthfully. Did you lead the captain to believe that *I* was supplying you with information?"

"I may have suggested that he was not wholly unsupervised, Lucifer, yes," Essex said stiffly. "And the heretic in your troop - Cowthorpe? Gowland? What discipline does he face?"

"Aaron *Calthorpe*? None, sir, none whatever. Aaron's beliefs are between himself and the Lord and he would be the first to tell you as much. Calthorpe is one of the stoutest men I know, uncle. He is faithful unto death to-" Luce swallowed and crossed his fingers behind his back, "this cause." Rather than the specific person of one slightly damaged redhead. He didn't think Uncle Essex needed to know that bit.

"Young man, I am rapidly coming to the conclusion that Captain Babbitt's perpetual questioning of authority is endemic in that troop!"

"Then I'm sorry for it, sir." He was mostly sorry that it saddened his uncle, who seemed worn and weary enough already. "But uncle - Captain Babbitt has done nothing wrong, nothing to merit his punishment. I'd be the first to tell you." His fingers were beginning to ache with being perpetually crossed and uncrossed. "We have had a bit of a falling-out of late, I'll admit that much. A degree of confusion. The captain is - over-sensitive, at times. Nothing we can't sort out. *If* he keeps his troop in its current format."

Uncle Essex was starting to look as though he'd just opened a drawer and found a dead rat within. "Lucifer, it begins to sound to me as though you consider that insubordinate ruffian a personal friend."

"That was the point of our misunderstanding. I rather think we are. Will be. Possibly. He - I think he came to depend on my -" he took another gulp of wine, "friendship, after Edgehill. He needed - he *needs* - a friend rather badly, after Rackhay's death."

Essex waved a hand in dismissal. "Don't be sentimental. The man's a professional soldier."

"He is a feeling man as much as you or I," Luce said reprovingly. "He deserves better than this."

"Are you directing my affairs, young man?"

"You broke him - *you* fix him!" Luce snapped, then blushed fiercely, stammering apologies.

Uncle Essex was staring at him in disbelief. "Young man, you have changed beyond recognition."

"Possibly, sir. It's the company I keep." He smiled ruefully. "Of all creatures, sir, Hollie Babbitt is faithful. Not sensible about it, but faithful, in his own perverse fashion. And he hasn't got anything to be faithful *to*, now. He has no family - no home - no other friends than myself, nothing except his command. And that must be very lonely, I think."

Essex gave Luce a long, thoughtful look, and nodded

slowly. "It can be, Lucifer. God knows it can be. Though how I am to blame for this -?"

"You took him off the flank at Edgehill. He says Rupert wouldn't have broken through if you hadn't."

"*I* did?"

"Tom Corston gave us your very specific orders - to move back with the reserves in the centre."

"*I* said - but Lucifer, I never gave any such order, why should I have done so? Why should I have given an order to weaken the flank - knowing we faced Rupert's elite? I assumed the captain had had some personal objective in defaulting his position, some - . When I called him to account, it was my impression that he considered himself above my governance, not because - And he thinks *I* -" Essex gave a sigh. "Oh, Thomas, what have you done?"

Luce held his breath and said nothing. It was dark outside, now. There were still carts rolling by outside, voices raised cheerfully or otherwise – someone downstairs singing. Essex took a light from the sullen fire, kicking the logs into flaring life, and lit the candles. "Well, Lucifer. I owe the captain an apology, it seems. I had assumed that his actions were the result of an ungovernable arrogance. It appears -" he poured himself another glass of wine - "that Babbitt is more sinned against than sinning. On this occasion. Tell him he can keep his troop."

"*Thank you,*" Luce breathed fervently. "Uncle, that assault on the guns at Edgehill was possibly the bravest thing I have ever seen."

"If not the daftest," Essex said dryly. "And *you* went with him. I suspect you two may be as wild as each other."

He sounded rather proud of it, too, if slightly astonished. Luce blinked at his uncle innocently, and did not voice the suspicion that he'd been nurturing since

Brentford bridge - that Hollie hadn't meant Luce, or anyone else, to go with him in that assault. That it hadn't been a daring act of courage, but the hope of oblivion. "Sir, would you give him leave of absence? Over the winter, while you have no use for him? I think if we leave him unemployed for much longer, he will be mad in truth. And there's a farm in White Notley where an extra pair of hands will be welcome, especially accompanied by a sturdy horse."

"White Notley?"

Luce shrugged. "My father's younger sister, sir. Not a lady who tolerates shirking. A few days under my Auntie Het's direction and the captain will be too tired to contemplate rebellion."

Essex poured himself a third glass of wine, shuddering. "Lucifer, there are times when you frighten me. Fine. Leave granted. I suggest you accompany him – giving my love to your lady mother, of course – before you are tempted into any further devilish machinations."

55 NONE TO MATCH HIM IN THE ARMY OF PARLIAMENT

"Dinner, my lord."

Venning looked smug, dishevelled, and ever so slightly stiff. Luce frowned at him. "Have you met with some accident?"

"Had to hand deliver one or two invitations, bor." He grinned.

It became abundantly clear which invitations he'd hand delivered as Luce walked into the hall and a good half dozen of Essex's personal lifeguard looked back at him with varying degrees of recognition and welcome. Sergeant Cullis, flaunting his newly-impeccable linen. And a very wet and scrubbed-looking Hollie Babbitt, who caught Luce's eye and visibly stiffened.

"Scrubs up nice, don't he?" Venning muttered close to Luce's ear. "Arsy lil' bugger, mind. Told him he weren't a-comin' to none of my lord's dinners looking like that, like a bag o' rags. Kicked up suffen dretful, he did." He shook his head, and Luce realised that the aide's thick fair hair had been deliberately brushed flat to hide a raw and bloody split through his eyebrow. That sort of kicking up dreadful, then. "Held 'en down in the water butt, I did, till he cleaned up. Good man, that sergeant of yours. Took both of us to do it, see."

"I imagine it would," Luce said, stifling a wild desire to laugh. It explained Babbitt's unfamiliarly groomed appearance. "Did you take a yard brush to him as well?"

Venning shrugged. "Should of. He bites. Terrible."

"Lucifer – sit by me," Essex called jovially from the end of the table nearest the hearth. The bright, warm, well-lit end. "Meet *my* lads. Henry Ireton – Nathaniel

Rich – "

It was unreasonable. It was wilful, and dangerous, and stupid, and still Luce couldn't bear to stand in the doorway and look at that great yawning gap at the far end of the table where not a soul wanted to sit next to Hollie Babbitt and Hollie Babbitt was trying to look as if he didn't care. "My thanks, sir, but my place is here. With my *own* commanding officer."

The big redhead turned his head slightly. "Me? I'm not your commanding officer, whelp. Fuck knows what they asked me here for. I'm nowt."

"Don't be ridiculous, sir. You are my commanding officer. You've got your troop back."

The expression on Hollie's face was priceless. Still trying to look cold and disaffected, and failing utterly. "I've what?"

"Stuck with us, captain. Sorry. It seems Uncle Essex had taken you in aversion as a result of some - misunderstanding. *He* did not give the order to pull you off the flank at Edgehill. Tom Corston did. All by himself."

"The little *shit*," Hollie breathed. "The hell d'he do that for?"

"Because you shamed him before the garrison at Warwick. Is my best guess. And because you and the late Captain Rackhay didn't like him, and made no secret of it. But we're not going to speak ill of the dead, captain. *Are* we?"

"And *you* sorted this out?"

Luce shrugged. "I owed you that much. Are you going to move up and let me sit down, or do I have to stand here at your elbow like your shadow?"

The redhead was still looking up at him blankly when Venning came across – limping, very slightly – and sat down with a thump on the other side of Hollie, in the next empty chair. "I ent sitting with them lot, neither.

Imagine one o' my lord's Lifeguard brawling in a back alley. Disgraceful want of conduct, that. Just as well they never asked me in, ent it?"

"Kicked *your* arse, didn't I? *And* one-handed."

"Oh, ah, any time 'ee wants to try it again, Rosie, I'm ready. Ent had so much fun since we nailed Mun Ludlowe's hat to the table, that time - what?"

"*Rosie*?" Hollie said, stiffening in his seat, and Venning pushed the delicate Venetian glass goblet further in front of him.

"Heard you was known as Red, bor, but Red don't even come *close* to that hair. Sup up, lad. Thass good stuff, that is."

"Cornet Pettitt, do you know this bloody impertinent bugger?

Venning grinned, shrugged. "This afternoon, bor, same as I met 'ee. I take these unaccountable fancies, see. Luce is a decent lad, and *he* likes you, so I d'reckon I have to give it a go."

Luce refilled his own glass. "Apparently I like you, Hollie. So I'm told."

"Are you drinking on duty, whelp?"

"Possibly. I think since the Commander-in-Chief of the Army keeps sending more wine down the table, we might get away with it. He *is* sorry, Hollie. I think he's trying to make amends for the - misunderstanding - as best he can."

"Can't bring Rackhay back, can he?" Hollie looked down at the filthy, bloodstained bandages round his right hand. "Witless is going to shit a brick when he sees this," he said thoughtfully. "Just as well he had to break my little finger a week or so back."

"Ah?" Venning cocked his head, and Hollie grinned, looking somewhat awkward.

"Aye. I reckon I've gone and broke it again belting you, lad."

"Oh, honestly," Luce said crossly. "*Will* you have a care for yourself!"

And for the first time since they'd met, Hollie blushed, looking down at the table-top as pink and flustered as a flattered maiden. "You still reckon I'm worth the effort, then, brat?"

"When my uncle tasked me with keeping you out of trouble, Hollie, he failed to mention that *most* of the trouble I need to keep you out of is self-inflicted." Luce leaned across the table and poked at the unlovely linen strappings. "It's bloody hard work, you know. Any chance you can give me a hand, here?"

Hollie snorted with laughter and lifted his splinted wrist. "Uh - no. Not for another three weeks, Witless says."

Luce stared at him blankly, and then his lips twitched. Venning looked from one to another, suspiciously. "Oh, thass *all* we need, is a smart-ass officer."

"You don't like it, you web-footed bugger, we can always talk about it outside like gentlemen?" Buggered if Venning wasn't laughing at him. So was Luce. Just as well Hollie hadn't been serious, either.

Venning thumped him between the shoulders rather familiarly, chuckling, and Luce shook his head. "I imagine you will never prove predictable, captain. Serving with you will never be boring, at least."

And Hollie wasn't sure how it happened, but some hours later there he was, in the middle of the night, still at Essex's board, with one elbow on Henry Ireton's shoulder, leaning over the table re-fighting the battle at Edgehill with the remains of his dinner. The lot of 'em were warm, well-fed, and slightly drunk. Bloody miracle any of them understood each other, what with Venning talking broad Norfolk, Ireton the Midlander, and both Hollie and Matthew Tomlinson North Countrymen –

from opposite sides of the Pennines. Talk about Babel.

Even Essex was smiling, pox on him, shoving apples around with the point of his knife to represent the artillery. Hollie had appropriated a dish of preserved cherries for his own troop – well, he would, wouldn't he? - Rupert's cavalry was a very well-stripped chicken carcase. Mun Ludlowe was having a high old time being the King and his household with a jug of wine – or the dregs thereof, judging from the hilarity – bowling Henry Russell's scattered bread rolls hither and yon shouting down a plague on all rebels, till Russell belted him round the back of the head. All perfectly amicable, just unexpected.

Cullis was grinning, which was as alarming a sight as ever. Occasionally leaning over to push things into a more accurate position. A dish of raisins for Ramsey's horse. Hollie disengaged himself from Ireton, slid round to the opposite side of the table, and thumped a half-eaten pasty down beside the raisins. "Rackhay," he said. Moved the cherries. "An' me."

Groans from the opposition. "Oh, give it a rest, Red," Ireton grumbled good-humouredly.

"Thass where you started off, bor." Venning raised a hand and skated the cherries down the table. "Thass where you ended up."

"But –" Hollie swatted the dish back. "Should have been there, lad. Should have stopped right where I was. Watch. You ready for this, Matthew?"

Tomlinson winced. "Not sure I am, Hollie. You're right heavy-handed, you are."

"Oh, bloody Yorkshiremen, always bloody whining. Shut up moaning and brace yourself." Hollie shook his hair out of his eyes – looked up at Essex, met his dark gaze. Smacked Rupert's chicken carcase, flat-handed, across the table. Watched cherries and raisins scatter across the cloth.

Matthew caught the bird before it hit the floor, replacing it with some distaste on its platter and wiping his greasy hands on his napkin. "But what happens if you move the cherries out of t'way and just let the bugger go?" Hollie said, still holding Essex's dark, implacable gaze.

"You get chicken grease all over Matt's breeches?" Ireton suggested, in his deceptively dry Midland accent.

Which just about did for Hollie, and he laughed till he had to sit down. For the first time in the best part of eight years, God help him. For a dinner he'd had to be dragged to – and it took two of 'em, he thought with pride – he was having a reluctantly good time. Hadn't expected to, hadn't meant to, but there it was. Bloody Venning – hit on him like the kick of a mule – stubborn bugger as well, wouldn't give up no matter how hard you hit him.

Stubborn little buggers seemed to find their way to him, damn it. He found himself looking down the table at Lucey Pettitt. A slightly less violent stubborn little bugger. Tenacious, that was the word. He had balls, did Lucey.

Table was a bloody mess, though. He'd forgotten what a riotous lot officers out on the hoy could be. Forgotten what it was like being one of 'em, too, which was probably for the best. He might not actually be the oldest man at the table but he imagined he was going to feel like it tomorrow morning. The talk had drifted into horses, dogs and women, with an occasional side venture into interesting legal cases of the past ten years. Hollie cornered the cherry preserves and paid absent attention to the conversation. By Christ, the Inns of Court must be a lively place if all the young lawyers were like this lot. God knows what it'd be like in there when the war was over and this shower went back there.

"What would you do?" Tomlinson was poking at that

poor benighted chicken again. "Sir? What would you do different?"

Essex smiling ruefully and it occurred to Hollie it hadn't been wine and roses for him either by the look of him. "All manner of things, Matthew. The joy of hindsight is that one sees with perfect vision the things which should have been attended to. What should I do –" He set the wine jug upright again. Returned the stripped chicken to its place to the rear, and on the right flank, of the apples.

Set out the dish of raisins and the half-eaten pasty, squarely facing the chicken. A row of little tartlets, facing the wine jug. Essex looked directly at Hollie. And moved that dish of cherry preserves, behind the tarts. "I should do the same again. I should use what I had to hand – experience, bravery –"

"Sheer bloody-minded cussedness," Venning muttered, not quite inaudibly.

"A certain strength of purpose," Essex said. "I should wish to keep those strengths to hand."

Hollie leaned over and put the preserves back with the raisins. And the pasty, in a scatter of crumbs, behind the tartlets. Raised an eyebrow at Essex.

Ireton was shaking his head. "No. Wouldn't serve, Red. Wouldn't have worked. You'd have ended up chasing halfway to bloody Worcester after Rupert instead, you mental bugger. Which would have left this side wide open –" he swept the chicken carcase and the raisins to the floor with a clatter "- expecting your man Balfour to come through in the centre and pull that trick of yours off, Hollie? Not his style, and you know it. He'd have waited for the order, like any other sane man. Wouldn't have got it, neither. I doubt anybody but you is daft enough to pull a stunt like that one, charge the guns off your own bat – *and* have the brass neck to order your troop to go with you."

Hollie dipped his finger in the cherry preserve and sucked it. "Wasn't me, owd lad. I never give any such order. I might be cracked, but I'm not like to take anybody else with me. That was all my cornet's doing." And it hadn't occurred to Hollie till all of about a minute ago to be bloody proud of the little bastard. "He might look like a girl, but don't mess with Lucey. Here's to Lucifer Pettitt-" he raised his glass in the lad's direction "- there's none to match him in the Army of Parliament. For which , believe me, I am thankful."

Venning nudged him, discreetly, under the cover of the ripple of laughter that followed. "Speaking of whom, I do reckon it's past his bedtime. Want a hand getting him home?"

He followed the direction of the freckled aide's amused gaze. All that could be seen of Pettitt was a sheaf of fair hair where the lad was resting his head on his folded arms atop the table.

"Looks like a bloodthirsty owd bugger, yon lad," Tomlinson agreed. "You want to watch that mate o' yours, Red. The quiet ones are allus t'worst."

56 PLAIN CIVILIAN HOLLIE BABBITT

Not much of a parcel, to hold a life in it. Not for the first time since Nat's death, Hollie wished for some kind of keepsake, not for himself, but to take to Mistress Rackhay and her children. Would have been good to take their father's sword. Would have been better, mind, if their father's sword wasn't buried in an anonymous pit in Worcestershire. Hollie wasn't even sure if any of the Rackhay offspring were male. Just his luck if he had rolled up with Nat's weapons, to find himself faced with a pack of little wenches.

Now there was a thought to send a chill down his spine: he had no skill and less patience with weeping women. If there was a heaven, and Nat was in it, he'd be howling with laughter by now. There was no way on God's green earth that Hollie was delivering a parcel of grubby linen and Rackhay's collection of explicit literature to his widow.

"*Bloody* Nathaniel," he grumbled. He'd sort of got into the trick of talking to Nat in his head as well, these days. Didn't get an answer from him any more than he got one out of Griete, but he was fairly sure they were both listening.

There really was nothing he could give her. He wasn't much of a one for sentiment, but even Hollie thought it wouldn't be wholly appropriate to deliver up a bloodstained sash to Mistress Rackhay. Anyway, he wouldn't part with that. That was an officer's sash and it stayed with the troop. (Not much of a one for sentiment. Ha.) Well, he'd see her provided for. He was enough of a bare-faced liar to pretend Nat had been assiduously saving his pay for the joyous day of their reunion, rather than spending it on unsuitable women and overbred horses.

Ah well, he'd dithered long enough over it. It wasn't like he was courting the bloody woman. He could always pretend a pressing engagement and shy off if she did turn maudlin. He straightened the cuffs of his one decent shirt – crumpled but clean, he wasn't wholly lost to propriety – and tucked his hair behind his ears. Reminded abruptly of Nat again, and that habit he had of licking his palms before he smoothed his hair back, as if that ever made it lie flat.

Tyburn was gleaming like wet marble, even his tack glowing with polish. It wouldn't last, as soon as they were out on the road on a wintry grey day with the mud belly-high in the lanes in places, but he'd made the effort. Christ, he'd made the effort, he'd groomed the black for hours last night till every tangle was out of mane and tail, every speck of mud off the horse's coat, and his new-healed wrist ached like fire. He'd even rubbed the horse down with a square of silk wrapped over a soft brush, in the hope of getting a well-bred gloss onto his winter coat. It was worth it. The black turned his head and Hollie automatically stepped back but for some reason of late the horse seemed to have changed his ways, he was more inclined to dribble chewed grass down your arm than bite. Probably the hours of grooming: that, or an understandable desire to be out of Windsor, and Hollie was with him on that one.

Summer in Yorkshire, summer in Devon, and cold winter at Windsor, that was what they said. Having spent seventeen winters on the edge of the Lancashire moors, he thought that December in Yorkshire probably couldn't be described as summery by any sane man, but then that was poets for you. Bloody Essex for you, as well. Hollie thought that if he had to spend another day in Windsor, sat mending harness in the kitchen of that infernal damp house watching the mushrooms growing up the kitchen wall – well, he'd run stark mad, was what. No doubt Essex was involved in sensitive political intrigues, far beyond the imaginings of rough fighting men like Captain Babbitt, and not just sat on his indecisive arse writing soft letters to His Royal Majesty whilst the fight went on in other counties.

Like Yorkshire, from what Tomlinson said. There were doings afoot in the West Riding, Newcastle and his Whitecoats attacking Tadcaster, Bradford attacked, and though Hollie didn't care too much what took place on the wrong side of the Pennines he was damned if he'd sit up here in Windsor growing mould, whilst the Malignant bastards crept up on his own home turf. It was nowt but spitting distance from Bradford to Bolton, thirty miles if that, half a day's ride if you pushed.

Christ, he could be of some *use* to Lord Fairfax. He was damn-all use to Essex, sat here in Windsor staring into space till the spring. So what if Essex hadn't pulled him off the left flank out of spite, at Edgehill. He'd pulled Hollie's troop off the left flank because he was a useless, dilatory, dithering *bastard*. The prospect of a nice damp day's ride out to Ingatestone to see Rackhay's widow didn't fill his heart with delight, either. Still, it was an excuse to get out of the city before he really did lose his mind altogether. No surprise he spent half his time talking to dead people. He got more sense out of them than he did out of most of the live ones on my lord Essex's staff. He mounted the black, pretended he hadn't noticed the smirks of the troopers lounging about the yard trying to look busy. Some people had suspicious minds, assuming that just because a man was wearing his good suit, he must be about nefarious business.

"Expecting to be back by curfew, captain?" Eliot said innocently.

"Possibly. Entirely depending on the state of the

roads, trooper." And mind your own business.

The roads were flat, and wet, and bleak, passing through mile upon mile of leafless hedges and bare woodlands. He stopped at the White Hart in Brentwood just after noon, with the black horse scarcely sweated. He could probably have gone on, but he was beginning to feel slightly sick. She was one small woman, not a troop of Rupert's cavalry. She evidently hadn't scared Nat, or they wouldn't have had three children. A stunted groom ran out into the inn courtyard to grab Tib's bridle and Hollie dismounted quickly. "I shouldn't, lad. The horse is – shy with strangers."

Out of perversity, the black rested his head companionably on Hollie's shoulder, the very picture of good fellowship. "He bites," Hollie clarified. Did worse than bite, if provoked, but best not to mention that in civilised company. Chances of this undersized rat of a stable boy finding out that the beast in his keeping was a murderous battle-trained warhorse were, hopefully, negligible.

The boy was still staring at him with his eyes narrowed. Hollie shrugged. "Fair enough. A penny for your patience if he behaves civilly. A shilling if he takes a chunk out of your hide."

"Come off it, sir. You're making out he's worse than what he is." The urchin's grubby hand was scratching the black under his noseband, and Tib standing there as mild as milk, letting him do it, with an expression of idiotic bliss. There were times when Hollie swore the beast had a sense of humour. Truthfully, he'd have rather stayed outside in the stableyard, with the good warm smells of straw and leather and hot horse and the company of one undersized youth to admire Tib's finer points. One thin, dirty young man whose wrists were shot out of the sleeves of his unmended, outgrown doublet and whose dark hair fell on his shoulders in dirty strands.

Hollie was aware in a way that he didn't think he'd been aware for a very long time that he was probably a hand's width taller than most of the men in the inn and that even in the gloom of the low-beamed room his hair was a most distinctive deep red. He kept his eyes on the stone flags. He wasn't going to trip over any of the outstretched boots, those days were long gone, he was just a bit nervy, that was all. Plain civilian Hollie Babbitt, no more. No one was even looking at him. Other than in idle curiosity, at least. He drank his ale without tasting it, crumbled the bread to crumbs, absently pocketed the cheese. Sat for a while staring at the blank, smoke-grey plaster wall opposite him, hardly aware of his surroundings. Aware that his right hand was shaking after the hours of brushing yesterday, and that his wrist ached in the winter damp. It was a welcome distraction.

"You seem distracted, sir." The tapster, collecting the untasted bread. "Not bad news, I hope."

Hollie shook his head. Not in the business of sharing his affairs with every inquisitive stranger in the locality. He wondered if Nat had ever drunk here, and then looking at the respectable travellers sharing the room, doubted it very much. No, Nathaniel would have been bored in here. "Considering the best way to Ingatestone," he said. "I have business there."

"Any house in particular, sir? I know Ingatestone well."

And hope to know my business better, Hollie thought dryly. "No, I can find the house without aid. But it's a kind thought." He felt the tapster's eyes on his plain grey suit and plain linen collar and he had a pretty good idea that it didn't matter how much he tried not to, he still looked like a bloody Puritan. He hoped that Mistress Rackhay didn't have any particular prejudice against

Puritans.

He left a scatter of small coins on the table – almost heard the mental upwards reassessment of his worth as he tucked his purse away – pulled his hat well down as he went out into the grey afternoon. The boy had groomed Tyburn in his absence. The black had been restored to his former condition of glossy perfection. "He's a lovely horse, sir."

"Aye, he is that." When he wants to be. Hollie looked at the young groom. "Are you treated well, lad?"

You can't do this, Hollie, you can't go around acquiring every street rat who takes your pity. No matter who might have done the same for you twenty years ago. You've already got an cornet who's young enough to be your son, you can't conjure a second cornet's commission out of thin air, no matter how thin the boy's wrists are or how filthy he is. He's probably infested with fleas and before you know it the whole damn troop will be scratching. The youngster looked sideways at Hollie, suspiciously. "Well enough."

"Fed well?"

The answer was no, he could see that for himself. Without waiting for an answer he handed over the hunk of cheese he'd pocketed. The boy's grubby throat worked. Hollie knew that look as well – he'd been half-starved himself in his time, and just as suspicious. "It's not poisoned, I can promise you. And I'm not after your skinny backside, so you can stop looking at me like that. I owe you a shilling."

"Penny. He never bit me."

"Shilling. I can spare it," Hollie said.

Another hour's ride wasn't nearly long enough for Hollie to steel his nerves for his meeting with Mistress Rackhay. Still didn't know what to say to her. Didn't even know if she'd know who he was. He owed it to Nat to go to her, though. To be sure for himself she was taken care of. Nat would have done it for him. Probably a lot better, come to think of it. Ingatestone was a prosperous enough village, a long straggling row of neat houses down a long straight high street. He could see a squat church at the top of the hill on the rising ground to the left of him and that had to be the tiny hamlet of neighbouring Fryerning. He halted Tyburn in the middle of the road, taking deep breaths. He could smell the wet leaves in the orchards of Ingatestone Hall. Smoke from cottage chimneys. A sudden waft of something cooking. Keep going, Hollie. Past the Hall – and you think you're awkward now, going to see the lady at a respectable little manor, think how bad you'd feel if you were going there instead.

Through the bare woods with the wind rattling the branches and the leaves coming down in red and gold drifts. A tiled roof, sway-backed as an old mare, russet through the trees: a long, low timber-framed house, old-fashioned and homely, with the sun glinting amber off the panes of glass in the mullioned windows. He reined Tib in, leaned forward for a second with his cheek against the solid warmth of the black horse's neck. And that, lad, is why you never got asked to Rackhay's wedding, nor to see his children christened – because the noise of generations of Rackhays turning in their graves would have been deafening, at the sight of their heir rubbing shoulders with the offspring of a ranting Puritan preacher.

Well, here he was. He straightened his shoulders and gave the black another nudge. Hooves ringing on the cobbles as he walked Tib round into the stableyard. A groom's head appeared, unshaven and surly looking, over one of the loosebox doors. "What's your business, mate?"

Hollie dismounted with a thump. The more he thought about it the less he took to this civilian lark. Any trooper who'd called him mate would have received a brisk kick up the backside. "A matter of *personal* business, with Mistress Rackhay."

"Mistress don't have no personal business with the likes o' you, cully, so I suggest you get back on your horse and shog off."

The yard was clean, swept, weeded: the harness he could see hanging over the box door was clean and well-tended. Just the staff who were arseholes, then. "Friend of the late Captain Rackhay - *mate*. So I suggest you keep your gob shut and your opinions to yourself."

"Kitchen's that way. Like to see how far you get."

Hollie stopped on his way back across the yard. Shook his hair back off his shoulders and straightened his cuffs again. Hadn't realised he had a powder burn in the sleeve of his decent doublet, but there you go. Also hadn't realised he looked so perpetually shabby as he evidently did. Perhaps he ought to stick to the officer's black, faded as it was.

He rapped sharply at the front door. A small body – a series of small bodies – hit the door at about knee height, yapping wildly. The door neither creaked, nor dragged at its hinges, despite its evident weight: clearly Mistress Rackhay kept her household in good order. He didn't get much of a warmer reception from the footman who opened the door: the man – who must have been twice Hollie's age and half his height, a wizened little manikin with meagre shanks and the pinched mouth of the long-standing toothless – eyed him with such frigid hauteur that Hollie's instinctive reaction was to go back outside and wipe his feet. "Your business, sir?"

"I wish to see Mistress Rackhay. On a matter of personal business." One of the spaniels had returned and was trying to out-stare Hollie. How the hell could Nat stand being surrounded by bug-eyed, ill-natured balls of hair, without wishing to use the little sods for target practice?

"What is it, Chase?"

And Hollie was prepared to like Mistress Rackhay on sight. She was tall, and slender, and shapely, and she walked across the rushes with barely a rustle of her dark silk skirts, she was that graceful. Smooth dark hair drawn back into a knot on the back of her head, smooth linen collar and spotless cuffs edged with fine lace. Then he saw her eyes and changed his mind. She was undeniably beautiful, about as approachable as a fortress, and he'd seen less coldly appraising eyes on goodwives in the Amsterdam fish market. "This – man – claims to be here to see you, madam, on *personal* business," the manikin mumbled. "Shall I see him sent him away?"

"Oh, I think so, Chase –"

"Madam, I am –" he stopped himself in time, "I *was* an old comrade of your husband's. Babbitt. Hollie – Holofernes – Babbitt. He might have mentioned me. He used to know me as Red - " And worse, depending how much drink he'd taken, but that wasn't for mixed company.

"Of course. I am so sorry for not recognising you." Her brow furrowed, neat pencilled eyebrows closing together – dear God, why did women feel the need to pluck themselves bald in the name of vanity? – "Do you need money, my good man?"

The yappy dog was still eyeing him belligerently. He eyed it back. "Not – not quite, my lady, I –"

"We have no service for your sort, I fear."

"Mama!"

Rackhay's children. He closed his eyes briefly. The little boy was the spit and image of Nat. "Who is that *ragged* man?"

Until the boy spoke, and then he took after his mother for sure. Nat had been full of his own importance but he'd never looked down on anyone for their appearance.

Well, not when he'd been sober. Mistress Rackhay looked down at him fondly, rested her hand on his fair curls. "He was one of your papa's men, Thomas, and I'm sure he was *very* brave."

"I don't think he can be a very good soldier. He hasn't got a *proper* sword." The little boy was looking at Hollie with disgust. "And he's very dirty, mama."

"Soldiers are, sweeting. It's not really a very good job for a gentleman. I hope *you* don't grow up to be a soldier."

No, Hollie hoped he didn't, either, but he rested his hand on the hilt of his munitions-quality backsword anyway, for the familiar comfort of it. Didn't look like much, but it was a proper sword, right enough. Not pretty, but efficient. Like Hollie himself, then. "Madam, I – I brought – I'd always promised your husband I'd see you cared for –" But he knew the answer already. They were very well taken care of, very well indeed. Hollie might be forgiven for thinking that Nat hadn't been missed at all.

A little girl's voice suddenly cut across his awkward mumblings. "That's not kind, Thomas. You're not nice." Two little girls, one little boy, all with the white-gold hair that he guessed would darken over time to Nat's amber, and their mother's elegant features. Two of them had her eyes, cold and assessing as a Cheapside whore, calculating his worth to the last farthing. (Wrongly, too, if he was any judge.) The third didn't. The youngest girl was pulling on the top of Hollie's boot and looking up at him. She had Nat's slaty-blue eyes, wide set and thoughtful. That figured. Nat had gone home after the battle at Rheinfelden. Nine months after Rheinfelden... she'd be just about rising three. Her face was still baby-round, but he could see her father's cheekbones under the puppy fat. One day, she was going to be lovely. But she might also be kind. "Do you know my papa?" she wanted to know.

Carefully, he bent to her eye level. "I did."

"Did he send me a *present*?"

"Cassandra! That's enough!" Mistress Rackhay frowned. "I don't believe that's a polite question for a young lady! Your nurse deserves a whipping, girl, for teaching you such manners –"

Hollie fumbled for his purse inside his doublet. Lass her age wouldn't be interested in gold or silver. And the Lord knew her mother evidently worshipped both and was short of neither. "This belonged to a very kind lady," he said slowly. "Would you look after it for her? She doesn't want it now."

It was a single pearl. Just the one, a great rough teardrop of freshwater pearl the size of a thumbnail, strung on a faded silk ribbon. It was the first trinket he'd ever bought for Griete. She'd worn it every day, though it looked daft with her workaday bodice, but she didn't care. Her nephew had given it back to him, after she'd been buried. Then he'd worn it himself every day until the ribbon wore through, and then he carried it against to his heart instead.

"Give it back, child, it's filthy," Mistress Rackhay snapped – glanced at Hollie, flushed a pale rose, and dropped her gaze guiltily. It was the first sign of anything other than whalebone under that smooth bodice. "May we provide you with some refreshment, Master Babbitt? I am sure Chase would be delighted to show you to the kitchen, where you can be comfortable –"

"It's *Captain* Babbitt," Hollie said – remarkably mildly, he thought. "Let the lass keep the bauble. I've no need for it. I don't think I need take up any more of your time, madam. I give you good day."

"Captain?" Her lip curled, faintly. He wondered if she knew she was doing it. "My apologies. I had not realised you were an officer."

"I must return to my duties, Mistress Rackhay. Pressing business. I'm sure you understand - having been married to a soldier for these many years." And one who'd rather spend his time with ruffians and tarts than with his loving family. Well, now Hollie could see why. It must have been something like Sunday best, all day, every day, in this household. No wonder she didn't recognise his name. He could just see Nat sitting across the table from her, telling her about his good friend Hollie whose late wife had run a tavern in dockside Amsterdam. "My condolences, madam. I am truly sorry for your loss."

She inclined her head coolly. "Thank you." Like he'd passed the salt at table, no more. And there he'd been, fretting lest she throw herself at him in a fit of hysterical weeping. Chance would be a fine thing.

Hollie turned to leave. He probably should observe the proper courtesies, but he wasn't going to. She didn't expect it of the likes of him. He planned to see himself out, and if that bloody dog continued to growl at him he was going to put a ball between its stupid fluffy ears. Then he stopped. "Do you miss him?"

Her eyes widened slightly in affront. One didn't ask a lady such questions. One didn't get an answer, either. "Chase, would you be so good as to see this gentleman out?"

Nat hadn't been dead three months, yet there was no sign of mourning in this house. It was as if he'd never been there. (Well, he hadn't, most of the time, had he?) His widow clearly wasn't prostrate with grief, though her fashionably sombre silk gown observed the proper custom. His children didn't miss him, with the possible exception of the baby, who was likely too young to remember him for long anyway. Christ, what a memorial.

The next thing he knew with any surety he was standing in the yard with the black's reins in his hand, leaning against the warm, solid shoulder. He felt oddly light and hollow, like a blown soap bubble. Rather afraid, as befitted a man with no past and a future that didn't seem to have a shape yet.

There was a chestnut mare standing placidly in the lane, rider wrapped up well against the late autumn chill. He could smell woodsmoke from the hall. He recognised his cornet's fair hair, even under the derelict felt hat. He probably ought to be furious, and not conscious of a rather shaky sense of relief. Not much in the way of roots, but - "Lucey, what the *hell* do you think you're doing here?"

Luce shrugged. "You asked me to write to the lady, sir. When your hand was strapped up. Eliot said you were headed this way, and - here I am."

"You *followed* me?"

"No, sir, I knew where you were going. There's a difference. I would have come, if you'd asked me. You could have, you know. I wouldn't mind."

"You didn't miss nowt, brat." A second figure dismounted from the mare. "And what, pray, is *that*?"

"His name's Matthew, sir. Matthew Percey. He said you spoke to him at the White Hart in Brentwood?"

Hollie sighed. "I did. I don't recall telling you my intentions, Master Percey. Am I so transparent?"

Bright dark eyes peering up at him from under a fringe of dirty brown hair. "They don't grow many your size, mister. And both of them is officer's horses. I got eyes."

Pettitt smiled somewhat uncomfortably, rubbed his chin. The lad was sprouting bristles. The age of miracles was not yet passed. Matthew jabbed his thumb at the cornet. "'E was asking after you. I might have happened to mention as I'd seen you. Thought I'd come along of him."

"To do *what*?" Hollie was glad the light was fading. With his hat pulled down over his eyes, he might pass for stern, rather than trying not to grin.

The dark eyes never moved off his face. "Hold your horse, mister?"

"You have nothing but the clothes you stand up in, Master Percey – you are filthy, doubtless lousy, and I suspect you scarcely know one end of a blade from another."

Luce scowled at the captain. "No doubt he'll fit right in with the rest of the troop, then. You don't get away quite so easily, Hollie. We need you. *I* need you. I believe Prince Rupert is still outstanding one, ahem -" the brat looked uncomfortable, "arse-kicking."

"And you reckon you're the man to do it, Lucey?"

"With appropriate tuition. And practice."

Hollie took a deep breath. "Tha can start practising wi' me, if tha's a mind to. God knows I probably deserve it."

The cool grey eyes met his. Laughing, the little bastard. "I'm not sure that giving you the hiding of your life would give me much satisfaction. Not standing out here freezing would, though. Shall we?"

Hollie looked sceptically at his unwanted new recruit. "I've no desire to be infested. *You* can ride pillion with the cornet."

"Oh, thanks a *lot*," Luce muttered.

"Shut up, Luce. You brought him, you're stuck with him, fleas and all. Till we find him a horse of his own."

The brat was grinning. "You know, it's funny you say that. I think I know where I can find one. My Uncle Stephen's old horse is out at grass in White Notley, an hour or so's ride from here."

Hollie bit back the retort he was tempted to make about Luce's relatives. This *was* the county of Essex, and everyone seemed to be related to everyone else. Luce blinked innocently, and went on, "We might as well, Hollie. I've leave of absence until the New Year, so my time's my own."

"How delightful for you –"

"Oh, so are you. Did I not mention? Uncle Essex thought we might as well both -"

"Leave of absence. And what the hell am *I* supposed to do with a leave of absence? Go fishing?"

Percey grinned, teeth flashing remarkably white in the gathering dusk. "You know something about this, don't you?" Hollie said suspiciously. Bloody Lucey Pettitt was managing him again.

"I know it's a way to Uncle Stephen's farm, and we'd better get on if we want to get there before midnight. Auntie Het would set the dogs on us."

"Funny, that. I know exactly how she feels."

Luce sniffed. "I hope you realise that while you're standing out here in the cold complaining, Auntie Het's probably got supper on the table. And I promise you, Hollie, there is nobody makes rabbit fricassee like my Auntie Het's cook. Thing is, I sort of promised we'd give her a hand. Since Uncle Stephen died the place has been going to rack and ruin. A couple of weeks' help would set her straight for the spring – she'd be ever so grateful. And she did say, you'd be no trouble at all."

By God, it was tempting, though. Not to be responsible for half a hundred surly troopers and their draggled mounts. Not to have to think, or argue, or fight his corner. No politicking. No danger. A roof over his head, and someone other than Moggy Davies cooking. Dry boots. A warm bed at nights. No Earl of Essex. Just – himself, and the work of his two hands, making things right instead of, for once, breaking them. Working till he was too tired to think any more, and he could go to his bed and sleep dreamlessly.

It was too good to be true, of course. "I hardly think your aunt would be delighted at the prospect of a stranger at her table, lad, especially another mouth to feed. I'm flattered by the offer, but –"

"Auntie Het," the lad said smugly, with the air of one breaking out the decisive weapon in his armoury, "*always* keeps open house at Christmas. She'll hardly notice."

The image those words conjured up –of being a part of something, of belonging – oh, damn the lad, he knew how to tempt a man. Especially a man with fuck-all else to hold to. "You realise that attempting to bribe a superior officer is a hanging offence, brat?"

"Absolutely. That's why I thought I'd best make it worthwhile."

Hollie sighed. He suspected his duty was to bristle with indignation. Currently he felt drained of either indignation or morals. Fine. Leave the brat in charge. Plain civilian Hollie Babbitt. He might start to get a taste for it. You never could tell.

Plain civilian Hollie Babbitt. Celebrating Christ's birth - by invitation, mind – with the worldly relations of the Earl of Essex. By God, that was a long way up in the world for a lad brought up strict and Puritan on the edge of the Lancashire moors. It was almost worth it, just to think what his godly sire would have made of the heathen proceedings. "Brat?"

Luce cocked his head enquiringly.

"D'you reckon your Auntie Het's cook might go as far as, say.... apple dumplings?" Hollie turned the black horse's head back the way he'd come. "Best make a move, then. It'd be a shame to waste 'em."

57 ENDINGS AND BEGINNINGS

Matthew had been asleep almost before his head touched the pillow: had been near enough asleep before that, sat swaying at the table between them just about wakeful enough to keep shovelling in Mistress Sutcliffe's good mutton stew.

Hollie had been on his best behaviour, he thought. He hadn't been rude to anyone, hadn't spilled anything, had passed dishes when asked, hadn't stared too conspicuously at the sight of Luce's proper company manners. He didn't think much passed Mistress Sutcliffe's notice, though. Funny, how quickly she'd engage Luce in conversation whenever that creaking old manservant hoved into view, so the brat didn't notice that most of what was going on the table was placed conveniently between Hollie and Matthew, where it was most needed. And Hollie hadn't talked with his mouth full, nor wiped his knife on the tablecloth, unlike Matthew, who did both. That lad's table manners wanted some mending. He thought he might leave that to Luce.

She wasn't daft, Luce's Auntie Het. He'd caught her eyes resting on Matthew's bird-thin wrists, but she never made a fuss about it. He couldn't imagine her making a fuss about much. Looked bugger-all like the brat, being neither fair nor slight of build, but that trick of just getting on and quietly doing when the doing was needed, was pure Pettitt. She was also considerably younger than the lad had implied. Luce had said his aunt was a widow, and she was. He'd never said that Het Sutcliffe must have been widowed before she was thirty – which he guessed, by the state of the place, must have made the late Master Sutcliffe just the itchy side of Methusaleh.

Never mentioned that the lass was sturdy-built and darkhaired and freckled like an egg, with a smile that never quite seemed to leave the corners of her mouth even when she was flat serious. He'd never said she was beautiful, either, but it would have been a lie, because she wasn't, not the way the world counted it. She was wholesome and peaceful and comfortable and more than anything else, more than his hope of heaven, Hollie wanted her to think well of him.

No more than that, Christ, he wasn't wholly deluded. What would a woman like her want with a half-mad rebel, out of favour with half the world and with no looks or breeding to commend him?

Just like she'd looked at Matthew's knobby wrists and known the lad was starved half to death, she'd looked at Hollie and known what ailed him. Not behind the door, that one. Subtle – that subtle he hadn't even noticed it at the time – but by the end of supper she'd had him agreeing to walk out at first light and check the hedges on the river meadow for gaps. He'd volunteered of his own accord to mend the paddock gate, because there wasn't much else between Tyburn and mischief once the black was rested. She hadn't treated him as an honoured guest, or as a distant friend of the family. She'd spoken to him like he'd never been away. Like he belonged there. Like she wanted him there, even.

What frightened him most was the once or twice he'd looked up from his plate and found those great dark eyes of hers resting on his face. He'd had a mare with eyes like that, once, near as damn-it pure desert blood, though he doubted she'd thank him for the comparison. Whatever she was seeing he'd bet money on it that it wasn't a scruffy, worn, weary rebel officer in all his dirt. He had the unsettling impression that she was reading his heart: and that whatever she saw, she approved.

The wind was rising again, pulling at one of the

wooden window-shutters downstairs with a howl and a rattle as it found a loose hinge. He'd have to deal with that when it was light as well. Let the lass work him for his keep. By Christ, this place needed some work. No job for a lass on her own, and half a dozen ageing servants. All the place needed was time and bodies to do the work, from what he'd seen so far. Being, believe it or not, too polite to pass remarks on the way the chimney smoked in the parlour, or the broken pane in the window-glass stuffed with rags up here in the guest chamber. And that was before he'd even seen the farm itself in daylight. Not that he knew much about farming, but if someone directed him, he could knock a nail in with the best of them. What the lass needed was a wealthy second husband, he thought wryly. Preferably some merchant who'd spend most of his time about his business elsewhere and give her free rein setting the house to rights.

"Hollie?"

He hadn't thought the brat was asleep. "What?"

He heard a rustle as the lad turned over and sat up on the truckle bed, his face ghostly in the moonlight. "Will you be all right, with Auntie Het?"

Across the river, a fox barked, shrill and clear in the frosty air. Matthew mumbled something, rolled himself in his quilts against the chimney breast, warm from the kitchen fire directly underneath.

Tomorrow, the brat was going to ride on to his loving family in Witham. He had a suspicion Matthew would go with him, rather than stay on this benighted farm in the middle of nowhere. Leaving Hollie with Auntie Het, a selection of decrepit servants, and a farm falling to bits about his ears.

Het, with her fine dark eyes, and her spotless linen that smelt of the lavender bushes it had been spread on to dry, if you happened to be standing close enough to notice. Het with her blunt, capable hands, who'd looked at the three of them standing on her doorstep in all their dirt and never asked a single question, but taken them in and seen them fed and warmed and comfortable as if they were as welcome as the King himself. (Or perhaps *not* the King himself, in this part of Essex.) Freckled, plump, comfortable Het, who barely stood higher than his shoulder.

Oh aye, Het was pure Pettitt, straight down the line. Just like the brat, God love him. Decent, and kind, and generous even when you didn't want generosity, and – what was it in the Bible, loving-kindness. He laughed to himself. Would he be all right? He didn't know. He took a deep breath – even the sheets smelled of her, of lavender, and fresh air – and closed his eyes. The house was quiet around them, with a deep-country stillness that he hadn't felt since he'd been a boy on the edge of the moors. He must have known peace then, in the gaps between his father trying to beat grace into him. Must have known it then, to recognise it now, or the beginnings of it.

Peace, and the first, awkward stirrings of desire. The other thing he knew - don't ask him how he knew, he just knew - was that, above all else, Het Sutcliffe would be kind. She was as dead straight as he was. If she didn't want him, she'd tell him. It might not be romantic, but it was deeply comforting.

"Will you?" Luce said, sounding anxious.

"Aye, lad," he said. "I reckon me and your Auntie Het will suit each other fine."

ABOUT THE AUTHOR

M J Logue has been passionate about the English Civil War since writing her first novel over 20 years ago. After a brief flirtation with horror and dark fantasy, she returned to her first love, historical fiction, and now combines the two. She has a degree in English literature, trained as an archivist, and likes Jacobean theatre, loud music, and cheese.

When not attempting to redeem the reputation of the Army of Parliament, she lives in Cornwall with her husband and son, three cats, and a toad under the back doorstep.

The further adventures of Captain Hollie Babbitt can be found in the rest of the Uncivil Wars series - available on Amazon Kindle and in paperback:

Red Horse (1642)
Command the Raven (1643)
A Wilderness of Sin (1645)

And the forthcoming
The Smoke of Her Burning (1644)

Stay in touch with the author via:

Twitter: www.twitter.com/Hollie_Babbitt

Printed in Great Britain
by Amazon